FOR *ABBY AND WILLIAM*

*AND FOR MY BROTHERS,*

*HARRY HURST and GEORGE HURST.*

*"The world was on fire and no-one could save me but you, strange what desire will make foolish people do."*

CHRIS ISAAK.

This is a work of fiction.

Names, characters, businesses, places, events and incidents are either the products of the author's imagination or used in a fictitious manner.

Any resemblance to actual persons, living or dead, or actual events is purely coincidental.

"His demise would take some time, and it would be fun, watching his reactions, as She, very slowly tore piece after piece of his life away from him, until, he'd be left with nothing but tatters and rags…and regret."

Also by the same author:

1. *Round the Ragged Rock.*
2. *Chasing Shadows.*
3. *Joyriders.*

# CHAPTER ONE

## LOCKSLEY ESTATE. EAST LONDON 4am.

The forensic team were already here by the time Sam Hargrieves arrived at the scene of the crime. On this sixteenth floor of the block of flats, every tenant had been instructed to stay indoors until they'd been interviewed by a police officer. No-one on this whole level was allowed to leave, or indeed enter, other than anyone who happened to be a tenant.
The concrete corridor was filled with curious tenants, trying their best to find out what exactly was happening at this ungodly hour. The wiser ones knew instinctively that it wasn't a drugs bust, because they were usually over and done with within a couple of hours or so. The police had been here now, for almost four.
Eventually, all the tenants had been marshalled back into their dwelling places, and order had finally been restored. Thick blue polythene sheets had been draped over the doorway of number 86. A C.I.D. officer stood outside of the door with his back against the wall, smoking a cigarette.
"Morning Sam", he said, smiling at his superior. "You're going to love this one".
Terry Mercer had been in the C.I.D. for coming up to sixteen years. Until this morning, he thought he'd seen just about every type of homicide there was to see. A man in his mid-forties, he thought he'd been familiarised with every possible method of murder, and he'd seen some vicious ones in his time.
"Is it a multiple?" Said Hargrieves, pulling on a polythene suit he'd picked out from the cardboard box placed outside the door.
"Two" Replied Mercer, "Although when you look in there, you'll think there has been a dozen slaughtered, Jeeezzuusss."
Mercer took another draw of his cigarette, and hooking his thumb behind him in the general direction of number 86, he said, "I'll tell you what Sam, whoever did this, well, let's just say they're off their rockers, they're knitting with one needle, let me put it that way, its'

bad Sam, very bad."

Sam Hargrieves, a fifty seven year old veteran, smiled to himself as he continued putting on the white forensic suit.

"Who's this"? Mercer said, pointing to the young man who accompanied Hargrieves.

Without looking at Mercer, he replied, "He's new, he's coming with me for a few days, he's going to try and learn the ropes. He has to learn first-hand experiences of what it's like in the weird and wonderful world of homicide."

"Not today he's not Sam, hell you can't take him in there, he'll make a mess."

*"Make a mess"* was slang in the C.I.D. for not being able to keep the contents of your stomach where they were, when confronted with a horrendous sight.

Hargrieves handed the young man a polythene suit. "It's up to you kid" he said, "but I'll warn you now Billy, it's going to be messy, there's been-

"You can't Sam, he'll-"

"You shut your mouth Terry, he can decide for himself. Now, sooner or later Billy, you're going to have to face sights like this. I'm afraid it's part of the job, if you want to get into forensics, that's all I can say to you, it's just part of the job, this is what we do."

William McDermott sighed and said "I'll give it a go sir, I'll come in with you, I have to start somewhere, it may as well be here."

A wheezing rasping laughter came from Terry Mercer, as if he knew already the outcome of the situation, and he did. Thirty-seven seconds after entering the premises with Sam Hargreaves, Billy McDermott blasted his way through the polythene sheets, and proceeded to empty his stomach onto the concrete floor in the corridor.

Looking at his mobile phone, Terry Mercer said, as he lit another cigarette, "I see Arsenal beat Spurs last night Billy, they reckon it was some game."

Billy continued retching and spewing.

"They won't win the league though", continued Mercer, " not consistent enough."

Sam Hargrieves could scarcely believe what he was seeing. Even for him, this was unbelievably shocking. The forensic team, dressed in their pale white polythene suits and masks, were showing him where he could stand, and where not to stand.
There was hardly a square foot of space in the living room where there was not a body part of some description. To his right, there were a number of severed fingers on the floor. To his left, half of a lady's arm, still wearing the watch. Directly in front of him, in the kitchen sink, the severed head of a woman, and a man's arm. On one of the easy chairs a pair of jeans with a man's leg, and half of his torso. The other leg belonging to the jeans lay behind the television set at the far side of the room. In the bathroom, the severed head of a man lay in the bath, with eyes staring into oblivion. There was hardly a space on any of the walls that wasn't spattered with blood. One of the forensic team had come across the rest of the woman's remains and the man's other arm in the one and only bedroom
A forensic officer spoke to Hargrieves.
"Two constables came here Sam after receiving a call from someone complaining about loud music being played."
Sam recognised the voice of the man behind the mask to be that of his friend Andy Phillips, head of the forensic team. Phillips continued. "Well, if this is a neighbours tiff, let's just hope they never *really* fall out."
Even Sam Hargrieves couldn't resist a smile underneath his mask. That was the secret though about being in homicide. You had to have a sense of humour. You had to be able to deal with the horrors of your every day job, and remain light hearted. If you didn't, then there was no place for you in this profession.
"It's the worst I've ever seen Sam, without a shadow of a doubt" said Andy, making his way over to where his friend stood.
Phillips spoke again, appearing to Sam, like some kind of astronaut from a B movie. The cloth piece over his mouth moved as he spoke.
"Get yourselves away bud, for a cup of coffee or something, you can't do anything in here until we're finished, and that could be some time by the looks of it. This is what you call a blind rage, God

almighty."
"Yeah" Sighed Sam, "We'll go and see how the officers are doing with their inquiries in the neighbouring flats."
As Sam was making his way back out, Phillips shouted after him. Hargrieves turned somewhat laboriously. "What is it Andy"?
Again the cloth moved around Phillips's mouth as he said to his friend, "Look Sam, I know that Mercer is a good cop and all that, but please, keep him away from me and my men. The very first thing he said on his arrival here was, "Find her pussy boys, you'll probably find there's a cock in it, I mean, he's a sick man Sam honestly, he's a bad influence on my men. Just take a look around you, huh? He had my men laughing, can you believe that? He's not well Sam."
As Hargrieves turned to leave, he smiled once again underneath his mouth mask. He knew what Mercer had meant. Someone had come home and found their misses in bed with another man. Phillips had been so filled with hatred, or jealousy of Terry, that he had missed his meaning by a country mile.
Sam pushed through the polythene sheets and was back in the corridor, where he found Terry Mercer consoling junior officer William McDermott, with an arm over the young man's shoulder.
"There's nothing to be ashamed of kid, we've all done it, and I'm sorry to tell you, but you'll probably do it quite a few times until you get hardened to it, but you will, you'll see. You must be a good cop Billy, or else you wouldn't be walking around with Sam Hargreaves, that much I do know."
Mercer turned, suddenly realizing that Sam was there.
"That was a bit nasty what you did there Sam, you've got the boy all fucked up man, bloody hell."
Hargrieves matched his friend's sarcasm.
"Come on" he said, "Let's go and get coffee, they're too busy in there looking for male and female genitalia."
Mercer smiled broadly at Sam.
As they made their way along the corridor, McDermott continued to retch.
There was police tape everywhere, and the three Scotland Yard men had to stoop down no less than three times before they

reached the elevator. Hargrieves told one of the officers standing at the elevator door, to go and talk nice to one of the occupants of the flats, and borrow a basin of hot water from them, and then go and clean up the mess outside of number 86.
The policeman's face changed from complete admiration, to that of utter disgust, but reluctantly set off to do what he'd been told.
"I should have done that sir" Said McDermott, clearing his throat.
"No you shouldn't" Replied Mercer, smiling. "One of the perks of being in the C.I.D. kid, you get other people to clean up your sick."
Mercer looked at his superior and said, "I wonder how our inquiries are doing Sam"?
"Surely somebody heard something" Said McDermott. "Someone's bound to have been spotted."
" Afraid not Billy" Replied Sam. "These inquiries never bear much fruit. No-one will have seen or heard anything. I'm afraid you'll find we're looked upon as an enemy of these communities, very close nit they are. Even if someone *had* seen something, it's a slim chance they'd confess to as much, either from fear of their own lives, or honour. Either way, we'll get nothing from them.
Thank God for forensics Billy. Mister Phillips and his team will soon have something for us to get our teeth into. As far as asking questions here is concerned, well, I'm afraid we'd have more luck asking a cat."
Mercer smiled as they waited for the elevator.
The door opened, and two young women, who looked to be in their twenties, stepped out into the corridor.
Mercer surmised that they had either been on a night out to a night club, or, they were working girls, it was getting harder to tell the difference these days, they all looked like porn stars to him.
"And where might you two delicious specimens be heading off to?" He said, smiling. The first young lady to answer was tired and cold.
"Nowhere with you creep" She said, sarcastically.
"Do you live here ladies"? He continued.
The girl who had answered him sighed, and said; "Look, here's an idea, why don't you go away home and take off your trousers and fuck yourself with a fish fork."

With lightning speed, Mercer produced his ID badge and repeated, "Do you live here ladies"? He smiled broadly.
The young lady sighed again and said, "Yes, I do, why?"
"And what number would that be miss" he said, glancing at their legs.
"You're a pervert" She said.
"Yeah, that's right, you're standing there half naked wearing a skirt shorter than a wash-cloth, but I'm the pervert, what number?"
"Eighty six, that's what number, now can we go?"
"No" Said Mercer, "You most certainly cannot go, we need to have a little chat with you miss."
"Listen" Said the young woman, "I can only speak for myself here, but after you give me a lecture on the dangers of prostitution, and on morals and principles and self-preservation, it is not going to change the way I feel about anything, I do what I do, and that's that. You can lecture me all you want on morals, but I could give you a lecture about survival, if that is what this is all about, so save your breath giving us any lecture you may have planned, and just let us be on our way, we're both cold and very tired."
A sudden gust of wind blew making the two girls wince against the bitter cold.
 Sam stepped forward and put his hand to his mouth as he cleared his throat. "Listen Miss, we really need to talk with you, and before you say anything else, this is not about prostitution or morals, we just need to speak to you, and believe me Miss, it is of the utmost importance. Now, my friends and I are off to find a cafe somewhere, so as we can warm ourselves up with a nice cup of coffee, so, what do you say, you two fine ladies join us, breakfast is on us, ok?"
The young lady looked at him suspiciously.
Sam continued, looking menacingly authoritative.
"Look, I don't want to have to take you to a police station at this ungodly hour, but, if we have to…"
"Fine" The girl snapped. "There's a cafe not far from here".
"Good, let's go" Said Hargreaves, smiling gently, and once again looking like a friendly old man, himself wincing against the bitter

wind.

The two young women and the three C.I.D officers all boarded the elevator. Fifteen minutes later, they were all seated around a couple of tables in Frankie's twenty-four hour snack bar.

It was all McDermot was worth not to be sick again as he turned away from Mercer, who was filling his mouth to full capacity with a burger absolutely saturated with tomato ketchup.

The two girls sat eating a hearty breakfast which consisted of bacon, eggs, sliced sausage, black pudding, and mushrooms. McDermot and Hargreaves each sat with their mug of coffee. Fifteen minutes later, they began to interview the girls.

"Ok" Said Hargrieves, "Let's start with your names shall we?"

The girl who'd said she lived in number 86 said, "My name is Mandy Smith".

"And yours"? said Hargrieves to the other girl.

"My name is Lizzie, em, Elizabeth Keaten."

Mandy said, "I live at 86 Temple Road, Locksley Estate, East London. I live there with my sister Jane, and her boyfriend."

"What's his name"? Said Hargrieves.

"His name is Thomas Felton; he works over at the brewery, not far from here."

"Your sister, could you describe her to me?"

"What do you mean, describe, do you mean her general behaviour, what?"

"Give me a physical description please Mandy."

Again Mandy sighed.

"She's thirty two, about five six I would say, she is of a slender build, about seven and a half, eight stones, something like that, long straight dark hair, and she hasn't touched heroin for more than two years, so don't tell me this has anything to do with a drugs bust, because if you've found heroin in that flat, then it most certainly belongs to Tommy, not Jane, is that what this is all about, have you found drugs there?"

McDermot shuffled uncomfortably in his seat. He had just had a flash-back of the woman's severed head in the kitchen sink.

Mandy continued. "It is isn't it, you've found drugs, and you're

trying to pin it on Jane aren't you. So that's the reason for the free breakfast and shit isn't it, well, you've just wasted your fucking money I'm afraid, because I'm not telling you shit!"
Sam smiled. "Mandy, this is not about drugs darling"." *If only it were."* He thought to himself. "I'm afraid you will have to accompany us to the police station after all."
"What the hell is it? Don't tell me Jane has done something wrong, she's not been in trouble for ages, is it Thomas? What the fuck is it, I'm not going anywhere until you tell me what all this is about."
"Listen Mandy" said Hargrieves," Let's get down to the station and I promise you all will be revealed when we get there."
"What was all that shit about going for coffee and breakfast then? You said there wouldn't be any need to go to the station, you lying fucking prick!"
In all of his thirty-five years in the police force, Sam had learned in the early stages of his career, that a full belly was very beneficial to a victim in a situation like this. He knew through experience, that if the girl did not eat now, then she wouldn't for days to come, because of the news she was about to receive about her sister.
"Well then, at least let me go home and change into jeans or something, this piece of shit can't keep his eyes off me and Lizzie's legs, he's a copper and he's standing there lusting after us, he's a perverted bastard."
"Yes I know that Mandy" Replied Hargrieves, making McDermot almost burst into laughter. "But I'm afraid it's not possible for you to go home just now, so come on, let's get down to the station and sort all this out shall we"?
"Make that twat walk in front of us then, he's making my skin crawl."
"Get in front please Mister Mercer" said Hargrieves .
" He makes my skin crawl as well Mandy, but I couldn't do without the ugly perverted pig, he has his uses."
Ten minutes later, Hargrieves was in one of the interview rooms in Locksley police station with the two girls and his new recruit, Billy McDermot. Upon their arrival Sam had spoken on the phone to Andy Phillips to hear what he'd came up with.

Andy had explained to him, that although he was ninety-nine point nine percent certain that the girl in the flat was Jane Smith, he would have to wait for confirmation from the laboratories.
By the time the two young ladies had drank two cups of coffee and smoked several cigarettes, confirmation came through to Sam Hargrieves that the two victims in the flat were indeed Jane Smith and Thomas Felton.
Sam walked back to the interview room heavy-hearted, where Elizabeth and Mandy were waiting with growing impatience.

"Look" Said Mandy, as Hargrieves entered the room. "I don't know what's going on here, but you'd better tell me soon, because any minute now, we're walking out of that door!"
Sam held his hands up; "Mandy, I'm sorry, really, but we have to check up on certain things, find things out for certain."
"Certain about what, for God's sake, I am so sick and tired of hearing shit, just tell us or we're out of here!"
"William", Hargrieves began, "Go and fetch the girls another coffee please."
McDermot left the room, taking the empty mugs away with him.
Again Sam cleared his throat. "I'm afraid Mandy, I have some bad news for you girl. Your sister has been found dead in her flat, along with her boyfriend Thomas Felton. I'm sorry to inform you, they've been murdered."
Mandy sat staring at Hargrieves hardly able to comprehend what Sam had just told her. She lit up another cigarette and eventually said, "Are you sure? Are you positive you've got the right flat? Mandy doesn't fall out with anyone, nor Thomas, she doesn't have an enemy in the world. Who could have done this to her, do you have anyone in custody"?
"Afraid not Mandy, that's where we thought maybe you could help us out, you know, like if you knew of any enemies she may have had, or her boyfriend, maybe someone who has a grudge on one or both of them, anything."
Mandy began to cry, as did her friend. Sam stopped asking questions.

Through her tears Mandy said; "How? She doesn't have an enemy in the world."

"*Oh yes she did*" Sam Hargrieves said to himself, remembering the cut-up pieces of the corpses' on his arrival at Locksley.

Mandy continued. "I've never heard her having an argument with anyone, apart from Thomas. She's lived in those flats for over six years". She began to sob again.

Sam watched the two young ladies consoling each other. Mandy was beginning to accept the situation she obviously thought the world of her sister.

So many times in his career he'd seen this. So many times he had to be the bearer of such sad tidings, such as these today. One of the down-sides to working in this profession, that you knock on someone's door, and within a few seconds you have delivered the news that is going to devastate a family. It feels almost like you are the one who has caused this horrible situation. You are the one who has broken their hearts, it's you, you have caused all this pain.

The door opened, jolting Sam out of his depressing thoughts. Billy McDermot entered the room carrying a tray upon which was four cups of coffee.

"I made us one as well sir" he said softly, realizing by the state of the girls that the bad news had been delivered.

"Good man" said Sam, equally as quietly as McDermot had spoken. "Come on kid, let's leave them for a few minutes."

Sam stood up and placed his hand on Mandy Smith's shoulder.
"We'll come back in a few minutes Mandy, I'm so sorry."
The two C I D. officers left the room.

On their way down the corridor, McDermot said to his superior, "She's taking it bad sir, about her sister."

Sam glanced at his favourite recruit. "She's taking it well kid, she's responding perfectly naturally...she'll heal."

"I'm sorry for before sir, showing myself up like that, you know, in front of all those people."

Hargrieves shook his head and then sipped his coffee.
"There's no need to apologise Billy, it was worse than I thought it

would be, in fact, if I'm honest, it was probably the worst I've ever seen."

"It was some mess sir. I certainly got the shock of my life, it was horrendous."

The two men sat quietly in another interview room for a few moments, and then Sam broke the silence by saying, "The head of the forensic team thinks that whoever done that, done it in a blind rage, what do you think Billy?"

McDermot looked to his superior and said, "Well sir, they may well have committed the crime in a blind rage, but they didn't leave in a blind rage sir."

"What makes you think that Billy?"

"Well sir, look at all the mess in the flat, blood everywhere".

"And?"

"Well there is only one entrance to the premises, there was not a single drop of blood outside of the door, not a single stain, so if the culprit or culprits *had* left in a rage, there would have been blood out in the hallway surely. They would be only semi-conscious of what they were doing, that's my theory anyway, I could be wrong sir. "

"You could be wrong Billy, but I don't think you are."

"I just can't believe sir, that human beings could do that to their fellow man. What on earth have they done to deserve having that done to them."

"I've asked myself that question Billy, many times over the years, and I don't suppose I'll ever find the answer. People kill for so many different reasons, revenge, jealousy, financial gain, or as far as we've seen here today, just for the hell of it. The ferocity in this case is confusing me. We can tell straight away, from the mess they have left, that they are psychologically damaged, perhaps beyond repair. They will no doubt be institutionalized should we be lucky enough to catch them. A hundred years ago or so, they would have been brought before the church and a decision would have been made whether or not an exorcism would be required."

Sam sighed and looked up to the ceiling, as if seeking divine interception. "That's how they would have described the crime

back then, and I'll be honest with you Billy, it would make our job a lot easier if they still held this point of view today. Blame it on the demons. Simple, the poor buggers are possessed, end of story. But today Billy, there are some very clever recidivists, and they are escorted into our courts by some up and coming fancy-pants solicitors who conveniently defend them on the grounds of temporary insanity. Off they go to some institution to serve their, undecided sentence, and where, after five or six years, they sit before some goody two-shoes committee, who decide that they have made a remarkable recovery, and that they are no longer a danger to society. Five or six years Billy, a far cry indeed from the fifteen years they'd have served if they'd been tried under normal circumstances. I've seen so many killers walking free from our courts, knowing full well, that the judge, as well as most of the jury knew in their hearts, that they were letting a murderer walk free. The justice system William, I'm afraid, is nothing more than a joke. A polished performance from a good solicitor and a cooperative defendant can turn an absolute dead-cert life sentence into a rehabilitation holiday. To those in the know Billy, it is very easy to beat the system. So, the solicitor sings out his harmonious defence, while his defendant sits phlegmatically awaiting the mercy of the kind-hearted judge and jury. The judge and jury are merely spectators, an audience, as the clever solicitor plays out his jurisdictional symphony."
There were two loud thumps on the door, as Terry Mercer came bounding in with his cup of coffee in his right hand.
"You've told her Sam"?
"Yeah, a few minutes ago Terry."
"Well" continued Mercer, "As you can imagine, no-one in the neighbouring flats have heard anything, typical."
"Well somebody did Terry, so we'll just trace the call to whichever house or mobile phone made the call."
"I already done that Sam" said Mercer. The call was made from a land line."
"And"?
"It was from Jane Smith's land line, bastards eh?"

Sam sipped his coffee.

Terry Mercer studied Sam's face. He couldn't help but notice that the ageing process was speeding up on his superior. He focussed on the whips of grey hair around his temple. His face seemed to have aged as well, there seemed to be more lines, permanent ones, creasing his brow and below his eyes. He looked closer to sixty-seven than fifty-seven. Mercer knew for certain, that he would never have been half the cop he was if it hadn't been for the man in front of him. He had been with Sam now for coming up to fourteen years, and together, they had brought to justice no less than one hundred and thirty-seven criminals, twenty-six of them receiving life sentences. Mercer knew he'd been trained by the best. He would do anything for this man, and without question.

On the few occasions he had doubted Sam's theories, he had been proved wrong, apart from the time when Sam had thought that his wife had been having an affair.

"Don't be so fucking stupid Sam, the woman loves you with all of her heart...fucking stupid clown."

Sam's reaction that day to Terry's opinion was the reason Terry wore a dental plate containing three teeth, but it turned out after some investigating by Terry that he'd been right to say that to Sam. Beth had not been seeing another man behind Sam's back after all. The two men she had had secret meetings with, were in charge of the venue and the cake for Sam's surprise fiftieth birthday party. Sam, to this day had never forgiven himself for that, for doubting his wife's loyalty. He spoke now, bringing Terry out of his reverie.

"What about Jane Smith Terry, is she clean? Does she have form?

"She used to be a runner Sam, I don't know who for. She used to collect as well, she and her boyfriend. This Felton guy, well he used to carry the threat. From what I can gather, he was a bit of a hard nut, he would dish out the punishment to late or non-payers."

"So" Said Sam, finishing off his coffee. "We just may have a motive then?"

"Revenge?" said Terry.

"Possibly, or it could just be what it looks like."

"It looks like the fucking killing pen in the slaughter house Sam,

that's what it looks like", said Mercer, answering a message on his mobile phone.
"Fuck, Phillips wants you to go back over there to see him, says he's got some interesting news for you concerning the bodies, what the hell? I've just came from there, the dizzy bastard, why in the name of God couldn't he have told me...the ignorant twat!"
Sam rose to his feet. "I'll tell you why Terry" said Sam, "The man simply can't stand the sight of you, in fact I would go as far as to say, he hates your guts."
Mercer looked, open mouthed, first to Billy, and then to Sam.
"What on earth for? What have I done to him for him to hate me?"

"I don't know Terry, he says he just doesn't like you. You are a bad influence on his men...I don't know Terry, he just doesn't like you and that's that, now, you take Billy over there with you, and tell Andy I'll be over there in about half an hour or so, I'll have to talk with Mandy for a few minutes, try and sort out where she'll stay and whatever."
Mercer stood up and said, "That's another thing that bothers me."
"What's that"? Said Sam
"Well, Mandy there says she stays with her sister and her boyfriend right?"
"Yes" Replied Sam, "What's discombobulating you about that?"
"The flat contains only one bedroom, with the living room and the kitchen being combined, it's just strange don't you think Sam? I mean, what kind of a set-up is that? You would think that her sister and her partner would like some kind of privacy wouldn't you."
Hargrieves looked at Billy McDermot, smiling, "You see that William? Everything is connected to sex with this man, everything. Mandy could and probably does sleep in the living room Terry. There are two people lying brutally murdered over there at Locksley, and all he can do is think about what the sleeping arrangements were, is it any wonder why Mister Phillips dislikes him so much?"
"He's just a fucking prick" Exclaimed Mercer.
"You see Billy? Just sex sex sex, oh, and when you get over there?

Stay outside Billy."

. . . . . . .

On their way over to Locksley, Billy said, "I appreciate everything you're doing Terry, to help me, I just want you to know that." Mercer sighed. "No problem Billy, we all have to start somewhere." Nothing more was said for a few moments, then Mercer said, "I don't think Sam realized just how bad it was in there. He wouldn't have taken you in if he'd known how bad it was, I did try to tell him. Do you think you're the first to empty your guts Billy, huh? You should have seen me, fuck I was in some state the first time I walked into a mess. I know we get training programs and all that, you know, when they take you down to the morgue and all that shit, but there are certain things that they can't train you for, like when you enter a house, and you haven't got a clue what you're going to see. Then the stench hits you, and your nostrils inform you that the victim or victims have been lying here for some time. First one I saw Billy, was an old woman, poor old bugger died on her chair, nice and peaceful like, trouble was, she had sat there for eight days before we were called. I swear Billy, I was still smelling her two months later, God, it was bloody awful, spew? You've never seen the likes' kid, so don't be too harsh on yourself about this morning, you done well Billy, considering what you were confronted with."
McDermot said nothing, he just smiled.
"Straight up Billy", said Mercer, sensing that the young man felt he was being patronised. "Sam must think you have a future or else he wouldn't be letting you anywhere near him. You just do exactly like he tells you, and you'll be fine. Everybody back at H.Q told me he was just a bad tempered bastard who just went out of his way to make everyone's life a misery. It was a load of shit. Oh he was a bad tempered bastard, still is, but he gets the job done, in fact he lives for the job, I don't know how his wife has put up with him all these years, but she does, God bless her...fuck, he's never home. Are you married Billy?"
"No sir, and I have no intentions of getting married, not for a long

time yet."

"Yeah" Mercer smiled, "You and Sam will get on just fine kid."

They arrived back at Locksley estate. It was now 9.23 am.

"My God Billy" said Mercer, "Imagine having to live here." Mercer was referring to the three giant blocks of concrete and glass which protruded from the ground and rose up, disappearing somewhere in the clouds above, each one indistinguishable from the other.

"Wouldn't fancy it" said McDermot, "Mind you, if you were in a situation where you had nothing, like you were on the street, and then someone offered you one of these, then I believe you'd be accepting it rather enthusiastically."

"Well, I suppose" said Mercer, "though I'm not a hundred percent certain I would be accepting it enthusiastically though Billy."

McDermot smiled at his superior.

"A home is what you make it sir" he said, as they approached the entrance.

"Yeah"? said Mercer, pressing the appropriate buttons on the panel in the lift shaft, "Tell that to the residents of number eighty-six Billy."

Two uniformed officers stepped out into the hallway a few moments later. "Good morning sir" One of them said to Mercer.

"Good morning boys" said Mercer, "Have you been to visit the great slaughter house in the sky then?"

"Yes sir, although we weren't allowed into the eh...you know. They say it's a mess sir."

"Yes, it's all that boys" Mercer replied, smiling.

They were once again on the sixteenth floor. Already, the police tape had been torn down from the entrance of the hall, and now the strips flittered in the winter breeze up here, one hundred and twenty-seven feet from the ground, like some kind of ceremonial streamers.

"I wonder why this bastard dislikes me Billy". Mercer was referring to Andy Phillips, the head of forensics, and McDermot could tell that his superior was slightly on edge about the whole matter. He struck McDermot as the kind of man who could take a lot of flack, but would be one of those people who, when their temper eventually did crack, would take a bit of stopping. He was mumbling something incoherent to Billy now, as they approached the murder scene.

As they approached the dreaded flat, two forensic officers came out, taking off their suits, and taking huge gulps of the fresh air, filling their lungs with life, as opposed to the putrid air they'd been breathing for the last few hours. Outside of the threshold there was a large cardboard box containing polythene shoes and suits for the officers. Pulling one of the packages out from the box, Mercer said, "Taking a breather boys?"

"Yeah Terry" One of the officers replied, "We're finished."

"Hmph" Grunted Mercer," We're just starting."

McDermot felt a flush of gratitude in the fact that Mercer had said "We're, and not "I'm". So he *was* to be part of this team.

"Andy's got all of the details for you and Sam, only, it's the weirdest case I've ever known", said one of the forensics.

"They're all fucking weird if you ask me" said Mercer, fully kitted up now. To his surprise, McDermot had kitted up as well.

"What are you doing Billy? Sam said you were to stay outside."

"Yeah, well I'm not going to learn anything by staying outside sir, don't worry, if I should embarrass myself again, I'll clean it up personally."

"Well, if you're sure Billy" said Mercer, who admired the young officer's attitude.

Mercer and McDermot pushed the polythene sheets to the side and entered the flat.

Phillips was standing with a note book in his hands, writing something down. He turned and looked at Mercer.

"Oh, you're back"? He said, sounding rather disappointed.

"Yes, my back my stomach, my legs, the whole lot of me is here" Replied Mercer cheerfully.

"Where's Sam? Did you tell Sam I wanted to see him?"

"Which question do you want me to answer first I know the answers to both of those questions."

Two of Phillips's men turned to look at Terry, who could tell that they were smiling underneath their masks.

"You've always got a fucking smart arse answer haven't you Mercer, eh? You can't just talk normally like the rest of us, can you, and everything is a bloody joke to you, I asked you a simple question and you have to act like the fucking jack ass...you're a complete prick, do you know that?"

Mercer pulled the mask from his face and said, " To your first question, the answer is yes, I told Sam you wanted to see him. To your second question the answer is, he's spending some time with a couple of whores, Sam always deals with things in the order of their merit."

This time Phillips's men turned away completely .

"Now" Continued Mercer, "seeing as how Sam is otherwise occupied, I am the investigating officer on this case, and I want *you* Mister Phillips, to go through every single detail with me, with a fine toothed comb and I want to know everything you've found out, from the D.N.A. samples to the last mouse to have a shit in the pantry, and I don't care if we're here all fucking day. You will give me the respect that my badge demands, or you will go flying over that fucking railing out there. Don't you forget who you're addressing Mister Phillips, or you and I will fall out big time. You want me to be serious? Well here's serious. You will address me as sir, whenever I choose to come into your company, and if I get any more shit out of you, I will pop your fucking head like a zit, have you got that, Phillips? You never mind where Sam is, that's got nothing at all to do with you, your main concern is the fact that I'm here, and I am here to investigate the murders of those two unfortunate people, now, what have you got?"

Mister Phillips looked suddenly shaken, he had been well and truly pollardised.

# CHAPTER TWO.

## 22B CALLINGDON SQUARE.

## ISLINGTON.

He stood at the window, looking out at the rising sun. She stirred in bed, her arm semi-consciously reaching out for her lover. As He stood watching this part of the city slowly come to life, or rather, shift up a gear. He began to go over in his mind, the course of events from the last day or so.
These killings had been different to their first. The first one had gone practically unnoticed two months earlier. The young woman was a down-and-out. He had offered the girl, a hot meal, some money, and some heroin, in return for three-way sex with his lover. The hot meal alone would have been enticement enough for the girl to agree to it. They had kept the girl there for four days, a play thing for She. However, after an attempted escape, She had lost patience with their prisoner. They nailed the girl's hands and feet to the wall, and proceeded to slash both of her wrists. Then they made love on the floor in front of their dying victim, her blood spraying over them as they rolled around banging and thrashing their bodies together rhythmically in total ecstasy.
"Did you make me a cup of coffee?"
Her voice made him jump slightly. Without turning around from the window, He said softly, "You looked so peaceful I didn't want to disturb you."
"I will have to go soon." She whispered. "I'll have to make an appearance at work, plus, my husband gets back from his work tomorrow, so I won't be able to see you for a while."
He didn't answer at first. Eventually, He turned to look at his beautiful lover and said, "You won't be able to stay away, you know that don't you?"
She smiled, as She walked over to the window, embracing him.
"What we done yesterday" He said, "would you like to do that again

sometime?"

She kissed him on the shoulder.

"Yes, only leave one of them alive for longer next time, kill them slowly, while we rape their partner, it'll be much more fun. What we've done this time will undoubtedly get their attention, we made a bit of a mess my sweet, did we not?"

He smiled and looked at his lover.

"They'll never catch us, we're far too clever for them, and yes, next time we'll inflict a little more in the way of torture on our victims."

She headed to the kitchen. His eyes followed her.

She was exceptionally beautiful, and He was completely smitten. He would do anything for this woman. He stood at the entrance of the kitchen watching his goddess making her coffee.

"I've got my eye on another victim for us. She's very pretty, and from what I hear, very promiscuous indeed, just the kind of young lady you like, and best of all, she's a whore. Nobody, certainly not the law, gives two jots about a whore, we could have endless fun with this one before we dispose of her. We'll have to wait a little time though, until the dust settles from last night's little episode."

She turned and smiled at her lover.

"That will be lovely my sweet, I'll leave you to sort out all the details. You just let me know when you've arranged it."

## LOCKSLEY EASTATE. EAST LONDON.

Mercer's sudden outburst of anger had done the trick. Andy Phillips's attitude towards him had changed completely. Sam was here now, and Phillips was explaining to the two detectives what had taken place in this house of horror.
McDermot was once again outside in the hallway, retching.
"I'll tell you what boys" said Phillips, you've got some job on your hands this time, I kid you not. This is probably the sickest thing I have ever seen."
He pointed to the kitchen table. "You see that? They actually-"
"Wow Andy", said Sam, holding his hand up.
"They"?
"Oh yes Sam, they, there were two murderers in here, and boy, did they go to town."
"Ok Andy, tell us what you think happened here."
Phillips took a deep breath. "Right, there is no sign of forced entry into the premises, so we can presume that the victims knew who their attackers were, or maybe the victims just answered the door, and then the attackers just barged their way in. There's no damage to the safety-chain on the door."
Phillips cleared his throat, aware that Sam was becoming impatient. "Once inside, they have set about slicing off limbs here and there. Now it's my guess that-"
"Guess"? Interrupted Hargrieves.
"Please Sam, let me finish. Right, what I think has happened is, they've rendered Felton helpless, and then one of the monsters has raped miss Smith, while her boyfriend watches on helplessly, and missing at least one limb at this point. The woman has-"
"The woman"? You mean a woman is partly to blame for this?"
"Oh yes Sam. Her saliva is all over Miss Smith's body, including her eh...her intimate parts, if you know what I mean. They've raped the girl, and this woman has had just as much fun as her male accomplice. So, at least you know that one of your attackers is a female bi-sexual."

Phillips pointed to the table again, and grimaced as though in pain, when he said, "There are vaginal fluids and traces of semen on there, the bastards have made love on there, after they'd finished butchering these poor people."

Phillips let the information hang in the air to let Sam Hargrieves' brain take in all the gruesome details.

Sam stood there shaking his head as he looked around the devil's living room.

Mercer broke the silence. "And no-one in the neighbouring flats heard a thing, no screams or cries for help, nothing, huh?"

"I'm afraid not sir" Replied Phillips.

Sam looked at Phillips, and then at Mercer.

"What about the D.N.A." He said, still looking around the room.

"Whoever they are Sam, well, they're not on any criminal file" Said Phillips, exasperatingly. As he looked at Mercer and Hargrieves, he said, "I know this sounds crazy, but I don't think that these people in here were their first victims."

Sam looked up to the corner of the ceiling, pointing to an air vent. "Where does that lead to"?

"That's how they left Sam. That goes anywhere you want it to go. Further up the tower block, or down. It's an air vent big enough for a man to crawl through, and there's hundreds of them. They left traces of blood in their escape, along with articles of discarded clothing. I have officers trying to find out the stores where the clothing was purchased...so far we've heard nothing. So gentlemen, that gives you an idea of what you're up against. There's just one more thing I have to tell you about our friends."

"What's that"? said Mercer, lighting up a cigarette, knowing that it would annoy mister Phillips.

"Well, when we first arrived, the cooker was still hot, the oven. I never gave it much thought at the time, until I discovered that Miss Smith and Mister Felton's kidneys had both been removed."

"Oh for crying out fuck" said Mercer, "You don't mean-?"

"I'm afraid so" said Phillips, just as McDermot was returning to the living room.

"They've feasted themselves on their victims' kidneys."

McDermot was once again out in the hallway, with nothing left in his stomach to come out, except bile.

"There are traces of their DNA in the oven, on the forks and knives, plates, on the table, they are...well, you tell me what they are Sam, I'm at a complete loss, honestly, I can't believe what I have seen here today. There is not much hope for humanity. Good luck boys in finding your demonologists, because that, my friends is what I think you're looking for. These guys are beyond your average loony-bin material, oh hell, way beyond."

As the detectives were making their way to the elevator, Mercer said, "Demonologists? Sam, don't tell me we're looking for occult freaks here, those sacrificial idiots who make a pact with the devil weirdoes."

"Don't know Terry, we don't know what they are yet, and more importantly, we don't know who they are. We know that they are not stupid."

"But Sam, cannibalism? In the twenty-first century? What kind of sick fucks are these people, bad enough killing, but eating their body parts? I've seen it all now Sam."

McDermott's face was ashen. His system had been subjected to an almighty shock. He was fast learning about the world of forensics and violent crime. The textbook days were over.

This was the real world, a very explicit unpleasant real world.

"No you haven't Terry, you've only been told about it. I wonder what shape we'd have been in, if we'd been there, watching this couple, sitting there at the table, dining on two human beings' kidneys, sitting naked no doubt, and all the other body parts lying around on the floor, legs and arms and heads. Good evening sir, we have an evening reservation, psychopath's the name, a table for two please mister Beelzebub."

Terry laughed as he pressed the button on the wall for the elevator.

"Joking aside Sam, these fucks could well be devil- worshipers you know."

"Are you alright Billy?" said Sam, glancing at his new recruit.

Ever so quietly, McDermot replied, "I'll be fine."

"You don't look fine kid" Said Mercer. "You look as pale as a ghost. Your face is colourless."

"I'll be fine" Repeated Billy, even more annoyed with himself now, after his second bout of vomiting.

"Tell you what boys" said Sam, "Just cruise around the area for the rest of the day, maybe check out a couple of local pubs or cafes, anywhere where you think these two killers could have frequented. Ask some questions, you know, with the locals. Try not let them know who you are. Ask them like you're gossiping, see what you can find out."

Terry knew what Sam was doing he was effectively giving them the rest of the day off. It wasn't like him to feel sorry for anyone, but he quite obviously felt sorry for Billy McDermot.

As Sam walked away from them he said, "I see you and Mister Phillips have sorted out your differences then."

He had a good idea of what had gone on. He was familiar with Terry's temper, and how he hated leaving things undone. Whatever Phillips's complaint had been against Terry, he knew that his colleague would bring it to a close one way or another.

Terry smiled at his superior.

"Yes, yes we did. It was just a misunderstanding Sam. He seemed to be under the impression that I didn't care enough about my job."

Sam Hargrieves knew what was coming next.

"Everything is crystal clear now between he and I Sam, we've sorted out Mister Phillips's pugnaciousness."

Sam Hargrieves walked away smiling to himself.

## DOVER STREET. KNIGHTSBRIDGE. LONDON.

She sat with her glass of white wine on the chaise-longue, dressed in a blue silk evening dress. She wore the diamond necklace her husband had bought her for her forty-second birthday. He had just sent her a text message informing her that he had boarded a taxi at the airport and that he would arrive home within half an hour or so. "Can't wait" She had said to herself sarcastically.

Her husband worked for a large oil company and was away from home, on average about eight months of the year, which suited Her down to the ground. She had married him for financial gain, and for no other reason. He was completely hopeless in bed, and was very poor at making any kind of worthwhile conversation, but She was very well off. She was in possession of two good cars, this house, a healthy bank account, and of course, his limitless credit cards, of which She made good use. She had a life, a good life, and what he lacked in bedroom skills, hardly mattered. She had He, and He dealt with her the way She liked it. He, however was not important in Her life. She could choose any man She pleased to fulfil her sexual needs, and quite often did, when She felt like a change. But He, at this moment was serving a purpose. There was a goal that She was aiming to. It would take a long time to reach that goal, but time was not of the essence at this point. Her goal was to hurt someone in as many different ways as She could, and to make their life as miserable as humanly possible. This person had hurt her so badly when She was his girlfriend. She had made a pact with him that they would stay together until they grew old. Then he had rejected her like a whore, explaining that She no longer had any place in his life and that he felt it would be better if they both moved on. The young man at the time had only been sixteen, and She fifteen, but it had devastated her beyond belief. She genuinely loved him, and pinned continuously for months after they broke up. Soon after this, her mother died, and She was left with quite a substantial amount of money, which she inherited on her eighteenth birthday. Soon after this She sold the house. She had no siblings and hadn't

set eyes on her father since he left her mother. She was only five years old when he'd left. She had never had to work and lived by moving around from town to town and city to city, staying in hotels and boarding houses, all the time, setting out her plan of revenge against the bastard who'd sworn that he'd loved her.
Wherever he went, She went, keeping a safe distance from him, but watching his every move, literally. She traced his career, step by step, and watched helplessly, as his life flourished.
Then came the day that cut her to the bone, he was going to marry. She had watched this woman with him, and how he was always smiling and laughing whenever he was in her company. They had gone out together for about two years, and now, the cow was going to marry him. This woman was going to spend the rest of her life with the man that She loved beyond words. "So be it" She had said to herself. "You marry him, but it won't be happy-ever-after dear, I can assure you of that."

*She was completely unaware of the multitude of mental illnesses she suffered from. One of which was schizophrenia. She was aware that some of her behavioural patterns were not what the average person would call, normal, but certainly had no idea of the mess her mind was in. Whatever had caused her to fall so deeply in love at such a tender age, she had no idea, but the hurt had never really diminished, and so now, he would have to face the consequences of breaking such a promise as he'd done. Her heart was unfixable, and inconsolable.*

She had met her present husband on an evening out with one or two friends She had made. They dated for six months, although it could hardly be referred to as dating. She looked upon it as more of a convenient way to top up her wealth, for She knew, even at this early stage, that he would do anything for her.
She already possessed an abundance of costly gifts. Gold earrings, bracelets, dresses, and not just dresses but designer dresses. He'd bought her a new car when She had made a comment one evening about an adolescent dream of owning her own red Ferrari. Soon after this evening, he'd proposed to her. Thinking it through for a

few days, she accepted his proposal, and for an engagement present he fulfilled her dream. Now, she had this beautiful house in the west end of London, and was in the perfect position to continue her plan of devastating her ex- boyfriend's life. She had more money than She needed and not one financial problem in her life. She had total freedom.

The price She had to pay for this freedom and the beautiful house would arrive home any minute now.

Because her husband was beginning his senior years, there was no chance of any awkward discussions about children. She had long since decided that children were not for her. She was far too self-indulgent to be bothered with that." Stretching your body hideously out of shape, and committing so much of your time bringing them up to be the people you hope they'd be, only, after all this, they leave you and then return with a partner who probably couldn't stand the sight of you, to hell with that!"

She heard the front door opening. "Hi baby-bee, I'm home, you lucky girl."

"*I hope it's not for long fuck-face* " And then, "Hiya babes, did you have a good flight my darling?"

## SCOTLAND YARD. BROADWAY VICTORIA.


Sam Hargrieves was in his office, studying a file on his computer, of convicted criminals, in particular the most violent ones. None of them however seemed to slot into place with this case. Most of the criminals he was looking at now were delinquents who acted impulsively, but none were capable of what he was investigating. There were three perhaps on his file who may have been crazed enough to commit murder this way, but they were already inside, and not even due for parole for another four years.
He took a sip of his coffee, and took off his reading glasses. At 9.15.am, he had already been here for almost three hours.
"I sometimes wonder Sam, why you ever wanted to get married, really." His wife Beth had said to him." Especially unbeknown to me of course, that you were already married to the force. Why did you get married Sam? Was it to punish me?"
He was going over last night's conversation with his wife.
"I mean, you don't like me going out with the girls, I know that much, but when I suggest that you and I go out, you've always got an excuse why you can't. "I've got a difficult case on just now babes, but it will soon be all tied up, done and dusted, then we'll go out and I'll make all this up to you." And do you know something Sam? I always believe you, and true to your word, the difficult cases do all get tied up, done and dusted, but then guess what happens next Sam? Can you guess? That's right, along comes the next case, and this one is even more complicated than the previous one."
He knew she was right. They'd been having this conversation for most of the twenty-two years of their marriage. Sam had never been one for going out drinking until the wee small hours. He was a homely man. He liked to come home at nights and put his feet up. Relax and unwind, have a couple of drinks with his wife by the fireside. He also knew, that there were two people in this marriage, and that he would have to be a bit more considerate to Beth's needs, "God knows she deserves it."
He would call up one or two of the theatres in the west end and see

which shows were on tonight. He would splash out and treat her to an evening meal and a show, and then perhaps a few drinks.
Already he felt better, although the selfish side in him was laughing his head off, because he knew, if he done this, then that would keep Beth quiet for months, and then he could get his teeth into this case. Suddenly, the voice of Terry Mercer was in his head, and reciting something said in a previous conversation; *"You are Sam, you're just a manipulative selfish bastard."*
Sam grimaced as he swallowed a mouthful of cold coffee.
His secretary knocked on his door and entered his office carrying a fresh cup for him.
"Good morning Sam" She said, smiling, and taking the mug of cold coffee from him, " I thought you could use a fresh cup."
"Thank you Rose, don't know what I'd do without you, do I have any messages?"
"No, but there's an officer here would like a word with you, if you can spare them ten minutes."
Rose Milton, another loyal female in his life. She had been his secretary now for six years, since he was promoted to this post. A woman of the same age as himself and with an outlook to life very similar to his own, many times he had jested to her that he had married the wrong woman. Sam looked at his watch.
"Ok Rose, tell him to come in, ten minutes, I'm very busy."
"She sir, I'll tell her to come in."

A minute later, there were two soft taps on the door. Rose opened the door and said, "Inspector Sandra Neal."
"Thank you Rose" said Sam.
"Good morning Inspector Neal, what can I do for you?"
"Good morning sir, I em...I might have some information here that could help with your present case."
Suddenly she had Sam's full attention.
"Really" He replied, smiling, "And what might that be Miss Neal, please, take a seat."
The officer in front of him was no more than thirty years of age. She was very attractive. Shoulder length dark brown hair, and neatly

cut. She had a full face with what looked like a natural rosy complexion, with beautiful green eyes. She wore a light grey trouser suit, which looked like it had been tailor-made. The young woman sat down. "Well sir" She began, "about three months ago, I was called to the scene of a murder over in Bridge Way Street, near Euston Station. The victim in the flat over there sir, was a down and out. It took us over three weeks to trace someone related to her. Well sir, I heard about the case you are currently investigating, and so I went over to take a look at the, eh, at the mess sir. It was the blood all around the place that caught my attention. You see, the young lady over in Bridge Way Street had been brutally murdered as well. My forensic team informed me that a man and a woman had eh, made love in front of their victim, as she bled to death." Sandra Neal cleared her throat and then continued.

"They nailed her hands and feet to the wall sir, and then they slashed the girl's wrists. These two, em, people, had then made love whilst their victim's life-blood sprayed over them. Bodily fluids were found on the floor sir, you know, eh, male and female bodily fluids sir. Now that I've seen the mess over at Locksley Estate sir, well I think that we are both looking for the same two people. I have taken samples from Locksley and given them to my forensic team, to see if the D.N.A matches up, I think they will sir."

"I see" said Hargrieves, rubbing his chin. "One of my team said that, you know when we had no-one on our records who matched the D.N.A samples. He said he had a feeling that these were not their first killings. Did they eat any part of the young lady, over in Bridge Way Street?"

"I beg your pardon sir?" said inspector Neal, aghast.

"Oh yes inspector Neal, the ones at Locksley didn't just slice their victims to pieces, they proceeded to remove both sets of kidneys, and then cook them in a pre-heated oven, at, I would say at one hundred and ninety for about half an hour, and then they sat down at a table no less, and began to eat their victims."

Inspector Neal found it very difficult to believe that Sam Hargrieves would make a joke about such a subject.

"Oh my God" Exclaimed Neal, utterly sickened.

"And mine too" Said Sam, sipping his coffee.

"No sir, nothing like that with my victim."

"No, but the sex thing though Sandra, and all the blood and guts and everything. It's looking pretty much like it isn't it, all the rolling around in the blood. You're right Sandra, I think the samples will match, and if you're right, then that means they've killed three people in as many months, and we know, without a shadow of a doubt, that they enjoy their handy work...in every sense. I have two detectives working on the case just now, as well as uniforms making door to door inquiries."

"May I ask the names of your two officers' sir, in case our paths should cross."

Hargrieves shifted uneasily on his seat.

"Yes, I, eh, I will have to apologise in advance for the behaviour of inspector Mercer, he's, well, lots of people are offended by him, you know, his language for a kick off. He's em, he's unorthodox, let's just say he's not your average run-of-the-mill detective, but he is effective and he's very successful miss Neal, so just go with him, you know, his eh, his banter, it would save me an awful lot of paper work if you don't make complaints about him."

"Sir" said Sandra Neal, rising to her feet, "With all due respect, I think I can cope with an ill-tempered officer, I have dealt with similar officers before, so long as he doesn't interfere with what I am doing sir."

"That's fine" said Sam, "but I warn you inspector Neal, just don't get in his road either, it works both ways remember."

Sandra Neal smiled at her superior.

"I know that sir, I won't."

"Oh, just one more thing Sandra."

"Yes"?

"He's a bit foul-mouthed from time to time, he doesn't mean to offend, I blame it on a bad education myself, he may even have that, what do you call it when they swear a lot?"

"Turrets."

"That's it turrets."

"Yes, I doubt if he has that sir" she said, smiling again at her boss.

"I think we'll find that he has other reasons for his continuous profanations, old habits for a kick off, inability to express himself."
"I don't know what he's got Sandra, the way he goes on sometimes. He talks about women's bums and legs, and what he feels they need.
Sometimes he gets a bit graphic in his descriptions. He makes comments on the amount of cleavage they show at work."
Sandra pushed her chair back under the desk, smiling. She knew that Sam was trying to prepare her for her first encounter with Mercer. "Sir, I shall not be making any complaints about inspector Mercer, no matter how abrupt his mannerisms may be. I can give just as much as I take sir."
"Of course" Said Sam, "I'm sure you can, please stay in touch."
"I will sir, and thank you for your time."
"Thank *you* Sandra, bye."
As the door closed, Sam mumbled to himself, "Huh, she won't be thinking that after she meets the course bastard."

As inspector Neal walked down the corridor towards the elevator, she saw two men coming out from one of the lifts about fifty feet in front of her. One of them was young, about twenty-five she guessed, the other looked to be in his late thirties or early forties. As she drew closer, she noticed the older man's eyes, and how they had taken in a physical description of herself, and how they stared blatantly on the area of her genitalia.
He managed at the last moment, to take his eyes away from there and to look into hers.
"Hello" He said, cheerfully.
"Hello" She responded, as she walked past the two men, "I expect I will talk to you soon inspector Mercer."
Mercer stopped in his tracks, turning to address the woman, who had not broken her stride.
"Do I know you miss?"
Without turning around, and just before she boarded the elevator, she replied, "You're going to."
The two men just stood still watching her, she could feel their eyes

on her. She glanced back to them as she stepped into the lift, smiling to herself.
Before the elevator door closed, she heard a man saying rather enthusiastically; "Fuck and fuck Billy boy!"

## CHAPTER THREE.

## DOVER STREET. KNIGHTSBRIDGE.

She applied the finishing touches to her make-up, in her marbled-walled bathroom. She hadn't appeared for a while at Saunderson and Blakeley estate agents, where She "worked" part time. She had called in and asked if they had anything in, that She may be of assistance with. Reginald Saunderson was only too pleased to oblige. Although She only worked part time, her success rate at selling properties was second to none. She had an eighty-seven per cent success rate in sales. This year alone, She'd sold no less than six properties over the value of three million pounds, two of them over five million. She was as elaborate as the dwelling places She was selling. Saunderson and Blakeley called her, "Their secret weapon".

She licked her lips, admiring her handy work, and staring into the mirror. The diamond incrusted mirror which had cost Charles, her husband, no less than four thousand pounds. Such was his love for her. She could ask for just about anything, and he would get it for her.
She walked into the bedroom where She retrieved one of the ninety-six pairs of shoes she owned, from her own walk-in wardrobe. Carrying her selected footwear in one hand, she stepped over to the king sized bed, stooped down, and almost kissed her husband on the cheek. She whispered in his ear, "Sweet-pea, sweet-pea, I'll have to go now."
Waking up and smiling, he said, "Oh, you didn't tell me, I thought you'd have taken time off to spend with me baby-bee."
"I know my sweet darling, but I'm afraid that Mister Saunderson has a property to sell, and he's simply desperate for a deal to be done. He says that he needs my charm and beauty to sell it for him, and he informed me that three different agents had attempted to sell and failed, so, he wants me to pour on the charm and sell it for

him."

"Oh well then baby-bee, if you put it like that, how long do you think you'll be?"

"Charles, darling, how can I possibly answer that question. I could do the job in half an hour, or it could take me all day, it's just like when you're fishing darling, you've got them to bite, so now you have to pull them in, and you can't hurry that process now can you, you've explained *that* to me many times, haven't you Charles. I promise you this though, my darling, I will be as quick as I can, ok? I can't be any more specific than that. Now, I've made you a pot of coffee, you just enjoy your day sweetheart."

"I might go for a game of golf with Trevor" Said the sixty-four year old devoted husband.

"You do that my sweet" said She, as She padded out of the bedroom.

"Bye my darling" she said, descending the stairs. "I will see you as soon as possible, wish me luck."

He shouted down to her, "You don't need luck baby-bee, the house is already sold."

"*Oh fuck off*" She said to herself, as She entered the garage and climbed into her cherry-red Ferrari California.

# SCOTLAND YARD.

# BROADWAY VICTORIA.

"Do you know your way around London Billy?" Said Mercer, as he and McDermot left the building.
"I'm ok" Said Billy.
"Right then, we're off to the morgue, you know which one?"
"Yes sir."
"Ok then, you drive Billy, and take your time, there's no hurry. The people who we are going to see are dead, and they won't mind how long it takes us to get there."
McDermot smiled, as they climbed into Mercer's own Vauxhall Astra.
"Now don't you be trying to impress me with any of that speeding shit now, do you hear me, there's no fucking hurry whatsoever."
"I won't sir."
"Well ok then, let's be off, don't know why Sam wants us over there anyway, fucking waste of time if you ask me."
"I think he said that the Smith girl, you know, the victim's sister, well she's coming to identify the body, you know officially."
"What fucking time?"
"I don't know sir, I thought Sam told you."
Mercer was frowning. "Here goes" Thought Billy to himself.
"Did he fuck tell me, she could be there now for all we know."
He pulled out his mobile phone from his pocket and pressed a digit.
"Hello Sam, for fuck sakes man, what fucking time is this Smith girl going to be at the fucking morgue, can't you tell me anything? I've got to guess what's going on now? Nobody tells me anything anymore, how the fuck can I be punctual when I don't even"-

Mercer was quiet again, as Sam was obviously informing him of something. All Mercer said in reply to what Sam was saying, was, "Oh, oh right, right you are Sam, sorry about that pal, ok, right Sam."

"Right" said Mercer, "that Smith girl Billy. She's not the reason why we're going over there. There's another officer going to be there, and the pathologist, we've to meet up with them. That's why we're going. He wants us to talk with them about the comparisons in our case, to the ones in this other officer's case, don't know why you have to jump to all these conclusions Billy, fuck sakes boy."
McDermot drove on, smiling.
"Now listen Billy, are you going to be alright in here, you're going to have to be looking at these bodies, you know, from the flat?"
"I'll be ok sir."
"Yeah, well, you said that the last time didn't you, eh? Next thing you were spewing out like fucking Moby Dick.
I'm only saying Billy, don't want you embarrassing yourself in front of strangers. Oh, and I have to watch my p's and q's, can you fucking believe it?"

Twenty-five minutes later, they arrived at the morgue.
"Hate these places Billy" Said Mercer, climbing laboriously out of his car.
"They're not my favourite places in the world either sir" Said McDermot, offering the car key to his superior.
"Just keep it Billy, you need to find out what it's like to drive around London all fucking day, that alone kid, is a sanity test."
Again McDermot smiled.
He liked Terry, despite all of his blasphemies. He liked his ways, saying things exactly as they were. There was no sugar and spice in his words, just cold hard facts.

As they walked across the car park Billy said, "I wonder who that woman was who spoke to you yesterday sir, she seemed to know you."
"Don't know Billy, and I can assure you, if I'd ever been in her company I would have remembered her."
"She was very nice sir."
"Yeah well, maybe she was a secretary or something, she looked like that type of a girl, you can always tell Billy by the way they dress. You remember that trouser suit thing she had on? Well that's

to let us males know that she is important, I mean, female solicitors wear the same kind of thing. It's to say, look at me, you'd better not waste your fucking time talking to me, I am more important than you. That's why they wear them."

"Don't you think they wear them because they're very smart and appropriate for work sir?"

"Billy, Billy, Billy, Billy, you have a lot to learn kid, and I mean in every department fuck. Women dress to send out messages, to the opposite sex. Now, you remember the two hookers? Look at the way they were dressed. They are dressed to let us know, that they are available for all kinds of fun, I mean, they didn't cover up much flesh now, did they? Skirts were so short you could almost see their knickers. Now, that woman yesterday, probably married, and I'll bet you her man is pussy whipped. When she gets home, she keeps those trousers on. Poor bastard will have to do the washing and everything, and God help him if he forgets to get the milk on his way home."

The two officers entered the morgue by the front door. They approached the reception desk, which was decorated with vases of colourful flowers, lending the place an ambiance of friendliness and comfort. To Mercer's delight, a middle-aged woman who was dressed in a lemon blouse and dark grey trousers addressed them. The jacket which matched the trousers was draped over the shoulders of her chair.

"Yes" She said, "And what can I do for you two gentleman?"
"We're here to see"...
Mercer fumbled in his inside jacket pocket for a few moments, finally producing a card. He looked at it briefly and said, "A mister Andrew Glover, we're here to see a mister Andrew Glover...pathologist."
"And you are?"
"Oh I know who I am" Said Mercer, smiling. "I'm here to see Mister Glover."
The woman's expression did not alter, she obviously hadn't caught on to Terry's attempt at humour.

"Yes, but who are you, what's your name?"
Mercer sighed, pulling out his id card and said, "I am inspector Terrance Mercer of the C.I.D, and this here is Mister William McDermot, also from the C.I.D. We are here to meet with a doctor Glover, with regards to a couple of brutal murders, very violent murders. We are here to examine the corpses along with the good doctor, well, what's left of the corpses...very messy you see."
The woman looked at Mercer disdainfully.
"Just a moment please, I'll inform the doctor of your arrival, take a seat please."
She disappeared through a door behind her chair, in rather a hurry.
"Fuck" Said Mercer, does she think we'll steal the flowers. See that Billy, fucking nosey bitch, wanting to know every detail, I'll give her details alright."
"Sir" Said McDermot, "She was only doing her job, making sure she knew who we were, that's all."
Mercer smiled at his trainee. "Well kid, she knows who we are now, and remember what I said about the trouser suits? Huh? She's another one, so fucking important." The woman returned and came around from her desk.
"Could you come this way please, Doctor Glover will see you now."
"Will he". replied Mercer. As Billy and Terry entered Glovers' office, he was already in conversation with a young lady, the young lady in fact, who had greeted Mercer in the corridor the day before back at H.Q.
"Good morning gentlemen" Said Glover to Mercer and McDermot, "This young lady here is inspector Sandra Neal, Inspector Neal? These two gentlemen are inspectors Mercer and McDermot, am I right gentlemen?"
Mercer sighed.
For forty minutes Terrance Mercer listened to Doctor Glover going over in great detail, the injuries afflicted to the victims at Locksley Estate. His patience was fast running out. He thought he was here to gather some important information that would perhaps enhance the chances of catching the murderers. Instead, he listened to the pathologist going on and on about how the fatal injuries had been

inflicted, and how much blood the victims had lost before finally losing consciousness.

"Another one" sighed Mercer inwardly. "Trying to impress the young lady seated before him, who was in turn, trying *her* best to fool the pathologist that she was listening intently.

Throughout Glover's lecture he'd hardly given Mercer or McDermot a second glance. He seemed to be talking to the young woman specifically, and was merely being courteous to Mercer and McDermot, by allowing them to listen in, and giving them an odd fleeting glimpse.

Mercer decided enough was enough.

"Well, thank you for your time Doctor, but we'll have to leave now sir" He said, looking at his watch.

"Don't you wish to see the bodies inspector Mercer?"

The pathologist rose to his feet. The man was immaculately dressed. Around sixty years old, he was dressed in a navy blue suit, with pale blue shirt and a red and blue tie. His brown brogues were of the highest quality.

"With all due respect Doctor Glover" said Mercer, now openly sighing. "How would that help us find the culprits sir. Personally, I am sick to the back teeth, as is my assistant here, of looking at those bodies. Granted, this would be the first time that we'd see them all pieced together, because any time that we have viewed them, well, there were bits of them all over the place. So, Doctor Glover, what our job is now, is to find the bastards who done it, not to look at the corpses every day of the week just to remind ourselves that there are some very sick people out there. Now, perhaps inspector Neal would like to accompany you to eh...look at the bodies, but my friend and I here, are detectives, we're off to find the bastards who committed these dastardly crimes. Our job is not to stand and scrutinise *how* they done it, now, if you'll excuse us."

At that point, Sandra Neal took the opportunity to excuse herself as well, leaving Doctor Glover rather speechless.

Outside the morgue, Mercer was lighting up his long over-due cigarette. "Jesus Christ my nerves Billy, I just wanted to smack that fuck in there, prattling on about how their legs and arms had been amputated, and how he had painstakingly put them back together again, what a fucking prick!!"

Sandra Neal came outside moments later. Her face looked like it was burning as she stood on the top step taking in the fresh air. Mercer, who was standing a little way off in the car park, was genuinely surprised when inspector Neal fumbled in her hand bag, and then proceeded to light up a cigarette. He would have sworn that she was a non-smoker.

She spotted her two colleagues and walked over to them.

"Thank you for that Mister Mercer" She said, smiling. "The silly bugger was driving me mental with his pointless bloody banter. Allow me to introduce myself properly. I am Sandra Neal."

She put out her right hand. Whatever she'd been told about Mercer, and most of it was negative, she couldn't help but feel attracted to him. Yes, he was rugged, but there was an unmistakeable attractiveness about the man. A woman would feel safe in his company. He was quite sexy.

Mercer and McDermot shook hands with inspector Neal.

"Have you had any more luck with the Locksley murders then Mister Mercer?"

Mercer shook his head, as he took a large drag of his cigarette.

"Call me Terry, and this is Billy."

After a few moments of light-hearted conversation Sandra said, "By the way Terry, just out of curiosity, was that flat for sale over at Locksley, by any chance?"

"For sale?" said Mercer, snorting. "Hah, who the, em no, it's a council property isn't it Billy?"

"Yes sir" Replied McDermot, grinning.

"What on earth made you ask that Sandra?"

"Well, it's just that the murder that I'm investigating, The Bridge Way Street murder, well, the property was up for sale at the time. The people who killed that girl, kept her there as a prisoner, before they finally murdered her. Oh and by the way Terry, the D.N.A samples match."

Mercer looked at her bemused. "The D.N.A samples?"
"You know, from Bridge Way Street and Locksley."
"I don't understand Sandra, what do you mean?"
"Didn't chief inspector Hargrieves tell you. I took samples from Locksley, and put them up against the samples from Bridge Way Street, they match. The people who committed those murders at Locksley are the same two who killed the girl at Bridge Way Street, they match. You and I Terry, are looking for the same people. That was why I asked you if that apartment was up for sale."
Mercer looked at Billy, exasperated. "For crying out fuck! Does nobody want to tell me anything anymore, fucking Sam!!"
"Don't be too angry at him Terry, I expect he knew I would inform you of the situation."
"It's not the fucking point though, is it Sandra, I should be informed at all times of all the relevant information. And what would have happened if Billy and I had got straight into the car and drove away, when would I have been told then?"
"Well" Said Sandra, completely unmoved by Mercer's sudden temper outburst, "we all know now, so there's no harm done. Now, would you like to accompany me over to Bridge Way Street, you know, just to look at the place. These murderers may have some kind of pattern they work to. I'll show you what they done to that poor girl over there."
Mercer looked at his junior officer and smiled.
"Yeah, are you coming in our car?"
"Well I thought that you could come in mine, Billy, do you know your way to Bridge Way Street?"
"Yes, no problem."
Mercer smiled now, as he looked to the ground. That was Billy's reply to every question that was asked of him. Mercer surmised that you could tell McDermot to drain the Amazon with a teaspoon in fifteen minutes and relocate it a hundred metres to the left, and Billy would give you that same answer. However, because of his present situation, which was, that he was going to be travelling in a very attractive young lady's car, he would let Billy's answer go unpunished, just this once.

"You go to your car Sandra, I'll be there in a minute, just want to show Billy something about my Sat-Nav."
"Right you are Terry, I'm just parked over here."
Mercer made sure Sandra was out of earshot.
"Ok then Billy, this is what's happening kid. You go to"-
"I'll find it no problem sir. It's just over by Euston"-
"Don't want you to find it, stupid cunt!" said Mercer through gritted teeth. "Fucking hell boy, this is my chance to bang her, fuck, she's crying out for it, why do you think she wants me in the car with her?"
"To look at notes sir, on the way to the scene of the crime?"
" Yes, that too, fuck, but that's not all Billy, she's gagging for it kid. Now, you are going to get lost, and you're going to call my mobile in an hour and a half, got it?"
"Ok sir, if you say so, where will I go?"
"Where will you go? How the fuck should I know, just get lost that's all, fuck it's a big enough city Billy, use your imagination for god's sakes. See you later, and remember, you take it easy with my car do you hear me?"
"Yes sir, I will, good luck sir."
"Yeah, that's right, you laugh you little twat, let's just see who laughs last huh, Moby dick."
"Remember what you were saying about the trouser suits sir, well, she's far too important for you."
Mercer smiled as he made his way across the car park, His sense of humour was rubbing off on the boy...he could tell.

## 22B CALLINGDON SQUARE.

## ISLINGTON LONDON.

He stood by the mirror in his lounge, adjusting his tie. This promotion was long overdue. He had worked hard since the day he had walked in the door. Burlington and Hedgewood were very good solicitors and estate agents, highly sought after, both for their work in the courts and as agents of property. At last, they had decided to promote him, giving him a company car, and this new job, which was to oversee the properties that their clients wished to sell. He was gratified in the fact that his employers trusted his judgement. He would overlook the property, and then return with a verdict of whether or not the property was good enough for Burlington and Hedgewood's reputation. Every property on their sales board and web-site were of the highest quality. At this moment in time, they had eight properties for sale, none of which could be purchased under three million pounds. He lifted his jacket from the coat hanger which He had hung over the door handle, and slipped it on. It fitted him perfectly. He stood now, admiring his reflection in the full length mirror. He had half an hour to spare before He had to set off. He sat down on the sofa and took a sip from his coffee mug, and then lit a cigarette. The morning newspaper sat on the table before him. He began to glance at the pages as He turned them, not giving any of the headlines any particular attention, until He read, on page five; Brutal Murders In Locksley Estate.

The report hadn't gone into any great detail about the condition of the bodies, other than to say there had been multiple amputations. He smiled as He thought to himself; *"There's no need to tell them any more than that, is there? The reader's imaginations would inform them of anything else they needed to know, all the gory details."*
The police spokesman had told the reporter that they were searching for a man and a woman, and pleaded to any members of

the public to step forward if they had any information whatsoever regarding the murders. *"There is a substantial reward available for anyone who can lead us to the culprits of this very horrendous crime. Full protection will be given to anyone who tries to help us with our inquiries."*

"Good luck boys and girls" He said to himself, rising to his feet. In his hallway, and hanging criss-crossed on the wall, He pulled out from its' sheath, one of the two razor-sharp Samurai swords which had made short work of Thomas Felton's attempts at defending himself and his girlfriend. "Good luck to you all."

## BRIDGE WAY STREET. HENSELTON ESTATE.

"Wow, this is pretty classy is it not?" said Mercer, stepping into the premises behind Sandra Neal.
"These are top dollar luxury apartments Terry" She replied, slipping off her coat.
"You said on the way over, that the girl murdered here was homeless. What the hell was she doing in here then? She wouldn't be able to break in would she?"
"No, she was invited here, or driven here, and apparently, not against her will either. According to the sweepers, they had all dined in here several times. There had been settings at the table, traces of meals shared together. They'd probably made some kind of deal with her. Money, or drugs, or both, who knows, but she wasn't a hostage. Not at first anyway. She was dining with them."
Mercer smiled at Sandra's reference to the forensics as *"sweepers."* He mused at what Andy Phillips would think of the young detective's description of him and his kind. He pictured Andy wandering around the scene of the crime armed with a whale-bone brush and a bin-bag.
As the two detectives wandered through the apartment, she said, pointing to the kitchen wall, "This is where they nailed her body, naked of course."
The walls had since been re-plastered and repainted. Then she pointed to the floor. "They had sex right here Terry, right here in front of the girl."
"Fuck. What kind of buzz did they get out of that? Was that it? The sick fucks, making love in front of their helpless prisoner pinned to the wall? Was that their thing? Was that their purpose?"
"They slashed her wrists Terry, in several places. The victim's blood would be spraying all over them, as they...eh...you know."
"They made love in front of her while she was dying?"
"Exactly Terry, makes you feel good about the human race doesn't it."
"Yeah, just the same as they've done over at Locksley it would

seem. But the locations of the murders Sandra, I mean, no offence to the people of Locksley, but look at the difference between the two apartments, fucking chalk and cheese, excuse my French."
Sandra smiled. "Yes, these are all owned by businessmen and women. Or by people who have so much money, that they purchase one of these places just for the hell of it. Someone told me that they're mostly used by the men and women who are having affairs behind their wives' or husband's backs."
"It's just the way of the world Sandra, I'm afraid, they're all at it, they're all doing it these days, I must be one of the old school."
"Which is why I haven't married Terry", Sandra put in. "My life is my own. I don't have to sneak around, or keep my mobile with me at close quarters, for fear of my husband snooping into my personal business."
Mercer couldn't resist, even though his next line was a lie.
"Me too Sandra, I think if truth be known, I enjoy my job too much to be bothered with long term relationships." He wasn't lying about his attitude to his job.
She knew Terry had a crush on her, and, if she was honest, she also knew, that she wouldn't refuse an offer to go out for a drink with him, should he offer. She smiled to herself as she made her way across the huge kitchen, knowing full well where Terry's eyes would be.
Without turning round, she said, "Fancy a coffee?"
"Don't mind if I do." He walked over to her as she filled the kettle. She put the switch down and turned to face the man. Mercer reached out, and the two began to kiss passionately. They both almost jumped out of their skins as the security buzzer rang out deafeningly loud. Sandra picked up the hand set which was mounted on a wall bracket, and spoke into it. "Hello?"
"Hello?" came the reply.
"Who is this?" said Sandra, her heart thumping.
"It's me Miss Neal, officer McDermot, may I come up?"
Mercer grabbed the hand set from Sandra. "Can you fuck come up! I thought I told you to go over, to eh, to go over to Locksley Estate officer McDermot, and spend some time over there, making

inquiries, did I not tell you that? Hmm? Didn't I make it clear to you, to lose yourself in the job?"
There was a few moments of silence. Eventually, when there'd been no reply, Mercer barked, "Hello?"
McDermott's voice boomed in his ear. "I can't sir."
Mercer lost his patience. "Why fucking not Mccuntmot?"
More silence, and then..."Got a flat tyre sir."
Sandra smiled at Terry, and kissed him on the cheek. "Never mind Terry, there'll be other opportunities, and anyway, this is neither the time nor the place, we're supposed to be on duty."
McDermot's voice once again boomed through the system.
"So, can I come up sir?" Mercer sighed.
"Yeah, you come up kid, come and get a cup of coffee, and fuck it!"
Sandra smiled to herself, remembering what Sam Hargrieves had told her about Mercer's blasphemous rants. Perhaps he did have turrets. "You're such a fucking half-wit aren't you McDermot...a simple fucking task...bastard!"

DOVER STREET.

KNIGHTSBRIDGE.


Another successful sale completed, she stood at her lounge window watching London's hustle and bustle shift up a gear as darkness began to descend. It had taken her the best part of four hours to land the deal. The property She had sold was every bit as luxurious as her own. The trouble was, out there in the property market, there were two kinds of buyers, People who had money, and people who knew people who had money. The gentleman today who had finally put pen to paper, had made no less than eight phone calls to friends or financial backers before finally giving in. She had treated the couple to a meal which would cost Saunderson and Blakeley, the princely sum of nine hundred pounds, but, in comparison to the price of the property, and the commission they would make, it was chicken feed.

She sipped her white wine, pleased with her day's endeavours. Her husband was not yet home, from whatever he'd been doing, and in all honesty, she couldn't care less. When he did finally arrive home, She would talk him in to taking her out to a show, and then drinks with some friends, some of his many friends.
She would drink more than She should, and quite purposefully, anything to quicken the time in his company. The evenings out were only to kill as much time while he was home. Other than that, they were pointless. Of course, all of her husband's friends had money as well, most of which had never worked for their fortunes. Inheritance is a wonderful thing. If there were any positives about these nights out, it was watching these men's wives squirm at the tables as She flirted blatantly and provocatively in front of them. She so enjoyed this game, making these women's evenings as tortuous and embarrassing as She could. Most of them were the jealous type, frightened that some attractive beautiful bitch, like herself, would come along and steal their meal ticket away from

them, from right under their noses. Most of them were like that, but not all of them. Some of them were very similar to herself, marrying for the financial convenience. She knew of two, who, when their husbands were gone, would be out scrutinising the best bars and clubs in the west end, for one reason, and one reason only. Society would refer to them as devious and manipulative whores, sucking like leeches from their providers. She called them opportunists, clever, inventive, even sexy, and most definitely, friends.

She was actually very proud of herself and her, *friends*. They had all learned from an early age, how to use their looks, and their bodies. Never would they have to set their alarm clocks for six am, and go out there to work themselves into an early grave, just to be able to obtain a mortgage that would tie them down for two thirds of their lives, to jobs that they despised, and just so they could drive a half decent car, or go abroad once a year on a cheap-package holiday, with a husband who looked as attractive as small-pox, and then pretend to their neighbours when they got home that they had been away on some exotic holiday, and not Majorca.
Life to her, was about taking opportunities when they arose, and never being ashamed of putting herself first, after all, She thought, if I don't look after myself, no-one else will. Society could think whatever they wished of her and her like-minded friends, she cared nothing of what *they* thought, and besides, society was corrupt, from top to bottom. Everyone, or at least, most of them, were driven on by that age-old policy that continuously stands us in good stead. "What's in it for me."

She watched the traffic down below and wondered if He was out there driving. She knew He saw other women, but She cared nothing about that, only telling him to make sure He was using proper protection. She stood now, wondering if He'd picked up a slut somewhere and was entertaining her at his home.
The relationship She had with Him, was in no way romantic. It was just that they had this sexual fantasy about committing murder a certain way, and inflicting pain as well as receiving sexual

gratification. Her mind was poisonous; she was aware of that. Why else would She be spending so much time tracking down the bastard who'd rejected her. She knew that it was a long long time ago, but still She felt this uncontrollable need to torture him and inflict as much unpleasantness into his life as She could.
The man in question, to be fair to him, had handled everything She'd done to him, quite well. He was strong, stubborn, hard, like a rock, but he would fall, oh yes, he would fall, and his descent would be lengthy, there would be no quick infliction of pain, and then, that's it over with, oh no, his demise would take some time, and it would be fun, watching his reactions, as She, very slowly tore piece after piece of his life away from him, until, he'd be left with nothing but tatters and rags…and regret.

Her mind wandered back to her lover again, knowing that She would be visiting him quite soon. She loved these sessions She had with Him. He was good, very good. He knew exactly what a woman's needs were, and He was never selfish, in any way. He would give her hours and hours of oral attention. She remembered on one occasion, when he'd used only his tongue and fingers and had given her countless orgasms. She also remembered the little homeless teenager, and how He had her crying out for joy as He continuously hammered her with his enormous gift, as orgasm after orgasm flooded through her writhing body. But alas, perhaps there *was* a tinge of jealousy in her after all, although she had grown fond of the teen, and the girl's enjoyment had turned her on, but such a pity, and why on earth had she gone and done something so stupid like trying to escape them. "That, inadvertently had sealed her fate, well at least prematurely. Which really was a shame, she tasted really sweet."

# CHAPTER FOUR.

## LOCKSLEY ESTATE.

"Let me make one thing clear to you Billy, ok? You want to make it as a CI.D officer? Well, the very first thing that you have to learn is, you follow your orders. You obey, even if you disagree with what you've been told to do."
"Look Terry" Said McDermot, exasperated," I have lost count of how many times I've apologised to you, can't you just leave it? I'm sorry. I screwed up and I'm sorry, there, now that's the last time I'm going to say it, so just lay off, anyway, you'll see her again, it's not as if you'll never see her again is it, she said she'd be in touch."
"Oh yes smart ass, I'll see her, with no thanks to you, clown boy. How the fuck? She doesn't even have my number numb-skull.-"
"For God's sakes Terry, she's a detective, not a plumber, she'll find you. Your paths are bound to cross, hell, we're on the same case Terry, she'll find you."
There was silence in the car for a few seconds.
"No thanks to you Moby."
McDermot shook his head as he parked the car.
"That's you, fucking Moby McDermot."
As they approached the tower block, Billy smiled to himself as he watched Terry Mercer laughing at his own joke. Terry was so caught up in his own humour that he had failed to notice Sandra Neal's vehicle, parked only four spaces from their own vehicle.
He would allow Terry to rant and rave continuously all the way up in the elevator, and all along the landing, until, at last, they would reach number eighty-six, at which point, he would change, from this howling lunatic, into a well-mannered politely spoken officer of the law, and who would pour compliments onto fellow officer Sandra Neal, smiling broadly. True to form, Mercer done exactly that, informing McDermot, that in all of his years in the force, he had never once encountered, such a jealous cunt-in-the-mud as him.
When they entered the premises, Sandra was standing at the sink

with her back to them. "Oh" said Mercer, "What a lovely surprise to see you here sweetheart."
"Thank you" Said Chief inspector Hargrieves, who had been standing behind the door out of view. "It's nice to see you too sweetheart, how have you been Terry?"
Andy Phillips was here from forensics as well. The sarcastic burst of laughter which was about to protrude from his mouth, was quickly dampened down to a polite smile as he caught the steel in Mercer's eyes.
"So" Said Hargrieves, "It turns out that Officer Neal was correct in her assumption, we are indeed looking for the same two as she. Now then Terry, I want you to split into two teams here."
"Sir?"
"I want Billy here to go with inspector Neal, and I want you to team up with, where is he Sandra?"
Hargrieves was referring to the young trainee officer, who was, at this moment in time, boarding the elevator, laden with fish and chips and cans of cola.
"He won't be long sir" She said, smiling, because she knew what Mercer would think of this arrangement.
"Right Terry" Hargrieves continued. I want you to do a bit of researching. Find out from Mandy, all the names of her sister's friends, people who visited here, and of course, all Thomas Felton's friends as well. You might want to start over at Tomlinson's brewery. See how many friends he had there, or enemies, and take, what's his name Sandra?"
"John sir, officer John Smedley."
"Take officer Smedley with you for a couple of days or so, you know Terry, show him the ropes so to speak, I'm sure Billy will do just fine with Officer Neal."
"I'm sure he will Sam. And this eh, Smidgey"-
"Smedley" corrected Sandra Neal.
"Smedley then, has he had *any* experience in the field?"
"Not really Terry, but I can assure you, he's a fast learner" Said Sandra, smiling.
"Aren't we all". Mercer looked at Billy McDermot, who was

beaming.
"Put it this way Terry, if you tell him to do something, then come hell or high water, he'll do it, he'll follow your orders to the letter."
"To the letter? Hear that Billy? To the letter, sounds like just the kind of man I'm looking for."
"Yes sir" Replied McDermot. "And Officer Neal sounds like the kind of leader that I am looking forward to working with, I think I'll learn a lot from her sir."
At that moment John Smedley entered the living room. Sandra introduced him to Mercer.
"You'll be working with detective Mercer until further notice, ok?"
"Yes mam."
The young recruit turned to face his new boss. "Sir, I'm afraid I wasn't previously informed of your arrival. I'm afraid I haven't bought you or officer McDermot anything to eat sir."
Mercer grinned at Sandra Neal, before replying to the trainee.
"Oh now don't you be worrying yourself about that officer Smiggy, Officer McDermot is finding it rather difficult to keep anything down these days, now what have you bought yourself to eat Smiddly?"
"Smedley sir. I have fish and chips sir."
"That'll do me" Said Mercer. "Give me yours and I will eat them, you go and get yourself some more. Try not to be too long though, Mister Hargrieves has found us lots of work to do."
"I'll be as quick as I can sir" Replied the young officer.
Mercer had already turned his back on the lad and was busy rummaging through the packages to find his meal.
"Right, I'll be off then." Said Sam Hargrieves, "We all know what we're doing do we?"
"Oh yes, we know what we're doing alright" Said Mercer.
Sam sighed and said to his friend, "Come and see me in my office tomorrow morning Terry, I need to go over a few things with you, about eight?"
"I'll be there" Said Mercer without turning around.
Sam shook his head and turned to leave.
"Good luck everyone" He said as he left.

Terry Mercer felt deflated. He hadn't expected Sam to react this way. He was deliberately splitting himself and Billy up for a reason. He surmised that the reason was Sandra Neal. Some loud mouthed bastard in the squad had opened their big fucking mouth and went running to Sam to inform him that officers Neal and Mercer were becoming too close to be able to concentrate fully on their work, and therefore putting the case in jeopardy, hence, this separation. Sandra approached him.
"Do you mind if I take a seat here beside you Officer Mercer?"
"It's a free country, or at least it used to be."
"Oh come on Terry, it won't be for long. He's just desperate to bring this case to a close. He's under pressure from higher up, to solve this before public panic sets in."
"He's like those bastards in H.Q. Sandra, doesn't want to see me happy. I used to be good friends with him you know. At one time we were inseparable, used to have a laugh whilst we got the job done. Used to go for a beer together before we went home, huh, hardly see the fucker now since he was promoted. He's a changed man Sandra. The young recruit had taken Billy with him, at Mercer's request. Mercer had also informed Phillips to make himself scarce. They sat eating together, not saying anything, as if they were contemplating the situation. Finally, Sandra broke the silence.
"He won't stop me seeing you Terry."
"That would depend upon what mood he was in."
"No, I don't mean that Terry, I don't care what mood he's in, or anybody else for that matter, I mean, they, they won't stop me seeing you, that's if you still want to see me of course. They can split us up on the job, all they want, but they're not going to dictate who I see in my own time, Christ I have a life you know."
Terry looked at her, rather taken aback. He'd thought that the deep feelings had been his alone, and that a closer relationship had been nothing more than wishful thinking on his part. He felt quite exhilarated.
He wiped his mouth with a paper towel and reached for her. He kissed her on the cheek. "You're right Sandra. I feel the very same as you. Why the hell should we stop seeing each other, thank you

for saying that, you've no idea just what that means to me."
She smiled back at him. "So you would like to see me on a permanent basis?"
"You bet your life I would."
He had something to confess to her about his past, and hoped that it wouldn't make a difference in their relationship, but he would have to tell her. Right now, wasn't the time though, there'd be time enough for that. At least he knew how she felt about him. It wasn't just wishful thinking on his part after all. For the first time in an age, something had gone right for Terry Mercer.

## CUMBERLAND GATE. WEST LONDON.

Everything had gone well for Him. His salary had been increased, and he'd been given a company car. He switched off the engine, the B.M.W three series engine, and looked up at the property he'd came to assess.

Another class apartment close to the Marble Arch. He entered the sandstone building, and then after scrutinising the name-plates on the wall, he entered the elevator. He stepped out onto an immaculate marble floor. Every door along the hallway was glossed black, with gold name-plates. The walls were white, and decorated with numerous hardwood framed professional sketches of famous land marks from around the city. Finally, He found the apartment He was looking for. He took the key-card from his inside jacket pocket and swiped it across the magnetic lock.

There was a loud click, as the lock disengaged.

He opened the door and stepped into the apartment. It was designed very similarly to Bridge Way Street, only in here, there were security cameras everywhere. There were two in the hall down stairs, and another two in the hallway up here. He looked around the house for others. Scrutinising the plan of the house He now held in his hand, He noticed that nothing had been mentioned about security cameras in the premises itself, that didn't mean there weren't any.

Many people who owned properties these days had secret cameras installed, hidden cameras. One would have to be extremely cautious, especially if one intended bringing back a whore to play with. In the lounge of the house, there was a three-piece suite, brown leather, and of good quality. There were also good quality carpets on the floor although the colour-clash was hideous. It hardly mattered, most people threw away any furniture and carpets which had been left behind. He had never known anyone to keep the furniture left behind. He stepped into the main bedroom. Everything in here was lavender, including the lace drape over the four-poster Victorian-type bed which took precedence in the room.

The current owners must have thought they were doing the buyer a favour, by leaving this. Everywhere in the room aubergine and lavender, not unpleasant, but certainly not his cup of tea. Even the drapes were of a shade of purple. He closed the door and entered the kitchen. It was the usual, fitted with all-mod-cons. The cooker placed directly in the centre of the spacious room. A breakfast bar circled almost the entire kitchen, leaving enough space for a large dining table if required.

After overlooking the second bedroom, and then, the bathroom-come shower room, He sat down to write out his report. He done everything by hand, and wrote with a very expensive pen and ink, one of the things his employers were impressed with. It was all too easy these days to open up a lap-top and print out something in seconds, with a pen you had to actually think about what you were writing, and of course, take time to write things neatly and correctly. He wrote out his report, which done the property no harm whatsoever, and deemed it acceptable for Burlington and Hedgewood's sales web-site. The place would sell, there was no doubt about that. The location alone gave it a favourable advantage. He sat back and enjoyed a moment of quietness, before He would head back to his office. He had no idea how long this place had been available, or how long it would remain unoccupied. If He decided to bring anyone back here, He would need to be very careful, especially if anything happened to that someone. After some thought, he dismissed the idea completely, too many cameras.

SCOTLAND YARD.

BROADWAY VICTORIA. 8am.


The thick grey laden skies that loomed over London appropriately matched Mercer's mood as he entered the building. Sam had changed, he thought to himself. He was no longer the man he used to be. He used to be one of the boys, laughing and joking with everyone, whilst dealing with the cases in hand. Now, he hardly had the time of day to pass with anyone. It was acceptable that Sam's new job would be more time consuming, and that he had a lot of responsibilities that he hadn't had before, but that said, he had still changed, and not for the better. His whole personality seemed to have changed. His attitude to people he'd known for years, people who were used to sharing a joke with him. Now, it was all stone-faced business, and don't arrive at his office door unless you've been invited or you have some *really* important information for him...otherwise.

He arrived at Sam's office, where Rose Milton sat outside in her little cubicle, typing away merrily and faithfully.

"Good morning Terry" She said, without taking her eyes from the screen. "You've just to go in, he's expecting you."

"Thanks Rose, and good morning to you blossom". He had called her this name since the day he found out that her name was Rose. He tapped on Sam's door and walked into his superior's office.

"Ah, come in Terry, would you like a cup of coffee?"

"There's no point, I'll hardly be here long enough to drink it."

Sam ignored the sarcastic remark. "Take a seat Terry."

Mercer removed a document that was on the chair in front of Sam's desk, and sat down, sighing.

"Do you know why I want to see you?"

"Nope" replied Mercer, though he had an idea of what the meeting would be about. Sam rested his elbows on the table, clasping his hands together, as if to pray. The two friends sat in silence for a few seconds. Terry knew from previous experiences that Sam was about to say something serious. And then it came.

"I could take her off the case Terry. I could even move her if I felt it was necessary. I could send her up to Birmingham or even further north, to Manchester or"-

"Excuse me, but what or who are you talking about Sam?"

Now it was Sam's turn to disclose his anger.

"You're my friend Terry! I'll punch you on the fucking mouth if you try and take the piss out of me, you know fine fucking well who I'm talking about, don't try and make a fuck out of me! Come to think of it, it might even be easier if I relocate you, I could think of twenty or more people who would sing the hallelujah chorus if I did!"

Sam took a deep breath. He rose up, grunting, and walked over to the door, opening it, and asking Rose if she would be so kind as to bring in a couple of cups of coffee. Upon returning to his desk he said, "You and I go back a long time Terry, do we not?"

"I'm glad you remember Sam". Mercer's words weren't in any way sarcastic, but a genuine reflection of a special time in his career.

"How could I ever forget it Terry. Because of the work we done then, is the very reason I'm sitting here at this desk now, how could I forget?"

"You've changed Sam. You're not the same guy I used to hang out with. Let me ask you something, when was the last time you and I went out for a beer? When was the last time you told me something funny about you and Beth, or something Beth said, can you remember? because I sure as hell can't."

Sam stood up and placed his hands in his trouser pockets. He stood with his back to his friend nodding his head.

"You're right Terry, I know you're right, but there's something you don't understand. I haven't got the time to have a joke, not with this job. You think I don't talk to you enough? You should speak to Beth Terry. I could lose her quite easily, I don't know how long her patience will hold out...bloody pressure Terry, this job is so different to the one I used to have, your job, and I'm not for one-minute suggesting that your job is easy. I never get a minute's peace Terry.

Some days I could...I...I could just jump on a plane and fuck off from it all."
Sam's phone rang.
"Hello? Yes, yes I will, that's no problem sir, pardon? No, I haven't, but I will, as soon as possible sir, goodbye."
He placed the telephone back onto its cradle and pointed to the clock on the wall.
"It's twenty past eight Terry, and that thing will ring all day now."
He hardly got the words out of his mouth, when his mobile buzzed loudly on his desk.
"Hello? Oh I know Beth, I forgot darling. Tell you what, you book the tickets for any night this week, and I'll –.
" She's switched off."
The phone on his desk rang again.
"Hello? Mister Walker, I'm dealing with it today, I'll get back to you just as soon as I can."
Once again Sam placed the phone back on to its cradle. This time Terry reached over and knocked it off onto the desk. He pointed to the clock on the wall now.
"You should take things easy Mister Hargrieves, give yourself time to take five now and again, and I once worked with a man who would have head-butted Jesus if he'd interfered with his free time. I've known you Sam for some time now, and I'm saying this to you as a friend, so please don't take offence. The job's killing you Sam. It's already killed the jovial detective I had the pleasure of learning my trade from, it's killed him. It's not happy with that though, now it's proceeding to do the same with your marriage bud. You're going to lose Beth if you're not careful, hell, you used to admit that you didn't spend enough time with her before, when you worked with me, God knows how all this is affecting her, all this time you're spending in this fucking office. Ask yourself a question Sam. Are you happy? Is Beth? Then ask yourself what's more important, this job? or your marriage, because in my opinion, one of them has to fall. Which one do you want it to be? That man I was talking about, he told me something once Sam, can you remember? He said, sort out your own head first before you attempt to advise others. You will

get three times the work done if you are happy. Now, are you happy, is Beth happy? Kick this job into touch Sam, and get your life back, and by the way, if you move Sandra or me away from this case, I will personally break every fucking bone in your body mister. Don't you fuck up my chance of being happy, you miserable fucking son-of-a-bitch that you are, ok? Now think on smart-ass and get on that phone to Beth and tell her to get ready to go out tonight, you sorry arsed miserable fucking miser."

There was a soft tap on the door. Rose came in with her usual friendly smile that would cheer anyone up, and carrying two mugs of coffee. Sam had already made his mind up about the job. Terry was right it was either this job or his marriage, and his health. There was no competition.
"Here she comes Terry, my sweet summer rose, isn't she beautiful?"
Rose looked first to Sam and then said to Terry, smiling.
"What have you given him Terry, you haven't given him one of those illegals have you, one of those E pills, you could get into serious trouble for getting him high Terry."
"Rose, my little darling, I'm going to resign from this post my angel, that's why I'm happy. Hog breath here has just made me see sense, isn't that strange Rose? The thickest man in the entire force, and he opens my eyes up to the bloody obvious, he's in love with inspector Neal did you know that Rose?
The girl must need her head looked at, but there you go, he's always been jammy like that. I don't know what women see in him to be honest with you, petal, I mean could *you* bring yourself to kiss that? His face"-
"Now that'll do Sam" said Rose, continuing to smile, lots of people round here could say the same about you and Beth. Some of the men round here thought that you were drugging Beth, and keeping her prisoner."
Mercer smiled. He was glad that Sam had made this decision, and truth be known, he hoped he could team up once again with the man who had helped and nurtured him through his career, and

through some very difficult times in his life.

## 22B CALLINGDON SQUARE.

## ISLINGTON. 9am.

He had been busy. For the past three evenings he'd brought back a different prostitute with him, who had all been impressed with his dwelling-place, His elaborate furnishings, his paintings, all the things in fact about this luxurious apartment which they could only dream of owning. He hid his actual circumstances quite well, the fact that He practically lived from pay-cheque to pay-cheque, and that all the furnishings in here had in fact been stolen, or gifted to him, including the crystal glasses that He and his latest prostitute-friend now drank from. The girl on his sofa now was smiling up at him as she brushed her long auburn hair. She sat with her legs crossed, exposing their appeal. She wore a short black mini-dress which was decorated with large golden-coloured autumn leaves, matching the colour of her hair perfectly. Her fee of three hundred pounds lay on the coffee table in front of her.
"You're very beautiful" He said to her, smiling broadly.
"Thank you for a lovely evening."
"Thank *you,* and I mean that, I've had the best time in ages, wow, you know your stuff don't you, and you must be the most unselfish man I have ever known, please, come and hunt me out again, you know where I drink, but I will also inform my girlfriends of you, well, two of my best friends anyway, I just know they'll be bursting to meet you when I inform them of your skills, and eh...your em...your gift."
He continued to smile at her. "Thank you for the compliments."
"Oh, you're welcome, trust me."
"What's your name"?
"Veronica, my friends call me Ronnie."
"Would you like another drink Veronica?"
"If it's no trouble."
"It's no trouble at all, bring your glass over please."
He acknowledged, that even without her high-heeled shoes on she

had very shapely legs. She padded over to him, handing him her glass. "Thank you."

"How long have you been a prostitute then Veronica?" The question seemed to whack her like a brick on the face. It was probably the last thing she'd expected him to say to her. Decent people she'd had parties with, tended to keep from using such a cold and callous word. It was a mute reminder of what she did for a living, and she would have to face up to the fact that a *Prostitute* was exactly what she was, and that, no matter how bubbly or attractive she may come over to people, she sold her body for money, which cheapified her in societies' eyes. She was a whore. He picked up on her sudden shame.

"About three years I've been a whore." She replied, as coldly as the question had been asked.

"Well Veronica, you must be like me in that department, I just love sex, especially with beautiful women like you, you are a remarkably beautiful woman you know, I have had a truly wonderful time, and I *won't* be telling my friends about you. I want you all to myself, and you can bet your life I'll be coming to seek you out, definitely."

She smiled at him, although it was more of a polite smile, a business smile. He had only been trying to heal the scar he had just inflicted. "Thank you for saying that, but all said and done, I know what I am."

"And I know what I am Veronica." He studied the young woman's face with mild curiosity, as if trying to read her mind.

"I detect something in you Veronica, guilt perhaps about what you do, and if that's the case then think of this. Who is more immoral, you, for taking money for services rendered? or me, for paying for your services? The way I look upon the situation is this, I have had a good time, and you have had a good time. We've caused no-one any heartache or misery, we've caused no-one any harm, we certainly haven't broken up any homes, so, why feel guilty at all. It is simply a business transaction that has taken place between yourself and I, it has nothing whatsoever to do with anyone else in the world. Immorality, don't forget Veronica, is merely a matter of opinion."

"You're very kind, especially when you know that I will be with other men today, and every day, different men...it's what I do."
"Yes, and I will be with my girlfriend later today, and someday soon, I hope the three of us will be together, what do you think about *that* Veronica, would you be up for that?"
She sipped her drink and said, "Oh I would be up for it, but I doubt very much if your girlfriend would be as keen on the idea."
"Ah, but you're wrong there young Veronica, I know for a fact that she'd be up for it, especially with a beautiful woman like you, and of course, we would pay you double the fee."
"Well, you know where to find me, and if it turns out that she is up for it, well then, what a night *that* will be, one for the scrap-book I'd imagine."
"Indeed" He said, lighting up a cigarette.
He sat down opposite Veronica and admired her.
"Can I ask you something Veronica? A favour really, it's for my girlfriend. Would you mind if I took a photograph of you? I'd like her to see for herself just how beautiful you really are, otherwise she won't believe me, she'll think I'm lying or exaggerating."
"I would hardly describe myself as beautiful, but, I'll give you a photograph if you want. You'll have to wait until I get my shoes on, I'm rather petite without them."
"I was hoping more for an erotic photo Veronica. I was hoping to take one of you showing off your promiscuousness, that's the kind of girl my girlfriend likes, you know, wild and carefree."
"Are you sure it's for your girlfriend? I don't usually have photographs taken of me, you know, like that, that's not what I do, and anyway, I don't take very good photos, the camera doesn't like me."
"On the contrary, I think you'll be wonderful, so, will you allow me, I know this is short notice, but I'm keen for her to see you, and it certainly won't do your business any harm, I can assure you of that."
Not exactly reluctantly, but then not enthusiastically either, Veronica agreed to let him take a few photographs. At first, she thought that he only wanted the photos to enhance his hedonistic

life-style, but then after some thought, she decided that good business was where you found it, and all said and done, one could never get enough `Good business`.
He continued to encourage her.
"Here" He said, "Let me show you some of my girlfriend, budge over".
He sat down on the sofa beside her.
He showed Veronica several photographs of Her. There was one where She was sitting exactly where Veronica was sitting now, with Her head back and Her legs wide open, exposing her womanhood.
"My God, she's not shy is she?"
"Goodness no, she loves her body, she's very proud of the way she's kept herself."
"She has every right to be proud, she's very beautiful.
Is she a model?"
"Not as far as I know, I haven't known her all that long, although it wouldn't surprise me if she has been."
"Her hair as well, it's absolutely gorgeous, look how it shines."
Veronica made small talk all the time He was taking the photos, trying her best to look relaxed about the whole affair. She found that after one or two, she no longer felt as uncomfortable as she initially had.

"That's it, that should do the trick, I think she'll be very attracted to you Veronica, I take it you're comfortable with bi-sexuality?"
"To be honest, I've never thought about it, well, not since I was a teenager at school". She lit up another cigarette, slightly nervous again, and more than a little embarrassed.
"Listen, I've never done it with another woman before, I don't know how I'll be when or if the occasion arises. I'll do my best to give you both a good time, but I can't sit here and say I'll be, you know, a success, but I'll try"...-
"Veronica, please, don't you worry about that. If you're going to enjoy the experience then you'll know within two minutes, and I can assure you, she will please you, trust me on that score, I've seen her in action. She'll have you feeling at ease with yourself in no time

at all."
"You've done this before with another woman?"
"Of course, and that's why I'm so confident about the whole matter. You are very attractive you know, young lady, your beauty is very powerful."
"And she doesn't mind you making love to strange women in her presence?"
"My dear, trust me when I say this. If you take a liking to what's happening, then I assure you, it'll be all I'm worth to get anywhere near you, She will dominate proceedings, She always does."
If Veronica was being honest with herself, she would have to admit that she felt quite turned on at the thought of sharing this man with a beautiful woman, and by the way he was describing things, she really had nothing to worry about. In fact, she felt quite exhilarated. He smiled at her as he rose from the sofa, looking at the photographs on his phone he had just taken, and nodding his head in approval. He pulled out His wallet and peeled out some notes, placing them on the coffee table next to the money He had already placed there.

"Oh no now, there's no need to give me more money, I don't mind giving you a photograph or two, after all, you've given me a wonderful time as well, here, take this back, I"-
"Ah uh, no arguing please. Accept it as a gift, for me putting you in a spot at such short notice. I want you to know how much I appreciate your trust, and that's exactly what you can do, you can trust my girlfriend and I, when I tell you that *this* will go no further than the three of us. It is our private little transaction that has nothing at all to do with the rest of the world. Now, can I use this number you gave me at any time, you know, at short notice?"
"Yes I'm almost always available". Her face immediately reddened as soon as she'd completed her sentence.
"Ok then Veronica, we have a deal. I don't think it'll be too long until you hear from me, are you alright about it now? Tell me I've made you feel at least marginally more confident about the affair."
"Yes, I'm eh...I'm fine I think. I'll see myself out, talk to you soon, I

hope."

"Oh you will, make no mistake about that Veronica, you will."

## CHAPTER FIVE.

## SCOTLAND YARD.

## BROADWAY VICTORIA.

Terry Mercer and Sam Hargrieves walked together along the corridor towards the elevator.
"I should have done this a long time ago Terry. I might have known the job would be too time consuming, and that it would cause problems between me and Beth."
"Well, that's you all over isn't it Sam, you always think you know better than everyone else, you know, a know-all, you've always been the fucking same if truth be known, such a stubborn hard-headed twat you are. At least you've seen sense though, before it's too late. It breaks my heart Sam to watch you fade away, because that's what it's doing to you, and don't just take my word for it, all the guys are saying it."
"Well Terry, I'm not packing it in for them, I'm doing it for me and Beth, and for my health, not that I'm saying being a detective is an easy job, and anyway, there might not even be a job for me, they could easily make me retire completely, honestly, that bastard in Downing Street is cutting back on everything, except his own salary. It's not a foregone conclusion that I can just step into another job." Sam sighed as he walked. "But do you know something Terry, I don't care, what you said in there was true. I think I knew what I needed, I just needed to hear it from someone else."
"What Sam, there's something else bothering you, I can tell."
"I don't want to lose her Terry she's all I've got in the world. I just hope I haven't left it too late to turn a new leaf. She's stood by me all these years and she deserves better than me if I'm honest, hell,

there's many another woman wouldn't stand for half of what she's had to put up with. I'm going to treat her like a woman from now on, you wait and see." Hargrieves looked at Terry Mercer.
"Stop it you soppy bugger. And stop worrying, the woman loves you to bits, you're one of the lucky ones you jammy sod, now get a fucking grip of yourself before you have me in tears."
Sam smiled as the two most ill-tempered detectives in Scotland Yard made their way along the corridor.
"I wonder who they'll get to take my place Terry, do you not fancy a go of it?"
"Are you trying to be sarcastic? Anyway there's no chance of that, and even if there was, do I look stupid? I've just watched what the job's done to you in six years...chief inspector indeed, fuck, there'd be more chance of Dagenham and Redbridge winning the champions league than me being selected for *that* post."
The two friends entered the elevator.
When they were out in the car park Mercer said, "Before you make any changes, I'm telling you this, I'm taking McDermot back Sam, he's coming with me, that fucking Smuggly, can go back with Sandra."
"How are you two getting on? I mean you and Sandra?"
"Don't even go there Sam, I know what you're doing, you fly old bugger, but for your information, we're doing just fine.
One step at a time Sam."
"Well, I'm off to explain to the chief of police why I'm resigning as chief inspector."
Terry frowned at the very thought of Sam having to explain himself.
"Hit him a smack on the mouth Sam if he tries to get silly. He is of the same calibre as that fucking ponce idiot in Downing Street. Both of them are out of touch with reality."
Sam climbed laboriously into his car. "I'll see you later Terry."

THE AVENUE RESTAURANT.

WEST LONDON.

Christine Smith sat with her husband Thomas, awaiting the arrival of their one remaining daughter. Already, Mandy was fifteen minutes late. Christine mumbled to herself, "*Hmph, how could we expect a bloody prostitute to be punctual, little bloody scrubber.*"
The restaurant was beginning to fill up. A skinny waitress dressed in a skirt no larger than a tea-towel approached their table, and politely asked them if they were ready to order.
Christine Smith looked at the young lady as if she had the plague, automatically associating the skimpy dress code as that of the same profession as her daughter.
"No, we're not ready to order yet", She sighed. "We're waiting for a third party if it's all the same to you. Don't worry, I'll call on you when we're ready to order, now if you'll excuse us, we're in the middle of a private conversation."
Emily Jenson lived for moments like these. When there were customers who thought for some reason, that they were a law unto themselves. Putting them in their place was almost a hobby for Emily, who was working here for no other reason than to put herself through university. She smiled sarcastically at the middle-aged, and quite obviously, sexually-frustrated hag in front of her, who was dressed like an extra in a nineteen thirties gangster movie, and sighed.
"Listen to me, I don't care if you're in a private conversation, or a comma. You are in this restaurant at its busiest time of the day. Now if you wish to eat elsewhere, then that's your prerogative, but I am under orders to enforce the restaurant's policy, which is, after

fifteen minutes, you order, or you leave, now, what's it to be, because I have not got all day to stand here and listen to your senseless banter."
At this point, Thomas Smith took over the situation, not because he wanted to, but knowing that, if he didn't, his wife's mouth would end up having them both removed from the premises in front of all and sundry.
"Excuse me miss. We're waiting here for our daughter to inform her of something of the utmost importance, I wonder if you could please give us just five minutes more, I'm quite sure she'll be here any minute now, I'm so sorry for the inconvenience."
"Five minutes", said Emily, scowling at Christine Smith.
"After all, rules are rules, I don't write them, my job is merely to apply them."
"Thank you so much miss, we appreciate it very much."
"I'm sure you do" Replied Emily.

Thomas had decided on this restaurant, way over in the west of the city to make sure, as far as they could, that they would have Mandy all to themselves. They knew what Mandy done to earn a living, and so had no desire to be sitting eating somewhere where they could quite easily be disturbed by one of their daughter's kind. Thomas had had quite a battle to convince his wife to come to *this* respectable diner. Finally, Mandy arrived.
When her father caught sight of her, he stood up and waved to attract his daughter's attention, but not because he was pleased to see her. He and his wife wanted this over and done with as soon as possible. As Mandy arrived at the table, she had to pull a chair out for herself. She was dressed in smart new jeans and a matching jacket, with beautiful suede boots, all of royal blue.
"Hi" She said awkwardly. "Sorry I'm late, but the taxi I took got caught up in heavy traffic, road-works you see."
Neither her mother nor her father responded to her explanation.

At last her mother said, coldly, "What do you want to eat?"
"I'll get fish and chips" Mandy replied, "I'll pay for this, you two order what you want."

Christine Smith was looking disdainfully at the menu.
"Indeed you will not pay for your father and I's meal, my God, to know how you get the money, the very thought of it sickens me to my stomach."
"Even at a time like this mum, you can't bring yourself to be civil can you, you can't even pretend to be nice to me, well, suit yourselves, I'm ordering fish and chips for myself."
Eventually, they all ate their meals. There was not one word spoken in the fifteen minutes it took them to consume their food. Then, it seemed like Mandy's mother had been saving every possible insult she could think of, for this moment in time.
"God works in mysterious ways indeed" Said Christine, wiping her mouth with a paper napkin she had retrieved from her own handbag. " Why does He take our real daughter, who has worked hard all her life, keeps a job, keeps her house clean, and has had the same partner for over six years. He takes her, and leaves us with this pathetic excuse for a woman who whores herself out to any Tom Dick or Harry, who happens to have a ten pound note on them, my God I feel sick even talking to you, you dirty little bastard that you are."
Mandy's father joined in.
"Why the hell would He take Jane and leave us with you, you little slut that you are. Don't upset yourself Christine. Tell her what you have to, and then let's get away from her."
"Thanks dad."
"You listen here you two-penny scrubber that you are, don't you ever refer to me as your father!"
"Fine" replied Mandy, smiling, although she felt torn to pieces.

"We know what you get up to" He continued. "You little slag. Your mother and I have heard all about your gutter habits, making pornography and constantly whoring, don't think we don't know what goes on up here."
"I don't care what you do or don't know, it's my life, and I'll do whatever I please. That's why I left home in the first place, to get away from you two, and it's strange isn't it, you even had a low

opinion of me before I left school, didn't you, and Jane, you used to accuse her of all sorts didn't you, none of us could please you, so don't sit there and sing her praises like you were in constant touch with her, or had regular conversations with her."

"I spoke with her a lot more than you did, you little cow, when did you last speak with your sister, slapper, Jane wouldn't pass the time of day with you, you bloody crow that you are, look at you!"

Mandy sat back in her chair and scrutinised her parents.

Her father, who was fifty-eight, dressed the same way now as he had twenty odd years earlier, like a frump. He sat with his diamond patterned vee-necked jumper and sports jacket, and his black trousers and shoes. Her mother, who was the same age as her husband, dressed in pale pinks and blues complete with pink-rinsed hair.

"I've got news for you two know-alls" said Mandy. "I've been staying with Jane for the past three years. She and I got on like a house on fire for your information."

This information, true or false was too much for Christine Smith.

"You lying whore!!" She cried, causing quite a few people in the restaurant to turn and look at her, and bringing Emily Jenson to the table and issuing a final warning that if she uttered one more obscenity she would have no choice but to throw her out. Emily continued; "I don't know what your problem is lady, but you, are on your last warning, now take a telling. Don't make me kick your ass out of here, `cause` I will lady, make no mistake about that." Emily deliberately scratched her backside to further annoy Mrs Smith.

"Bloody rif-raf. I'm so sorry ladies and gentlemen for this woman's outburst, but rest assured she's been warned, please continue with your meals."

Emily pointed to Christine Smith, and then the door, then her eyes. Emily was having a simply wonderful day.

Christine, who's face now was the same colour as a no-go traffic light, calmed herself.

"Once the police have finished examining Jane's body, she's coming down to Basildon where she belongs. She'll be buried with her grandmother."

"Oh, her grandmother, not mine?"

"Listen here whore, you have burned your bridges with us. We want nothing more to do with you, do you hear? Now, in my bag, I have a cheque for you. Your sister had an official will written out, and she's left you four thousand pounds of her hard earned money. As much as I tried to stop the payment, I have been informed by her solicitor that you must receive it. And don't phone either, ever, and anyway, we're having the number changed. Only people we class as friends or family will get the number. The last thing we want is to be bothered with filthy scum like you. I hope with all my heart that you catch a horrible disease like aids or cancer or something, and I hope that you die a very slow agonising death that will allow you the time to reflect on just how much of a plague you've been in our lives. Even if I wanted to give you a cuddle, I couldn't, for fear of catching some sexual disease from you. You choose to be a disgrace to this family by turning into a slut and a whore? Then you live with the consequences of your decision, huh, you were a slut even before you walked out of the school gates, I hope you rot you little scum-bag."

Christine and Thomas Smith rose to their feet. Thomas threw some notes down onto the table to pay for their meal. Christine threw down the cheque, put on her jacket, picked up her hand-bag and then, walking arm in arm with her husband, headed for the door. Mandy watched them, as did Emily Jenson, lifting her skirt marginally for the benefit of Christine Smith, and then pulling it back down, before waving good-bye to her.

Mandy sighed heavily. She knew today was going to be difficult, and she could have tried to explain to her parents that Jane had struggled with a heroin problem, and that the only reason she had got into prostitution in the first place, was to help fund her sister's insatiable habit, but they were beyond even trying to understand, let alone listen. In truth, Jane had been as much a whore as she was, until she'd met Thomas Felton.

As Thomas and Christine Smith reached the door, Emily Jenson moved in for a final confrontation with the `hag`.

"I have been instructed to inform you ", she lied, and keeping her voice down," that you are not to return here ever again.
The owners of the establishment do not wish their regular customers to be subjected to language like that, you should think yourself lucky that that young lady even takes the time to speak to you, you miserable piece of fucking shit that you are, now fuck off and don't come back here or I'll take great pleasure in kicking your fucking arse right back out, ok? madam?"
Christine Smith began to speak but was abruptly stopped.
"Goodbye now!" said Emily as she closed the door on the couple.
Mandy watched her parents disappear from view, and from her life. A few minutes later Mandy left the restaurant and took a taxi cab back over the city to Locksley. Back to where she had the only friends in the world. The girls, like her, who had got into prostitution for so many different reasons. When she returned, she would drop in and visit Veronica. She would cheer her up, she always did. Whatever happened in her life, she knew she had in Veronica a friend who would never let her down and a caring person who always had time for her. Mandy considered herself extremely lucky to have a friend such as she, especially the way she was feeling now. It wouldn't have made one bit of difference to Christine Smith even if she'd turned out to be a solicitor.

## TEMPLE ROAD. LOCKSLEY.

All the way over to Locksley, Mandy had gone over everything her mother had said to her in the restaurant. She knew she shouldn't let it get to her, but it did. *"Nothing but insults for the best part of fifty minutes, come to think of it, nothing but insults for the best part of her life".* Mandy knew why her parents had been this way with her, and her sister. It was because both her father and mother had wanted sons. It wasn't so bad for them, after the arrival of their daughter Jane. They would simply try again. But after she had arrived, Christine had been informed that she couldn't have any more children. The news had devastated her, and of course, Mandy was to blame for damaging her mother's womb and for causing her this terrible heartache.

The taxi arrived at its destination. Mandy paid the driver who had tried his level best to keep some form of conversation going all the way over here, but he could plainly see in his rear-view mirror that the young lady was troubled about something. She thanked the driver and made her way into the tower block. In the elevator, there was a little boy about four years old accompanied by his young mother. The aggressive graffiti on the elevator walls did not seem to attract the young mother's attention. Maybe she had read it all before. Just about everything she read was insult to women, sexual insult; *Veronica needs cock like she needs air. Sally eats sperm for breakfast. Blow-job and anal from cheap-at-the-price Chelsie. Carol takes the train.* The elevator came to a halt. The young mother stepped out into the hallway with her infant. The doors closed again. *Alice is a sperm whale.* The walls were covered with insults, from ceiling to floor. But that was just the way things were. The graffiti only depicted how the youth of today looked upon her and her kind. Compliments and kindness came only from the men who used their services. No-one but they, would understand the kindness and the coldness, and the loneliness of the working girl. None of the insults had been put there by any of their customers. They were put there by youths who lived in a world of little or no prospects whatsoever, and so, it was their way of hitting back at a world who cared nothing of their predicament, or indeed, their very existence; *For a tenner, bring your friend to meet Julie-two cocks.*

Mandy stepped out into the hallway, floor eighteen. It could have been floor level six, or sixteen, or one, or twenty-one. They all looked the same. She knocked on number 108, Veronica's flat. No-one answered. *"I should have text her first"*. Just as Mandy was walking away, she heard the safety chain on the door rattling. The door opened marginally. Veronica stood with a huge white bath towel wrapped around her body, with a smaller one wrapped around her head.
"Come in, come in babes" she said, kissing Mandy on the brow. "How have you been my little angel, haven't seen you for ages it seems." Her friend's voice was like music to Mandy's ears.
Kind words. Veronica's melodious tones were comforting her already.
"I've just made coffee baby doll, do you want a cup?"
"Yes please Ronnie I'd love one." The two young women embraced. Mandy sat down on the sofa while Veronica poured her her coffee. Veronica came through with Mandy's cup.
"Have they heard anything Mandy? Have they got any ideas who it could have been?"
"Not as far as I know, anyway, they won't be in any hurry to catch them, my sister and her boyfriend were known only to society as useless fucking junkies, there may as well have been two rats killed in there. Anyway, that's not why I'm here Ronnie. You and me and Lizzie, I'm going to take you out for a meal and a few drinks. I'll have to wait until the cheque clears, but next week or the following week, I'll treat the two of you."
"I'll look forward to it Mandy, but I was thinking more along the lines of me treating you, I've met this guy you see, he's loaded Mandy, his house is over in Islington, a beautiful apartment. He pays me three hundred pounds a night and I'm not kidding you, I

should be paying him."
"What's the catch Veronica, there's always a catch."
"No, honestly babes, he's as straight as the day is long."
"Is he married?"
"No, and that's just it Mandy, he's shown me photographs of his girlfriend, you know, bloody hard core photographs, doing all sorts of things with her, and he's em he's well equipped, if you catch my drift."
"There's got to be a catch Veronica."
Veronica was excited and only half listening to Mandy's voice.
"He showed me one photograph of her lying back on his sofa with her legs open, I'm not kidding you Mandy, she could be a model, she's so beautiful, anyway, I'm meeting her tomorrow night and"-
"What?!! Are you for real Ronnie? The minute she finds out you've been with him, she'll kill you, you stupid woman, God Veronica, wake up for goodness sakes."
Veronica smiled at her friend as though Mandy hadn't even spoken a word. She walked over to her unit, opened the top drawer and pulled out a bundle of notes.
"There's just under twelve hundred pounds there Mandy ok? Four nights, and four of the most wonderful nights in my life I don't mind telling you. Now I know that I would never be lucky enough to land a guy like that, you know, to marry, so I'll take my chances Mandy, while lady luck is smiling upon me, because God knows, her appearances in my life have been few and far between. He wants to pay me six hundred quid for a session with him and his girlfriend; she's bi obviously, so I'm up for a bit of that. He says that she likes to watch and masturbate while he pleasures the other woman, they've done it before Mandy, she's not the jealous type."
"Just you be very careful Veronica, I stand by what I say, there's always a catch."
"Mandy, give me a little credit kid will you? You know I'm no fool, nobody will take me for a mug. It's the best thing that's happened to me in ages, can't you just be happy for me, he's really nice babes, and if his girlfriend is not happy about the arrangements, then that'll be the end of it."

"I am happy for you Ronnie, it's just that I've lost my sister, and I couldn't bear it to lose any more of my friends, and I know you're nobody's fool...but neither was Jane."

## FINLAY STREET HOLBURN. 7am.

Terry Mercer stood shaving at his bathroom mirror. There was a lot of work to do today. For that, he was grateful. Work was good it kept the mind occupied, and healthy. Work helped you focus on the present. It did not allow you time to dwell on things. Things like when your wife takes off with your kid and doesn't tell you where she's gone, or why, whether she's met someone else, or she's just taken off to make a fresh start somewhere under a new name and identity. That was five years ago, and he'd never heard from her since. At the time, he'd initially thought they'd been kidnapped, until he discovered that she'd taken every garment of clothing she owned, and Daniel's. She had also drained their bank account of twenty thousand pounds, and left an unpaid gas bill of three hundred and twenty pounds. What had hurt him so badly was that, the night before she left, they had made love and shared a bottle of wine. After that, they had cuddled up on the sofa and watched a late night horror film. They went to bed together, and in the morning when he got up, Carol was busy in the kitchen, as usual, making up junior's packed lunch for school. When he got home that night at around eight thirty, they were gone, and so was the money, and so were all his dreams, and his faith, and his hope. She'd taken everything.
Terry wiped steam from the mirror and looked at his face. He couldn't talk about Sam Hargrieves, he was ageing fast himself. He padded through to his bedroom and put on clean underwear and socks, then his jeans. His phone rang in the living room. It only took him a few seconds to get through, but by the time he picked the phone up, it had just stopped ringing. "Bastard!" He roared as he replaced the receiver. He headed back into the bedroom to put on his clean shirt, but upon reaching the bedroom door, the phone began to ring again. He bounded back through to the living room and snatched up the phone, stubbing his toe en-route.
"Hello? Who is this?"
"It's me sir it's Billy."

"What in the name of fuck do you think you're playing at, phoning me at this time of the fucking morning? And what kind of detective are you going to be? It takes you two go's to make a fucking phone call, you fucking prick, and anyway, who gave you this number, tell me!"
The surge of excruciating pain in his big toe had just reached its peak.
"Hello?"
"Hello sir."
"Well, who gave you the number, was it that cunt Hargrieves?"
"No sir, it was you. You gave it to me last night, remember? You told me to phone you at seven o clock, pick up a car at the depot and come and get you. You said we had lots to do today so you wanted to get an early start."
"So I did" Said Mercer, more to himself than to his junior officer.
"Right well, get your arse into gear and get over here, do you think you can find Finlay Street?"
"Yes, no problem sir, I'll"-
"Hey, stop fucking saying that, no problem, because you have a problem with everything you do, don't you. You have a problem about trying not to be sick, you have a problem with making a phone call, and you most definitely have a problem following orders don't you, fucking flat tyre you twat. You just get your arse over here pronto, I've been standing here waiting for you for the past hour and a half, it's nearly time to get back into bed, now just get a fucking grip will you!!"

Mercer slammed the phone back down and made his way back to his bedroom. He put on his clean white shirt and was fastening the buttons when his phone rang again. Once again he bounded through to the living room, snatching up the phone.
"Let me fucking guess, you can't find the depot, and you think you're going to be sick, is that it?"
"Hello"? said Sandra Neal, "Terry?"
"Oh, eh...sorry Sandra, I've just had Billy on the phone, and eh, I thought it was him"...

"Well, I was just going to say, if I don't see you today, do you fancy going out for a couple of drinks tonight, you know if we don't get finished too late?"
"That would be lovely Sandra, thank you, em, where will I meet you?"
"I'll send a taxi over for you and they'll bring you to my place ok?"
"Ok that'll be brilliant, see you later Sandra."
Terry Mercer buttoned up his shirt and made himself a cup of coffee. The phone call that Sandra Neal had made would make William McDermot's day an awful lot more pleasant than it would have been.

It was going to be one of those days for Terry Mercer, even though he now had a date for this evening. He suffered these days from time to time. Days when everything Carol had done to him, came back to him with a fresh rawness that burrowed into his heart with the same painful ferocity he'd felt on the very day she'd left him. On days like these it felt like she had left him only yesterday. He picked up the photograph of himself and Carol, taken on their wedding day. He had never been happier in his life, with their whole future in front of them. It had all seemed set out before them, a course of successfulness, happiness, achieving goals along the way, building a family, and then some day, their dream home. Then, after seven years, all the dreams of building homes and achieving goals, of building a family, they all came crashing down around his feet, like a house of cards. He picked up the photograph of his five-year-old son Daniel, taken on his first day at school. People used to say he was his double. That was then, five short years ago. His boy would be twice that age now. *"I wonder what you look like now captain"* he said to the photograph. He took a drink of his coffee and lit a cigarette, a luxury he would not have been allowed, if Carol had still been here. In all this time since she had left him, he had never once been out on a date with another woman, perhaps subconsciously believing that she would return. Two months after Carol had left, his mother died, and that was it for Terrance Mercer. From that day onwards he cursed fate, and he cursed life, he cursed the criminals he pursued and he cursed at just about everything he came into contact with.

There had been some bitter rows between himself and Sam Hargrieves, but Sam had helped him the best he could, and dragged him screaming and kicking through that corridor of darkness and misery. He kissed the image of his son and replaced it along with the others. His mother smiled up at him from another photograph. She had deserted him too, although for very different reasons.
"I'll need to get over there ma, and get some fresh flowers put on your grave...I haven't forgotten you, God knows you're the only woman in my life who never done me wrong...I've met a new girl ma, I think you would have liked her." Terry Mercer asked the photograph of himself and Carol, as he had on many an occasion, why?" Then he sat down on his bed and cried...again.

## PARLOUR STREET. SOUTH KENSINGTON.

Sam felt like a new man. He felt as though an enormous weight had been lifted from his shoulders, and it had. He informed Beth of what he had done, and why he had done it. He had resigned without informing her because he knew if he'd discussed the situation with her, she'd have blamed herself for him taking this action, and that she'd forced him into doing this. "Beth" He had said to her the previous evening; "Believe it or not girl, you are all that matters to me. You are the reason I wake up in the mornings. Without you, I don't know what I would do. You've supported me throughout all these years, through all those ungodly hours I've worked, and I have just come to my senses recently. That job was killing us, and it was killing me, so I had to do something about it. Terry advised me to kick it into touch, can you imagine that Beth? Terry Mercer giving *me* advice, but it was the best bit of advice I've had in years. From tomorrow Beth, I am simply inspector Hargrieves. Now, you and I are going out tonight, and if you fancy a bit of company along with us, then say to one or two of your friends and their husbands if they fancy a meal and a show, I'm paying." "My God Sam, what's came over you"? said Beth, smiling broadly. "Common sense Beth, that's what's came over me. I have given the best years of my life to the force, and I don't regret that for one minute, but I'm damned sure it's not taking the last of my years. You and I deserve some quality time my angel. Now, I have one or two things to sort out in the morning, but I'll be done by lunch time. Have a look on the internet and decide which show you want to see. We're going to start living now Beth, and this time I mean it."

Beth gave her husband a kiss on the cheek. "I love you Sam Hargrieves, I hope you know that."
"Oh I know it Beth, I'm just grateful that you do."
"Yes and I'm just grateful to Terry for talking some sense into you."
Sam laughed.
"What's so funny?"

"Nothing Beth, it's just the thought of Terry Mercer talking sense."
Sam was thinking of the words Sandra Neal had used.
"You have to dissect the coherent words from his continuous profanations."
Beth spoke again.
"He's had a hell of a lot to cope with Sam, since Carol left him. He thought the world of that girl you know, and I can tell that underneath all that cursing and swearing he does, there is a very distraught man, struggling to keep the faith in himself alive.
Now I know you were jesting there Sam but spare him a thought now and again. He lost everything, his wife and his little boy. It's going to take a very special lady to heal *that* man I can assure you. And now that you've resigned from this post, try and spend a little more time with him. Bring him back for dinner Sam now and again, because I'll tell you something sweetheart, you're all he's got for a friend in the world, so don't you let him down Sam."

## TEMPLE ROAD. LOCKSLEY ESTATE.

"Ok" Said Terry Mercer, "Let's go and see what Miss Smith can tell us Billy. Now before we go in here, let me remind you of the situation. As with the rest of the tenants in these apartments, we will not be made welcome, so be prepared for short cold remarks. People change when they move into apartments like these, their actions become almost animalistic. They live by their wits Billy, so if they know something or witnessed something of importance, then, for their own safety, they will deny any such knowledge, a kind of self-protection policy, for want of better words. They may have moved into this block, perfectly normal human beings, but after some time when they realize that there's not much hope of ever getting back out, they change, almost metamorphous-like, into unrecognisable beings, shadows of their former selves."
As if to enhance everything Terry had said, the walls of the apartment halls screamed out to Billy about just how dangerous it was to live here. As usual, the broken plaster off the walls, the names of gangs spray-painted everywhere, the threat of physical violence to anyone who would dare to enter the premises uninvited. He looked all around as they walked. A discarded lipstick, a used condom, several empty beer tins, broken glass everywhere he looked, blood stains on just about every wall. Although he and Terry had been here before on numerous occasions, this was the first time he'd actually given the place any kind of close inspection.
Mercer continued. And Billy McDermot listened, intently.
"To say they'll be discourteous would be an understatement, so we have to be patient Billy, and we have to learn for ourselves what are truths, and what are lies. Through time, you'll learn how to read their faces, see the signs, and obtain the information required."
Terry Mercer pressed the button on the elevator panel.
"She's staying with a friend here Billy, our friend Mandy, a Miss Veronica Wells, chances are, she'll be a working girl as well, so, if she is, then we find out if she's been in the habit of going over to

the other block of flats to visit Jane Smith and her partner."
"Look at this sir" Said McDermot, grinning and pointing to the graffiti on the elevator wall. "Sally's arse sucks canal water."
Mercer offered no reply. Today for some reason, he was behaving differently, seriously, business-like, and no cursing, strange.
They stepped out of the lift and made their way along to Veronica's apartment. To Mercer's surprise, the door was answered almost immediately. Veronica stood inside the doorway with the safety-chain on.
"Yes? Can I help you?"
"I sincerely hope so Miss, are you Miss Veronica Wells?"
"Yes, oh you must be inspector Mercer."
"Yes I am Miss, may we come in?"
"Of course" She said, "But please, don't upset Mandy, she's having a Hell of a time just lately, can I get you a cup of tea or something?"
"Eh, thank you Veronica, that would be lovely, tea please, milk and two for both of us" Mercer said, knowing full well that Billy didn't take sugar. McDermot just smiled and looked to the floor.
"Just go through there" Said Veronica, pointing to a door. "She's not long out of bed so you might have to wait a little until she comes round a bit, she's not at her best first thing in the morning, she's like me, a bit of a slow starter."
Mercer and McDermot entered the living room, where they found Mandy sitting on the sofa watching TV. On the chair opposite Mandy, the other girl they had met at the elevator sat eating a piece of toast. Elizabeth Keaton looked up when she saw the two officers enter the room.
"Mandy" Elizabeth said to her friend, "The police are here."
Mandy did not take her eyes from the television screen, but merely replied, "So?"
"Excuse me Miss Smith" Said Mercer. "We just want to ask you a few questions, and then we'll be away again, out of your faces. Now first of all, I'd like to start by apologising to you for my abruptness the other day, it wasn't very clever of me was it, and it didn't get us very far, and so I am here today to make amends, if you would permit me."

Mandy continued looking at the TV screen, taking a bite of her toast. "Does that mean that you have suddenly ceased to be a pervert then?"

Mercer smiled. "Probably not Miss, I'm afraid my eyes wander when confronted with such natural beauty, such as yourself and this young lady here, I wasn't expecting such a treat to be walking out of the elevator the other day at shortly after four in the morning miss, but I think what you mistake for perversity, is in fact admiration , you are all beautiful young women you know, it would be difficult indeed for any man not to glance at your obvious beauty, with all respect."

"We are *all* beautiful women you say? There was only Lizzie and I in the elevator."

Again Terry Mercer smiled. "I was referring to the young lady who's making the tea miss as well."

Veronica came through from the kitchen carrying a tray with all the cups of tea, and completely contradicting everything Terry had said to Billy down stairs in the hall.

"Here we are gentlemen."

"Thank you very much" Said Mercer, taking the tray from Veronica's hands. "Thank you, you're so kind miss."

Five minutes later, Terry began his questioning.

"Now then Mandy" said Mercer, "Do you mind if I call you Mandy?"

"Well, seeing as how it's my name, it might be a good idea."

He smiled at her.

"Ok then Mandy, now the first thing you have to understand here is, we want to catch the people who done this to your sister and her boyfriend, so if my questions seem a bit, em personal, it is only to get a clearer picture of the situation. So, let's start with Jane shall we? Did she have many visitors?"

"Not really, about three or four close friends came to the flat, no-one else as far as I recall. If there were any more than that, then I didn't know about them."

"Do you know their names Mandy?"

"Yes, and so do you, you're talking to two of them right now, Lizzie and Veronica."

"I see", and who would the other two be?"
"That would be Rose, Thomas's sister, she works as a receptionist over at Tomlinson's brewery, it was she who helped Thomas get his job there."
"Jane and Thomas, did they go out much Mandy?"
"Very rarely about three or four times a year on average, they weren't big drinkers if that's what you mean. Sometimes Lizzie and Ronnie and I would take a bottle of wine over, well, not me, because I live there, lived anyway, God knows now what will happen."
"Who's Ronnie? Is this one of your sister's friends?"
Mandy looked at Mercer and smiled, pointing. "Ronnie, Veronica, the one who's legs you keep glancing at, at her natural beauty of course."
Veronica tried to pull the short towelling dressing gown down a bit, but it was a half-hearted attempt.
McDermot smiled and looked to the floor, gloating slightly at his superior's embarrassment. Mandy clocked him.
"You needn't laugh you're having a good time there looking at Lizzie's tits, are you not? Are you another one who is attracted by natural beauty, are you?"
"Ok Mandy", interrupted Mercer," so you can't think of anyone else who visited your sister's apartment?"
"Nope."
"Where did they go, you know when they did go out do you know?"
"Yeah well, if Thomas was still alive he'd kill me for saying this. Thomas had a deep interest in the opera. He liked to go to the west end and watch the shows, it costs a fortune to go to those kind of shows you know."
"Yes, I do know Mandy, said Mercer, recalling the one and only time Sam had persuaded him to go along with him and Beth, and how much it had cost him. "They are very expensive indeed".
"My sister loved it in the end, she used to tell me to get myself over there and experience it for myself, never fancied it much though, you know, men running around with tights on, and jumping about the place on their toes, not my scene really."

McDermot jumped in with both feet. "That's ballet" He corrected, "You know, where the men dance with tights on, it's ballet, not opera."

"Ah well, you'd fucking know wouldn't you" Said Mandy. "It's all the fucking same to me, it's all poncey shite to me. Do you like that detective? Do you like watching the men in their tights, exposing their, em, natural beauty huh?"

McDermot's face turned crimson.

"Indeed I do not Miss."

"You seem to know all about it then", she said, laughing, as were all the others, Mercer included.

"Look at you" Said Mandy to officer McDermot, "All red faced and everything at the thought of liking the men in their tights, d'you like a bit of cock then detective? Think we hit a nerve there girls, what d'you all think?"

"Look, I don't like cock, I mean men, I'm not gay!"

"If you say so officer" Said Lizzie, "But you've gone all red, bring your head over here, because I could light up a cigarette off your ears, your face is burning."

Mercer could plainly see that they weren't going to get anything else out of these girls today. He could smell cannabis as well, and who could blame them, he thought to himself.

He politely excused himself and McDermot as they rose up and made their way to the front door.

"Officer Ballet? What do you think of these?"

Lizzie lifted up her top and exposed her breasts to officer McDermot. "If you're not gay, then you get yourself back here to see me, prove it that you're not gay." McDermot smiled and stepped out into the hallway, so very grateful for the cooling air. He was raging inside at his superior, and was trying his best to bite his tongue, and not land himself in any trouble.

As they walked along the corridor Mercer said, "It's only a bit of fun Billy boy don't-"

"Yeah, just a bit of fun, it's always at my expense though isn't it, the joke's always on me, you're good at that Terry aren't you, dishing out the abuse, but you can't take it when it's handed back to you."

"Billy, they were just having-"
"I know, I know, they were just having a laugh, well fuck you Terry, don't say another fucking word, I mean it, not another word or I'll smack you on the fucking mouth, I mean it, fuck you and your little games, you were encouraging them as well."

Suddenly Mercer stopped smiling. He looked at McDermot.
The joke was over.
They made their way to the elevator in silence. Not another word was spoken between the two men until they reached the car, whereupon McDermot offered the car key to his superior.
"You drive" Said Mercer.
They both got into the vehicle.
Just as McDermot reached for his safety belt Mercer swung his left fist round and landed a solid punch into the stomach of the young officer.
Billy began retching and stuck his head out of the door as he began to vomit.
"Sorry `about that kid, but I'm afraid you and I don't know each other well enough yet for you to talk to me in that manner, don't you forget your place kiddo, you're still learning your trade, and you've got a long way to go in learning how to address your superiors."

## QUEEN ELIZABETH THEATRE. WEST LONDON.

"This is more like it Beth" Said Sam Hargrieves, "I'm looking forward to this."

"You're not just saying that Sam to pacify me, are you?"

"Of course not, you know I enjoy the shows, well on the few occasions that I've managed to get here, but my angel, we'll be here more often now Beth, you'll be able to catch up with all the shows you've missed."

Seated up high in the balcony, Beth took her husband's left hand in both of hers, and then tapped his hand in an act of gratitude.

"Thank you Sam, you have really surprised me with your actions, I know how much that job meant to you, and you sacrificed it for us, that's a wonderful gesture Mister Hargrieves."

"Yes, but I'll still be out on the cases Beth, it's just that I won't be working as intensively as I have been in the past, I'll be allowing more time to spend with you, and I must admit, I could get used to this kind of living pretty quickly."

Sam was referring to the elaborate furnishings and decor of the theatre. The lights went down, and so too the volume of the audience's voices, until you could almost hear a pin drop. Everywhere in complete darkness now, except for the stage, where bright colourful lights lit up the scene for the first act.

Sam looked at his wife. She looked so beautiful with her royal blue evening dress. She had spent almost three hours at the hairdressers having her hair done especially for this evening. Her silver hair shone in the colourful lighting, and catching her eyes, making them shine like bright blue sapphires, her dress revealing just enough cleavage for a respectable woman, Mercer would have thought, Sam observed, showing off the beautiful pearl necklace he had bought her for their first anniversary.

He was almost overcome with emotion. He was a proud man.

"Beth? I think-"

"Sshh" she said, placing a pointing finger up to her lips.

The woman of the couple sitting next to them smiled at Sam.

He had seen her before, but he couldn't remember where.
The lights on the stage changed colour, and then the woman's face disappeared, then re-appeared. Now she was whispering something in her husband's ear. The music began from the orchestra pit, and the show was under way.
Strangely, and for no apparent reason, he wondered how Mercer was doing, this being the first date he'd been on for quite some time.
Sam needn't have been concerned for Mister Terrance Mercer, for he at this very moment in time, was consummating his relationship with Miss Sandra Neal, and was burying ghosts from way back when Carol had left him. He hadn't forgotten how to entertain a woman after all, and if inspector Neal had been asked about Mister Mercer's performance thus far, she would have replied, "He's doing just fine."

She sat next to her husband in the theatre, but her thoughts were over at Islington. She glanced at her watch and wondered who He would be making love with at this moment in time, she had another week or so to tolerate the man here beside her, before She would once again have her freedom. It was the first break in the show, and they were just about to be heading off to the bar for refreshments. Charles had reserved a table for them. The man had glanced at her on one or two occasions in that first act.
She knew She had got to him, first with a polite smile, then by exposing a bare leg as She crossed them, allowing one of them to be fully exposed through the split in her long silk evening dress. On one occasion, she had run her hand up and down it, slowly, as though She were caressing it erotically, and She was. Every now and then, as the lights changed colour on the stage, she saw him looking, and at one point, swallowing hard. As she stood up, she momentarily turned her back on her husband, and bent down to retrieve her hand bag, allowing Sam a bird's eye view of her ample cleavage. At one point Sam thought they were going to pop out.
"Shall we go and get a drink Sam" Said Beth, smiling, "You poor man, you must be thirsty after that show."

If the woman heard Beth's sarcasm, she made no reply, nor gave any response.

"What makes them be like that Beth, is it to get to you? Do they like annoying other women? God almighty, did you see her flashing her legs?"

"Let's go babes, and get you a cold beer, poor darling, or perhaps a cold shower." Beth smiled.

"Hell Beth, her husband is sitting right next to her, what the hell is he thinking?"

"I don't know Sam, but I know this much, that necklace she has on will be worth about fifty grand, I know that much, and God knows how much all of her jewellery will add up to. I'd like to see her collection at home. And as for her perfume…"

"Mercer has a name for women like her."

"I don't want to know Sam what Terry calls them."

"He calls them gold-digging fuck bitches-"

"Sam! I said I don't want to know", although she couldn't resist a smile at Terry's description, and truth be known, he probably wasn't far off the mark.

## CHAPTER SIX.

## EUSTON ROAD. 10am.

Billy McDermot had tried three times to get in touch with Terry Mercer, but for some reason, he wasn't responding. He had forgiven Terry for punching him in the stomach, realizing that he'd been out of order, and anyway, whether he was or not, there was no excuse for threatening a superior officer. Terry and he had made friends again, so it wasn't that that was stopping him answering his phone. As far as Billy was concerned, there was only one thing that could be stopping him. Sandra Neal. Billy didn't want to go back to HQ, and discover that Mercer or Sandra weren't there, and then land Terry in trouble, owing to the fact that he was supposed to stay by Mercer's side at all times unless otherwise instructed. He had been shown by Sandra the other day where the key for Bridge Way Street was kept, and so decided he would spend an hour or so over there, keeping out of the way, and allowing Terry time to communicate with him.

As Billy approached the apartment, an elderly gentleman was coming out, and held the door for Billy, passing the time of day politely with each other as they passed. Two minutes later Billy was standing in the kitchen of the apartment, waiting for the kettle to boil. Through the kitchen window he could see trains silently coming in and out of the stations. He could see traffic running to and fro on the roads beneath him, again, in complete silence. He made himself a coffee and wondered if he was doing the right thing, after all, if he was going to be investigating anywhere it should be over at Locksley and not here. "Oh well" He thought to himself. "I'll just spend an hour here or so, and then I'll head over to Locksley, surely Terry will contact me by then." He sipped his coffee and leaned on one of the work tops, looking at the freshly painted walls, where, according to Sandra that poor girl had been pinned. "My God" He thought to himself, "What was going on in the mind of someone who could do something like that." Worse still, they were out there, in one of those vehicles, or maybe on one of those trains. Maybe they work in a local shop. That's just it, how do you spot a psychopath, unless you actually catch them committing a crime, it was almost impossible. But it was this that had attracted him to this profession in the first place, the challenge. He was learning his trade with Terry Mercer who was, to say the least, unorthodox in his methods, but he had been entrusted to Terry by Sam Hargrieves, who had the whole departments' trust, and so, if he felt that Terry was the man to learn him his profession, then so be it.

As he sipped his coffee he noticed a cigarette packet on one of the work tops and a gold lighter on top of it. Nodding his head and smiling, he deduced that Sandra must have left them here on her last visit, either that, or, she was here now. "That would explain a lot". If she was here, then without a shadow of a doubt, Terry would be here as well. He took one of the cigarettes out of the packet and lit up. Now he was in a bit of an embarrassing situation. If he went to one of the rooms and disturbed them, Mercer would give him hell, and maybe even another punch in the stomach. He would never hear the end of it. Then he thought, if they were in here, then they quite obviously hadn't heard him coming in. Billy made a decision. He would drink his coffee and smoke the cigarette, and then he would leave. He could go back over to Locksley, maybe even try questioning the girls again, even though he knew that he would be targeted with sarcasm, sexual sarcasm. No matter, that's exactly what he'd do. He sipped his coffee. "Was Terry and Sandra here though? She may have left the cigarettes the other day." He lay the burning cigarette in the ash tray and made his way as quietly as he could, down the hallway towards the bedrooms. He stood outside of the largest bedroom, listening. Yes, they were here. He could hear the muffled moans of pleasure coming from Sandra. He almost burst into laughter, as he remembered what Terry had said a few days earlier, romantic Terry. "It's my chance kid, to bang her, fuck she's gagging for it fuck."

Billy almost burst into laughter again. He suppressed his laughter thinking of how much trouble the two of them would be in if Sam Hargrieves found out about their behaviour, after all, they were supposed to be hunting ruthless killers, not spending their time in luxury apartments making love, and taking full advantage of the facilities, beds included. He returned to the kitchen, again, as quietly as he could, closing the door behind him and sitting by the table with his back to the door. Five minutes and he would be out of here. Surely Terry could last that long.

As he sat smoking, Billy began to think about something. How many card keys did Sandra have for this apartment? She must have more than one otherwise that key would not have been in the hiding place she'd shown him. He had hardly thought about this when he heard the bedroom door bursting open. He could hear footsteps coming down the hallway on the tiled floor, a woman's footsteps. It sounded like she was wearing high heels. She was striding with purpose.

"Oh my God" He thought to himself "How embarrassing."

The kitchen door burst open.

"Sandra, I can explain everything, I didn't realize you'd be here with Terry."

Just as Billy turned round, he had barely enough time to acknowledge that the naked red head wielding the axe was not Sandra. He had no time to defend himself, the woman had already begun to swing the instrument and landed him a blow to the head with ferocity, cracking Billy's skull with the blunt end of the axe. Billy felt blinding pain in his head, and then felt himself falling and slipping into complete darkness.

When he regained consciousness, he was tied securely to the upended kitchen table, and he was gagged. There was a man lying on his back on the kitchen floor in front of him. A naked man and the red head was administering oral sex to him.

When She saw that Billy had regained consciousness, She stopped sucking, and lifted a small hand axe.

Still dazed and confused, Billy looked in horror as the woman raised

the axe above her head and brought it crashing down on his left foot, blade first this time. He screamed with the fresh burning pain under the gag. The axe had practically severed his limb just above the ankle. She began performing oral sex on the man again.
Without stopping what She was doing, She picked up a large razor-sharp kitchen knife, and began stabbing Billy wildly with it, everywhere.
Two stabs on one of his legs then a stab in the stomach, one in the chest, one right through his ribs, one on his testicles, still sucking. She was not even looking at Billy, only at her lover. She continued stabbing everywhere as she continued performing her sexual act. Billy's vision began to blur. The stabs were becoming less and less painful, until, he could no longer feel them, then he couldn't see or hear anything…and finally, he couldn't even think. There was only darkness and silence.

## LOCKSLEY ESTATE.

Veronica had bought herself some new clothes. She was going to meet with Mister money-bags tonight. This time she would meet his girlfriend as well. If all went to plan, she would be six hundred pounds and God knows how many orgasms better off in the morning. She had spoken to Him on the phone, and She seemed eager enough for it to happen, and so, Veronica had bought some new things, at least to try and compete with the woman's appeal. She was beautiful there was no doubt about that.
Why She wanted to share her man with anyone else was not Veronica's business, and she had no intentions of asking her.
She ordered her taxi to come and take her down to `The Merry Widow`, where she was to meet the couple. She arrived there ten minutes early at eight-twenty, just enough time to order herself a drink and calm herself down. He was a strange one. She had never met anyone like him. There was nothing strange about his looks though. He had all the correct attributes, tall, dark, perhaps slightly on the slim side, but very handsome, with piercing sea-blue eyes. He was always immaculately dressed, clean shaven, and blessed beyond belief where it mattered. A man maybe in his early forties, a good catch for any woman, which only added to confuse Veronica more, why you would be prepared to share a man like that with anyone else, albeit for sexual fun only.
You would still feel that they'd lose the intimacy in their relationship, but, none of her business. Having said that, who could be more perfect than a working girl to try out all your sexual fantasies with, it's not as if they're going to tell anyone about them, well, no-one of any importance to them anyway.
It was now, eight thirty-five. He was five minutes late. Maybe the woman had backed out of the idea, although he had told her on the phone that she was as keen as he was, and she'd certainly sounded enthusiastic enough on the day she'd phoned her.
A couple of young men approached her and asked if she'd like a drink. She informed them that she was waiting for company but they were welcome to come and sit with her until they arrived. One

of the young men went to the bar to get the drinks, the other sat down beside Veronica. She knew one of them.

"You stick out a mile", said the youth who sat down.

"I stick out a mile Simon, what the hell is that supposed to mean, are you trying to give me a compliment?"

"Yeah, of course Ronnie, I mean, you stand out…you eh, you look different to all the other whores."

Veronica slapped his face hard and loud enough for two lads who were playing pool to look over.

"Sorry Ronnie, I mean working girls you look too good to be doing that you know? I mean, don't get me wrong, I love it when you spend some time with me, and I know Veronica, that if you didn't do this, that there'd be no chance of getting a date with you, I know that, but"-

"Simon, are you trying to tell me that you think I'm beautiful?"

"Yes."

"Ok then pet, thank you, goodness me man what a state to get yourself into, calm yourself down."

Simon's friend returned from the bar, clad in jeans and t-shirt that looked like neither had seen a washing machine in quite some time. To make matters worse, if that was possible, one of the laces in his baseball boots flapped loosely as he walked, reminding Veronica of a five year-old out playing.

"Are you going to be busy tonight Veronica?" He said, sniggering like a school boy.

"Is that drink for me?" She said, pointing to the tray.

"It most certainly is." More sniggering, and laughter.

"Well put it down then, and thank you, now, please remove yourselves from my table until you can learn how to speak properly, you know, like the adults you're supposed to be, go on, before my friends arrive and think that I'm deranged for talking to you, and tie your laces you silly boy. Honestly lads, take a look at yourselves, there's not much chance of you having sex with a girl without paying for it is there, I mean look at yourselves, you look like you've stepped right out of a Charlie Dickens book, goodness me, Oliver was never in it, and as far as Great Expectations are concerned,

Christ, now just go away, and for goodness sake, at least try and act like men. Instead of spending all your money on beer and glossy magazines or DVD's or whatever it is that you purchase to relieve yourselves, try spending it on some clothes, you'd be surprised how young ladies react to men who keep themselves well dressed, after all lads, if you don't respect yourselves, then don't expect any-one else to respect you, especially attractive girls, now, on you go, and take heed to what I've told you."

"It's been nice talking to you Veronica" said Simon, dressed almost identically as his friend, complete with the tomato sauce stain on his t-shirt from his last meal.

"I'm sure it has" She replied, now, on you go, quickly, disappear please."

The two youths made their way over to another part of the pub, and almost out of sight, thanks to the dim lighting.

She glanced at her watch and then at the clock on the wall. The pub clock was the correct time, it was 8.50.

"What's wrong with you Ronnie?" She asked herself. "Don't you think they're coming? And what are you more disappointed about, not collecting six hundred quid, or not having the three-way-sex you've been thinking about all week. Mandy was right, there is always a catch." It didn't look like they were coming, but she would give them until 9.30 to appear. If they hadn't arrived by then, she would go home and have a drink with Mandy and Elizabeth.

One hour later, Veronica was back home sitting with her feet up on the sofa wearing her towelling dressing gown, and a large glass of vodka and coke in her hand.

"I told you Ronnie, didn't I tell you there's always a catch."
Mandy poured herself another gin and tonic.
"You broke the golden rule Veronica you got too close to him. I've been listening to you going around the house all week, singing and humming along to the radio, and do you know something Ronnie, you haven't been with a single trick since you've been with that man, bloody weeks ago."

"I know Mandy" Veronica admitted, "I know you're right, I let him get to me but it wasn't intentional, I couldn't help it, he's the kind of guy I would have loved to have married."

"Yeah" Said Lizzie, laughing, "And I wonder why, can you guess Mandy?"

"Yes ladies, I know what I've told you about his money and his, you know, but it's more than that, he's just so kind and considerate, he's a breath of fresh air, compared to the lonely broken inadequate men who hire our services."

"It sounds to me Ronnie that you've actually fallen in love with this man" said Elizabeth.

"I know, I know, don't keep reminding me, I've been trying to convince myself otherwise, so, there's only one thing to do ladies, tomorrow, I'll just get myself back into the saddle so to speak, I'll just forget about him and his money, and his girlfriend, lucky bitch that she is, but I know you're right Mandy, I'll just have to get on with my life, the life that I'm *so* used to, maybe I'll win the lottery or something, and then we can get away from here. Perhaps we can go and live in one of those exotic countries. Go and live abroad somewhere instead of living up here in the clouds where the cold and damp air will eventually set into our lungs and we'll succumb to bronchitis and die before our time, lugubriously...forgotten."

## BRIDGE WAY STREET.

## HENSLETON ESTATE. 11.45pm.

"What the hell is Sam doing here at this time of the night Sandra?"
"Don't know Terry, but he doesn't look too pleased with himself does he?"
"He's stepped down from chief inspector, maybe that's why he looks a bit doleful" said Terry, parking up the car. He and Sandra walked over the car park towards the entrance of the luxury apartments, where Sam Hargrieves sat upon the top step.
"What have I told you Sam about wasting your nights man, you should be home with Beth, and you'll be giving yourself piles sitting there on the bloody cold step, you stupid fossil."
Sam pulled out a cigar from his overcoat pocket and lit it up.
"I'm waiting for forensics to arrive Terry, where have you been all day?"
Terry sighed. "Sam, you told Sandra and I to go over to the morgue again and listen to what the pathologist had to say. So, we went there, and we've been there for almost four hours, you told us to Sam, you said he had some details you wanted us to hear about the killers. Then we went for something to eat."
"Where's Billy Terry, do you know?"
" He'll be off home Sam, I know, before you say anything, I haven't seen him today, he and I kind of fell out the other day, I thought I'd give him a break, I've been a bit sore on him lately, and why are you waiting for forensics Sam, have you found something else up there?"
"Something else?" Said Sam, puffing furiously on his cigar to keep it lit. "Oh you bet I have Terry, just found it about forty minutes ago, on you go and take a look, the doors' unlocked."
"What have you discovered sir?" said Sandra, feeling slightly ill at ease in case Sam had found something that she should have.
"Oh, you just wait and see Sandra, you go up Terry, go and take a look pal you wait here with me Sandra."

"What the fuck am I looking for Sam?" said Terry, himself feeling a little out of sorts. It sounded rather sinister to him, the way Sam was talking. Whatever he'd discovered, he was as keen as mustard for him to see it, but what the hell could it be?

Three months had elapsed since the murder in this apartment. Terry stepped through into the open hallway and decided to take the stairs up to the second floor.

Outside in the cold crisp frosty night, Sam and Sandra could hear Terry's footsteps climbing the concrete steps. Then they heard him opening the heavy door. A few seconds later, they could hear Terry letting out a terrible hopeless cry of despair, and then a kind of guttural scream, almost animalistic, similar to that of a lone wolf.

"What the hell is it Sam" said Sandra, what the hell have you discovered in there?"

She left Sam sitting on the steps and ran inside and up the stairs as fast as she could.

She found Terry Mercer on his knees outside in the hallway, crying like a baby, sobbing and clutching the cigarette case Billy had bought for him by way of an apology for his outburst.

"Billy, Billy, I'm so sorry kid, oh my God I'm so sorry son...you were going to be..."

Sandra stepped past Terry and walked gingerly into the apartment. The upturned table faced her as she stepped into the kitchen. Billy's corpse was fastened to the table, his head bowed, as if looking to the floor. Sandra let out an involuntary gasp. He was just pulp, human pulp. As she stared in disbelief, there must have been a hundred stab wounds around Billy's body. Both of his eyes lay in the red pool which covered almost half of the kitchen floor.

"What is it Sam, what's wrong, why are you sitting down here bud?"

Andy Phillips stood with his team of two women and two men, the best there was in the field of forensics, at least around London.

"Come on Sam, let's be getting you to your car old pal, where's Terry?"

"He's up there Andy, go and help him, I'm alright, I'm going home."

"Is there a mess up there Sam?"
"A mess? Oh yes Andy, there's a mess alright."
"Well look, I'll have to chase Terry out of there just now, he hasn't got that kid with him up there has he? Don't want the lad spewing all over the evidence."
"Oh don't you be worrying yourself about our Billy Andy he won't be spewing up today. I'm off home, I'll talk to you in the morning pal."
Police cars began to arrive along with an ambulance.
Sam Hargrieves climbed laboriously into his car, and drove off into the city, heading back home and longing for that loving embrace from Beth, who understood everything about evenings like these.

When he arrived home, he parked his car in the drive and switched off the engine. He sat in his car now, going over in his mind, what he had just discovered in Bridge Way Street. He felt numb. A feeling of complete disbelief came over him. If he could just wake himself up from this nightmare, because that's exactly what it felt like. But there was no waking up from *this*. This was here, and it was here forever. All these years in the force, all these years of discovering bodies, bodies with bullet holes, with knife wounds, people who'd had their throats cut, people who'd been poisoned, some who had suffered petechial haemorrhaging. One particular victim of that, he remembered had had their tongue forced down their throat. Up until this evening, he thought he'd seen everything there was to see. He thought he was immune to shock. How wrong he had been. He had gone over to Bridge Way Street, just to take a look at the apartment. Sam had always done this. He would return to the scene of a crime, even after all the forensics were finished, and he would walk around the place, trying to recapture the events which had taken place there, using the information given to him by the forensic officers. Sometimes he was blessed with thoughts of inspiration which would pay off, and sometimes he got nothing from it, but every time, he done it. When he and Beth had got home from the theatre, he was anything but tired, and so he had come over to Bridge Way. Tonight, as he'd entered the apartment,

there had been what he called a strange silence in the place. Most people, including Terry Mercer would tell him not to be so stupid, and that silence was silence, and that was that. But Sam knew, or rather, believed, felt, that the quietness in an empty house was different than that of the silence in an empty house, with a dead body present. Besides he remembered that, upon entry of the apartment, he could smell the blood, enhanced by the fact that the central heating system was on, and the place was really warm.
Sam opened the window of his car and relit his cigar.
Tears rolled down his face now as his mind relayed to him what he had seen when he'd opened the kitchen door, and knowing too, that if Terry hadn't fallen for inspector Sandra Neal, then the chances were, Billy McDermot would still be alive. Having said that, it was not a case of unprofessionalism, after all, it was his idea that Terry and Sandra went over to the morgue to speak with the pathologist. Terry and Sandra were only following orders, and Terry thought he was just giving young Billy some space and time, realizing that he'd been a bit hard on the lad lately, and confessing to Sam that, *"The boy must feel like he's joined the fucking Scuhtzsaffel rather than the CID"*.
The kid had been through a lot these past few weeks, and to top it all, the fall out he'd had with Terry had really hurt his feelings. Terry thought that the lad would have just hung around HQ taking phone calls or running errands. But Billy, being who he was, thought he'd keep himself active and visit the crime scenes unaccompanied, a big mistake, and one really in all honesty, he should never have made. The boy had always been eager to please, always trying to better himself, but he had broken the golden rule, which was, never under any circumstances, return to the scene of a crime unaccompanied, unless you were given permission to do so, even if the crime there had been committed weeks before, as was the case in this instance.
Sam climbed once more laboriously out of his car. His house was in complete darkness, with the exception of his bedroom light, which burned brightly. He could see Beth at the window watching him. She had obviously heard the car pulling into the drive, and, she'd probably watched him in the car smoking and crying. He could tell

that she sensed something was wrong, otherwise she would have waved at him. Such a lovely evening they'd had at the theatre, what a bloody shame for her, that it had ended like this.

He climbed the stairs wearily, feeling exhausted and deflated. As he reached the top of the stairs Beth said, "Who is it Sam, I know someone close to you has died, who is it?"
Sam fell into his wife's arms and began sobbing.
Beth patted his shoulders, making him feel like she was the only person in the world who cared about what was going on in his life, and with the exception of Terry Mercer, he was probably right.
"Just a kid Beth, he was just a kid, a bloody good one. We left him unattended, stupid kid went to a flat, there had been a brutal murder there, Terry was...he was just... Sandra took Terry away to the morgue, stupid Billy."
In all of their married years Beth had seen her husband upset on numerous occasions, but never like this. He was standing at the top of the stairs with his arms wrapped around her neck, and sobbing bitterly. From what she could make out, one of his young recruits had been murdered, and that he was to blame. She knew that he was in fact, letting out all these pent up emotions and frustrations of all the years he had felt he'd let her down. He was doing his best to please her. He seemed to think she would leave him, and that she would just suddenly walk away from him. He had stepped down from the post of chief inspector for that very reason. He felt he'd let her down because of all the nights she'd spent at home alone over the years. All the broken promises he'd made, all the last minute cancelled holidays, everything.
They were all coming out now in these sobs. He let go of Beth, and leaned his back against the wall, sliding slowly down onto his hunkers. "Jesus Beth" He stammered, they've stabbed the boy a thousand times." He put his hands up to his face and continued crying. "They took the boy's eyes out Jesus Beth, oh dear Christ...I don't...I can't do this Beth any more, I love you my darling, I love you so much, and I am so sorry for neglecting you all these years Beth, they stabbed the boy like a pin cushion...I don't want this

anymore…I can't do it baby, they've beat me babe, don't leave me now Beth, I am so sorry angel."

Beth, down on her knees, cuddled into the only man in her life she had ever truly loved. She cried now along with her husband, feeling the love, and the strength, and the weaknesses that make us the people we are. She would never leave this man, no matter how many hours he worked. How can you walk away from yourself, because that's exactly what she would be doing.
She just kept tapping his shoulders and saying, "I love you Sam Hargrieves, don't you ever forget that, and I'll be here by your side until I die."
Sam Hargrieves had trained successfully, eleven recruits including Terry Mercer. All of them had turned out to be excellent detectives and had played major roles in Scotland Yard's most successful achievements. He'd had big plans for Billy McDermot, and could see that the boy was going to be one of the best. There was not a shadow of doubt in his mind about that, but before the lad could be sent out on his first assignment, his life had been taken from him, ironically, by the very criminals he was about to pursue.

## DOVER STREET.

## KNIGHTSBRIDGE. 2:30am.

Satisfied that her husband was fast asleep, she sat outside the back of the apartment, dressed only in her underwear and one of her six fur coats, smoking a cigarette and sipping a glass of brandy. She went over in her mind, the course of events of three days prior to this one, when She had taken the life of the young detective.
The young man's life had been a bonus, and was unplanned. Her accomplice had sent her a text message informing her that He would be in the Bridge Way Street apartment for the next three hours, if she cared for some 'dangerous' sex.
He made it clear to her that the detectives were still investigating the premises and that they made random appearances from time to time. She had then made an excuse to her husband, and ordered a taxi to take her over there. When She arrived, He explained to her in great detail about what He intended to do with the beautiful prostitute He'd been seeing, and how much She would enjoy her, until the time was right to kill her. She was completely turned on when He described just how much the whore enjoyed oral sex.
He'd even gone as far as telling her how desperate she was for the three-sums to begin. She had looked at the photograph of the girl, and informed him to arrange it as soon as possible. They would take their time with this one, as she was far too pretty to kill quickly. They would have lots of fun with this one, before they decided they'd had their fill of her.
He and She had then went into the master bedroom and began their fun, both of them turned on thinking about the whore named Veronica, and with what was to follow over the forth-coming weeks and months. She had got up from the bed to retrieve her cigarettes from the kitchen, when She'd heard the key-card lock buzzing. Someone was entering the apartment.
At first they had felt apprehension about being caught by police officers, but after a few moments, it became clear to them that

whoever was in here, was unaccompanied. They even heard the person outside of the bedroom door, and so began to make love again, hoping that they would enter the room. When that didn't happen, She decided to take matters into her own hands.

She took the small hand axe which He always carried around with him, from his large valise. Naked, except for her shoes, she threw open the bedroom door and strode down the hallway towards the kitchen. When She opened the kitchen door, the young man sat at the table with his back to her. He had no time whatsoever to defend himself. She drew hard on her cigarette now, remembering the look of shock on his face, when, for that split second, he realized that She was not the woman he'd expected to see.

He came through to the kitchen and helped her secure the young detective to the table. Once secured, they both sat smoking and discussing matters about the prostitute they were soon to meet up with.

The young man in front of them stirred into consciousness.

This was what She was waiting for. She lay her partner down in front of their prisoner and began performing oral sex on him. The young detective began muttering something. She had then lifted the small axe, making sure that the unfortunate detective could see what She was brandishing and then brought it down as hard as She could. She almost succeeded in taking his foot off with that one single blow. But for a small splinter of bone, the foot had been amputated.

She then left him allowing time for the shock to kick into his system, as She continued performing oral sex to her smiling accomplice. Between waves of consciousness and unconsciousness, Billy could faintly hear the woman speaking to him;

" You shouldn't have come nosing around here, should you young man, especially on your own. That was a big mistake, and one which has unfortunately cost you your life. What did you think you could possibly achieve by coming here, it's been months since we done the little drop-out. You're going to pay the price now you silly boy."

Through his hazy vision, Billy saw the naked man tying a blind fold around the woman's eyes.

" I love this game". She said, laughing and groping around the floor until She finally found what her hands had been searching for.
"Found it" She shouted cheerily.
She picked up a large pointed knife, shaped like a dagger.
Billy began to pray that Terry or Sandra would appear miraculously and dispose of these insatiable blood thirsty monsters from Hell. He braced himself for the pain as She prepared to apply the first of many thrusts.
She stabbed haphazardly at his anatomy, laughing all the time, like a child of nine or ten, playing innocent party games with her friends at a birthday party.
The blade penetrated just under his ribs on the right hand side of his body. The next stab pierced his stomach, the burning hot pain making him scream with agony, and crying out for mercy, but he knew there was no mercy coming from this bitch, he had already witnessed her handy-work. Only Terry or Sandra could put a stop to this tortuous frenzy, but that wasn't going to happen. He was going to die, right here, right now.
The laughter continued as did the oral sex and the stabbing, some of the penetrations hurting more than others, finally he couldn't feel anything, nor could he hear, only blackness and silence, eventually washing over him and giving him sweet release.
She stood up and leaned over the corpse of Billy McDermot, staring at his wide open eyes.
Smiling, She bent down and with the point of her knife, gauged out both of the young man's eyes onto the kitchen floor.

She drained her brandy glass, her husband still fast asleep.
Soon, he would be gone again and She could see Him as often as She liked. She slid the patio window closed again and poured herself another glass of brandy, smiling to herself, and thinking about how impressed the whore named Veronica would be when She brought her here for the fun to begin This victim would be treated differently, *she* would actually be released, time and time again...at least for a while she would.

SCOTLAND YARD.

BROADWAY VICTORIA.

A young woman named Polly Sheppard had been promoted to the post of chief inspector, and as far as most of her colleagues were concerned, including Terry Mercer, she had thoroughly deserved the promotion. She and Terry had been accepted into the CID on the same day fourteen years ago. Although Polly had married, unlike her friend Terry, she had no intentions of starting a family. A husband could understand if she was distracted for weeks on end on an important case, and be able to adjust, children couldn't, and so for that reason she had never even discussed family with her husband. A woman in her late thirties, she had kept her figure well. She had shoulder length blonde hair which she kept tied back with two butterfly clips. Her appearance was immaculate, her looks, stunning, and she was as radiant now as she was when she first stepped through the door of Scotland Yard, turning every male head, and female in some cases on that day, in her direction. She had been turning heads ever since, and still did, even though there were far younger women than she in the department now.
She sat across the table from Terry and Sandra Neal, beside Tony Chrysler the chief of police. Chrysler, a man in his mid- sixties, was also an acquaintance of Terry's. Chrysler sat now with his elbows on the table reading the pathologist's report and running his fingers through his pure white hair, inhaling and exhaling through his nose. Polly actually looked like a teenager sitting next to him. It was Polly who spoke first to the two detectives.
"It is a tragedy what has happened Terry, a real tragedy." She looked at her fiend across the table.
"I know you Terry, and I know you well, and I know that somehow, you'll be blaming yourself for the death of William McDermot. So, let me put you right on that matter. Officer McDermot, if he could speak for himself now, would be the first to admit that he had only himself to blame for what happened."
Mercer attempted to say something, but was stopped by Polly

raising her right arm.

"Please, let me finish Terry, I know what you're thinking. You're thinking that if you hadn't spent the day at the morgue with Sandra here, then Billy McDermot would still be alive, well, Billy was twenty-five, big enough and old enough to know the rules. He's had lectures like the rest of us explaining the dangers involved in acting on impulse unassisted without informing any of your colleagues of your whereabouts. The fact remains Terry, that if Billy had taken someone with him, then perhaps, and it's still only perhaps, he may still be alive today. I understand your disappointment Terry, I happen to know that you and Sam thought the world of the young man. Whatever way you look at it though, or however sorry we feel for him, the fact remains, that he failed as a CID officer, and that failure cost him his life, his failure Terry not yours or Sandra's, or Sam Hargrieves'.

Now then, you two have been summoned here for two reasons. The first is to inform you that you and inspector Neal have been put in full charge of this case. The second is to let you know that Sam has suffered a slight heart attack. Now before you get yourself up to high doh, don't worry, he's fine, he'll make a full recovery, but he has decided to retire."

Polly sighed heavily as she looked down to the sheets of paper on her desk. The forensics' report on how William McDermot's life had come to an end. The report spared no detail of McDermot's injuries, and how they'd been afflicted, but the horrible descriptions written by the forensic officer was only an unfortunate part of the job, and a necessity.

Cold truth, hard facts, hard core descriptions, but necessary.

"Sam's had enough Terry he said that this nearly killed him."

She smiled as she read out what else Sam had told her.

She looked at Terry and said, "He said losing the boy was bad enough, in fact it was like losing a son, the loss was that deep, but if he were to lose you, he wouldn't be able to bear the joy, it would be overwhelming, it would be too much to bear, far too much happiness to cope with at one time, so he's decided to step down while he still has some of his health. He also went on to say, that you were the cause of his ulcers returning, and that, in fact, it was you who gave him his first ulcer with your unbelievable stupidity and blatant disregard to orders, but, he wishes you well Terry, and hopes you'll be jammy enough to catch these ruthless murderers and bring them to justice.

Now then you two, that's all the formalities over with, the seriousness of these murderers' actions stares us straight in the face.

The press are beginning to play with the public's heads now, and so any time they ask us if we're any closer to catching these killers, and we have nothing to give them, then they write something to start panicking the people. Very soon Fleet Street will have the citizens of London as frightened as that of the days of Jack the ripper, the only difference being that we have two killers, and neither of them are as meticulous with their blades as our Victorian friend was, at least he made clean cuts, so, off you go Terry, and please, try and get a result, although I know how difficult this is turning out to be. We get it from both ends folks, we have these maniacs cutting away at our general public, and we have Westminster cutting away at our numbers and our budgets, however, we must continue, cuts or not. Our job is to protect the public, so good luck to the two of you. Terry? You and I go back a long time, and, in all the cases you and Sam Hargrieves solved, there is none of them as important as this one.

If you catch these animals, then please, do us all a favour, and put them to death. Let's not waste any more of the tax payer's money by having to feed these animals and putting them on trial."

Terry Mercer rose up to his feet smiling and nodding his head, because whether Polly Sheppard had told him or not, he had already decided what he was going to do to them on the night he saw Billy McDermott's body in the Bridge Way Street apartment. Polly looked at Terry as he opened the door.

"I mean it Terry I don't want you and Sandra blaming yourselves for this unfortunate event. He's gone Terry, and that's that. It's a shame I know, but like I say, we've all had the lectures, he shouldn't have gone there himself."

Polly could see by Terry's face that she needn't have bothered opening her mouth.

LOCKSLEY ESTATE.

EAST LONDON.

Mandy Smith and Elizabeth Keaten each sat upon an easy chair painting their toe nails. Veronica Wells was in the kitchen preparing their meals. Veronica was forever making sure that her friends ate regularly, and although she was only twenty-eight she was looked upon as a kind of surrogate mother. She was appreciated more than words could tell, especially by Mandy, which was why Mandy in turn looked out for Veronica. She was more than just a friend to Mandy. She was a confidante, a precious friend.
Veronica came through to the living room carrying two trays. On each tray there was a plate of shepherd's pie and a glass of low fat milk.
"Come on you two, come and get this while it's hot, can't have you going out there with nothing in your stomachs." She sat the trays down on the coffee table and returned to the kitchen to retrieve her own meal. On returning, she barked at her friends, like any other mother would. "Come on and get your tea, you can finish that after you've eaten...now!"
And just like two daughters, Mandy and Elizabeth put down their nail varnish and reluctantly made their over to the table.
The three young women sat down to eat their meal, all of them in good shape, a necessity in the business they were in.
Veronica believed that one square meal a day was enough for any woman. She started her day with a bowl of cereal, mostly skipped lunch but would sometimes indulge in an apple or banana, and then, the one hearty meal at around five or six o clock in the evening. Of course there were the numerous bottles of water throughout the course of the day as well, which served two purposes. One, it kept her hydrated and therefore regular at the toilet, and two, as she had learned from the days when she had absolutely nothing, that water was very good for keeping the pangs of hunger at bay. All that remained now was for the three of them

to kick this nasty habit of smoking into touch, easier said than done, when you so enjoyed it.

The three women sat now, smoking and discussing their plans for the evening. Most of the deals these days were pre-arranged on mobile phones or on the internet, although there were still some of the old-fashioned punters who still preferred meeting in bars, or the ones who still enjoyed rolling around in their cars, the old tradition. Even with all this technology, there would always be, the street girls, and therefore, there would always be the dangers involved in selling yourself from the corner of some deserted pavement, but try telling that to a young lady with a raging heroin habit who is desperate for a twenty quid bag.

Because the police had not yet finished their investigations in Mandy's flat, Veronica let her use one of the rooms in here to entertain her tricks. Mandy and Elizabeth worked around each other's schedules. The arrangement seemed to be running without a hitch, so far.

"Have you got anyone coming round tonight Veronica" Said Elizabeth, as she picked up the empty dinner plates.

"Not really, I was thinking about going down to the pub later on, maybe pick someone up there, I don't really know what I'm doing tonight, haven't made my mind up yet."

Mandy couldn't resist. "You're not still waiting for your dream guy are you Ronnie? I told you, he's not for real. You had a couple of good nights with him babes, and he paid you well, just put it down to experience and move on, you won't hear from him again I can assure you. Get yourself out babe, and back among the trolls, it's easier, and it's much more fun."

Veronica looked at her friend. "Yeah, and they pay you peanuts, because peanuts is all they have. We can't charge them any- more, because they don't have any more. Hell, some of them are spending their wives' gas and electric money on us, and the ones without wives are spending money borrowed from loan sharks. We are the closest thing they'll ever have to, "The other woman"._

Veronica sighed, looking down at her mobile phone on the table.

"Yeah I know Mandy, you're right, I may as well just carry on, better the devil you know huh?"

"That's it Ronnie, that's the way I look at it. When I get down I try to think of the people who are far worse off than me, and there are millions babes. I look around me and I count my blessings."

Mandy thought of her poor unfortunate sister and brother-in-law.

"If I had been in the house that night Veronica, I might not have been here tonight. You just have to make the best of your life when you're here, and that's exactly what you should be doing Ronnie. I know the sun will shine again babes, it always shines after the rain has gone...you've got to keep looking for the rainbows Ronnie."

## SCOTLAND YARD.

## BROADWAY VICTORIA.

Terry Mercer was grinning like a school boy as he departed from The Thames Valley Police Headquarters in a brand new BMW 318d M sport saloon, metallic silver, with Sandra Neal sitting by his side.
"Are you sitting comfortably there Madam?"
"I'm fine Terry" She replied, smiling to herself at Terry's reaction to the car they'd been given to use.
"This is what it's all about Sandra, the fucking Germans, they sure know their stuff. We've got here Sandra, Dakota leather upholstery, a six point five inch colour display screen, eighteen inch alloy wheels, sports seats and M aerodynamics body styling, as standard my angel."
Sandra laughed at Mercer's mock salesman jargon.
"Seriously Sandra, wait till you drive this thing, hell, there's no way the bad guys are getting away from us in this."
It had been just over a week since the death of Billy McDermot, and today was the first time Sandra had seen Terry even smiling, let alone laughing.
They were on their way to Burlington and Hedgewood estate agents and solicitors to interview the agent who was in charge of sales at the Henselton Estate.

Every year without fail George Burlington and Graham Hedgewood took their wives to a warmer climate for three months of the winter. Misses Rosemary Hedgewood suffered badly from asthma, and so the winter break for her was medicinal. As fate would have it, He had been left in charge, and so, if He was careful what He said, He could tell the CID anything He wished, provided of course, that the rest of the staff were kept well away from earshot whilst He was being interviewed. That wouldn't cause him a problem seeing as He was in charge of everything, and everyone.

Sandra and Terry had an abundance of questions to ask whoever

was in charge when they arrived at the estate agents. She had tried unsuccessfully on three different occasions throughout the week, only the answering machine came back to her, explaining that Mister Burlington and Mister Hedgewood were extremely busy and that one of their staff would be in touch as soon as possible. Today, she and Terry would arrive unannounced and would muscle their way in to speak with whoever was in charge of Bridge Way Street.
"Let me do the talking Terry when we get in here. We need to handle the situation with kid gloves, rather than your usual roller coaster style."
"What the hell's that supposed to mean? I know how to handle situations like this missy, I can be gently gently when I have to be, I've been a detective for some time you know I'm not exactly new to this."
" I know Terry that came out all wrong there, I wasn't trying to intimidate you, sorry babes. All I'm saying is, we'll stand a better chance of co-operation with a...female approach, if you catch my drift."
"Right, so you're going to flirt with the fucker, is that what you're saying?"
"Terry, do you need to be, yes, I'm going to flirt with him if I have to, but only if I have to. These solicitors actually think themselves way above us you know."
"They charge us plenty of money for their fancy fucking talk, I know that much, and what if it's a woman in charge are you still going to flirt with her, I would pay good money to see that babe."
I bet you would Terry, and I'll bet you have, you and the forensic team, when you were all out on that stag night a couple of months ago. I heard all about it Terry. You should all think shame on yourselves making the young man do that with the stripper in front of everybody. My God if his wife ever found out about that she would divorce him immediately, and the stripper should think shame on herself as well, squatting over him like that, it's disgusting."
Terry only grinned as he remembered the evening in question.
"It's all just part of the initiation into the C.I.D. Sandra, you should

know that, and I'll bet you had a good night out with all the girls when you first joined the department."
Now it was Sandra's turn to smile, and blush… "Oh yes," she said, "We all had a brilliant night."

PARLOUR STREET.

SOUTH KENSINGTON.


Sam and Beth Hargrieves sat in their patio each of them with a mug of tea. Beth was reading a paper-back Sam was reading his daily newspaper. The November sunshine weak as it was helped to warm the room, its rays intensified by the double glazed windows.
"I wonder how Terry's doing," said Sam, taking a sip of tea.
"He'll be doing just fine, now don't start that again, because you're not going back in there, and that's that. I know what you're like so please, get that idea out of your head."
Beth was referring to the conversation they'd had the day before, and how Sam felt that maybe he'd made the decision to retire prematurely, and now that he felt a bit better, he could perhaps work on a part time basis.
"I never said I was going in, I'm just saying, I wonder how he's doing, that's all, hell Beth."
"I'm not biting Sam, you want to know how he's doing, then give him a call, but don't blame me if he snaps the head off you, while he's busy, because you would do the bloody same, and anyway, he and Sandra are coming over for dinner in a few days, ask him then how he's doing, ask them both."
Sam knew what was on Beth's mind. She was afraid that he would want to return to the job and therefore put his health in jeopardy once again. If he was honest with himself, he would realize that he'd had a lucky escape, and that other poor buggers never got a second chance. Yes, he was retired, and he was staying retired. He would spend the remainder of his life with his long-suffering wife who deserved a medal of honour for what she'd put up with throughout these years. She was only trying to protect what she loved.
"Yeah, you're right Beth, I'll wait until they're both here."
Sam stood up with his mug of tea and waddled over to the house plants on the window sills, and began inspecting them, looking like

he knew what he was doing when in fact he knew nothing whatsoever about anything horticultural.

Then Sam said something that completely took her by surprise.

"I don't know what I'd do without you Beth, really, I mean people say that don't they, to their partners, others say it in songs or poems, but I really mean it. These last few weeks I've been thinking about loneliness, something I've never done before. I really feel sympathy for the people who live on their own.

How awful for them, to have nothing but memories to wake up to, or to go to bed with. My little breakdown has left me thinking about stuff like that Beth, and I'm just grateful to God that He saw fit to bless me with someone like you. I am a very lucky man, and I will never again take you for granted."

Beth tried being light-hearted.

"Oh, so you take me for granted then?"

"I used to, not deliberately, but yes, I did. I took it for granted that you'd be home at any godforsaken hour I would arrive. I took it for granted that meals would be prepared for me and served on the table, that my laundry would be done for me, that our bed would be changed, that the house-work would be done that the cupboards would be stocked, that the bills would be paid in time, all of it Beth, I took it all for granted". He sipped his tea. "I won't ever take you for granted again."

Beth put down her book and looked at her husband. He had changed alright, but she wasn't sure she was comfortable with these changes. Certainly she was happy that for the first time in their lives she had him all to herself, but it was that just lately, he seemed so insecure, always wanting to be near her, really near her. Maybe this would have been the point in their lives where grandchildren would have taken over, or filled a gap, or something, but there would be no grandchildren it was only them. They would have to grow old together in the knowledge that it would always be, only them.

Once again Sam surprised her, like a bolt of lightning out of the blue.

"Do you fancy a week up in the Lake District Beth? I'll bet it's beautiful up there at this time of the year. You could take your brushes up with you, it's been a while since you've done a landscape, what do you say?"

"What about dinner with Terry and Sandra, we've made arrangements."

"We'll just reschedule, come on Beth let's think about us for a change."

"Well I'll have to get my equipment down from the attic, you'll have to help me Sam."

"Of course I'll help you, come on, let's get your gear and start packing some clothes, and don't forget the cameras."

Beth Hargrieves was herself grateful to God for gifting her with such an unpredictable husband, and he could get as close to her as he damn well pleased.

## DOVER STREET. KNIGHTSBRIDGE.

She lay in her scented bath once again going over the course of events in Bridge Way Street. He and She had decided to lay low for a while, there were cops everywhere and it was no wonder.
The detectives who were in charge of the first Bridge Way Street murder must have been scratching their heads when the second murder had taken place there. It would have been the very last place they would expect another victim to be taken out.
Mockery to them it would seem.
They would be thinking that the second murder had been meticulously planned, when of course it had been anything but.
She lay in her bath, very slowly masturbating with her fingers, remembering how she'd executed the young officer.
She kept thinking about the shock on his face when he turned to look at her, expecting to see an entirely different woman.
Instead, he saw her, naked save for her shoes, and how terribly erotic to be standing there wielding an axe and saying absolutely nothing, and then, knocking him out with the dead end of the instrument.
She was abruptly brought out of her reverie as her husband banged on the bathroom door.
"That's me off now baby bee for a game of golf with Trevor. We're supposed to be going for a game of ten pin bowling after that, so I could be quite some time today angel, just to let you know."
"Ok my sweetheart, I'll see you when I see you, have fun with Trevor."
"Another four days and he'd be off again", and then She could relax. He'd spent most of his time in Trevor's company, which suited her to the ground. It suited Trevor's wife Grace down to the ground as well, because it left her plenty of time to get banged silly by the handsome young architect she'd met at her Yoga class. Grace had married Trevor for the very same reasons. An abundance of gifts, good car, elaborate house, endless credit card facilities, but at least Trevor was young and handsome, and from what She could gather,

worth-while going to bed with, It was just that Grace had an insatiable appetite for sex, and not even Trevor could satisfy her needs. "What a beautiful world we live in" She thought to herself, as She reached orgasm. "Sweet deceit indeed."

## BURLINGTON and HEDGEWOOD ESTATE AGENTS.

## W. LONDON.

Terry and Sandra Neal sat in the waiting room having been informed by the receptionist that all the staff were extremely busy today and that they may have to wait some time before anyone could see them. Terry smiled at Sandra when the elderly lady had said this to them. She obviously didn't realize that, if they wanted to they could summon every solicitor in the entire premises into the waiting room, right now, and in their underwear if they so desired. Instead, the two detectives decided to give it half an hour to see if anyone would see them. If no-one had seen them by then, then they would insist on seeing someone.
Terry rose up from his seat and began looking at the advertisements on the walls. Elaborate houses with even more elaborate prices.
"Look at these properties Sandra, I would need three life-times to pay for some of these houses. Of course, like everything else here in the capitol, they are over-priced. Over-priced and over-rated."
"You got that right Terry. I never thought I'd ever see the day when we would pay thirteen pounds for a portion of cod and chips, and I noticed yesterday that you paid more than ten quid for a packet of cigarettes."
"That's your government for you Sandra. I honestly think they'll be taxing the citizens of London a tax just for being born here, we already pay for our cars parked in our streets, it's just anything to take money from us, that's their answer to every problem that arises. Charge them more money. Huh, they've cut the police force's numbers right up and down the country. Some of the smaller stations have been closed down. So we have fewer officers now, and yet we're expected to do the same amount of work. The cuts were necessary they said, notice how there are never any cuts in the houses of parliament Sandra. The whole country is on a wage freeze, no pay rises for anyone, oh but the government give

themselves an eleven per cent rise, and then they flaunt it in the faces of the working people, and blame it on the unemployed.
Is it any wonder why people are beginning to stay away from polling stations. It's because we've came to despise these greedy fat bastards who are lining their pockets at the public's expense and declaring to us that they're working their socks off.
Is it any wonder we hate the corrupted bastards every one of them."
" For God's sake Terry, calm yourself down. Whatever possessed you to build a career in nomology you'd have made an excellent politician with your constant bloody ranting about things which are totally out of your control."
The door opened and the elderly receptionist poked her head though.
"You're very lucky, someone has found the time to fit you in, please come this way."
Terry and Sandra followed the woman, who was surprisingly nimble, down a maze of corridors all carpeted in deep red, with dark natural wood panelled walls.
"We're very lucky are we?" Terry mimicked.
The receptionist did not respond to his sarcasm.
"Oh yes you're very lucky, everyone here are run off their feet, here we are." She stood and knocked on the door, fixing her blouse and straightening her skirt, as if the person she was about to see was going to judge her on her appearance.
"Come in" Came the reply.
"Sorry to bother you sir, we have here a Mister Terrance Mercer and a Miss Sandra Neal, they are from the CID and wish to ask us a few questions."
"Fine Janet, show them in please, and bring us coffee as soon as you like."

The secretary come receptionist come waitress showed the detectives into the room. A woman in her late sixties Terry guessed. He prided himself on his observational abilities.
He also guessed by way of her "Chores" and duties that the woman

would be grossly underpaid for the work she was doing.

The young man in the office introduced himself as Mister John Burlington, grandson of the late John Burlington and founder of Burlington and Hedgewood estate agents and solicitors.

"Good day to you officers, and how can we be of assistance to you today?"

Terry glanced at the man. For some inexplicable reason he'd immediately taken a disliking to him. One of these sassy young come-uppers who had inherited everything they possessed, but who looked upon you as though it was a privilege for him to spend any time at all talking to you.

"Bridge Way Street, Henselton estate, who's in charge of the property that is for sale there, the property as you will know by now, where two brutal murders have taken place," Said Terry, looking the young man in front of him, straight in the eyes.

"It seems to me Mister Burlington that these murderers possess card-keys for the premises, because they come and go there as they please."

"It's a terrible state of affairs I agree with you, and a situation that Burlington and Hedgewood could well do without. I'm afraid quite a few of us have access to the card-keys for all of our properties. I think we've all had an attempt at selling that house. On top of that, there are thieves working overnight, creating card copying machines, and producing cards for houses and hotels all over the city, it is terrible and we're forever battling against such crimes."

"I see, well then Mister Burlington, when you say we, how many people are we talking about, how many agents or solicitors have access?"

The young man flushed slightly as he sat back down on his chair, trying his best to look calm and collected.

"Oh, I'd say about eight, eight or nine of us have access to all the premises on sale."

"Eight or nine Mister Burlington? said Sandra Neal. "You run, and indeed own the company, and yet you can't give us an exact number of employees?"

He was back in full control of himself again, his composure

regained.

"Begging your pardon Miss Neal, you didn't ask me how many employees I had, you asked me how many people had access to the Bridge Way Street apartment. Janet for example, who'll be bringing you your coffee with any luck, is an employee of Burlington and Hedgewood, but does not have access to the afore-mentioned property."

No-one said anything for a few moments, but Terry sat staring into the young man's face making Sandra feel uncomfortable, as if Terry would strike the man at any moment, but the young solicitor didn't flinch.

Eventually, Sandra broke the awkward silence.

"I'll tell you what Mister Burlington", she said, retrieving a piece of paper from her bag. "Here are the dates of both murders, now, we'll come back in a couple of days or so and we'll interview any member of your staff who has had anything to do with Bridge Way Street, two days prior and up until two days after the dates of each murder".

"How on earth do you expect me to find out who was where and when, we don't make reports after each visit or we'd be up to our necks in paperwork, for goodness sakes, you can't expect me to produce accurate figures for something like that, it's preposterous."

"I don't care what it is Mister Burlington, we're coming back here in two days, and we'll expect a list of names of the appropriate members of staff, and have them ready for interviewing, failing that Mister Burlington, we'll have no alternative but to close your premises down until we've interviewed every employee. Oh, and these interviews will be lengthy and individual, so if you are busy "these days" then I suggest that you get yourself some cover, if you can come up with a list, if not, we'll just shut shop until we've done what we have to do, is that clear Mister Burlington?"

He sighed and nodded his head. "Crystal". He mocked.

"Good" Said Sandra, rising to her feet. "We'll skip the coffee."

"Is it just me Terry or was he acting like he was hiding something, for a minute there I thought you were going to strike him."

"He's a cocky bastard, I'll give him that, but then his kind always are, he's one of the privileged Sandra. That little twat in there has never known a hardship in his life, certainly not a financial one. He's never known what it's like to worry about a bill, he's always had money, his kind, and they love to rub it in to mere mortals like us. That suit he's wearing? About two grand Sandra, and by the way, well done for your verbal aggressiveness, you get full marks for that, letting him know who is boss."

As they walked across the car park, she replied,

"I'm getting lots of practice."

Terry smiled as they reached the car.

## LOCKSLEY ESTATE. EAST LONDON. 10pm.

Veronica Wells sat with her feet up on the small footstool watching Tom Cruise on TV. His character was arguing with his autistic brother played by Dustin Hoffman about underwear, boxer shorts to be precise. It was one of Veronica's favourite films. A heart rending story about the difficulties encountered every day by those affected by Autism.

Without taking her eyes from the screen, her fingers searched diligently the chocolate box perched on the arm of her easy chair for the last three remaining sweets. Mandy and Lizzie had gone out to work, although none of them had returned home yet with any tricks. She looked at the clock on the wall. It was only ten o clock there was still plenty of time. Mandy had been pressing on her again tonight, to get herself out and making money.

In her heart she knew Mandy was right, but still, she couldn't get that man out of her head. Veronica rose up from her chair and headed for the fridge where she still had half a bottle of white wine left from the other evening. As she approached the fridge, her mobile phone buzzed, vibrating the empty chocolate box off the arm of the chair and onto the floor. As if Mandy could hear her from where she stood, Veronica shouted out to the phone, "I'm not coming out tonight Mandy, so please give it a break girl...having my wine babes, and I'm watching Tom Cruise, and that's that. Gonna take a shower and then I'm going to get my Rabbit out, and Tom's going to give me a good seeing to, he'll sort things out with me." She poured her wine into a half pint tumbler and made her way back to her chair. She glanced at her phone, taking a sip of her wine as she did so. Her heart skipped a beat. It was him. The text message was from him. "At last" She said, with shaking fingers, "Let's hear what you've been up to mister."

After texting each other three or four times He decided to phone her. Now he apologised verbally for not turning up the other night, explaining to her that something unexpected had turned up which had to be dealt with.

"You could have sent me a text message it wouldn't have taken you long, and as far as the other night is concerned, where on earth do you get that from? It's been almost three weeks and I've never heard a thing from you, I have almost given up on anything happening between us."

He didn't answer her at first, making Veronica think that He'd switched off.

"Hello?"

"I'm still here, and the offer is still on. If you still wish to have a party with my girlfriend and I, then be in the bar, you know which one, on Tuesday night at nine o clock, it's entirely up to you. You'll be paid the amount of money previously discussed.

Now, Veronica, just a little reminder of who we both are. I am a man attracted by your sexual attributes and abilities, I am a customer. You are a prostitute looking to sell your wares to the highest bidder, please don't think of our relationship as anything more than that, I only apologised to you out of decency, that's all, I shan't ever apologise to you again, for anything. So, you either want the business or you don't. If you don't, then my girlfriend and I will find another prostitute who'll be glad of the money, so we'll see you Tuesday perhaps."

The phone went dead. Veronica was devastated. Her feelings had been shattered. He sounded so cold, so bitter. She didn't need to be reminded of what she was, she knew what she was, but she was still human, she still had feelings. Is that what these people thought? That prostitutes didn't have feelings? The fact that we sell ourselves to make a living, tears us apart from time to time. The battle of morality. Sometimes it felt like they'd sacrificed their humanity," and then you get this." She had waited for so long to hear from him, hoping that they could continue their business, but when he cut her deeply with remarks like that, it just made her feel even more cheap than she was. She sighed and then came to her senses. She would deal with them as coldly and unfriendly as they were being to her, after all, it's all about the money Veronica she told herself. Yeah, she was no more than a whore, and that's how she was going to be with him from now on, and any other punter she pulled in future. Being nice to people was just a complete waste of time in this game.

## SCOTLAND YARD. BROADWAY VICTORIA.

Just before Terry and Sandra left for the day to continue their investigations, a young female officer approached them carrying a polythene bag which contained an item of clothing.

"Excuse me" She said to the two detectives. "This has just come back from the labs, it's from Locksley. This garment is sold in only two premises in the whole of London and nowhere else, other than fashion shows. I am informed that it would cost somewhere in the region of eight hundred pounds, so it doesn't look like money is the motive sir for these murderers".

"What the fuck is it Katy?" Said Mercer, squinting his eyes at the bag.

Kathlene Oconnor smiled.

"It's a top, well, what's left of it, it's just a top, a lady's top."

"Eight hundred quid for a top? I'd want a sexy blonde bitch along with it if I was paying that for a top."

Sandra Neal and Kathlene Oconnor just stood and looked at Mercer.

"A bit of your personal fantasies slipping out there sir" Said Oconnor, herself being blonde.

She continued. "If you think that's bad just wait until you hear about the perfume."

"Come on, tell us Katy, the suspense is killing us" Mercer said, looking at his watch.

"Ok, it's specially imported into Britain and usually only bought by celebrities and the likes.

"Come on, how much, and what do you call it?"

"I don't know what it's called but I am informed that a small bottle of it, and I mean small, will set you back three thousand pounds."

"Three grand? for a bottle of perfume? So the fuckers have money Sandra, and plenty of it. You can get on with what you were doing Kate, thanks for the information. If you find out anything else give us a text message."

The young officer headed off.

Sandra stood smiling at Terry Mercer.

"What?"

"That wee Irish girl has the hots for you Terry did you know that?"

Mercer smiled back.

"She's just a kid, eager to get on that's all, she's a very good forensic officer as well."

"Yes she is, and she's no kid, and you mustn't let her on do you hear me Mister Mercer, or else all of your privileges will be taken away, is that understood?"

"Fucking hell Sandra, she's only-"

"Is that understood?"

"Understood" Said Mercer. "Now I wonder if I'll be able to find the people who sell that three grand perfume, I need to buy that for some-one I know who has the hots for me."

"The words balls and branding iron comes to mind Terry, if that person's initials who you're buying the perfume for, is not SN."

Terry Mercer was flattered at the thought of a woman being jealous of him. All of his self-confidence had been stripped away from him when Carol had departed from his life. She had stripped him of any trust in women as well in the manner in which she had exited his life. If anyone could do that to you, whilst pretending so well that they loved you, then they could do anything. Their deceitfulness was unlimited. Sandra Neil was very slowly and gradually rebuilding his faith in women, reminding him that not all women were evil-scheming bitches with no other intention but to inflict heartache and misery into the hearts of their victims.

## CHAPTER SEVEN.

## LOCKSLEY ESTATE. EAST LONDON.

Veronica stood with her mug of coffee in her hand staring out onto the surrounding flats of Locksley. It was going to be one of those deep dark November days, when the sun wouldn't shine through at all. Instead, drizzle would sheet down from the heavens constantly for the full duration of the day.
Grey, everything was grey. The sky was grey, the flats were grey, and the horizon, or what she could make of it, was grey.
She sipped her coffee, day-dreaming, as she had done since she was a teenager, about living in California, and waking up to the sun every morning.
She lit up a cigarette, thinking about all those lucky bitches who were fortunate enough to be able to go shopping in Rodeo Drive, and dress themselves in bright colourful clothes and drive around in fancy cars. They had husbands who provided for them, or lovers, or both. The best she could wish for was to save up her money and spend a couple of weeks there, and even then, it would have to be some-one else's cancelation, a cheap cut holiday.
"Someday though" She sighed, "I might get lucky someday."
She almost jumped out of her skin as the letter-box in her hall rattled, followed by the thump of her day's mail landing on the floor. Even the letters were soaking wet, along with useless scrunched up junk mail. She threw the unwanted rubbish into the pedal bin, cursing the TV companies, attempting to sell her an additional bundle of shit over and above what she was already contracted to.
"Fucking twats you really are. You already fuck us up the ass with the deals you've given us, but you're not satisfied with that are you, you greedy bastards."
She had to fight to control her temper, a temper which had landed her in trouble more than a few times throughout her life, beginning at primary school.

She poured water into her kettle and put down the switch.
She sat down at the table with her coffee and picked up her cigarette, and began to read her mail.
None of the letters were even worth opening. Bank statements, TV licence reminder, house insurance.
At the bottom of the bundle, an unmarked envelope.
This letter was bone dry. "Perhaps it wasn't the post man who delivered this". She thought to herself. Once again, her temper began to play up. "I hope to fuck this isn't one of those junk letters, or I'll be..."
She opened the brown envelope and to her total astonishment, pulled out a rather large bundle of fifty pound notes. There was a small piece of note paper enclosed which read; Tuesday night 9.pm. don't be late.
She counted out the money. There was eight hundred pounds in the envelope. Veronica smiled to herself. Now she couldn't give a flying fuck if they turned up or not, that was entirely up to them. They had paid her in advance. They would turn up this time she surmised. They had a good reason for turning up this time.
Right there and then she decided she would say anything to Mandy or Elizabeth about this. Although she meant well, she was sick and tired of listening to Mandy's lectures about moving on. She thumbed her way through the fifty pound notes again.
She would move on alright. The excitement of the cash and the sexual endeavours she would perform with the couple had given her a new lease of life. Suddenly this bleak dark November day felt like the first day of spring. Her cigarette had burned away in the ash tray. She lit another, taking a deep draw and enjoying the kick to the back of her throat.
"I'll move on alright babes" Veronica said, hatching a plan in her head of how to cover up this excitement of her rendezvous with Mister money bags, and his beautiful and quite obviously, kinky-bitch girlfriend.
She would finish her coffee and cigarette, and then she would dress up and go and pull a couple of punters, making sure that Mandy and Elizabeth seen her in action. This way, if she showed any

excitement, the girls would just think that she was pleased to return to normal. In truth, Veronica had never been as sexually excited as this in all of her life. Even when her high school maths teacher had done her good and proper in the store cupboard whilst next door, through the wall, a class of sixth formers were busy sitting their exams, and she being only a second year pupil. Even that didn't match this. She would have to calm herself down. Her heart raced at the thought of what lay ahead, and of course, she had already been paid. His cold phone call had now all but disappeared from her memory.
"Calm yourself down girl, you're going to bloody hyperventilate you silly bitch" she found herself saying.

Veronica stood in the shower feeling the warm soothing jets of water cascading down her body. She was thinking about the beautiful woman she was soon to make love with, in front of her boyfriend, and indeed, make love to her boyfriend right in front of her. "What was it he said? She would probably play with herself using her fingers while he made love to her. He said she loved to watch other women with him, kinky bitch indeed".
As she continued showering, her mobile phone played her favourite song out loud.
"Oh I know Mandy" She said, stepping out from the cubical.
She lifted her phone. It was an unrecognised number.
"Hello"? Came the soft female voice in Veronica's ear.
"Am I speaking to Veronica?"
"Yes, who is this?"
"Did you get the money? I told him to pay you in advance."
Veronica suddenly became a stammering nervous over-excited school girl.
"Eh...yes, I em...I eh...I just received it em...yes, I got it."
"Good, that's good, are you ok for Tuesday?"
"Yes definitely, I eh... yes I am."
Veronica could hardly contain her excitement.
"That's good Veronica, because we are looking forward to sharing your body for a few hours, sharing's good, isn't it?"

"Eh...yes, I em...yes sharing's good. You don't mind, you know...sharing, him I mean, you don't?"
"Relax girl, I wouldn't be doing this if I were the jealous type now would I? You just be there on Tuesday night, because I am looking forward to eating you alive. I've seen your photographs Veronica, you are a very beautiful woman you know. I don't mind sharing with someone as beautiful as you, and I want you to misbehave with that boyfriend of mine do you hear, I mean really, really misbehave, do you promise me Veronica?"
Veronica was actually feeling faint with the excitement. Even the woman's voice was turning her on.
"Ok I...em...I'll promise...if you're ok with everything...I mean."
She heard the woman laughing at her awkwardness. Even her laugh was sexy.
"See you Tuesday Veronica, bye sweetheart."
The phone was dead. "Oh yes"! She roared. "I'll misbehave alright, I just hope to fuck you're not the jealous type lady, because you're going to hear me howling like a banshee, I'll fucking misbehave alright missy."

After she had dressed, she counted out the money once again before putting it away in the assorted biscuit tin she kept in her chest of drawers. She would pull a couple of punters in the next few days and she would enjoy it. It would be practice for her, just in case she'd got "out of the habit." Her next couple of punters would be very lucky boys, as she would be thinking about what was to follow on Tuesday night. For the pittance they would pay her, they would be very lucky boys indeed.

## BURLINGTON AND HEDGEWOOD ESTATE AGENTS.

## W. LONDON.

It took Terry Mercer and Sandra Neal just over an hour to interview all of the appropriate staff concerning the Bridge Way Street apartment. As it turned out, there were only three employees to interview.

He sat smiling at the two detectives across his desk. He had taken a bit of a gamble on pretending to be Mister Burlington, but as long as the staff didn't address him by his real name he'd be fine. He had previously advised them, before the arrival of the detectives, that he did not wish to be disturbed while they were in discussion in his office.

"In all honesty Mister Mercer, we're seriously considering giving up the Bridge Way Street apartment. We're sick of it to tell you the truth, and let's face it, there won't be anyone in any great hurry to purchase such an infamous property, not after the course of events which have taken place there. As one of my staff so rightly pointed out, we'd have a better chance of selling Dracula's castle to a bunch of virgins than being able to sell that place now. Oh, and speaking of staff, we had a visit from one of your officers the other day, Mister Phillips I believe was his name. He said he was in charge of the forensic department, and that he wished to take DNA samples from myself and all my staff. It was to save detective Mercer and Neal some valuable time he said. Of course my staff and myself were only too pleased to oblige and so samples were taken from everyone who works here, including the maintenance chap."

"Well that's saved us some time indeed Mister Burlington, full marks to Mister Phillips" Said Sandra. "I think that that concludes business here for now, although we will be back for further interviews, and of course with the results of those DNA samples taken. Did Mister Phillips say when he'd be back?"

"He just said that he'd be in touch with us as soon as he got the results from the laboratories, a few days he thought. Oh, here's an idea" He continued, "Why don't I give you my mobile number, so as you can text me and let me know when you're coming, that way I can make arrangements, you know, with my staff, in case we're busy, otherwise you may have to wait some time before we can see you."

Mercer rose to his feet, sighing heavily and impatiently.

"Mister Burlington, let me make something quite clear to you now, just in case you've been disillusioned. If myself or my colleague here wish to have a discussion with you, or any of your staff, then regardless of how busy you may be, we will have a discussion, we do not need invitations, understood? We're detectives, we're not wedding planners. Night or day, we will arrive when we feel it necessary, ok? Are we all clear on that?"

"I understand perfectly detective Mercer, I was merely trying to be helpful to you, I apologise if I offended you."

Mercer raised his hand. "Mister Burlington, I apologise to you. That was out of order on my part, and of course we appreciate all of your help and cooperation, we are very grateful indeed. We'll be in touch with you when we get the results of the samples, and then you and your staff can then be eliminated from our list and you'll be able to continue with your business, good day to you sir."

Terry and Sandra exited the office, leaving Him wondering if He'd done enough to throw them off the trail. Mister Phillips had not just landed here out of the blue. He had asked for him specifically, and spun a lie, informing Phillips that detective Mercer required DNA samples from all staff at Burlington and Hedgewood. Of course, He'd gave another sample of DNA to Phillips, informing him that it was his, and so there was no fear of any match coming back to him or any of the staff.

Mister Phillips had no reason to doubt the man and so set about the task of collecting the samples the following day. After his recent fall out with him, Phillips had no intention of ignoring Mercer's request. If all else failed, and the detectives continued to come calling, then He would have to take matters into his own hands. He knew where both detectives lived, and hoped that He wouldn't have to go to their homes in the middle of the night, and put them off the track permanently. He would wait for the outcome.

# TEMPLE ROAD. LOCKSLEY.

## EAST LONDON.

Veronica stood in front of her full length mirror, admiring her new dress. She had deliberately chosen one that would hug her figure and enhance her attributes. Turning slowly around and running her fingers over her body, her eyes never leaving the mirror, she summoned Mandy and Elizabeth through to her bedroom for their valued opinion.
"Wow" Said Mandy as she entered the room, "How much did that set you back, my God Veronica, you look absolutely amazing."
Still looking in the mirror Veronica replied, "Plenty, I bought it over in Brentwoods."
"I can see that." said Mandy. "Put a pair of heels on Ronnie, let's see the full effect. My God girl, you're going to be a very busy lady if you wear that out I can tell you that much, isn't she Lizzie, doesn't she look stunning?"
"Yes she does, who's the lucky guy Ronnie?"
"They all are Lizzy, every one of them. Any man who has the privilege of any one of our company is lucky."
As far as Veronica was concerned, she was succeeding in bluffing out her friends. In truth, she could hardly keep her mind from wandering on to the thoughts of tomorrow night when she would meet up with Mister money bags and his super-slut. She had been with three tricks this week and had purposefully let Mandy and Lizzy see her in action, so now she could live in peace and not have Mandy going on all the time about dangers and catches or jealous bitches. Her plan was working.
"They're all bloody lucky Lizzy, whoever gets to play with us."

Veronica sat down on her bed as Mandy handed her a pair of shoes appropriate to the colours of the dress, which was burgundy and gold. Veronica slipped on the shoes and stood up, once more scrutinising the mirror.

"I'm telling you Ronnie, you should come and meet the people I work for from time to time Max and Grace, you'd make a fortune honestly babes, they'd love you, literally."

Mandy was referring to the couple who paid her two hundred pounds cash for an hour's work, which was having sex on camera with male or female partners, or both.

"Not for me babes." said Veronica. "That's not my scene. Don't get me wrong I like nothing better than watching a good old fashioned blue movie, but as far as taking part in them? No thanks, it's just not my cup of tea, and talking of such, who's turn is it to put the kettle on."

Lizzy was already making her way through to the kitchen. As she was heading back to Veronica's bedroom, she stopped to pick up the local newspaper which had been delivered. She entered the room, her face transfixed to the front page.

"What's wrong Lizzy you look like you're reading your own obituary." said Mandy, laughing.

Lizzie looked at her two friends. "It's ballet, you know officer ballet?"

"What about him pet."? said Mandy.

"He's been found dead, murdered. It says here he'd been stabbed over a hundred times, Lord save us."

## SCOTLAND YARD. BROADWAY VICTORIA.

Chief inspector Polly Sheppard sat in her office awaiting the arrival of inspector Sandra Neal whom she had summoned over twenty minutes earlier by means of her new top-of-the-range mobile phone, bought for her birthday by her husband. She was reading the report from the coroner and shaking her head in disbelief as she read how officer McDermot had met his fate.

There had been over a hundred stab wounds inflicted upon the unfortunate officer. It was the explicit fine details of how those wounds had been inflicted that was making her shake her head. According to the pathologist, the stabbing had not been ferocious, or venomous. There had been no aggressive attacks, but rather, a continuous soft poking, aimless and hap-hazard.

The pathologist seemed to be under the impression that whoever had done this had not even been looking at the victim.

The blade however, had been extremely sharp, as sharp as a surgeon's scalpel, so, there would be no need for any vicious stabbing. Any contact whatsoever would inflict major damage.

She cringed as she read on, learning that the officer's eyes had been removed after his death. Polly was almost physically sick as she read on. *The sperm had been placed inside McDermott's mouth, also after his death.*" Oh my God" She exclaimed. "What the hell is happening to us? Are these people even human?

Are they even worthy of being called human? What the hell are we looking for here"?

She had spent four years studying criminology and psychology, and had read of similar crimes committed in her psychoanalytical journals, but had never for one second believed that she'd have to experience them herself.

There was two soft taps on her office door.

"Come in" She said, still shaking her head as she read on.

"Ah, come in Sandra, this won't take very long."

Sandra closed the door behind her and took a seat opposite Polly Sheppard, who eventually lifted her head from the report.

She let out an exasperated sigh and then said; "Right Sandra, first things first. Are you and Terry having a physical relationship?"
The fact that it took Sandra more than four seconds to reply, let the cat out of the bag, and so now denial would be futile.
She knew, as did Terry, that this was frowned upon, especially if the two officers in question were working on the same case.
There was no escape. If she lied, they'd be punished accordingly, if she told the truth, then they would undoubtedly be separated and reprimanded.
"Yes we are Miss Sheppard."
"Thank you for your honesty Sandra" said Polly, writing something down on a sheet of paper.
Sandra braced herself for what she supposed was coming next, which would be, that one of them, namely she, would be transferred to another branch, probably out of the city, and most definitely taken off this case.
Polly sat with her elbows rested on the desk tapping her lips with her thumbs and looking intently at Sandra. Then she came to her decision. "Ok Sandra, I'm not going to take any action just now. I'm not going to split your partnership up with Terry, God knows the man needs someone to love him, but-"
"Oh thank you Miss Sheppard, you won't-"
"Please, let me finish Sandra."
Once again Polly Sheppard sighed, knowing that she was taking a gamble with this decision.
"If I think for one second that your relationship is jeopardizing your work performances, I will not hesitate to move you as far away from here as I can, now do I make myself clear Sandra? I am pushing the boat out for you two here, I hope you appreciate the fact."
"I understand mam, and thank you again for giving us this chance."
"That's quite alright Sandra, I believe that everyone deserves a chance to prove themselves, just don't blow your chance ok?
And how is he doing anyway, after the young McDermot incident, is he holding up alright?"
"Yes mam, he seems to be, although I can see it in his face, that he

still blames himself to a degree."

"Yes, well, it's the lad's funeral tomorrow, after we get that over with we'll see how we're going. I've got the pathologist's report here in front of me, and I can tell you Sandra, that poor boy died a horrendous death. These are very sick people you're searching for, let me tell you that."

"With all due respect mam, I know. Begging your pardon mam, you've just read the report, I saw him, I saw how that sick bitch and her partner left him, and so did Terry mam, and I think that's what's getting to Terry. That sight will haunt him forever. It will me, I know that much. As far as Terry's concerned, it was his job to look out for young McDermot. He sees it as some kind of momentary lapse of discipline, self- discipline, that he let himself walk away from the boy, thus leaving him vulnerable, something like that."

"Yes, well, you look out for him Sandra. I know sometimes he's a bit rough round the edges, his language as well, I know he is, but he's also one of the best detectives we have round here. He and Sam Hargrieves are spoken of as gods. Now then Sandra, back to business, under no circumstances whatsoever have either of you to investigate any premises unaccompanied, is that understood?"

"Yes mam, I promise you here and now that if Terry even suggests anything relating to that, I will not hesitate to inform you, I promise you that mam."

"Ok then Sandra" Said the chief inspector, "Please go out there and bring these two sick people to justice, and whatever you do, be very careful Sandra because these two are not your average criminals. Now and again, we come across crimes that shock even the hardest of officers. The psychoanalysis of these two will make some interesting reading, of that I'm certain. There is no crime too sick or depraved for these two, they've already proved that. Just be very careful Sandra, you and Terry, these two are very dangerous indeed."

As Sandra walked through the car park, sheets of drizzle soaked her almost to the skin. Squinting her eyes up to the sky she thought to herself, "Yeah, go and find these sick criminals and bring them to justice. So does that mean that if we don't find them soon they'll take Terry and I off the case, blaming our relationship for affecting our abilities as detectives?"

Nothing could be further from the truth. Both she and Terry were spending as much time as they could on this case. In her heart of hearts, she believed that Terry and her would succeed in capturing these sickos, she just felt it in her bones. The trouble was, as things stood now, they had not one single piece of evidence to be going on with. Forensics had gone over everything again and again to try and find something to give them a lead, but there was nothing to go on. Only the fact that it was the same two people who had committed the Bridge Way Street murder and the Locksley Estate murders, and of course now, the murder of officer William McDermot.

As she reached her car, she heard an almighty bang from the other side of the car park. Someone's tyre had blown out.

She climbed into her car smiling, remembering the day Billy McDermot arrived at the flat in Bridge Way Street, and foiled Terry's plans for the afternoon. Truth be known, it was as much her plan as it was Terry's. As she drove through the city, she was trying to get a picture in her mind of what these demons would look like. If, by any chance they'd actually come face to face with them before today, then her vision would in fact be prosopagnosia. According to what Kathlene Oconnor had found out about the garment found in Locksley, then it would seem that one of them had money, and plenty of it. She would ponder on that subject, the fact that they had money, and practically to throw away, otherwise you wouldn't be spending that kind of money on a top, and God knows how much on other clothes.

The question was, was it He who had the money? It didn't take her long to come to work it out, in fact it took Sandra only a few seconds to reach her conclusion. She had the money, definitely. If He had bought Her the top, there's no way She'd have left it there, and more than that, She'd have removed it if there was any threat of it being soiled with blood. Anyway, if a man had bought you a top costing that much, then you wouldn't even be wearing it to go and commit murder...unless they'd been out first for a few drinks, and the opportunity had arisen unexpectedly.

"So sicko bitch has plenty of money. That being the case, then she almost certainly doesn't work. Are these sexual crimes she commits, a past-time? Does she discuss with her sick friend what she intends to do with their victims? Are the victims hand-picked? Do they just come upon them perchance?" Sandra thought back to the Bridge Way Street girl, their first victim, as far as they knew anyway. She was the perfect victim, a very pretty petite young woman, who happened to be down on her luck, and who suffered from a heroin addiction to boot. Suddenly Sandra had a flash in her mind of a girl begging and pleading for her life, as her severed veins spurted out blood onto her naked sick captors, as they rolled about on the floor making love while she grew weaker and weaker.
`Inspiration.`
"These two bastards do not live together." She was as certain of that as she could be. "The sick bitch is married to someone other than the creep she kills with. She has a completely different life-style to the rest of us. She lives like a celebrity. Fancy car no doubt, maybe even a chauffeur, who knows?" One thing was for sure, she doesn't have beans on toast for tea. Fancy restaurants, exuberance, luxury, intellectual friends, a wealthy husband or partner. She is an expert at feigning love. She is beautiful. She has never had to ask twice for anything. Her husband may work away from home from time to time, if he works at all. Whatever, she has money though. And it would seem that she lives a pretentious life, a Jekyll and Hyde type of existence.
"Fancy meals in fancy restaurants with intellectual friends one night then making love with her secret lover whilst slaughtering their latest victim, and of course, let's not forget, sitting down naked at a table and devouring their victim's kidneys the next.
And why on earth would she be orally transferring sperm into their victim's mouth? What the hell is all that about? What possible kick could that be giving her? Was it her way of putting life back into death? Well, for whatever reason she done it, the girl is in desperate need of a frontal lobotomy, there was no doubt

whatsoever about that." She smiled to herself again as she thought about Terry Mercer, knowing that if he caught her, he would perform the operation himself with a rusted tent-peg.

Half an hour later Sandra pulled up outside of Burlington and Hedgewood estate agents, not one of the samples taken from the staff here had matched the DNA samples from bridge Way Street. The people at the labs had worked enthusiastically on the samples but were less than surprised when nothing matched up. Sandra had come here to inform Mister Burlington that he and his staff had now been removed from the list.
Terry Mercer was even more disappointed than she was. He had a strong dislike to the man, and apparently for no other reason other than the fact that he existed. He had a gut feeling that Mister Burlington was holding back on valuable information.
He came over that way to Terry, as if somehow he was playing games with them, like he knew the killers even, something, there was just something about the man. It was his mannerism, and it was that gut feeling that Sam had educated him on all those years ago.
"Always go on your gut feeling Terry, more than ninety-per-cent of the time, you'll be right."
The overworked lady who's name Sandra had completely forgotten sat faithfully tapping away on the keyboard of her computer. She looked up from the screen as Sandra approached the small glass hatch.
"Now then, good day to you constable, how may I be of assistance?" Sandra only smiled, unsure whether or not the old biddy was being sarcastic.
"Is he in?" said Sandra, taking out the sheet of paper with the lab results.
"Is who in dear?"
"Mister Burlington, that's who, may I speak with him?"
The elderly lady smiled and looked at Sandra rather strangely.
"Mister Burlington?" She repeated, "I'm afraid you've been mistaken Miss, Mister Burlington hasn't been-

"Janet!!"
Suddenly, He appeared at the door.
"For goodness sakes woman, show the inspector to my office immediately from now on instead of dithering away there. Any time she or inspector Mercer arrives here, you show them straight to my office, do you hear me? Now get on with those letters I told you to type, bloody old natter-hag that you are. Come this way Miss Neal, I do apologise."
He led Sandra into his office closing the door behind them.
"Please take a seat Miss Neal, make yourself comfortable. I'm afraid our Janet gets into one of her chatty moods from time to time, she becomes rather garrulous, and I'm sorry to say, I'm afraid you've been unlucky enough to catch her in one today, she'd talk all day so she would, if you let her when she's like this, under normal circumstances we could hardly describe our miss Rogerson as talkative."
"She wasn't doing anything wrong Mister Burlington, she was only doing her job, in fact I think you're rather fortunate to have a nice old lady like that working for you. Anyway, the reason I'm here today, is to inform you, that you and your staff have been officially cleared of any suspicion, you know, from Bridge Way Street, and suspicion is hardly the correct word. Anyway, all your staff's names have been eliminated from the lists and of course your name as well."
"Splendid", he beamed. "Are you any closer to catching these blood-thirsty maniacs then Miss Neal?"
Did she detect a note of sarcasm in his reply?
"I'm afraid Mister Burlington, I am not at liberty to discuss those matters with you. So, Mister Mercer and myself shan't be disturbing you or your staff any more, thank you once again for your co-operation."
Sandra rose to her feet.
"Would you like a cup of tea before you leave us Miss Neal?"
"No thank you Mister Burlington, I have to head back, but thank you for the offer."
As soon as Sandra Neal had left the building, He marched straight

into reception.

"I'm only going to say this once Janet, so you'd better listen to me. If anyone of authority comes into these premises, then you show them straight to me, do you understand that? You hardly open your mouth to any of your fellow employees in here, it's like trying to get blood from a stone, but as soon as someone of authority steps in the door, you're overcome with enthusiasm and you become loquacious and full of life. Now, do you understand what I've told you, because as long as I'm in charge here, you will do exactly as I tell you, do I make myself clear? Good, now go and fetch me a cup of coffee and ask the rest of the staff if they want one, and don't take all day doing it, and get all those e. mails sent out and letters written and posted by the time we finish tonight. Just because you've been here for a number of years, don't think that you're irreplaceable. Mister Burlington wouldn't even query the situation if he were to come back and find a nice young pretty secretary sitting there behind the reception desk, so you think on old lady!
He hoped that he'd frightened Burlington and Hedgewood's longest serving employee into avoiding another close-shave situation like the one he'd just experienced. If not, He would have to go round to her little flat and print out her little suicide note before she hanged herself from the ceiling. Depression is a terrible thing.

Janet Rogerson was heading down to the tea room, distraught, tears rolling down her face, wondering what on earth she had done wrong to deserve such an aggressive onslaught from her temporary boss. She was also wondering why he had not corrected the police lady when she had addressed him as Mister Burlington.

## FINLEY STREET. HOLBURN.

Terry Mercer and Sandra Neal had just returned from Billy McDermott's funeral. Sandra could see in Terry's face the pain he was feeling. Young hopeful recruits arrive at Scotland Yard hoping to become successful CID agents. Terry hadn't been keen on any of the latest batch to arrive, until Sam had introduced him to Billy McDermot. Almost immediately Terry had taken a shine to the lad recognising the boy's potential. As far as Terry was concerned, most of the latest recruits couldn't catch a criminal in a prison wing, although Terry had phrased it somewhat differently. But Billy McDermot had that rare gift.
She remembered what Terry had said to her; "Most of the trainees they send here Sandra are armed with certificates up to the back teeth, and qualifications which would suggest they could give Einstein a run for his money, when in actual fact they'd struggle to boil an egg".
Billy was different. If he was presented a piece of evidence that seemed to be unsubstantiated, he would scrutinise it until he found a flaw within, especially if he had a gut feeling about the suspect. It was that gut feeling thing that Sam had imprinted into him, and the importance of searching the evidence continuously until you found the crack. Billy had that gift.
Sandra brought Terry out of his revere.
"Could I make myself a cup of coffee please Terry?"
"Oh I'm sorry Sandra, I'll make it, I was just thinking about Billy, poor little bugger...had his whole life in front of him."
"I know Terry, I know he did" She said, putting her arms around his shoulders. "But it's like Polly said, he broke the golden rule, and he's paid the price. I know it's a tragedy Terry, but, and without being ruthless, it's a tragedy that wouldn't have happened if he'd followed the rules. The rules are there after all to protect us. We all came through our training, we all had to do it no matter how keen we were to impress. All said and done Terry, we have to move on. You and I have a job to do. Polly had me in her office yesterday, she

knows you and I are an item."
"Oh fuck that's-"
"No, she's not moving me away Terry, just as long as our love life doesn't interfere with our professionalism."
"What did she say Sandra?"
"She just said that everyone deserves a chance. She said that as long as we get the job done and don't let our feelings for each other get in the way of our thinking, then she was quite happy to let us work together. She also praised you Terry, you and Sam. She said that all the staff looked up to you both, you were like gods, or words to that effect."
As Terry stood putting spoonful's of coffee granules into two mugs he said, "She's nice, only she would give us the chance of working together. If it had been any of those other lot who got that job, they'd have been laying down the law and making a song and dance about it all. One of us would have been sent elsewhere."
"I know Terry, so we'd better get our acts together and start getting some results. Just because she's letting us work together just now, doesn't automatically mean she'll always allow it. If we could get a result with these sicko's we're searching for, then it would go well in Polly's eyes, the sooner we get those two, the better the chances of us being kept together. If all this stretches out for any length of time, well, I don't have to tell you what conclusions she'll come to."
"Yeah I know Sandra, I've been giving thought to that."
The couple sat talking until the early evening, whereupon Sandra made the decision to go back to her own place and have an early night. They would both benefit from a good night's sleep. She could see that Terry was hurting very much for Billy.
She smiled at him as he took the empty coffee mugs through to his kitchen. Even if she had stayed the night here, they would not have made love, an unspoken arrangement between them both, that they would pay William McDermot a token of respect, it was the least they could do.

## DOVER STREET. KNIGHTSBRIDGE. 6am.

She was excited. Her husband had received a phone call the previous evening. Something was wrong overseas and his employer had asked him if he could possibly cut short his vacation and come and sort out the problems. He was also informed that if he did, he would be financially rewarded as well as being given a brand new car of his choice. She had feigned disappointment to the best of her ability and hoped that She looked convincing enough to him. Her husband had been home for a total of five weeks and two days, and in all of that time they had only made love on a half dozen occasions. On two of those occasions She had practically been unconscious having deliberately consumed vast amounts of alcohol.
"I'm going to miss you so much my darling" She said. "I hope you're going to make this up to me when you get back sweet pea."
"I promise you I will baby bee, I'll bring you a nice gift back, maybe some more perfume and jewellery, I'll make sure the gifts are very special, for my very special little lady".
He took a last sip of his coffee as he looked out of the window.
"There's the taxi babe, I'll have to go".
He gave his wife a last kiss on the cheek, and then, as he attempted to kiss her on the lips, She turned her head, so that he managed only to kiss her on the other cheek.
"Have a good flight my darling" She said, as She hugged him one last time.
"Oh I will sweetheart, they've booked me a first class flight."

She watched from the window and waved as her financial security boarded the taxi and then disappeared down the deserted street. She had placed a bottle of wine in the fridge the night before as soon as She'd heard the news. She was free once again, an unexpected bonus, and by the way her husband had been talking, she would be on her own for at least six weeks. She retrieved the bottle from the fridge and made her way back to the bedroom, her bedroom. She then took out from one of her three chests of

drawers the photograph of the prostitute She had enlarged through her computer printer. She took a sip from the crystal glass She had poured her wine into. Sitting back up on the bed, She ran her fingers over Veronica's lips, and then down to her breasts, then between her legs.
"Not long now my little play thing" She said, smiling, "I bet you taste nice and sweet."

## FINLEY STREET. HOLBURN.

Terry Mercer had never been a good sleeper. Ever since he was a child his slumber had been constantly interrupted by bouts of involuntary coughing and, of course, the inevitable phlegm which had to be disposed of. Since the age of ten, he couldn't remember a single night where he hadn't been awoken at some point. It was at that tender age that he'd contracted pneumonia. The illness had been so severe that it had left permanent damage to his lungs. He had suffered it for four months before any treatment had been administered. When his mother had taken him to the doctors, she was informed that her son suffered from asthma. Terry was given an inhaler which done him no good whatsoever. His condition worsened. Finally, after sixteen weeks he was diagnosed with pneumonia. Immediately following the change of medication there was improvement, but the damage had been done. It left him now with asthma and he was prone to heavy colds, and sometimes, especially at this time of the year, bronchitis.
He felt really tired as he made his way back to the bedroom. Heavy and sluggish, and that was good. He knew he'd be back to sleep in no time, and he was.

As he drifted back off, he began to dream about all kinds of things. First he dreamed he was in a cafe with his mother, as a little boy, drinking a glass of juice while she drank her coffee. Then he dreamed that Carol had come back and begged him for forgiveness after causing him all this pain. Although, in the dream Carol had stayed the same age she was when she'd left him, his son had grown into a young man, who punched his father on the mouth as he made love to his mother. He stirred restlessly in his sleep. Then, he was with Sandra. He could feel her soft warm skin next to his. He put an arm over her shoulder and pulled her close to him. It felt good. She felt good. She lay naked next to him, whispering sweet nothings in his ear. He slid his hand down between her legs and felt the soft warm moistness of her sweet womanhood. She was still

whispering. What was she saying to him? *When will you learn."*
He tried to lower himself down so as to perform oral sex but was stopped by another hand, a strong hand, a man's hand.
*"When will you learn"?*
Who was stopping him, his son?
"This is not your mum captain, this is dad's new girlfriend, this is Sandra, you shouldn't be objecting to this, Sandra loves me, your mum doesn't, it's as simple as that, and anyway, you shouldn't be in bed with your father and his lover, get your hand away from-"
*"When will you learn?"*
"Come on, this is not right."
Sandra opened her legs to accommodate his son's fingers.
"Sandra!! What the hell are you doing?"
*SSShhh..mm it feels so good. Let him be, I belong to him, he owns me, now wake up bastard wake up you idiot, WAKE UP!"*
Terry sat bolt upright in his bed.
Sweat poured out from him, his mind in a confused state.
He looked in the semi darkness at the form lying beside him.
"Sandra? Is that you?"
Gingerly he put his hand on her shoulder and rubbed softly on her beautiful skin.
"Mm that feels good, come and lie back down."
"You came back Sandra, you changed your mind?"
"Switch the lamp on sweet pea and I'll explain everything."
Terry leaned over to switch on the bed-side lamp.
A man's voice. "I'll do it."
Terry felt the cold steel of the barrel of a gun on his brow just before the light stabbed his eyes.
"This, I would imagine would be the last thing you were expecting to happen inspector Mercer. You've been getting a little too close for comfort, so we thought we'd do something about it."
"It's you" Terry said, rubbing his eyes," and I take it that this is your sick bitch here."
The slap that She unleashed upon Terry's face surprised him. It was very powerful, and very painful.
"Tie him up babe."

There was nothing Terry could do. The gun was still firmly placed against his brow. There was no chance of a quick surprised attack from him. If he struggled, he was dead, it was as simple as that. He felt his hands being bound by masking tape.
The man who had imposed as Mister Burlington now spoke again. "Bring him down stairs babe, we can have some tea while we explain what we're going to do to him and his snooping girlfriend."
"I had a feeling it was you" Said Terry, his face blazing with the slap. "I get these gut instincts you see, it's my own fault, I should learn never to doubt them, I just fucking knew it, sick bastards the pair of you." He was forced to his feet, his eyes now adjusted to the bright light. Suddenly he felt the cold steel of a knife being placed under his testicles as She said; "If you speak again without first being asked a question, then I promise you here and now, you won't have any guts left with which to have any feelings, is that clear?"
"Perfectly."
The imposter to Mister Burlington looked so much different now to how Terry had been used to seeing him dressed. Gone were the smart white shirt and tie and suit. Denim jeans and black leather jacket was now his attire. His accomplice was dressed only in her underwear.

"Come on" Said the man, "Down stairs, I'm dying on a cuppa, you go in front babe, let him drool over your body. She has an ass to die for, don't you think Mister Mercer?"
"I've seen better, often." Replied Terry as they made their way down to the kitchen.
"Not in this life-time you haven't" Replied Mercer's captor, still with the gun against his head.
The couple sat opposite Terry at the kitchen table. They had released his hands from the binding but had secured one of his legs to the leg of the table. The beast spoke again.
"Drink your tea up Mister Mercer, God knows when you'll get your next cup."
There was procedures to follow in situations like this. Terry had done all this in his early days, and was quite surprised at how fresh

they were in his mind. There was an order to follow, a list. He thought the time was right to proceed with phase one.

"Whatever you have planned for me, I would do it quickly if I were you, because inspector Neal is an early riser. We have a code you see, and if I don't call her by a certain time, she knows something is wrong."

The beast smiled at Terry, waiting for him to continue. When he didn't, he said, "And.?"

"Well she'll be over here with reinforcements quicker than you can say, we are sicko's. So even if you kill me, she'll still get you, she'll get you both."

The woman with the imposter sat with one foot up on the table, still only dressed in her underwear. In her left hand she held a cigarette. In her right hand she held a necklace. There was a reason why she was showing him the necklace. He didn't recognise it. She sipped her tea and then smiled at Terry, one of the most sinister smiles he had ever seen in his life. It was malignant. He just knew something absolutely devastating was coming. She swung the necklace to and fro like a hypnotist, still with the creepy smile. Her next sentence brought Terry Mercer's world crashing down around him, making him actually dizzy with shock. She stopped swinging the necklace, pointed to her friend, and said; "He's already fucked her, your em...your Sandra, and although it's not for me to say, she eh...she fucking loved it so she did."

She almost whispered her next words. "Very big you see, very nice for a lady. She enjoyed sucking it too didn't she babes?"

"Oh yes" He grinned, "She certainly knows her stuff. She wasn't very keen on taking it through the back door, but when she realized she wasn't going anywhere, she succumbed to it. I think she kind of relaxed a little, and began to enjoy it in the end. She's in the van outside, you'll see her soon."

The sick bitch spoke again, her smile even more sinister, if that was possible. "I wouldn't kiss her on the mouth if I were you Mister Mercer, she's been swallowing...well, you know what she's been swallowing, more tea Mister Mercer?"

Terry had faced danger on many occasions throughout his career in the police force. What was sitting here in front of him, in his own kitchen, far outweighed any danger he'd ever faced.

He was face to face with, not one, but two psychological time bombs, she, it seemed being marginally worse than him.

The female monster was incredibly beautiful. It was unbelievable. She was stunning, absolutely stunning. No man in his right mind would ever dream of associating her with any of these horrendous sexual crimes which had taken place.

If he couldn't find a way to save himself and Sandra, then the pair would kill many more people before they were apprehended, if they would ever be apprehended. Who would suspect *her*?

Terry Mercer began to study the facts, if they were all facts.

Did they have Sandra in their van? Had they been telling the truth? Or were they merely trying to frighten him or prepare him for some kind of deal? But the fact that they now knew that Terry knew who they were made him realise the seriousness of the situation. He was in trouble here, real trouble, and there was no Sam Hargrieves to pull him out of the shit this time. He genuinely feared for Sandra's and his lives'. The odds weren't very good on their survival. It was what would be inflicted upon them first that worried him so much. The last place he expected to face a situation like this, was his own home.

## TEMPLE ROAD. LOCKSLEY.

Mandy Smith and Elizabeth Keaten sat watching TV each drinking a glass of wine. None of the girls intended working tonight, one of them because she'd had a good couple of days or so and was able to put some money away to give herself a treat at a later date, the other, because Mother Nature had arrived and intended staying for a week or so even though she was a very unwelcome guest.
"What do you think about Veronica Liz? Do you think she's up to something?"
Elizabeth looked at her friend.
"Well, she has seemed rather vivacious lately, you know, full of energy, sprightly, don't get me wrong, she's always cheering me up when I'm feeling depressed. I'm not for one-minute condemning her, but she does seem more cheerful these days, more than usual, why? What on earth would she be up to?"
"Not up to Liz, I mean, this cheerfulness, there's got to be a reason for it, and I think I know what that reason is. I think she's still seeing that man, you know, the one with all the money."
"You mean the one you think she's fell in love with?"
"Yes, I think she's still meeting up with him and there's nothing wrong with that Liz, it's just that she told me he has a girlfriend and that they wanted to have threesomes with Veronica. I kept telling her to be careful, and if possible, leave well alone. I mean this woman did not voice any disapproval, in fact she seemed as keen on the idea as her boyfriend, as far as I could make out. It's just that…oh I don't know Liz, I just smell a rat that's all. Perhaps I'm being over protective. I think Veronica's had it to the back teeth of me going on about the dangers of jealousy, that's why she's decided to meet them and say nothing to us about it. She's going to work as usual, pulling her usual punters, but that's just to disguise what else is going on in her life. Look at the clothes she's bought lately, not that I'm saying she doesn't look after herself, but just lately she's been buying top of the range outfits, really sexy outfits and, well, I don't think she's buying them for her usual fifty quid

punters."

Mandy rose up from her chair dressed in her pink dressing gown with floppy-bunny slippers to match, and made her way to the fridge. She took out a bottle of wine and poured herself another glass full.

"I don't know Liz" She shouted through to her friend.

"Maybe I'm just being silly, Veronica's old enough to know what she's doing. If there was any danger, she'd be out of there as quick as lightning, we'll just let her carry on as if we don't know anything, hell, if there's anyone who deserves a bit of luck and a bit of happiness it's her, and good luck to her if she's making herself a bit of money."

"Changing the subject Mandy" Said Liz, "Have you heard any more from that detective Mercer?"

"Nothing yet Liz, and I don't know what's going to happen now, after that young detective was murdered over in Bridge Way Street, you know, officer ballet?"

"That was a bloody shame Mandy, he was a nice looking young man, I quite fancied him you know."

"That's just my point Liz, even CID detectives are not safe out there, and they're bloody armed with guns and everything. If people like that can be brutally murdered, well, it doesn't look too good for us. That's why I fear for Veronica, one sudden burst of jealousy from that woman and Veronica could be history. We're just lucky that we know most of our punters Liz. I wouldn't want to be starting out now, with complete strangers, no fucking way."

"I'm sure Veronica will be just fine Mandy, but I must say, I take your point about the dangers, and I'm sure she'll be deeply grateful to know that she has friends who care for her and have her back covered. It's good to know you have friends".

Mandy sighed. "I think it's with what's happened to Jane that is making me like this. Jane and Thomas could look after themselves Liz, especially Thomas. I wouldn't fancy any man's chances on a one to one with him, under normal circumstances of course. Whoever done that to them must have caught them off guard. Either that, or Jane and Thomas trusted them wholeheartedly. And, it was in their own home, it wasn't as if they were somewhere unfamiliar to them. Whoever they are Elizabeth, they are very dangerous people, and very deranged people...sub-human I would say, asylum materiel."

## FINLEY STREET. HOLBURN.

There was a rule that Polly Sheppard had. Each and every officer working on a murder case must report back to their superior at least every forty-eight hours, to give details of their progress, if there has been any. Today was the morning of the third day and Polly Sheppard hadn't heard anything from Terry or Sandra.
Both of their mobiles had been switched off, and neither of them were answering their land line phones at home.
Polly sat in her car trying her best to work out the reasons why neither of her officers were replying to her calls and messages. She weighed up the situation, and reluctantly came to the conclusion that they'd been abducted, or worse. There was no other explanation for their lack of communication.
Sandra knew that there was no danger of her being moved away to another area. And Terry, he had never seemed so happy, until the murder of Billy of course. Polly had noticed him hanging around HQ a couple of days prior to Billy's funeral looking rather lugubrious. This was one of the reasons she'd decided to take no action against them when Sandra had admitted to their relationship. Anyway, for whatever reason, her two officers were not responding, and she was ninety-nine point nine percent certain that it was not through choice.

Polly sat directly across the street from Terry's house. She was awaiting the arrival of two people, a locksmith and a certain Mister Andy Phillips from forensics. All sorts of scenarios were forming in her head. Was there a possibility that these sick cold-hearted killers had put their sights on Terry and Sandra? She remembered the coroner's report on Billy McDermot and how the lad had been executed. Looking over to Terry's house, she shuddered involuntarily, thinking about what she might find over there behind his door. They were either dead, or abducted, these were the only two options she left herself with. One of them was reality. She hoped with all her heart it was the latter of the two, at least then, there was half a chance of getting them back alive. What made matters worse or shortened the odds of that happening, was that Polly had read Sandra's report and discovered that at least one of the killers had plenty of money, so there would be no phone call for ransom payments. She genuinely feared for their safety. She sat listening to the constant rain drops pelting off the roof of her car, and almost jumped out of her skin as Andy Phillips wrapped his knuckles on her driving side window.

Polly Sheppard had never uttered a single profanation in her entire career at Scotland Yard, almost twelve years.

"Fucking prick Andy, was that supposed to be fucking funny? Idiot fucking clown!"

Andy immediately realized he'd startled his superior, which was not the most intelligent thing to do given the present circumstances.

"I'm sorry mam, I didn't mean to scare you, I didn't mean to knock so loud."

"Yes you did, get in the car out of the rain, fucking banging. The lock-smith hasn't arrived yet, and I'm not knocking Terry's door in get in, you're soaking wet, what a thing to do Andy, you're such a clown, honestly, you're all like little boys playing games and tricks on each other, don't you try that shit with me mister, bloody juvenile tricks giving people frights, I'll fucking frighten you clever dick."

Just as Andy had made himself comfortable a white Transit van pulled in across the road from them.

"That looks like him, come on, let's go and see what's happened to Terry."

Phillips cleared his throat. "Excuse me mam, I think it'd be better if myself and my two colleagues who are in my car, went over there and find out what's happened. I'll let you know if they're in there, and may I say mam, that although Terry and I don't quite see eye to eye, I sincerely hope with all my heart that he is not here.

If there's a mess mam, I'll let you know not to come in. Go and have yourself a cup of tea until we check out the house."

Polly looked at Andy Phillips and knew that he was right, it would be best if she were not present. Terry Mercer and she had known each other for a long time, the last thing she needed to see, was pieces of him and Sandra scattered around his house.

"Whatever you do Andy, as soon as that man sorts out the locks you chase him away, do you hear? We don't want him spewing up all over the evidence."

"I will mam" said Andy sympathetically. "On you go mam, I'll call you shortly".

Andy Phillips could see the look of concern in his boss's face and so ventured. "Remember it was your idea mam to force Terry's locks. Someone will suffer for this when he gets back, we'll hear blasphemies then mam...I don't want to be held responsible.

Polly smiled at Phillips. "Don't worry Andy...I'll take full responsibility."

## CHAPTER EIGHT.

## UNKNOWN LOCATION.

They didn't have long to live. Terry and Sandra had been bound securely next to metal ladders which were pinned to a concrete wall. They had been gagged and so they could not verbally communicate. Sandra had been stripped to her bra but they had allowed her the luxury of jeans and trainers. Terry guessed that they'd been here an hour or so. They had been injected with something that had rendered them unconscious. The concrete ground was wet and cold where they were seated. Sandra sat struggling to loosen her ties, but it was useless. The concrete floor had rendered their backsides completely numb.
Water trickled down the walls in several places. As his eyes adjusted to the light, or rather, the lack of it, Terry could see movement in front of him. It was water, and it was flowing, quite rapidly, about ten feet in front of them, the size of a large stream. They could hear in the distance, a kind of rushing whooshing type of noise, like echoes. Terry listened intently. It was water, lots of it, and it was heading their way. He wondered if Sandra had realized where they were. If she hadn't, she would soon find out.
They were in a sewer, a storm drain to be precise, and it had been raining continuously now for almost four days. Then, and without warning, the water in front of them began to flow faster, fast and silent, like a tide, and wider, so that it was only a metre or so from their feet. Although they couldn't speak, he could see the fear in Sandra's eyes. He shuffled in vain to loosen the bindings. He felt a sharp pain in his back, the water now at his feet. He managed to find the source of the pain with his bound hands, a screw sticking out from the wall. Terry rubbed the masking tape furiously up and down and along its' length. The tape was beginning to give but the water was now soaking his legs and backside, not that he could feel it. His body was completely numb. He felt the burning pain in his wrist as the ragged screw dug into his flesh. Now the water was at

the base of his stomach. Ignoring the pain, he continuously rubbed the tape over the length of the screw. More skin ripped open. Still he rubbed vigorously, the water now half way up his stomach. Finally the tape gave way and his hands were free.
He struggled to his feet and put his hands under the water, searching frantically for the screw in the wall. He found it and began tugging. The knurls of the screw which had been his friend when trying to burst open the masking tape was now his enemy as it burned and tore at the raw flesh of his desperate fingers.
A miracle, the screw came loose. He moved as quickly as he could and tried his best to ignore the information in his brain, which was, if the water continued to rise at this rate then he had about a minute to save Sandra. He found her bound hands beneath the freezing water, which was now at Sandra's throat.
She kept her head up as high as she could. As luck would have it, Sandra's hands had not been bound as securely as his had been, and just as the water reached her chin, the masking tape gave way. Terry helped her to her feet. In almost complete darkness the water continued to rise.
They could not see the water flowing now, instead it filled the area where they stood, silently, an icy cold murderer that would numb their bodies, rendering them completely helpless and leaving them no strength whatsoever with which to swim, and anyway, he thought to himself, swim where?

Wherever the water had been travelling to, it had reached its' destination and was now back filling on them rapidly. Their only hope was to climb up one of the ladders. Terry climbed up first. The ladder seemed to go on forever. He climbed and climbed, looking down and making sure Sandra was behind him. Eventually he reached a concrete ledge about three feet wide. It was wide enough to sit on and take an essential rest to gather some strength. Almost completely exhausted the couple sat on the ledge huddled together. Within a couple of minutes they both freed themselves from their gags. Terry was looking upwards for a hatch or a manhole cover from which they could make their escape. In this poor light it was almost impossible to see more than ten feet in front of them. There was no alternative other than to walk along the ledge.

Surely there would be an escape route. He got to his feet, helping Sandra to do the same. He looked above him and cursed at what he saw. About six feet above them was a distinct water mark, two feet above that, the wall ended. The water below them was still rising quickly and was now only about ten feet from where they stood. "Follow me" Said Terry, and then felt so stupid for saying such an obvious thing. Together they carefully made their way along the ledge, taking small steps and keeping their hands flat against the wall. On and on they walked and seemed to be getting nowhere. Then, Terry thought he could see something ahead of him on the ledge.

Was it a person standing there?

The water was only two feet below them now. If it was who he thought it was, they were dead anyway. If they stayed where they were, death would come for them in an icy torrent.

They would have to move on. It would be better to die quickly from a bullet, than to drown in this freezing mixture of storm water and sewage. As they approached the shape Terry almost cried for joy, it wasn't a person but an old overcoat with scraps of paper and rags attached to it, It had been placed there by a previous storm surge, but it was what it was pinned to that made Terry cry out for joy, another metal ladder, and another manhole above it, and so grateful he was for the ladder, because now, the water was lapping at their feet.

Up they climbed, with limbs aching from their ordeal, and hands completely numb. Higher and higher they climbed.

"I know its agony Sandra, but just keep climbing babe, we can do this, higher means safer my sweetheart."

"I need to rest Terry."

"Just keep going babes, we're nearly there."

He looked down beyond Sandra and could just make out the water beginning to come through the manhole they had climbed through only minutes before.

It was marginally lighter in this compartment and he could see a ledge about eight feet above him. Finally he reached it and was able to help Sandra up onto the concrete haven.

They sat back with their backs against the wall panting and choking, their lungs heaving. Only adrenalin had given them the capability to reach even this far.

"Just leave me Terry, I can't go on, I'm finished, I'm exhausted."

Terry could not answer her. He sat back, himself exhausted and at the end of his limits. With his back against the wall, he looked up. The ladder continued high above them and through yet another manhole. Above that, and even in this poor light, he saw what he'd been praying for, daylight, but then there was a rasping rumbling noise and the daylight disappeared.

## FINLAY STREET. HOLBURN.

It had taken Andy Phillips and his two assistants a little over half an hour to obtain DNA samples from Terry Mercer's home and compare those samples with the existing ones.
Andy stood scratching his head in total bewilderment.
What the hell had Terry been up to? The DNA samples had matched those of the murderers, but what was confusing him was where those samples had been taken from. If the information given to him by his team was correct, and he had never known them to be wrong, then Terry Mercer had been in bed with the woman.
How the hell was he going to explain that to Polly?
She and Mercer had been friends for years, and she had heard Mercer on many occasions saying how much he was going to enjoy inflicting pain onto this sick bitch, and yet, here was evidence to suggest that, not only did he know her, but he had been in bed with her, and again according to his team, had been intimate.
His own personal opinion of Mercer did not help the man's situation. Polly would go bloody mental with him if he suggested to her that her beloved Terrance Mercer had been to bed with one of the killers. To make matters worse, Phillip's team had discovered DNA from the male killer as well, but he had been fully clothed.
Had that sick fuck arrived here to find his woman in bed with Mercer? And if so, why was Mercer not lying here with his brains blown out all over the floor.
He sighed as he pulled out his mobile phone. The good news, at least as far as Polly Sheppard was concerned, was that Terry was not lying here hacked to pieces, as for detective Sandra Neal?
"God only knows" he said, as he put the phone to his ear.
Twenty minutes later Polly Sheppard stood listening in total disbelief at what Andy Phillips was telling her.
"No...no way, I'm not having that Andy, no way. I don't care what it looks like, I'm not having that, not Terry, Jesus Christ no chance, there has to be some other explanation to all this."
Andy Phillips stood beside the chief inspector feeling almost guilty

for giving her this news, as if it were his fault that the forensic evidence had turned out this way.

Polly seemed to be in some kind of trance as though she was asking herself questions and then proceeding to answer them out loud.

"Well if Terry was in bed with her, and her accomplice was here, then why isn't Terry lying dead here?"

"I know mam I asked myself the same question."

She continued as though Phillips hadn't said anything.

"And what the hell has Sandra been doing here all this time? Has she arrived at the same time as the slut's lover?

Has she found Terry in bed with that? No, no no there's something not right here Andy, and anyway, if things had happened the way the evidence suggests, then there would have been some kind of struggle, have you ever seen Terry Mercer fighting Andy?"

"No mam."

"No, and you wouldn't want to either, I've seen him and there is no way he would let those sick fucks drag him out of his own house without first putting up a ferocious struggle, that much I do know. So, however this evidence looks, I can guarantee you that this is all wrong. Of course, you'll be over the moon won't you Andy, about all this, you'll be fucking loving this, well, I'll tell you now, you go around telling the staff that Terry slept with the monster, and I will remove your balls with a pair of blunt secateurs, understood?"

"Yes mam."

Polly left, slamming the door behind her.

Andy sighed with relief as Polly left the house. He'd never seen her *this* riled in all of the time he'd known her, but no matter what she said, the evidence was here that Mercer had been in bed with the murderer, of that there was no doubt, and it was that fact that was frustrating the chief inspector.

## UNKNOWN LOCATION.

They had rested on the ledge for almost five minutes now. It would take all the strength they could muster to make this next climb. Sandra looked down at the water which was rising at an incredible rate.
"Right let's go." said Terry, "That water has nearly caught up with us again."
"Why is there so much water Terry, we must be a fair old height up now, and still it rises."
"Somewhere down there those sickos have had access to sluice gates or flood doors and they've closed them. The water rising up now should be rolling its' way along to the Thames or one of the other rivers flowing beneath London. They intended us to drown there Sandra. If that water reaches us now, we'll drown alright, at least. We'll have to go to the doctors when we get out of here, you see the storm water drains mix with the live sewer drains."
"So what you're saying Terry is, that that is not really water at all, its sewage, I've been up to my neck in sewage."
"That's why we have to climb, we have to get out of here, and we have to save a lot of people's lives up there. They left us for dead Sandra, and we've survived.
We'll have to get treatment, injections, tetanus injections, even if that water gets into our cuts, it will eventually kill us, have you ever heard of Weill's disease?"
"No."
"You get it from rat's piss. It gets in to you through cuts and scratches. It'll travel through your blood stream and it will end up in your brain. If that doesn't get you then the Hepatitis will. So are you in agreement with me that we have to climb?"
"You have a way with words Terry" She smiled. "I'm just so very cold and tired, I'm shivering so much."
"I know babe, but you're going first this time, I'm right behind you, I won't let you fall, I promise. We'll get out of here and we'll catch those sick bastards Sandra. I'm going to burn them, that's why we

have to get out of here, and of course, now we know what they look like, we know who we're looking for now.

I have to kill them now Sandra, so please, don't let me down, move up that ladder babe so I can get them back, I need to beat them up so badly Sandra, before I pour petrol onto them. I need to hurt them so much. They're not fucking drowning us in live sewage or rat's piss I'll make the bastards drink rat's piss, that's what I'll do."

They climbed the metal ladder with Sandra in front. She listened to Mercer going on about what he would do to these sick dead-beats. Tears rolled down her face as she recalled her ordeal in her own home with the monsters, even before they'd set off for Terry's house. Terry seemed to be unaware that they'd been to see her first in fact, they'd been waiting for her in her house when she got back from Terry's place. They raped her and played with her for their own enjoyment. They raped her anally as well.

Even as she climbed now she felt a needle-like stab of pain in her anus. She retched as she climbed remembering what else that bitch had made her do... Terry was right though, they had to get out of here. A psychologist or psychiatrist could sort out her head once she got out of here.

"Come on!!" cried Terry, "Keep climbing, just keep climbing-"

"I'm fucking climbing you dizzy bastard!"

Terry smiled through his pain. That's what he wanted to hear, venom, adrenalin, temper, determination. She would make it to the top, her blood would flow now she would heat up with the temper surge.

"Come on move Sandra, don't want you falling in the shit girl, hell you smell bad enough as it is, talk about body odour hell, take a bath babe."

"If you don't shut your huge fucking mouth Terry, I'm going to kick you in the face and watch you falling into that shit, I'm warning you."

"Big deal bitch, just keep climbing and never mind the fancy talk. Just three or four more steps you useless bitch that you are, a fucking dog could climb this better than you, come on."

At last they reached the top ledge. They both looked up through the last man hole square. Their last climb would only be about ten feet. They could hear traffic above them. Traffic meant civilisation, life, normality as opposed to being trapped in this unknown labyrinth of deathly darkness. They would not die in this putrid rancid atmosphere of sulphureted hydrogen, the product of putrid decomposition. One final push and they would be free, although, where they would get the strength was anyone's guess.

They sat on the concrete ledge crying and cuddling each other. Suddenly, just above their heads, they heard a grating rasping sound, and then they were blinded by the light. A man in a blue hard hat looked down at them.

"What the fuck are you doing down there you stupid fuckers!!" Sandra looked up at the man who was now accompanied by another three of his work mates, and shouted; "I love you, thank you so much."

Terry Mercer and Sandra Neal sat on the ledge laughing and crying, completely exhausted. How they had done it, he did not know, but they had. They had made it back to life from the very bowels of hell. Even the sewage workers, who were hardened to the stench of the drains, retched as the gases hit them when they lifted the manhole cover from the pavement.

As it turned out, they were close to Clapham North underground station. The man who had shouted down to them was a fifty-nine-year-old gentleman by the name of Alf McAdam. He was the foreman of the three men who were standing beside him. Only he communicated with them. The other three men said nothing. These men were known in the sewage business as flushers.

Alf McAdam had been informed by one of his superiors that there was a serious blockage and the computer system was registering a massive back fill. Their job was to locate the blockage and flush it out, a job he had done since he was twenty four.

"How the hell have you managed to get yourselves down there? You're not the culprits for that bloody blockage I hope I'll have to notify the police. We'll get you out of there, but you're not bloody well going anywhere until the police have spoken to you."

Neither Terry or Sandra had the strength or the patience to explain to the man who they were, and anyway, Terry thought that they wouldn't be believed anyway.

Five minutes later, Terry and Sandra sat in the back of the worker's van sipping soup from a flask. Alf McAdam stood outside the van leaning on it with one arm and holding his mobile phone with the other.

"These two people are saying that we can't go down. They're saying that the water level is rising extremely fast, which suggests to me that one of the flood gates has been closed, at least one. Check with the computer systems, they'll tell you which ones have been closed off, somewhere in one of the systems, there's a red light flashing furiously, and there's no-one looking at it."

Alf looked down through the manhole again using his torch. He could make out, about twenty feet below, the jet black water, which, from where he stood, looked like liquid tar. The stench grew stronger.

"It's still rising" He said to his mobile. "There's no way we can get down there. If you don't find the source soon, then a lot of Clapham's streets are going to be flowing with foul smelling sludge. You'd better find it soon and hope that you can open whatever gates have been closed. I'm going to close this street off completely and warn these market stall traders to move their merchandise. Now you call me back the minute you hear anything ok?"

Alf McAdam lit up a cigarette and asked his men if they'd called the police, which they had. He had never been a man for panicking in all of his years with the Thames Valley Water and Sewage Works, but, as he looked yet again down the manhole and noticed the water only fifteen feet or so from the surface he was getting ever closer to losing complete control.

He opened the back doors of the van and roared at Terry and Sandra, "If I find out that you two are responsible for this, I'll make sure you both do time, you malicious bastards that you are!"

He slammed the door closed and said to one of his men, "You stand here and guard this van and make sure that they don't go

anywhere, you keep them in there, bastards, I'm sure they have something to do with this, they have to, why else would they be down there?"
"Alf" Cried one of the workers, it's only about six or seven feet from the surface."
Alf's record of keeping his cool in tricky situations went for a burton.
"What in the name of fuck do you want me to do, I'm doing everything I can for fuck sakes, I can't stop the water, I'm not Jesus you silly looking cunt!!"
He strode over to the manhole. Any minute now, the raw sewage would start to spill over onto the streets and begin to flow down towards the market place. His phone rang, just as two police cars arrived, sirens blaring.
"What"? He said into his phone, " I can hardly hear you for these stupid cunts."
He pointed to one of his men. "For fuck sakes, tell them to switch off that racket, What?" He said into his phone again.

Eventually, he was informed that the source of the problem had been located. Two flood gates had been closed off. They had now been reopened and any minute now he would begin to see the water recede. Just as the water was only two feet from the top, it began to drop. Slowly at first, and then it receded almost as quickly as it had filled. Alf breathed a sigh of relief. He removed his hard hat from his head and wiped sweat from his brow.
One of the police officers approached him.
"What's the problem?"
Alf stared at the officer, and then pointed to his van.
"There are two people in there. When we opened up this manhole lid, they were sitting on the top ledge looking as though they were at death's door. They've had a very lucky escape whatever they've been up to, and don't ask me how they got there, but those storm drains go down about eighty feet or more...fuck knows, anyway, they're all yours now. I haven't got a clue who they are but they're in pretty bad shape. You'll need to get them to hospital for

injections. They'll need antibiotics, tetanus and anti-histamines, in fact, if I were you, I'd get them away now in your car instead of waiting for an ambulance, you can interview them at the hospital. If they've been in contact with that water, well, I'd just get them to the hospital as quick as possible, and then no-one can blame you for wasting time."

"Ok" Replied the officer, "Thanks for the advice, we'll get them away right now."

Alf turned away from the officer and walked over to the manhole, once more fully composed.

"That was a close one boys." He said, as he looked down into the empty compartment.

"What was the problem Alf?" Asked one of his workers.

"Some idiot apparently shut off two flood doors, blocking the main storm water flow. I thought at first it was those two in the van who done it, you know maliciousness or something, but there's no way it could have been. The two gates that were closed off are over a mile and a half away, there's no way it could have been them, but how or why they have got themselves stuck down there, hell knows."

"It's a good job we came along when we did Alf." said one of the young workers. "Those manhole lids weigh over two and a half hundredweight they would never have been able to lift it, especially with only a slippery metal ladder to hold on to up at the top here."

"Well, they're out now lads" Said McAdam. He began to laugh as he lit another cigarette. "Tell you what boys, their arses are going to be like pin cushions by the time those lot at the hospital are finished with them."

## CLAPHAM ROYAL INFIRMARY.

Doctor Terrance Stevenson approached the small isolated room in ward C where Terry Mercer and Sandra Neal were recuperating. He entered the room, closing the door behind him, a tall thin gentleman about thirty five.
Terry did not like the look of this, the closed doors. Closed doors meant privacy, confidentiality, secrets, bad news.
Doctor Stevenson sat down on a chair at the foot of both patient's beds whereupon Sandra and Terry sat, fully clothed.

Terry braced himself in fear of what might be said to him within the next few minutes. He had several cuts and scrapes which he knew had come into contact with the sewage on several occasions. He also knew that he and Sandra had been down there for at least two hours which was more than enough time for Weill's disease to kick in and take control of his blood stream, or Hepatitis, or any number of fatal diseases, including diseases of the lungs, because he knew, that as that sewage rose higher, slowly but surely the air above it would become poisonous, and because the gasses had nowhere to go, it meant that the air they were breathing was becoming contaminated. Mixed with the air they were breathing was Sulphated-Hydrogen, this is the gas given off a decomposing corpse. There would also be Carburetted Hydrogen, which had been known to explode, and of course, Carbonic Acid. Years ago, the old miners called this killer, "Choke Damp."

Terry breathed out a massive sigh of relief as Doctor Stevenson finally said, "Good news you two, you both have a clean bill of health. You have not contracted any fatal diseases although we have given you both strong doses of various anti-histamines. Those tests we done this morning on the encephalogram were just to make sure that your brains are nice and healthy."
"And were they?" said Sandra.
"Perfectly inspector Neal, but after all the bacteria you've been in

contact with, we had to do a number of tests making absolutely sure you hadn't contracted anything fatal.
For example Encephalitis Lethargica this is a viral disease with symptoms very similar to Influenza. It is marked by Apathy and double vision, also extreme muscular weakness, Lethargic Encephalitis, you might recognise it by its' more common name of "Sleeping Sickness."
"But we don't have it doctor, right?" said Terry suddenly remembering the boring Pathologist who spoke to him for four hours and told him nothing.
"That is correct inspector" Smiled Doctor Stevenson.
"Everything is fine, you might want to rest up for a couple of days though, give your bodies time to build up your strength. Now then inspector Mercer, do you think you could leave inspector Neal and I alone for a few minutes please, I have some rather personal questions to ask her, she might appreciate the privacy."
"Look" Said Mercer, "I'm not letting her out of my sight after everything we've been through, and-"
"It's ok Terry, really, it's ok, go to the canteen and get yourself a coffee, and bring me one back would you? Honestly, it's alright Terry, don't worry."
Stevenson smiled at Terry. A tall lean man about the age of thirty five to forty, with jet black jelled hair, and with one of those partings his mother used to make him have in his primary school days.
"I'll take good care of your partner inspector, I promise you she's in safe hands."
Terry nodded to the doctor. "I'm sorry, it's just that we've been through hell and I don't want her suffering anything else unnecessarily."
"I quite understand inspector, but I assure you, she'll suffer no unpleasant experiences in my presence."
"Ok" said Terry, "I'll see you shortly babes."
Sandra smiled at Terry, grateful for his concern.

All the way down to the canteen Terry was recalling everything the sick bitch had said to him.

*"He's already fucked her."*

He had a lump in his throat and had to fight to hold back the tears. He knew very well what sort of questions doctor Stevenson would be asking Sandra, delicate questions. Sandra's ordeal had been far worse than his. Now, because of those sick monsters and what they'd put Sandra through, he would spend the rest of his life if he had to, finding them. One thing was nagging him in his mind as he thought about the psycho bitch.

For brief moments in her presence he felt as though they'd met before somewhere, indeed the way she addressed him seemed to suggest that they had been acquainted at some point in time. He kept shrugging the idea out of his head, after all, if they had met at some point, he would surely have remembered the occasion. Undoubtedly though, whoever she is, she is a very sick woman, in every sense of the word.

# SCOTLAND YARD.

## BROADWAY VICTORIA.

Terry sat explaining to Polly Sheppard everything that had happened in the last few days, including their narrow escape from the sewers.
"How the hell did they manage to infiltrate your house Terry in the first place, you've got that place secured like Fort Knox."
Terry shrugged his shoulders.
"They didn't even break any glass, or anything else for that matter, I don't know how they done it. Sandra said they didn't get the key from her, because it was still in the hiding place she has for it at her house, and come to think of it, how the hell did they get into Sandra's place? Her security system is almost as good as mine, but the fact remains, they did, may I smoke?"
"Go on just this once."
Terry lit up his cigarette.
Polly sat scrutinising her favourite detective.
He seemed different. There was something missing from him, she could see it in his eyes. His face seemed to her like it was set in stone. There seemed to be a determination in his face. The semi-naked girl in the calendar smiled at him, but although Terry's gaze was set in her general direction, he was not looking at her. Instead he seemed to be drawing on his powers of perspicacity.
It was understandable that he would be more determined than ever to catch these monsters after their ordeal in the sewers, but there was something more than determination in those eyes. Something she didn't recognise, something almost sinister.
"Where's Sandra just now Terry?"
Terry's gaze was set in the same direction.
"She's seeing a psychiatrist."
Polly smiled at Terry sympathetically, knowing how he must feel just now and how, yet again he would find some way of blaming himself for what happened to Sandra.

She sighed. "I think you two should take a break for a while Terry, you and Sandra, give yourselves some time to recuperate."
"No."
"Terry, I'm your boss now, and if I decide you need a break, then you'll take a bloody break, understood?"
Terry said nothing more.
"And anyway" Polly continued, "I have already decided that it would be best for all concerned that you and Sandra no longer work together, but don't worry, I'm not relocating her, she'll still be working in the city."
Terry sat staring into Polly's eyes. Even as he took a drag of his cigarette, his eyes never left hers. For a brief moment or two, she actually thought he was going to attack her.
Feeling his disappointment she said;
"Terry, I'm doing this for everyone's benefit, and I-"
"Fine, I resign, here."
He took off his shoulder holster and placed it upon Polly's desk, and then done the same with his ID badge and card.
"Terry, don't be so bloody stupid, what are you doing?"
"I'm making it easy for you Polly, you won't have to worry about me and Sandra working together anymore."
"Is this because of what happened to William McDermot Terry, because if it is-"
"It's got nothing to do with Billy McDermot, it's to do with what happened to Sandra Neal and Terry Mercer, that's what it's to do with, and the way they are being treated after a near death experience. We got ourselves out of that hell-hole as a team. We were tied and bound and left to die. If it had been any other two officers down there in that stinking cavernous immensity then you'd have been fishing out two corpses, but because of how Sandra and I feel for each other, well that gave us that extra bit of determination to get ourselves out of there. So don't sit there and tell me that our love for each other is undermining our professionalism, because it's not, in fact, it was our love that saved us, and now you want to split us up as a working team? Split up the two officers who stand the best chance of bringing those fucking

maniacs down.
We know them. We know first-hand how sick they are. We know how unstable they are, and I'll tell you this much Polly, they are going to disappear from the radar just shortly, and then you won't see them for a long time.
Sandra and I know what they look like, or at least, we did. They won't look like anything your artist impressionist can come up with. This is a big city Polly, and they'll stay out of sight for a long time. The killings will stop, for a while. But they'll be out there, watching and waiting for the heat to die down. If you take Sandra and I from this case-"
"I'm not taking you from the case Terry, I just feel that it's all been too much for Sandra. I thought I was doing you a favour Terry, giving you a break, I thought I was helping you. Hell Terry, Sandra's had to go to the psychiatrist you can't tell me she's in any condition to continue working?"
Terry stubbed out his cigarette. "I've been seeing a psychiatrist now for three years Polly do you think it's affected *my* work performances?" Polly sighed. "Tell Sandra to come and see me. And for Gods' sake, pick up that badge and gun before I shoot you...prick!"
Terry Mercer smiled. "Will do `mam`."
"Is that the truth Terry? Have you been seeing a psychiatrist all this time?"
"When Carol left me Polly, I struggled. I hit the bottle hard, and is it any wonder, her leaving me the way she did, and on top of that, having to babysit that senile old bastard Hargrieves, is it any wonder I have to see a psychiatrist?"
Polly smiled at Terry, knowing full well his true opinion of Sam Hargrieves.
"You were some team, you and Sam Terry."
Mercer nodded. "I learned a lot from that man Polly. Just leave me and Sandra alone and let us work together, because I truly believe that she and I can be as successful as Sam and I ever were, and that's the gods honest truth, just leave us alone Polly, and we'll tell you if the pressure gets too much for us. I have a lot of respect for

you Polly Sheppard, an awful lot of respect, and I happen to think that you are the best person to hold this post, certainly in *my* time here. And it was because of that respect that I was prepared to resign, because now Polly, I have to kill those dogs, not just catch them, but eliminate them. If I had taken leave as you suggested, I would have still been out there searching for them, only it would have been illegally. If anything had gone wrong, then no blame could have been placed upon your shoulders, so you see, I wasn't being childlike I was doing you a favour."

Polly scrutinised her favourite detective, smiling at his opinion of her and admiring his loyalty. But then Terry said something that rocked her completely, and took her by surprise, even shocked her.

"If I hadn't met Sandra Polly, then you and your womanising husband would have been parting company lady. Get fucking rid of him Polly, you deserve better than that."

Polly was shocked at the fact that Terry even knew her husband, let alone know everything about his hedonistic libertine life style, but then, he was the best detective they had here in Scotland Yard.

"I'm sorry, but he's nothing but a rat bastard Polly, and you're way too good for him. He bought you a new phone did he? Tell him to give you a real gift, something really useful, like a divorce paper. I'll tell Sandra you wish to see her".

Terry rose to his feet and thanked Polly for her understanding, and her patience.

"I know it's none of my business Polly, but I try and look out for my friends...my real friends. See you later Pol."

Polly sat in silence after Terry had left. She had just been hit by an emotional tsunami. Once again, Terrance Mercer had told her where everything was at. She looked at her mobile phone, smiling softly, and then she picked it up and pressed the digits for her husband's phone. His phone was switched off.

She smiled again, looking at the office door. "I know Terry, but I'm so damned scared of being on my own." Polly Sheppard broke down and cried.

## DOVER STREET.

## KNIGHTSBRIDGE.

She sat on one of her favourite chaise-longue sofas, sipping a dry martini.
"Did anyone see you coming here?" She said, annoyed that He'd taken such a risk.
He shrugged his shoulders. "I don't know, I wouldn't think so."
He sensed that She'd suddenly become disinterested in him, as if She was bored with him. What He was about to tell her would soon wake her up. This would bring her back to reality. He looked for a reaction in her face as he said; "They survived."
She sipped her martini. If She had been shocked by the news, She hid it well, there was no obvious facial reaction.
He continued, "I told you we should have just killed them there and then, now we're in grave danger. I can't go back to my job, I'll have to move away, completely away, from London I mean. This is the end for us, there's no other"-
"I'll miss you" She cut in sarcastically. "Where will you go?"
He looked at her disdainfully.
"You're not one bit interested are you? You couldn't care less what happens to me, could you, just as long as you've got your fancy house and cars and your money and your fancy friends, everyone else can go and fuck themselves as far as you're concerned."
He didn't really know what the outcome of this conversation would be, he just felt he had to inform her of the bad news in person. Her reaction to the news had surprised him. He'd expected her to have some kind of a panic attack.
"I'll help you out, I'll get you some money and then you can disappear somewhere and make a new start."
"I didn't come here for money" He said quietly. "I was hoping you would come with me, I thought maybe"-
"And why would I do that? Why on earth would I run away with you?"

"I thought we had something going on, I em, I thought maybe you loved me, obviously I was wrong."
"Obviously" She repeated." I'll give you ten thousand, that should be enough to get you away…from here I mean. You're something of an expert in computing you'll soon be able to obtain employment somewhere. One of your crooked friends will be able to sort you out with a false birth certificate and driving license passports and such, you'll be alright."
He sat shaking his head, smiling at her unbelievable cold-heartedness.
"I should have known. I should have known that this would be how you'd react. I'm alright Jack, that's you isn't it?"
"That is perfectly correct, now, do you want the money or not, because I haven't got all day to sit here and listen to your woe-is-me attitude. You knew the risks before we started. I also informed you that our relationship was nothing more than a means to sexual gratification, I told you not to expect any long-term relationship to evolve, and so, the time has come to part company, it was nice knowing you, but now it's over."
If He had arisen from the chair and accepted her financial offer and put all this down to experience, then perhaps He could have made a go of it somewhere else. Instead, He said something he thought would frighten her.
"It *will* be over, you're right. It'll be over if I turn myself in and tell them everything, or tell your husband just what an insatiable nymphomaniac he's married to, and that you fuck with men and women all the time behind his back, and that you're nothing more than a cheap mutton-dressed-as-lamb murdering whore. It would be over then, wouldn't it? No more fancy fucking house and clothes, you fucking whore that you are!"
"Look, stop it, just stop it" She said, rising to her feet and pouring them both another drink. "Ok, I was sharp, and I'm sorry, but you already know that's not what I think of you, we'll find you a house somewhere, don't worry, I'll see to it, here, have another whiskey. You know I'll come and see you."
She sat back down on the chaise-longue, and patted the space next

to her. "Come and sit down next to me. I'll make sure you'll have nothing to worry about."
He came and sat down next to her with his glass of whiskey in his hand.
"You silly boy "She said, "You know I can't resist you, I'm sorry I pretended not to care." She peeled off her blouse over her shoulders, and placed her glass carefully on the crystal coffee table then She gently took his whiskey glass from his hand and placed it beside hers. "Make love to me, right now. Make love to me like you're making love to the whore we're going to meet. Fuck me hard lover, fuck me really fast and hard!"
They began to kiss passionately and seduce each other, and began making love, violently, their bodies thrashing around in rhythmic ecstasy, until the opportunity arose for Her to take hold of the razor sharp ice pick.
She inserted the instrument into his right ear and pushed it hard, all the way up into his brain .His body convulsed vigorously, jerking and twitching in a final death-dance.
"Sshhh," She said soothingly, as if She were comforting a restless child. "Didn't I tell you, you had nothing to worry about, hmm?"
She rose up from the floor, retrieving her drink from the table.
" Now then we'll have to get you into the bath, I'll have to get my sharp knives out and everything." She looked at the corpse.
"I really wish now I'd let you fuck me to a finish. Oh well, there's plenty more fish in the sea...calling me a whore indeed."
She would semi-freeze the body, a favourite trick of hers from the past. When a body was semi-frozen it was easier to dispose of, and far less mess was made, not that She minded the blood at all, only in this instance, there was a lot of expensive flooring that would be ruined by bad blood. She began to speak out loud to herself.
"So, the freezer first, then half him in two, while the bones are nice and brittle, and then finally down to father Thames."
She used to wonder why people referred to it with that sentiment. She even made up a little poem. Her own personal definition was, that if you could bring to the river, your secret shameful package, whatever that may be, a gun, a knife, a husband, or a wife, a son, or

a daughter, or anyone you had to slaughter, the old Father Thames would forgive you, and like an old kindly priest, he would keep your secret forever. So far in her life She'd committed to the river Thames, no less than six bodies, one of those being the man who had raped her, and ripped her virginity away from her at the tender age of eleven years. Years later she'd came down here to find him, armed with an eight pound mash-hammer. She found him in his hotel room and allowed him the luxury of knowing who she was and why she was about to mash in his head. After sixteen consecutive blows to his skull, the job was complete. Fourteen years was a long time to hold a grudge, but she could hold a grudge forever...time was nothing.

Two hours later She stood in the shower having put the two parcels in the boot of her husband's car, after she'd finished disposing of the `parcels` She would contact the whore. She would let Veronica sample a taste of the good life.

## FINLEY STREET.

## HOLBURN.

"What did she say to you Sandra?" Terry Mercer and Sandra Neal sat by the gas fire, each with a cup of tea in their hands.
"Nothing really, she just asked if I was alright, and did I feel mentally strong enough to continue on this case."
"And what did you say?"
"I just told her the truth."
"Which was?"
"That as long as I was working with you I'd be fine, I told her that you give me extra confidence, strength, self-belief."
"And do I really?"
"Terry, there is no way I would have survived that the other day without you, and I mean that. I had a long discussion with my psychiatrist and I went through everything with her. All the things they done to me, all the threats they made concerning you. Do you know what they were going to do? They were going to strip us naked, tie us up and then throw us into your bath, fill it, and then throw in an electric fire in with us."
Terry heard the break in her voice.
"Yes but they didn't did they, and now, they'll have gone into hiding.
They've reached their limit. We were on to them. They couldn't just sit around as we got closer to them, so they had no choice but to take matters into their own hands."
Terry remembered what Sam Hargrieves had said to him all those years ago about gut feelings.
Sandra looked at her partner.
"They're both evil Terry, but it's her, she's the one who calls the shots. Oh he's a killer, don't get me wrong, but it's her, she's the dominant one she makes the decisions. She's also schizophrenic."
"Oh, you think? Sorry, I know she is Sandra."
"What was it Terry that Andy Phillips called them, demonologists?

Well, in actual fact, he's not far off the mark. The thing that gets me Terry is, why didn't they just kill us there and then?
Take us down the sewers, I get that, but why didn't they shoot us there and then, rather than leaving us alive."
"They probably thought we'd suffer more, having all our faculties but not able to do anything to save ourselves. Just leave us to struggle and struggle, until the icy water rose over our heads and finally drowned us, huh, drown in that filthy sludge of rain water and sewage. I'll bet the sick bitch had a couple of orgasms thinking about that one."
"Well we know she's well to do Terry, we know that."
He smiled at his partner. "You could have fooled me."
"She has money Terry, lots of it, she's intellectual you won't find her in your average restaurant I guarantee it. I think she's married, probably to a successful man who is completely devoted to her, and if not married, certainly living together. How does she get away with all these deeds without being found out by her husband? Simple, he isn't there, he's away somewhere, whatever it is that he does. He comes back home, and she's there for him with all the devotion you could wish for. The honest, faithful wife who loves him to bits, pardon the pun."
Terry took the empty mug from Sandra. "So what are you saying? That we stand a better chance of finding her first before we find him?"
"Exactly Terry, you said it yourself, they'll be off into hiding, only they won't be hiding together. He'll be off, and when I say off, I mean gone, he'll be away from London now. He's been found out, so he can't go back to Burlington and Hedgewood can he, so he's gone. For all we know, he could be in Loch Lomond, or he could be in Florida, that's how much chance we have of finding him. She, on the other hand, is still here in the capitol, playing out her role as the faithful little housewife. She can't go anywhere, not if she values her life-style." She looked to Terry for a reaction to her opinion.
Terry stood nodding. "You've got her all sussed out haven't you Sandra."
"Maybe" said Sandra. "It's what I think anyway, and going by the

amount of money she spends on jewellery and clothes-"
"Yes, and let's not forget perfume." said Terry, smiling broadly. Sandra smiled back at him and replied, "Yes, and let's not forget our little Kathlene O'Connor with her infatuation with you, and the threat still stands mister Mercer, let's not forget that."
Fifteen minutes later, Terry and Sandra lay in bed together, not making love, not even kissing. They just lay there in the darkness listening to the wind and rain whistling at the window, and each of them recalling the course of events from the past few days, and both of them very grateful for the other's presence. Terry said nothing to Sandra, but he was thinking back to the night that the female monster lay in this very bed, cuddling into him. She had said something that was now tugging at the temporal lobe of his brain. And then he remembered what it was. She had called him "sweet-pea". Somewhere in his memory bank there was a flash of someone in his life calling him by that term of endearment. It wasn't his mother, and it certainly wasn't Carol, who the hell? Then, in the darkness Sandra said; "Did you know Polly Shepard is splitting up with her husband?" Terry smiled and said; "Oh that's a shame," and then he cuddled into Sandra, still racking his brains. Why, of all the things the nasty bitch had said to him, did *that* spring to his mind?

## TEMPLE ROAD. LOCKSLEY ESTATE.

## EAST LODON.

When Mandy arrived back, Veronica and Lizzy were watching TV, she had been to visit an old friend who just happened to owe her a favour or two. The friend in question was a young lady roughly the same age as herself. The girl was currently going out with a young man who had connections with certain gang members in the city, and of course all these gangs had to protect themselves, and so fire arms were plentiful, in abundance in fact. The young lady had obtained three hand guns at Mandy's request.
When Mandy had come to see the girl and order the guns, she thought that the young lady would need time to get them, a couple of weeks or so. Mandy was quite taken aback when upon ordering the guns, the girl had said; "I'll need some time Mandy to get them, give me a couple of hours."
"A couple of hours?" said Mandy, well impressed.
The young lady had misread Mandy's reaction.
"I can't help it Mandy, these things take time, I'll have to go and collect them myself, and that on its' own is a risk, because the police are stopping people at random now on the streets for spot searches, and when you're as beautiful as me, well you stand a bigger chance of being searched and having your arse and tits groped in public."
Mandy shook her head, grinning at her friend. "I'll come back in a couple of hours Stephie."
Now, four hours later, she was back at Veronica's place.
"Can I have a word you two in the kitchen please."
"Sure" said Veronica, "What have we done?"
Mandy put on the kettle.
"You haven't done anything, I just need to have a chat with you both."
The three friends sat at the kitchen table. As soon as they all had their coffees Mandy began.

"The crime rate in this city is rising, and I'm quite sure you don't need me to remind you, in particular, violent crime, and violent sexual crime, and this, despite the government's pledge to crack down on it. The trouble is it's a load of bull-shit lies just to get us to vote for them, as we all know. So we'll have to take measures to protect ourselves in this hostile environment in which we live. Now, what I'm going to say next to you will no doubt come as quite a shock to you, but I value our friendship and I value our lives too much to put them at risk any longer, I'm afraid pepper sprays are not enough of a deterrent these days, and can only be used on one attacker at a time. If we were to be attacked by two or more people, we would be in serious trouble."

"Get to the point Mandy." said Veronica, "you've bought a gun haven't you.

"I've bought three guns Veronica, and before you say anything, I know your views on fire arms. You have the same point of view as my sister had. She wouldn't allow Thomas to have a gun in the house, and look what happened to them. Now, if she and Thomas had a gun hidden somewhere in the house, then just maybe, they would be sitting here now having a coffee with us. I'm not going to allow that to happen to us ladies, I'm making sure of that.

Most of the other working girls around here are already carrying a piece with them. None of them as yet have had to use them, but they all say the same thing.

They all say they feel a hell of a lot safer in the knowledge that they have it there with them in their bags, and knowing that if anything kicks off, they at least have a fighting chance of survival. So, what do you think girls? Will you carry one around with you?

Even if it's just for me?"

"I've never even held a gun." said Lizzy, "I wouldn't even know what to do."

"Don't worry Liz, none of us have, but I've arranged for a friend to come round, she'll learn us all we need to know, and of course, she'll give us demonstrations, so, what do you say. Just think of Jane and Thomas, would you want that happening to me, or I you?"

"Yeah, we'll do it" Said Veronica.

Mandy now felt a sense of relief, especially what she thought Veronica had going on at this moment in her life.
Elizabeth sat nodding her head.
"I'm still in shock with what happened to your sister and Thomas, and now officer ballet, I mean he's a C.I.D. cop and still he got murdered. They carry guns don't they? I think it's a good idea Mandy, and you're right. Hell, I couldn't bear it if I came home and found one or both of you lying here murdered, yeah I'll do it Mandy, I'll learn how to use one. I hope your friend has patience though, because I'm petrified of guns."
"You'll be fine Lizzy, you'll soon lose the fear. My friend Stephie, was one of the most timid girls I had met in my entire life, now she's...Christ, now she's eh...oh I don't really know how to describe Steph, apart from being a blatant flirt and cock-tease, but no-one will take advantage of her, let me put it that way...male or female."
Veronica smiled at her friend. "You know the nicest people don't you Mandy."

# DOVER STREET.

## KNIGHTSBRIDGE.

She sat at the table in her kitchen. It was done, she had disposed of the body. She had a particular spot on the banks of the Thames about three miles from the city. A nice little secluded spot where there was hardly ever any human activity. She felt frustrated, annoyed at the fact that She'd had to do such a deed.
"Why did He have to do that?
Why did He come here and spoil everything we had going?"
She couldn't risk him coming here. He did not exist in her world when She was here. Here was a place He was never meant to see, never meant to visit. Here had nothing at all to do with him.
She would join him in his world from time to time and do what they had to do, but always, She would return to the sanctuary of here. She would miss him, there was no doubt about that, but lately, He'd attempted to become more dominant towards her, taking over the reigns as it were, trying to be the alpha male.
"Now look where it's got him."
Now, She would go back to how She operated before She met him. She led him to believe that the girl they'd killed in Bridge Way Street was their first victim, but there had been many more.
Three of those victims lay at the bottom of the murky Thames having threatened her in a similar manner as He had just done.
She had been killing for a long time, long before She'd even met her husband, even before she'd exited the high-school gates for the last time. She was an accomplished killer, and the secret of being able to kill with a clear conscience was simple. You simply looked upon the world in the same manner as our friend Charles Darwin had. God hadn't put us here. God hadn't made man a woman from one of Adam's ribs. We are here today in our present form through evolution, the process of elimination, and if this is true, we are soulless. There will be no judgement day, and neither will there be any rapture, and there certainly wouldn't be any second coming of

Christ, because as far as She was concerned, He'd never been here in the first place. So if there is no God, then there is nothing to fear. And if we have no souls, then we are beasts of the field, we are animals, to hunt and to kill comes naturally to us, it is the reason we exist today.

Survival. The rule of the beast. Eat or be eaten.

Evolution, not God, has made us the superior species.

No man would ever rule over her though, and there were now four of them lying in the Thames that was testament to that fact...and that would never change.

She wandered through to her lounge with her coffee cup and stood at the window watching the Knightsbridge traffic moving silently to and fro. Christmas decorations were everywhere She looked. Giant-sized Santa clauses created from a million multi-coloured lights, raised bells or rode sleighs pulled by multi-coloured reindeer, or climbed imaginary chimneys with giant sacks on their backs, and all to impress and inspire us enough to enter their stores and spend our money. More lies. Primary schools all over the country would be making last minute adjustments to stage sets, constructed by over enthusiastic teachers, grasping, through the children of today, that childhood of theirs that seemed to have raced past them in a blink of an eye and was lost forever.

"But" She thought to herself, "If it keeps them happy, then so be it." She recalled that terrible day long ago in her childhood, when She was informed by some scruffy girl in her classroom, that Santa clause did not exist, and that it was your parents who placed all your parcels under the Christmas tree. Strange, that when she learned the awful truth about Santa clause, it tore her heart to pieces, but when She learned the truth about Jesus, who could potentially save her soul for eternity, She felt nothing.

The wind whistled at her window, pelting icy raindrops hard against it. She entered her kitchen once again and refilled her coffee cup. She felt kind of lonely, brood-ish, like she could use some company. Maybe She would arrange to meet the whore, do some Christmas shopping, spend some time with her. Perhaps She would treat her and buy her some nice things, after all, she mustn't have too much money, doing that to make ends meet. Yes, that's what she'd do. She would show her a wonderful world where she could have anything she wished for. She would give her a taste of that kind of unbelievable life-style, where anything her heart desired, would materialise, and then, when She had her hooked, she would take it away from her...just like we do with our children and Santa Claus.

# CHAPTER NINE.

## SCOTLAND YARD.

## BROADWAY VICTORIA.

Terry Mercer and Sandra Neal stood by the chief inspector's office door, awaiting the arrival of Polly Sheppard, who was now fifteen minutes late for the appointment she had made for them.
"Five minutes more" Said Sandra," and we're out of here, we can't stand around here all day waiting. I'd like to hear the outcome if it were us"-
"Ah there you are, sorry I'm late, bloody lawyers would talk all day if you let them".
Polly opened her office door, removing her scarf and jacket almost at the same time.
"Come in come in, take a seat". She made Terry and Sandra a cup of tea. The two detectives sat opposite the chief inspector.
"Any news on the sicko's, dare I ask?"
"It's just as we thought mam" said Mercer, "They've disappeared from the face of the earth. There is not a trace of them anywhere however we have discovered that He has a name. He's been posing as a young Mister Burlington at Burlington and Hadgewoods, to us anyway. The name He's been using to society is Anthony Smith. Tony Smith, but that could have changed by now, and probably has. He'll have been clearing out bank accounts and the likes, opening new ones under a different name. We have officers making inquiries around the banks in the city".
"Ah, so at least we know how he gained access to Bridge Way Street".
"That's just it mam. Sandra and I have interviewed the old lady who is the receptionist there, and she's informed us that any number of estate agents could have access to Bridge Way Street. People are not restricted to having their properties advertised by just the one agency. If you have the money, you can use any number of agents

to try and sell your property. Again, we have officers checking which agencies are advertising the property. Once we get a definite number we'll begin to conduct interviews. What Sandra and I think is, that the bitch, or her husband works for an estate agents as well, obviously, not Burlington and Hedgewood. What we have to find out is which one mam".

Polly smiled at Mercer, nodding her head.

"Cut out the mam shit Terry, everybody here knows your sentiments regarding authority, you're fooling no-one. Keep me posted on your progress, and be careful, whatever you do. Are you sure you're ok Sandra to continue? You've had a hell of an ordeal, and I'm not talking about the sewers, I'm referring to working with him".

She pointed to a smiling Mercer.

Kathlene Oconnor knocked and came into the office, handing Polly a printed e mail.

"Mm, that's lovely aftershave" She said, sniffing the air directly beneath Terry Mercer's chin.

"Mm...lovely", she continued, as she left the room, closing the door behind her.

Polly Sheppard and Sandra Neal both smiled...Terry dared not.

# LAKE DISTRICT. WINDERMERE

## CUMBRIA.

Sam and Beth Hargrieves walked hand in hand along the side of the lake, stopping now and then to take photographs.
"This has been lovely Sam".
She was referring to the week they'd spent up here in the Lake District. The hotel in which they were staying, gave them a view from their bedroom window that beggared belief.
A dusting of snow lay on the fells in the distance. To Beth, it looked like a scene from a fairy-tale movie. She had taken more than three hundred photographs in the time they'd been here, as well as doing more than fifty sketches.
Even Sam, who had never really been interested in photography, had taken a hundred or more photographs.
As they arrived back at the hotel from their walk, Sam said.
"You'll be spoiled for choice Beth, which sketch to get started on when we get home. This is an artist's paradise up here, talk about landscapes".
"Thank you Sam, this week has done us the power of good. It's one of the best holidays we've ever had, really. Why the hell do we pay over-the-top prices for overrated holidays, and we have *this* on our very own doorstep". Beth knew that she had left herself open for criticism, and counted the seconds in her head as Sam begun.
"Well that's you Beth, you're always wanting to go to bloody Spain or Portugal, and you know I don't like the sun. You sit out there tanning your arse, and then suffer the consequences for days after it, with the effect of sunburn. You moan at me sitting indoors all day, or if I'm at the bar, and you just get"-
"That'll do Sam, Christ. You can't say anything about Terry Mercer, you're far worse than him when you get started. I was only saying how nice it is here, that's all".
An hour later, Sam and Beth had lunch in a local restaurant and then made their way back to the hotel to pack. Sam sat in the room

while Beth done all the packing, not because he was lazy, but because he had a bad habit of forgetting to pack certain things, like the Rolex watch that Beth had bought him for their twentieth anniversary, a very welcome tip for one of the waiters or room-service girls in the Algarve.

Of course, when inquiries were made, none of the room service workers had set eyes on the watch.

He sat now, scrutinising his newspaper while Beth busied herself packing their belongings, and making small conversation with her husband in between.

Suddenly Sam said; "Look at this Beth, our Terry and Sandra Neal have had a lucky escape. Apparently, they'd been abducted and left for dead. Christ, according to this they'd been left tied up in one of the main storm water sewers in the city."

"Are they alright?" said Beth,

"Do they know who abducted them?"

"Doesn't say."

"How did they manage to get out?"

Sam read on. "God knows, but they've issued an artist's impression of the couple who abducted them".

As Sam studied the artist's drawings, he said, or rather, half mumbled; "I've seen her before, I'm sure of it, but where? I know I've seen her, and recently."

"Let me see." said Beth, taking a look at the newspaper.

After only two or three seconds, she smiled and looked at Sam.

"You really have retired haven't you Sam, you honestly don't remember where you saw her, really? I'm surprised about that. I wouldn't have thought you'd have been able *not* to think about her. You said plenty about her on the night you saw her, remember? her cleavage Sam practically in your face? Remember?"

"That's not her Beth, hell , it's nothing like her."

"Of course it is Sam, oh but you'd be concentrating more on her legs and breasts I expect, you probably don't even remember her face. That'll be the reason for your prosopagnosia, and don't deny it. Sam, it's not a photograph remember, it's only an artist's impression, and I'm telling you that that's her. When we get back

home, it might be worth having a chat with Terry. You might be able to help him find these people, but don't be getting yourself all worked up, I'm quite sure Terry will have everything under control." Sam pointed to the drawings again in the paper.
"That's not the man she was in the theatre with that night, if it is her."
Beth, who was placing the last of their belongings into the suitcase said, "Who said it was?"
All the way down the M.6 Sam was pondering about what Beth had said to him. She obviously knew what he was thinking about, because as they climbed out of the car to get refreshments in a service station near Preston she said, "Don't be thinking anything stupid Sam, like coming out of retirement. You can tell Terry and Sandra what you know, and then that's that. You're retired Sam, and you're not going back into an environment that is far too dangerous for a man of your age. You're not going back into those dangerous situations like Sandra and Terry have just experienced. If that had been you down there in those sewers, then we'd have lost you for sure, and anyway, I much rather prefer the Sam Hargrieves who is beside me now to the one I hardly saw for days on end, or the one who ended up having a nervous breakdown and then a heart attack, so please Sam, don't be going down that road again. You've done your bit, enjoy the rest of your life with me. Give Terry, or rather, point Terry in the right direction, and then continue these lovely little weeks away in the country with me." She studied her husband's face and couldn't help herself from sounding desperate. She knew only too well that people who had spent most of their working lives in the force could not just switch off from the job they'd been doing. It was second nature to them. Suddenly she found herself saying something she thought she'd never say to anyone. "I'm begging you Sam."

DOVER STREET.

KNIGHTSBRIDGE. 9pm.

Veronica was confused, she had received a call from His girlfriend asking if she could make her way over to Knightsbridge. She was to enter a pub called The Golden Arrow, get herself a drink, inform her of her arrival, and then wait there for her.
Veronica had done that, and now sat by a window watching the busy flow of traffic rolling past her.
The pub wasn't too busy, but busy enough for no-one to pay her any particular attention. After fifteen minutes or so, a young woman entered the pub, and sat down at a table next to hers. The woman ordered a drink and then pulled out a magazine from her bag and began to read.
She had taken off her coat, hanging it over the shoulders of the chair she sat upon. The waitress brought the woman's drink to the table. The young lady thanked her, and then turned her attention once more to her magazine, having briefly looked out of the window.
The waitress returned to Veronica's table asking if she required another beverage. Veronica ordered another vodka and coke. Glancing at her watch, she sighed. What was it with this pair? She sensed she was going to be stood up again. It had been forty minutes or so since she'd informed Her of her arrival. It didn't matter so much to her this time, because they had paid her in advance, but it was still frustrating, having to be dragged over the bloody city.
Even before the waitress returned, she decided she would wait long enough to drink her vodka and then she'd return to Locksley, by that time she'd have been here an hour, long enough for them to either appear, or at least contact her explaining why they weren't coming this time. The waitress returned with her drink and her change.
Veronica tipped the girl with a two pound coin, who smiled and

thanked her politely, but looked into the palm of her hand as though Veronica had just placed a lump of dog shit there.
"Fuck you madam." She thought to herself. She looked at her watch. "Right, fifteen minutes and then I'm out of here."
She felt rather humiliated, insulted, bringing over an overnight bag containing some sexy lingerie and a couple of changes of clothes.
"Why the fuck could they not just send her a text message saying they're sorry they can't make it. Was that too much to ask?"
Finally, she stood up, draining her glass, pushing her chair neatly back under the table. She picked up her bag and turned to leave the pub. As she did, the young woman sitting near her with the magazine done the same, and then turned to Veronica and said, "Shall we go?"
"Oh my God, it's you, oh, I'm sorry, I mean, I didn't even recognise you, have you dyed your hair?"
"And cut it shorter, do you like it?"
"Yes, it's beautiful, wow, oh my God I've sat here in front of you and I didn't even recognise you, that's amazing, you were brunette weren't you?"
"Yes, but I fancied a change. Do you really think I suit it or are you just being polite?"
"No it's beautiful, you're beautiful, I'm just, I can't believe it, that I've sat here waiting for you, and you've been sitting here right in front of me."
"Well" She smiled, "Shall we go now? I have a taxi ordered to take us to my place, do you still want to come?"
"Of course, yes, and thank you for trusting me."
"For trusting you? With what?"
"For paying me in advance."
"Let's not talk of financial matters, we're friends, and friends don't talk about stone cold financial arrangements, they talk about having a few drinks when we get home, and perhaps going out together tomorrow to do some Christmas shopping, that's what friends talk about."
She smiled broadly at Veronica.
Veronica had to admit, she was absolutely stunning.

As they were leaving the pub She said, "Oh, by the way, it'll just be the two of us this weekend, I'm afraid my boyfriend has been called away with his work for two or three weeks. He's going to miss Christmas and everything. Will you be alright with that?"

"Yeah, em yes, whatever, you're the boss."

"You must refrain from saying that Veronica, I am not your boss, we are friends remember?"

Outside the pub She linked arms with Veronica as they made their way to the corner where the taxi would pick them up.

An hour later, Veronica sat in the most luxurious house she had ever seen in her entire life, dressed in her new sexy top with mini skirt to match, and sipping champagne and strawberries.

She sat opposite her, just smiling and looking at her, making her feel awkward.

Veronica felt that she had to say something.

"I've em, I've never slept with a woman before, and em, well not like that you know, but I'll do my best for you, if and when"-

"Hush now Veronica. Tonight is not about sex darling, tonight is about becoming friends." She raised her glass and said cheerfully, "Cheers, here's to friendship, long and prosperous friendship."

"Cheers" replied Veronica, feeling a little more comfortable with the situation. And then, just like her boyfriend had done, She hit her with cold-hearted reality.

"You are very beautiful Veronica, what is it that makes you do what you do for a living? Surely there are other avenues of opportunities open to you, pardon my abruptness, it's a bad habit of mine."

Whatever anyone would say about Veronica Wells, no-one could say that she didn't speak up for herself or her friends. Although the question had stung her, more than a little, she responded immediately by saying; "Well, before I answer that question, I would like to know the name of the person who asked it, it's what friends do you see, they inform each other of their identity, now my name is Veronica Wells, I live at"-

"I know where you live Veronica, and"-

"Good, that saves me the trouble, now if you don't mind, I'd like to know your name, and your boyfriend's name come to think of it.

Listen, if I'm just your whore and my services have been obtained purely for sexual purposes, then believe me, I don't give a flying fuck who you are, but you were the one who said to me that you wanted to be friends, and that you wanted to go Christmas shopping tomorrow, well, call me old fashioned, but I'm not in the habit of going shopping with people whose names I do not know."
She sat smiling still at Veronica.
"You're feisty, I like that, you'll put up a fight."
"Put up a fight? What the hell are you talking about?"
"I simply meant that you wouldn't put up with anyone's nonsense Veronica, and that no-one will stand on you, now, as to my name? My name is Victoria, you may call me Vicky, ok?"
"Ok then Victoria, my name as you know is Veronica, and for the amount of money yourself and your boyfriend are paying me, you can call me anything you want. Now, as to your question, I'm afraid I wasn't born the brightest of sparks, and where I grew up, in Hackney, well let's just say there were more opportune places to be starting out your working life. As you will have no doubt surmised, I am not academically blessed, and so, after numerous shitty jobs, I decided, after some long and hard questioning myself of morals, to study the law of the streets. I have aspired to the dizzy heights of excellence in that field. Let me explain something to you. If you are not born into money in these parts, and, like myself, you have no academic qualifications whatsoever, then life here in the city is an uphill struggle, to say the least, and with each and every application form you fill in, you are constantly rejected, time after time after time, then there comes a time that you have to make crucial decisions in your life. Now I'm not saying that what I do is the ideal career choice, but when your rent goes up and up, along with everything else in this bloody city, then it comes down to survival. I was left with a simple choice. Sink or swim. If I wanted to remain living in London, I would have to find the means and ways of obtaining the financial requirements. And so, being unskilled as I am in just about every department, I turned to the one thing that I was good at. Pretty soon, morals and principles were excluded from my vocabulary, and my life-style, but I will say this in my defence

Victoria, if you don't mind *me* being abrupt. You called me remember"

"Oh my goodness me girl, come over here, I did not intend to offend you. Come and cuddle me, I apologise to you if I upset you, my goodness, come and let me kiss you and hold you."

Veronica was very confused. One minute She was verging on being nasty with her venomous remarks, the next, she would lick dog shit from your shoes, but, if she was honest with herself, she would not be refusing any request of going to bed together. Her beauty was powerful, mesmerising even.

Victoria held Veronica in her arms and began to kiss her passionately. Like it or not, Veronica was melting. She had never kissed with a woman in her life, certainly not passionately, and the feeling was very different to any man she'd kissed. But the feeling was taking her breath away. It felt amazing to her. It was at this point that Veronica came to realize, that in fact, this was the first time in her entire life, that anyone had actually kissed her with passion, real passion. She would go shopping with her tomorrow. She would do anything She asked of her tomorrow, and she would do anything She asked her to do tonight. Suddenly Victoria gently pulled away, and held Veronica's face in her hands, tenderly.

"You are my fucking whore. You are mine and I love the very air you breathe."

More passionate kissing.

"I want you so badly, and I love you and I will take care of you, and you are my whore, don't you forget that Veronica. I want to eat you and suck you, and I want to breathe you, you are my beautiful whore, and I am your whore, now tell me!"

"You are my whore." said Veronica softly.

"Tell me!!"

"You are my fucking whore!"

"Yes I am, we are lovers and we are fucking whores Veronica and I want you to lust for my body like I lust for yours."

"I do" replied Veronica, and much to her own surprise, she found that she wasn't acting.

"Now, stand up, and let go with your hands, no touching. Just stand

and kiss, and lust, come on kiss me, kiss me like you mean it."
The two women stood kissing passionately with their hands by their sides. Eventually Victoria pulled away, and smiled.
"Tomorrow we'll go shopping together Veronica. Tonight, we will sleep together, but we won't do anything except kiss. When we get home from shopping tomorrow, then we'll make love, and I will introduce you to feelings that you never even knew existed, my little whore."
"I believe you, you little whore that you are." Veronica had spent most of her life thinking that she was unique having this very powerful sex-drive. But here was someone who more than matched her appetite." She was actually dizzy with excitement and lust.

# FINLAY STREET.

## HOLBURN. 10th Dec. 4am.

Terry hadn't been in a deep sleep. He wasn't by any means a somnambulist, but rather, his sleep was sporadic. He drifted in and out of slumber throughout the course of the night.
Besides, he hadn't had a good nights' sleep since the psychopaths had broken in, although he could hardly use the term `broken`. They hadn't broken anything. He'd had all his locks changed since then, including his windows, and insisted that Sandra done the same for peace of mind.
Although they were deeply in love, they chose to have three or four days of the week when they didn't sleep together which seemed to serve to keep their relationship `keen` in Terry's opinion. He would always have the fear of their relationship going stale, which was what had obviously happened between him and Carol.
Why else would she take off like that, and in that manner? He had been lying in his bed listening to the wind and rain lashing against his window. Something was troubling his mind, and he couldn't for the life of him, think what it was. But he was restless, more so even than usual. He rose from his bed and made his way down stairs to make himself a cup of tea. If anything went wrong with Sandra and him, he surmised that it wouldn't be the end of the world. He had never been monophobic, and never would be. In fact, sometimes he relished the solitude. He stood waiting for the kettle to boil, still he felt restless. He was having one of those `feelings`.
That's all he could describe it as.
He'd continuously muttered imprecations upon the psychopaths since the night of his abduction, but he didn't think it was anything to do with that, that was making him feel this way. His thoughts were now with Sandra again, and how vulnerable she'd seemed. For no apparent reason he was worrying about her. In fact, his thoughts were becoming perspicacious. But why?
She'd be safe and sound in her own house, especially as she'd had

the new security system installed, and the very same as his own. So why was he feeling like this?
He'd take his tea upstairs and he'd give her a call.
She would be angry at him waking her up at this time of the morning, but if he didn't, there'd be no sleep in here tonight.
Still he felt solicitous as he climbed the stairs.
He climbed back into bed and lit up a cigarette having taken a few sips of his beverage, a luxury he'd never have been permitted if Carol still lived here. He sat up in bed drinking his tea and smoking his cigarette, listening to the sound of the rain being relentlessly hammered against his window, He loved the sound of it. It soothed his mind and always had, since he was a child.
He hadn't heard the car pulling up, but he heard the two car doors being closed outside of his house.
Terry was already dressed in jeans and tee shirt and half way down the stairs when there was three loud knocks on his door.
With gun in hand, he shouted from the bottom of his stairwell, "Who is it?"
There was no reply, but another three loud knocks.
Now, he was right beside his door, but not directly in front of it.
"Who the fuck is it I said?"
The letter box opened.
"It's officer Fisher sir, Miss Sheppard says you've to come to her office at once."
"At *this* time of the morning?"
"She says it's extremely important sir, in fact it's urgent."
"Tell her I'll be there in half an hour or so."
"She says you have to come with us sir, she insists."
Mercer opened the door. The two officers stood on his step wearing waterproof coats and holding on to their hats against the ferocious wind.
"Come in boys" said Mercer," I'll just be a couple of minutes to get some things gathered together. Do you want some coffee?"
"No time sir, if you could just"-
The officer's impatience kicked off one of Terry's rants.
His temper momentarily exploded, partly because of the officer,

and partly because he knew that something was seriously wrong. Polly Sheppard was not guilty of panicking.

"I'm fucking hurrying, twats, four o clock in the fucking morning, bastard. Did she say what it was about? What the *fuck* is so important that I have to come down there at this fucking ungodly hour?"

"She didn't say sir. She wouldn't disclose that to us sir, we're only messengers."

Two minutes later Mercer was at the foot of his stairs, plucking a jacket from the coat stand and slipping it on at the same time as trying to fasten his Cat boots.

"Come on then boys, let's go and see what's so important at this time of the morning. It can only be about those two fucking psycho's. They've probably been up to their shit again with some other poor buggers, has she sent for inspector Neal as well?"

"We don't know sir, we were just told to come and get you, as fast as we possibly can."

Nothing more was said in the car on their way down to headquarters, but Terry's mind was working overtime, wondering what all this was about. He thought about texting Sandra to see if she knew what this was about, but decided against it in case Polly hadn't summoned her to be here. Had those two bastards been up to their tricks again? Had they trapped some other poor sods in some cavernous shithole?  Surely they wouldn't be brazen enough to abduct someone else, not so soon after they'd almost been captured. Of course, we weren't meant to survive. That would piss them off. Maybe they felt an overwhelming desire to take their frustrations out on someone else. Less than fifteen minutes after the first knock had been applied to Terry's door, he was making his way to the elevator and up to Polly Sheppard's office.

As Terry walked along the corridor towards Polly's office, her door opened, and out stepped Doctor Glover.

Now he knew it was about the death of someone, Doctor Glover was the police pathologist. He was the man who had spoken to Sandra and himself and Billy for God knew how long, and told them absolutely nothing.

As they passed Glover said, "You've just to go straight in Mister Mercer."

His face was completely expressionless.

As Terry approached the office door he thought to himself, "Here comes that perspicaciousness again."

He tapped on Polly's door a couple of times and stepped inside the office. He knew straight away it was going to be bad news.

Whenever Polly Sheppard had news of bereavement to pass on to anyone, she found it very difficult to look the receiver in the face. She stood now with her back to him.

"Close the door Terry." She said softly.

Mercer had that feeling again. Whoever this was about was close to him, very close.

*"Please don't let it be Sam or Beth, please God, please don't let it be them."*

Someone once said that God answers every one of our prayers. It's just that sometimes the answer is not the one we're looking for.

"Where's Sandra? Have you not sent for her?"

Now he felt frightened because he could see that Polly was crying. He sat down, and for some reason, he felt completely drained of all energy.

Finally, she looked Terry in the face, and then she shook his world to its' very foundations.

"Sandra's not coming Terry."

She tried to keep her voice from breaking.

"It's not what we thought Terry. She hasn't been attacked...this time. She's em...she's done this herself, it's em...you know."

Terry lit up a cigarette, resting his arms over his thighs, and his head bowed.

"How?" He managed.

"She used her gun Terry. She was obviously hiding her pain from all of us, and not just us, she's been bluffing her psychiatrist as well. I've been reading her reports on Sandra's progress."

The shock was still kicking in to Terry, into every nerve and fibre in his entire body. He felt pins and needles from head to toes.

Of all the things he'd expected to happen between himself and

Sandra, this was the last of them.
She seemed so strong, determined. She vowed she would get those depraved lunatics brought to justice. He sighed heavily as Polly handed him a cup of coffee.
She looked at her friend as he sipped the beverage.
"Are you alright?" she finally said.
"I em...I don't think so Polly, really. I don't think I'll ever be alright. Someone up there has got it in for me babes, honestly. It's like I'm not allowed any happiness or contentment. No I'm just put on this earth to take other people's shit Polly. I fucking asked her if she was alright, if she was coping, I asked her Polly, and she told me she was fine. She said that me and her psychiatrist was helping her through it, and that her determination to catch them was more than enough incentive. The lying fucking bitch! What a selfish bastard. How could she do this to me Polly? How could she leave me like this?"
Cigarette ash fell to the floor. He flicked the cigarette again, allowing more to fall. He sat shaking his head, and sighing, wondering how he would set about filling yet another massive void in his life.
Again he sighed. He was too angry to cry. He was so disappointed with Sandra, taking this way out.
"I'm going home Polly. I'm taking a couple of days off, I'm not feeling too good."
"Terry, I don't want you spending time on your own, I can-"
"Why not Polly, the man upstairs seems determined that I do just that. Everything I touch Polly, turns to shit. Fucking lying bitch that she was, fuck you Sandra."
He stood up, crushing the cigarette stump underfoot on the floor, and then made his way to the door.
As he reached it he said, looking at Polly, "Don't you be changing your mind about divorcing that fucking rat Polly, you'll be just fine.
"Terry, are you going to be alright, really?"
"Well, I'm not going to top myself Polly, simply because I think it's what that bastard up there is wanting me to do. Fuck him as well."
He closed the door gently behind him and made his way to the elevator. On his way down the corridor, he lit up yet another

cigarette, causing one or two of his fellow officers to frown at him as they passed. None of them however, had the bravery to make any comment. As he walked, Tony Chrysler, the chief of police, appeared from one of the elevators.

Seeing the cigarette in Mercer's hand he roared, pointing to it, "What the bloody hell do you think you're doing man, get that put out at once!" As Terry boarded the lift, two secretaries who were passing by, put their hands up to their mouths in complete shock as Terry addressed the chief of police.

" Fuck off Tony, I can't be bothered with your shit today. I know I shouldn't be smoking in here, but then, we all do things we're not supposed to do, don't we. Are you still banging your physiotherapist down at the tennis club?"

Standing in the lift now, he flicked the cigarette in Chrysler's direction, making him duck and dodge the missile as it hit the wall with a shower of orange sparks.

"See ya" said Mercer as the elevator doors closed.

Once on the ground floor, he summoned an officer to obtain a vehicle and take him home. Twenty-five minutes later, Terry Mercer was standing in his back garden. At long last, the rain had stopped.

Tears rolled down his face as he carefully placed the articles of clothing that Sandra had left here onto the small fire he'd built. A dressing gown she had chosen, because of its softness and comfort. *"If I can't be with you Terry, this'll be the next best thing, nice and cuddly-cosy"*.

Terry sniffed the perfume from the garment, as he reluctantly let it fall onto the flames, making him feel even worse, if that was at all possible. He glanced up at the clearing skies, and looked, almost mesmerised by the golden beam of light that shone down onto the city in the distance. When he was a young boy, he used to think that this light was a blessing from God himself, and the golden light represented good news or happiness to the people it shone upon. He continued gazing up at the light as his tears now flooded down his face. That was the trouble with God's light though, he thought to himself. The light was always shining on other people...never him.

## Scotland Yard.

## Broadway Victoria.

"Listen here Polly, I don't care how good he is, there is no-one speaking to me in that manner, who the bloody hell does he think he is?"
Tony Chrysler had barged into Polly Sheppard's office, firing off from the hip without knowing about Sandra Neal.
Polly let him rant on about Terry's inexcusable behaviour and lack of respect for his superiors.
"This is not going unpunished Polly, he is going to be severely reprimanded for this, bloody smoking anywhere he feels like. mean it Polly, he's gone too far this time. I thought he was my friend; he's just humiliated me in front of staff. I've had enough of his bloody attitude. He can't keep blaming Carol for leaving him, hell that was years ago. He's getting away with bloody murder in here, well, no more!"
Polly looked at her superior with tear stained eyes.
"He's just received some bad news sir, we all have."
At last Tony Chrysler noticed Polly's face and immediately knew something was seriously wrong. His anger subsided considerably, as he said sympathetically, "What is it Polly, what's wrong?"
"Inspector Sandra Neal sir, we've just discovered her body in her flat."
"Murdered?"
"No sir, it's worse than murder, it's suicide, she em...she used her own gun."
Chryslers ageing face was ashen. "Oh sweet Jesus."
"I was just about to phone you sir."
Chrysler rubbed his hands over his face. "Oh dear Christ, that would explain Mercer's outburst."
"Yes sir, they were em...they were a couple sir...they were in love. That's what makes this all the more heart rending for Terry."
Chrysler sighed. "What the hell's happened Polly, suicide?"

"I know sir, we're all as shocked as you are, she seemed so strong...considering."

"Considering? Considering what Polly?"

"Well, you know, after their ordeal, when those murderers abducted them. They left them for dead. Terry and Sandra were bound and left down in the sewers somewhere beneath the city. He managed to get himself and Sandra out of there, but I think it's what happened before that, that's unhinged her mind.

They abducted her first sir. They raped her continuously for quite some time before they bundled her into a van, then they abducted Terry. I tried to get them to take some time off, but they were adamant they were fine. Obviously, Sandra was living in self- denial, she obviously wasn't fine. She's been seeing a psychiatrist for the past few weeks, you know, since it happened."

Chrysler studied Polly's face, as if he was waiting for her to continue. When she didn't, he said, "Did you think to speak with her psychiatrist without Miss Neal knowing about it?"

The question was an insult to Polly

"Of course I did, I have spoken with her on three different occasions, and she informed me that Sandra was doing fine, in fact she said that she was an amazingly fast healer."

"What's her name, I want to speak with her, today."

Polly opened one of the drawers in her desk and handed Chrysler the name and address of Doctor Elizabeth Kirkpatrick P.H.D.

Chrysler looked at Polly. "Surely if she's worth her salt, she'd have noticed abnormalities in inspector Neal's behaviour".

"I don't know, you'll have to ask her that." I went to see her sir to get an accurate assessment of Sandra's mental well-being. I thought Doctor Kirkpatrick would have spotted any weaknesses.

When she told me that Sandra was fine, well I took her at her word, and I accepted her decision."

"Well I'm not accepting her decision. I'm going over there, and she'd better be bloody convincing , because if she isn't, she'll have a bloody law-suit on her hands for professional negligence."

Chrysler stormed out of the office, slamming the door behind him. The fact that he'd slammed the door informed Polly, that he obviously felt that she was to blame for what happened to inspector Neal, at least partly so. She also observed that never once throughout their entire conversation did he take the time to ask her how Terry Mercer was feeling, and how this may affect *his* professionalism. How would this affect his every day functioning? But Tony Chrysler was not interested in Terry Mercer, other than to throw the book at him with regards to attitude and respect to senior officials For his own sake, she hoped that he did not plan in visiting Terry at his home to reprimand him. One dead police officer was more than enough to contend with. Terry Mercer's behaviour, at this point in time, would be very unpredictable...to say the least.

## DOVER STREET.

## KNIGHTSBRIDGE.

Veronica sat in the luxurious house wondering when the bubble was going to burst. This really *was* too good to be true. Her new friend had been treating her since she'd opened her eyes at eight o clock this morning. She had cooked Veronica breakfast and had taken hers through to the bedroom along with her own on a tray. As they ate their breakfast She informed Veronica of what She had planned for them in the day ahead. This was to be a special treat for her, marking the beginning of a long and fruitful relationship.
"I want to take you Christmas shopping" She had said, but it was to be Christmas shopping with a difference.
"We are going shopping specifically for you Veronica. Anything you see you can have. We are going shopping for clothes, shoes and jewellery, and before we go, I wish to make it clear to you that you mustn't object if I want you to wear something, something that you have not chosen, ok? And I don't want to hear anything about money or paying me back. I happen to think that you are one of the most beautiful women I have ever met, and I am honoured to have you as a guest in my home, so, today Veronica, is all about you, have you got that? Are you ready to go and enjoy yourself?"
That was ten hours ago. It was now a little after seven o clock in the evening. `Victoria` had insisted that she got everything she fancied and would not allow her to pay for a single item with her own money.
"Are you sure about this?" Veronica had said to her in one of the top stores.
"I'm as sure as I've ever been about anything" She replied.
" Just relax Veronica and enjoy yourself. I want you to remember this day for the rest of your life."
"I already will" Veronica said." I have only ever dreamed of days like these, and those dreams concerned winning the lottery. No-one has ever treated me like this. This really is a dream come true, you are

very kind Victoria."

"Nonsense, we haven't even started yet. You are going to feel special today young lady, because you are special, and you are going to feel appreciated. I am very fortunate Veronica. I live as I choose, and I have the means to do that, however, I am not oblivious to the fact that there are millions of people in the world who are not as fortunate as myself. Today I just want to let you see, and feel what it's like to be able to live like this, and this is not bribery or trickery, this is genuine friendship. I just want to make you feel happy, now do you mind if I make you feel happy? Just for once?"

All that was ten hours ago. Veronica sat now on one of the chaise-longue sofas, surrounded by all the bags and boxes, which contained dozens of dresses skirts and tops, underwear, goodness knows how many pairs of shoes and boots, jeans and jackets, blouses and jumpers, earrings and watches, necklaces and rings, plus items that she hadn't chosen and had not seen. Victoria had bought her some articles for a `surprise`. It was absolutely unbelievable. `Victoria` had gone for a shower and had told her to sit where she was until she returned. Then, after she'd showered she was to choose an outfit for tonight, as She was taking her out for dinner. Veronica sent Mandy and Liz a text message, telling them not to worry, and that she was *"being treated like royalty"*, by the girlfriend no less. *"So much for jealousy Mandy"*. Xxx.

## PARLOUR STREET.

## SOUTH KENSINGTON. 8am.

Beth Hargrieves sat at the breakfast table waiting for her husband who was taking a shower. She felt devastated. The paper boy had just pushed the morning papers through the letter box as she'd came down stairs twenty minutes earlier.
There it was on the front page; POLICE OFFICER COMMITS SUICIDE. There was a four inch square photograph of inspector Sandra Neal in the top right hand corner of the page.
The newspaper had claimed that,` *Due to intense pressure from her superiors*` she had suffered a nervous breakdown, and thus, ended her life.
The paper had gone on to say that Sandra had been investigating the murder of a young woman which had taken place in Bridge Way Street and also the double murder of a young couple in Temple Road, Locksley.
Beth did not read any further because she felt a horrible sickening feeling in her stomach.
She knew that Terry Mercer was changing for the better. Anyone who knew him would witness the changes in him recently. He had started taking pride in his appearance again. He was always clean shaven, he'd began ironing his clothes, and cleaning his shoes, and it was all down to Sandra Neal. Beth sat looking out of her kitchen window at nothing in particular. "Poor Terry" She sighed. She began to think what life had been like for him these past few years. "He never gets any warnings" she said to herself. She remembered how cheerful he used to be when he was with Carol, always laughing and joking, and so was Carol. She was always playing pranks on Sam and Terry, and Carol used to love going shopping with her, or so it seemed. They would exchange stories of their C.I.D. husbands. They would discuss their conversations and how boyish they both seemed to be, and of course, and best of all, they would share stories about both men's attempts at DIY, both men being equally

inadequate.

Beth was smiling at these memories, until she remembered the day Terry came here and informed Sam that Carol had left him. Sam's reaction to that was to tell Terry to eff off and not to joke about such matters. Sam hadn't even finished his sentence when he realized that Terry wasn't joking. She had taken off, and she'd taken his little boy Daniel with her. Daniel was Terry's pride and joy."
Sam had had a terrible time with him. At one point he had said to her that he wasn't entirely sure if Terry had the mental strength to get through it. He was pinning for Carol and Daniel daily.
He'd been cut to the soul. Sam had friends all over the country in the police force, but none of them could come up with any information regarding the whereabouts of Carol and Daniel Mercer. Terry and Sam had discussed everything, and after some considerable thought, Sam paid for a P.I. When no information had come, after six months, Terry told Sam to forget it because he was just wasting his money. Finally, Terry owned up to the fact that he had lost them and he would just have to face facts. Then, just as he was starting to show signs of his former self, he lost Sam, his best buddy. Sam had at last been successful in his application to become chief inspector. Terry had to adjust again. Sam had paired him up with countless partners, male and female, but he struggled to get on with any of them. Eventually Sam had given up, and reluctantly let Terry work on his own. Sam would come out and join him whenever he could, but it was becoming more and more difficult to do both jobs, and Sam was getting weaker all the time. Beth sat now thinking about the young McDermot lad, and how Sam had said that he would make a very good detective someday if he was given proper tuition, that was why he'd given the boy to Terry. And then Terry lost him as well, blaming himself for the boy's death, and always would...and now this.
"God only knows if he'll be able to get his head round this".
She could hear Sam whistling upstairs as he put on his clothes.
"He won't be whistling for long" she sighed. She had no idea how he would react to this news. One thing she did know, and it was this that was making her feel sick to the stomach, because everything

was at stake here. Her own happiness and Sam's, their life-style, these lovely little trips away for a few days at a time, they were all at stake now, for she knew in her heart, if Sam thought for one minute that Terry Mercer was going to fall, then he wouldn't even discuss the matter with her. He'd be back out of retirement as fast as he could say his name.

## CHAPTER TEN.

## DOVER STREET.

## KNIGHTSBRIDGE.

Veronica and her new friend` climbed out of the taxi, raising their jackets above their heads in an attempt to shelter from the torrential rain. The two women reached `Victoria's front door laughing at the ferocity of the gale forced wind.
Once inside Veronica closed the door behind her and said, "Thank you Victoria for the best day I have ever had in my life, I couldn't have dreamed of a better day than this."
Shaking off her jacket `Victoria` replied, "Don't keep thanking me, please you're spoiling my day, I'm having just as much fun as you."
"Trust me, you're not" said Veronica.
`Victoria had taken her to one of the most elaborate hotels in the West End. The meal had been absolutely beautiful and consisted of seven courses which had confused Veronica considerably when it came to using the correct cutlery. Victoria had lovingly kept her right.
After dinner, She had taken her to a top night club where Veronica had spotted more than a few celebrities throughout the course of the evening. This was better than a dream, you wake up from dreams. She wouldn't like to think how much Victoria had spent on her. It was frightening even to begin counting when she knew, that for one pair of shoes alone it was more than four hundred pounds.
"What would you like to drink Veronica" She said, kicking off her shoes.
"Anything at all, I don't mind."
"Tell you what, you make me a gin and tonic and you have whatever you want, I'm just going to change."
Veronica had become acquainted with the house in the day or so she'd been here, knowing where everything was. Just as she'd made up the drinks the telephone began to ring. She decided not to

answer it. Whoever it was would call back if it was important. She called up the stairs to Vicky, but there was no reply. After the phone had rung nine times, the caller had hung up.

A couple of minutes later Victoria came back down the stairs dressed in red silk pyjamas.

"Here's your drink Vicky. Your telephone just rang there."

"My telephone?" She looked at Veronica intently. "Who was it? Did you answer it?"

"I'm afraid I didn't. I don't like that Victoria. It's like an invasion on someone's privacy , I'm sorry if I've"-

Victoria stepped forward, taking the drink from Veronica, smiling.

"You truly are a remarkable woman Veronica do you know that? Let's go through to the lounge."

As Veronica took a seat on one of the easy chairs Victoria lay across the chaise longue, with her right elbow resting on the arm of it, supporting her head. In her left hand she nursed her gin and tonic.

"So Veronica, have you had a good day then?"

"A good day? Are you joking? God Victoria you have no idea how happy you have made me, and I'm not just talking about the presents, I'm talking about you, the person Victoria. You're really fun to be with. I feel like I've known you all my life."

"So, do you think you could spend a few days with me? You don't think that'd be too unbearable, do you?"

"Come on Vicky, you know how much I like you surely."

"Well that's good then, because I have a confession to make to you."

"A confession? You don't have to confess anything to me."

"I'm afraid I do Veronica".

She took a sip from her glass.

"I'm afraid Tony isn't coming back...ever."

"Tony? Oh I see, he's"-

"Yes, he and I have em...split up." She smiled softly. "He's married you see. He's em...he's gone back to his wife in Manchester, so I'm afraid we won't be seeing him again. Pity, but there you are, these things happen, that's life as they say."

"I'm sorry to hear that Victoria, you must be hurting, had you known all along he was married?"

"No, he only confessed last week. It came as a bit of a shock, but what can you do, you just have to get on with things."

"Victoria, why didn't you tell me this yesterday or this morning? Why did you take me shopping? You must be hurting inside now, you shouldn't have done all that today, and I could never pay you back. We could return all those things though, all the receipts are in the packages."

"My goodness me Veronica, why on earth would I do that? Heavens above girl that would be so cruel, I could never do that, and besides, we still have a deal do we not? Are you, or are you not my whore?" Victoria smiled at Veronica.

"Well?"

Veronica smiled back.

"Yes, I'm your whore".

"Good, then fetch me another gin and tonic bitch, as fast as you like." Both women laughed.

She took another sip of her drink. "There is just one more thing I have to tell you, just to get it out in the open. I am married as well, does that make any difference to you Veronica?"

"No, not one bit of difference, it has nothing to do with me, unless you're going to get into trouble for spending so much money. You're not, are you?"

"Of course not" Said `Victoria, smiling. "I have my own money, and besides, Charles would never question anything I do. Charles is my husband, he works in the oil industry, but don't ask me what he does, I couldn't begin to tell you, but I know that he gets bucket loads of cash for doing it, and that is the one and only reason I am married to him, I can't pretend otherwise. He's not a bad looking man, let's just say that he's totally inadequate in, em, essential matters. It doesn't help his cause that he has a pathetically small penis, but his bank account is massive, and that, to me anyway, is the most important statistic in any relationship, at least it is in my relationship, and sod what anyone else thinks."

Veronica smiled broadly and took a sip of her drink.

"Well, you certainly make a good point for argument Victoria.

Does he know that you see other men?"
"Of course not, but he is so much in love with me, that even if he were to become suspicious, I think he'd turn a blind eye just to stay with me."
Veronica poured her `friend` another gin and tonic and stepped over to the chaise longue to hand it to her.
"So, really Vicky, all said and done, you're just, for want of a better word, a whore like me, are you not?"
"I told you we weren't so far apart didn't I?"
"Is your husband due to come back any time soon?"
"Not soon enough to disturb our fun for the next few days."
Victoria took Veronica's hand in hers. "Did you enjoy Tony, Veronica?"
Veronica blushed slightly, but then found herself turned on by her own truthfulness. "You bet your life I did. I've been looking forward to making love with you both."
"Well, first things first Veronica, let's get acquainted with each other's bodies first, so that we know each other's preferences , and then we'll set about finding a replacement for Tony."
"He'll take a bit of replacing" smiled Veronica. "He is rather...em...gifted, is he not?"
Victoria swallowed the remainder of her gin.
"You'd be surprised how many well-endowed men I know."
Veronica almost burst into excited laughter.
"God, you really *are* a whore...a very beautiful one Vicky."
Veronica was now completely at ease with the situation.
This woman had a way of drawing out of her a level of promiscuousness that she wasn't even aware she possessed.
In her time as a working girl she'd learned how to be "turned on" even if her punter was totally useless. She had mastered the art of pretence which was quite beneficial in this business.
Many punters had left her thinking they had given her a wonderful time and that there wouldn't be any problems in negotiating further "appointments" and this worked out well for all concerned, sexually and financially. But with this woman here, there was no pretence whatsoever. Victoria reached for her and embraced

Veronica. *God even her perfume turned her on.* The two women began to kiss passionately.

## LOCKSLEY ESTATE.

## EAST LONDON.

Elizabeth Keaton and Mandy Smith could hardly believe their eyes. The living room floor had disappeared, having been covered with boxes and parcels, the gifts bought for Veronica by Victoria.
Mandy stood shaking her head and smiling.
"Do you mean to tell me Veronica that this woman bought you all these things, just like that, no commitments, no promises or bribes, nothing?"
"That's right Mandy, just like that, no promises. She's a really nice woman once you get to know her. She is so kind, honestly. I felt at ease with her straight away. You two were worrying about nothing, although I do appreciate you concern for my welfare, but I'm as safe as houses, really. If anything, she's more in danger from me, and that's the truth."
"What's her boyfriend saying about her spending all this money on you?"
Veronica looked at Mandy. Mandy had always been the same. If there was an awkward question to ask, or an awkward situation to be put into, then you could count on Mandy.
"He doesn't say anything, it's her own money."
"Well what does she do, because in case you hadn't realized Ronnie, she's just spent the best part of ten grand on you, and that's only a rough guess, it could be more, did you know that?"
"I don't know what she does Mandy, and I don't care, it's not in my interest to care, not in our line of work, you know that. Look Mandy, just look around us. When could I ever expect to purchase things like these? I went shopping in the west end. I have dinned in the best restaurants there are in London, when do you think I'd be doing that again Mandy. I'm just a two-penny whore in the east end of London, who just got lucky, that's all. Why can't you just be happy for me? Why have you always got to look for the black side Mandy? You're always suspicious of everything. I know what

happened to Jane and Thomas, and I can understand your protectiveness I really can, but I'm ok girls really, honestly. This woman is as kind as we are to each other, the only difference being, she happens to have more money than us. Look, I'm not sure where all this is going, it could end today, or it could end tomorrow, I don't know.
know one thing though, the good things in my life when they do come along, are never here for any length of time, so while I have *this* going on, then I'm grabbing it with both hands.
I'm being treated like a princess, which is ironic don't you think, because fairy-tales are all I've ever had.
There's no gallant knight coming riding out of the early morning mist on his trusty steed to sweep me up and take me away from Locksley, it's not going to happen, but this?"
She pointed to all the parcels, "Is the closest I'll ever get to living out that dream".
Veronica sat down sighing, cross-legged on the floor.
Mandy could tell that her friend had something more to say, something important. She watched as Veronica nervously lit up a cigarette.
There was silence for a few moments, and then Veronica hit her friends with, "She's asked me to move in with her."
Again, there was silence, as Veronica's words hung in the air, and stabbed Mandy and Elizabeth's hearts time and time again.
The words refused to go away, instead, they kept punching and kicking and stabbing at the girls who now felt sure, that they were going to lose a very special friend, forever.
Veronica may as well have told them that she'd contracted some fatal disease. And then, in that horrible, almost violent silence, Veronica drew the sword given to her by the woman who had made her fairy-tale come true, and ran it straight through the hearts of the only two people in the world who had ever really loved or cared for her
"I said I would."

## FINLEY STREET.

## HOLBURN.

It had been three days since Terry had received the devastating news about Sandra. He stood at his cooker turning over the fried egg he was about to place in between two slices of buttered bread. This would be the first intake of nourishment in that time.
As with any other crisis in his life, he dealt with it in his own way, which was, round the clock cigarette smoking, and the company of an old friend, hailing from Tennessee, who went by the name of Jack Daniels. Now, his professionalism was taking over, the professionalism which had been inculcated into him by Sam Hargrieves over the course of his career. His attitude to Sandra's suicide had changed considerably. The girl had been mentally unhinged by those two monsters. Her ordeal in the sewers had been bad enough, but it was what they had done to her before that, that had broken her. It was those two hedonistic evil bastards that had taken her life. He knew she'd been raped, and that was why he had refrained from making any sexual advances towards her since her ordeal. Maybe, in hind-sight she may have felt different if he *had* made some kind of sexual advances, perhaps, the fact that he hadn't approached her in that way, only served to constantly remind her of her nightmare. For whatever reasons, it was too late now.
All he had left to focus upon, was to bring these demonic monsters down. There was nothing else left in his life. Once again, doing the job was all he had, only this time, there was no Sam Hargrieves to help pull him through. *That moaning old bastard had gone into retirement.* And anyway, he wasn't fit enough to do the job any more. As Terry ate his breakfast, he recalled the encounter he had with Tony Chrysler, three days earlier. "Huh, I might not even have a job to go back to, after all, no-one from head office has called me, with the exception of Polly." She had text him and asked if he was alright. He knew he had let Polly down. She would no doubt of had

to face a raging Tony Chrysler following his outburst. Terry was prepared for whatever Chrysler had to throw at him, even if that was suspension. It wouldn't make one bit of difference to his way of thinking, whatever was said to him. Those monsters had taken the lives of two officers in the past few weeks, and he was going to find them, and kill them, it was as simple as that. He climbed into his car at eight-forty-five and began the lengthy drive to Broadway Victoria. What would happen, would happen, what would be said, would be said. He only hoped he could contain his temper when Chrysler began his ranting, because if he couldn't, he could very well be driving back home sooner than he wished, minus his badge and his gun. Thirty-five minutes later he was boarding the elevator and heading towards the Chief of Police's office, where he would learn how he would be spending his future. He hadn't ever suffered from tackipneea, but found himself taking deep breaths and trying his best to steady his breathing, and to slow his heart rate down. No wonder he felt breathless he said to himself. He had hardly been living healthily in the last few days, too many shots of Jack Daniels and copious amounts of cigarettes, not a healthy combination at any time, but when you're climbing fifty and carrying more stress than a van full of presidents then it could easily be a recipe for disaster. He approached Chrysler's door, and took one final deep breath and then knocked. Chrysler shouted for him to come in. Terry Mercer braced himself for the verbal onslaught that would inevitably come, reminding him of just who he had been addressing, and how his behaviour would look to junior officers, and that he should give himself some lessons in self-discipline and control. To his total astonishment, he was greeted by a smiling Tony Chrysler, and a quite healthy looking Sam Hargrieves. "Come in come in Terry, we were just talking about you, take a seat."
"Sir" began Mercer, "About the other day, I can explain my outburst, although, there are no excuses for such inappropriate behaviour, I apologise sir. I was tired sir and I had just-"
"Hold it Terry" said Chrysler. "I have been informed by Polly what you have been through lately, and I accept your apology, however, this does not mean that I would take such a light-hearted approach

should there ever be a repeat performance."
"There won't be sir, I assure you."
"Good, now there is someone awaiting your arrival down in the canteen, I take it you wish to remain on this same case?"
"Oh yes sir, definitely."
"Ok, I have chosen you a new partner to work with. She has come down from Manchester, and I can tell you Terry, they were very reluctant to let her come down here, I assure you, so I don't want to hear about you moaning to Polly Sheppard saying that she is as much good as a fucking glass hammer, like you did with Sam here when you were referring to officer Smedley, ok?"
"I won't sir." said Mercer, glancing at Sam who was smiling at the thought of Chrysler using Terry's own choice of words.
"Ok Terry, her name is Ava Cruntze, detective Ava Cruntze. Sam's going to walk you down to the canteen he's got some information for you that you will find very beneficial."
Sam had sat smiling directly in the face of Mercer as Chrysler had spoken the detective's name. He, more than anyone knew that Terry would find it difficult not to make a comment on the woman's name, especially as Chrysler had just informed him that she had come from Manchester. Cruntze could hardly be described as a typical English name. Hargrieves enjoyed the moment thoroughly as Terry's face almost cracked into a smile.
"On you go Terry, and good luck."
"Thank you sir."
Chrysler got to his feet and stretched out his hand to Sam Hargrieves. "It's been nice seeing you again Sam, now you take things easy, do you hear me? And tell Beth I was asking for her."
"I will Tony." said Hargrieves at the door.
"Pop in for a chat any time, you're always welcome."
As Terry and Sam walked down the corridor towards the lift, Polly Sheppard was making her way to her office.
"How are you Terry, are you feeling any better?"
"He does now Polly, he's had a cuddle and a kiss from Tony, and the two of them have made up, they've just spent the last half hour there licking and kissing each other's bums, it was quite emotional

don't you know, I had a lump in my throat Polly."
"I'll talk to you later Terry" She said, laughing to herself as she continued walking.
Terry and Sam walked on.
"Whatever you said to him Sam, I am very grateful, thanks bud, I owe you one.
"It's no problem Terry, Christ you've had some time of it lately, have you not?"
"I didn't see that coming Sam, I have to be honest. She said she was coping fine...I believed her."
"It was those bastards Terry."
"I know that now Sam, but I reacted like a maniac."
"Yes you did, but Terry, you are a maniac you always have been son, now, we're going to meet Ava so, best behaviour ok? and for goodness sakes, don't be falling in love with her, you're like a fucking juvenile, you really are."
"Is she nice Sam, I take it she must be with a comment like that."
"Best behaviour please Terry, best behaviour please." replied Sam, laughing.  As they entered the canteen Terry said; "So what's this news you have that could be helpful to me?"
"It might be nothing or it could be something, I've been reading yours and Sandra's reports."
"And?"
"Well according to Sandra, she thought that the female killer has plenty of money and-"
"Come on Sam, I fucking know that, tell me something new for goodness sakes. I know what she looks like, have you read my report? The sick fucking bitch was lying beside me in my bed. She gets off with inflicting pain and misery onto people, she masturbates in front of you as she informs you of what her sick boyfriend has done to your partner, for fuck sakes Sam, I thought by the way Tony Chrysler were talking, you had something useful for me."
Sam pulled out of his coat pocket, the police artist's impression of the killers. He was just about to say something when Terry interrupted him.

He sighed heavily and then said; "Sam, that's no fucking good, I've already explained to all and sundry that they won't look anything like that now. Jesus Christ Sam, you know as well as me that as soon as they heard that we'd survived the sewers, they would change their appearances, fuck sakes."

Sam just stood looking at his shoes, smiling sarcastically and waiting for Terry to finish. "Do you mind if I say something Terry? ranting on there like an idiot." He held out the sketch. "Just answer me. Would you say that this was an accurate description of the bitch of how she looked to you at the time of your ordeal?"

Mercer sighed again. "Yes Sam...at the time, at that time, not now, they'll be-"

"Right, that's all I was asking, you've got to make a song and dance about everything haven't you. I know all about how they'll have changed their appearances, I've been a detective longer than you, you know." The two men stood in the middle of the busy canteen unaware that they'd attracted an audience.

"Well why don't you act like it then, telling me all this shit I already know. Everything you're telling me, I fucking wrote. You're not telling me anything I don't already know. How the fuck is this supposed to be helping me?" Terry suddenly realized that he was being observed.

"What the fuck are *you* all staring at you bunch of fucking two faced crawling bastards that you are!"

Sam had to intervene, otherwise someone was going to get hurt, and someone else was going to be suspended.

"Come on and get a seat Terry, I do have something to tell you, something helpful."

They found a table in the corner of the canteen, and sat down, both men completely oblivious to the reason they were actually down here, which was to greet and welcome Ava Cruntze.

"I think I know her Terry. I think I've seen her, and by the way you've described her, the woman I saw would fit that description perfectly."

Terry stared across the table. "When, when did you see her, and where?"

"She was in the theatre, a couple of months ago, and I take it the man she was with was her husband, certainly not the killer, her accomplice, and while we're on the subject of him, I have some news for you. At approximately six-fifteen this morning, they pulled out the body of a man from the Thames, some dredger or river cleanser or something. They pulled out the torso of a man. We then sent some divers in, well, Polly Sheppard did, and about two hours ago, they retrieved the rest of the man's body. The labs carried out some D.N.A. tests, and discovered that it was him, the killer. It would seem that his sick bitch has had enough of him, or at least that's one theory, but whatever the circumstances, it is definitely him. Now you know why Tony Chrysler was in such a good mood. He now has something positive to inform the press."
"Are they absolutely positive it's him Sam? I mean, if he's been in the water for some time-"
"Terry, come on, don't insult the forensics, they know their stuff, disregarding how you feel about Andy Phillips."
"So Sandra was right."
"About what?"
"She said that this woman was living a double life. Living in Luxury with her husband or partner, and then having this affair with this other sicko, and murdering people in the middle of their sick fucking sexual games."
"In luxury you say?"
"Yeah well, if you can buy tops which costs hundreds of pounds and perfume that costs thousands, then I would say you'd be living in luxury, wouldn't you?"
Sam sat nodding his head and smiling at Terry.
"What? What's so funny Sam?"
"The night that Beth and I were at the theatre, this woman had been flaunting herself, right in front of me, especially for me, right in front of her husband, at various times throughout the show she flashed her bloody legs. She kept crossing them and rubbing her hands up and down, bloody smiling at me all the time she was doing it, and this, not only in front of her husband, but right in front of Beth as well. It was plain to see she was getting some kind of kick

out of it."
"Did her husband not say anything to her?"
"Not a word Terry, not a bloody word, in fact I think he turned a blind eye deliberately to what she was doing."
"Ever heard of swingers Sam?"
"Don't you dare try and be the cunt boy with me Terry, I heard about swingers long before you even heard about cornflakes. These people were not swingers. You know what you were saying about the expensive clothes and perfume?"
"Yeah, what about them?"
"Well, she bent down in front of me to retrieve her hand bag, huh, her bloody breasts nearly popping right out. Well, as she did, Beth clocked her jewellery and informed me that what she was wearing would cost at least fifty grand. Now you know why it was so important to me as to how accurate the artist's impression was, smart ass. I think it's her Terry."
Mercer looked at his friend nodding his head.
"She seems to fit the description, but will she ever return to the theatre, after all she knows that I know what she looks like."
"That's what I intend to find out Terry. Beth and I are going to go back there. Surely if she's leading a double life, she won't want her husband suspecting anything is out of the ordinary. She'll surely carry on frequenting the places they are in the habit of going to."
Again Terry sat nodding. "Yeah, even if she looks nothing like the way she looked the last time I saw her. I wonder what's happened that she's had to do away with her playmate, and she's fucking halved him in two you say?"
"If it was her who killed him, yes."
"Oh she's killed him alright, otherwise if it had been anyone else who'd murdered him, they would have just shot the fucker or cut his throat. It's her alright, but it's my guess that she won't be coming out to play for a while."
Terry was just about to continue with his theory when he was tapped on the shoulder.
He turned round to face a very beautiful woman.
"Excuse me" she said, "Are you Terry Mercer?" Terry swallowed

hard, and confirmed his name.

"Well, I've been waiting in here for the best part of an hour awaiting your arrival, only when you *do* arrive, you choose to deliberately ignore me and pick an argument with father time here. Let me make one thing clear to you, nobody messes me about, have you got that? My name is Ava Cruntze, and your manners are deplorable, I hope you know that".

The two detectives sat like scorned school boys, their back-biting sarcasm at each other now seemed so immature, their' faces went red with embarrassment much to the delight of the spectators in the dining hall. These moments were rare, when Messrs Hargrieves and Mercer were put firmly in their places, and made to sit still and listen to how childish their behaviour was. Even the kitchen staff were enjoying the detectives' reprimand and their come-uppance.

# TEMPLE ROAD.

## LOCKSLEY.

`Victoria` sat in her Ferrari California outside the blocks of flats waiting for Veronica. She felt almost claustrophobic sitting in between these concrete blocks where people actually lived.
How terribly unfortunate for them to be living here, although living wasn't exactly an accurate description though, was it?" she thought to herself. Rain pelted hard on the roof and windscreen of her car, making it seem even more miserable if that was at all possible.
The huge towers of concrete and glass were the same colour as the thick grey December skies.
The last time she was here was with Tony. She had met the couple at the theatre and while Charles had been talking to some of his friends, She had begun having a conversation with them.
The couple had invited her and Charles over to their flat for drinks, so that the young man could pick Charles's brains about all things to do with opera. She hadn't arrived here with Charles though, and they certainly hadn't come to talk about opera.
She shifted in her seat as she remembered the young man's face as Tony raised the samurai sword, and with one easy swipe, severed the man's arm. Tony and she had taken a lot of cocaine that night, and most of that evening was just a blur. She did remember though, how Tony had held the girl underneath her arms, whilst She had held her legs open and performed oral sex on her, while her boyfriend lay on the floor dying from blood-loss, minus an arm and a leg by this time. She was sure he was still conscious though as She lapped away at his woman. `Victoria` sighed, and lit up a cigarette. The flats looked so different back then because they'd been here at night, and so all the different coloured lights looked almost inviting, rather than these grey concrete prisons of hopelessness which protruded from the ground and rose up into the depressing skies. Most of the residents here had attempted to decorate their windows with Christmas decorations. "Huh Christmas".

She thought about these poor people existing in these concrete blocks, and imagined that most, if not all of them would be unemployed. Their Christmas celebrations would occur, only with the aid of money lenders who would no doubt charge them astronomical amounts of interest on the pittance they would borrow. But it would have to be done otherwise Christmas would not take place for their children.
"Santa Clause would be giving them a miss, and they couldn't have that."
Veronica came trundling out of one of the blocks of flats wearing a white fir Jacket and designer jeans with brown leather boots up to her knees. Even in her winter attire she looked extremely attractive. If she had lived anywhere else in the city, she would have been snatched up by a modelling agency, there was no question about that, but fate would have it that she lived here, in the land of nothing really matters, and where she would wake to a day that was exactly the same as the day before, and would be the same tomorrow.
`Victoria` smiled to herself. All around her were mute reminders of why she chose to live this pretentious life with her husband. Everyone who existed here, had inevitably been sentenced to death, even Veronica, she however would have a little taste of a different kind of life, a different kind of existence.
"Strange" She thought to herself. "She and Veronica lived in the very same city, and yet so many worlds apart."
"Hi Vicky"
"Hello babes" replied Victoria. The two embraced.
"And what would you like to do today Veronica?"
"I would like to do anything you wish Victoria, anything at all, I'm still waiting to wake up from this dream."
`Victoria` smiled. "I'm glad you're having fun babes, because that's all I want to do with you, have fun."
Veronica was beaming.
"Vicky, I can honestly say, at the ripe old age of twenty-eight, that I have been well and truly educated in the art of making love with another woman. I just didn't think it possible that another woman

could make me feel like that, thank you."
"Shut up Veronica, you'll make me crash the car."
The two of them made small talk as they headed off to the west end. Half an hour later, they were seated in a top restaurant eating lunch. After their meal and while they were having their coffee, `Vicky` said; "You know, the other night when we were lying in bed talking?"
"Yes, what about it, oh, did I talk too much?"
"Don't be silly Veronica, I was referring to your dreams, remember we asked each other what our wildest dreams were?"
"Yes?"
"Well in a couple of days from now, I'm going to give you a nice surprise, do you have a passport?"
The smile faded from Veronica's face. "I'm afraid not".
"Well after lunch we'll see to that."
"Won't that take time? You know, for a passport to be issued?"
"Not when you know the people I know Veronica, and as I was saying, I have a nice surprise planned for you. We're going shopping again. Oh I'll have to tell you, I'm hopeless at keeping secrets. All being well, in a few days from now, you and I are going shopping in Rodeo Drive, how does that sound?"
Since the tender age of fifteen Veronica Wells had dreamed about going to California. She put her hand up to her mouth and attempted to say something, her fingers shaking uncontrollably. She then burst into tears completely overcome. Her dream had just come true. Any doubts Mandy had put into her head about this woman, were fast fading into total oblivion. Circumstance had brought this woman into her life, just another financial arrangement, an act of lust. But now, she had met someone who had turned out to be kind, and very keen on her, she was going to America. A total stranger had just made her dream come true.

## SAUNDERSON and BLAKLEY. ESTATE AGENTS.

## KNIGHTSBRIDGE.

Parked about two hundred metres from the estate agents, Terry Mercer and Ava Cruntze began walking from the car park. Thirty-two-year-old Ava was dressed immaculately. She wore light grey trousers and highly polished black boots. Her black leather coat came down to just under her calves. The coat was worn open, revealing a cream blouse, open at the collar. On top of that, she wore a grey waistcoat which was also open upon which her I.D badge was pinned. Her shoulder length hair was somewhere between gold and blonde. She had a full face with a ruddy complexion. Almost as tall as Terry, she stood five feet nine, her one inch heels giving her that extra height. Her slim build gave the impression that she was taller than she actually was.
She was very attractive, but also business-like, stern, giving out a visual signal that this woman would stand for no nonsense.
She would intimidate men, and women. Even her stride was confident and authoritative.
Mercer, dressed in his jeans and sports jacket with a plain black tee-shirt underneath, pulled out a cigarette from his jacket pocket and lit up. Without breaking her stride, she looked side-ways at her colleague and said; "Must you? Such a disgusting habit and it stinks."
Tough." said Mercer. "Put in for a transfer if you're not happy with who you're working with." They continued walking and snapping at each other, until Ava came to a halt.
She turned to look at him.
"This is clearly not going to work is it Mister Mercer, you have already made your mind up about *that* haven't you. You're not even prepared to give it a chance, your head is so far up your own arse, that you're not even aware of what's going on around you."
"What's that supposed to mean?" Mercer barked.
"It means that you have some kind of death wish going on with

yourself. It means that you would like to think that you are responsible for the deaths of officers McDermot and Neal, well I've got news for you Mister, it had nothing to do with you I'm afraid. So just get yourself out of this hole you've dug yourself into and come back into the real world, and help me to find the people who really killed them, because as long as you have this attitude with yourself, you are never going to find them.

Now I have been informed, that you are supposed to be one of the best detectives they have down here. That means nothing to me Mister Mercer. You won't fool me or impress me with reputations I'm afraid. If you and I are to work together, then you'd better understand this, right from the start. I am strong. I am strong willed, and I will do my utmost to defend you in any situation. I will kill to defend you without any hesitation whatsoever, and I will put my life on the line to save you. I will share any problem you have and I will help you if I possibly can. That is what I'll do. Now, what have *you* got to offer Mister Mercer, because if you can't give me the same, then we are just wasting our time here!"

They walked on through the car park. Terry had given no reaction to Ava at this point. As they walked, Ava said; "I've read up all about you Terry Mercer, and without sounding pathetic, I do actually feel sorry for you with everything that's happened. I understand that you and Officer Neal were lovers as well as partners. Your loss must be very painful, but it's not your fault, and neither is it your fault about William McDermot, and it wasn't your fault about Carol Mercer. She hurt you the most Mister Mercer, and quite honestly speaking? She should feel ashamed of herself, but we both know that she probably won't. What I can tell you is this, although our relationship is strictly a working one, I promise you here and now, that I will never let you down in a time of need. Like I say, I will defend you with my life, because that's our job, but I will never desert you or leave you vulnerable in any situation. So what do you say Mister Mercer? Do we form a formidable team here and now? Or do we go back to the car and then back to H.Q?"

Terry stopped to look at the young woman beside him.

"You won't let me down?"

"I promise you. Do you promise not to let *me* down? And treat me with respect?"

Mercer nodded. "Yes I do Ava, I promise you, and we *will* make a formidable team. I like that word formidable. And will you give *me* the respect I deserve?"

"Fuck off" she replied, "That wasn't in the deal."

Terry burst into laughter as they reached the end of the car park. "Do you want to get something to eat Ava, before we go into the estate agents?"

"Well I don't know about that, how are your table manners?" She glanced him up and down disdainfully. "I mean, can you manage a fork and knife, can you?"

Terry nodded, laughing. "Oh yes, no problem, I've been using them now for almost two years."

After a light lunch the two detectives made their way to Saunderson and Blakley's offices.

"Who are we interviewing in here Terry?"

"Anyone who can give us a list of the names of personnel who work here, and any of them who have had access to Bridge Way Street."

"Do you think it was an estate agent who killed the girl?"

Mercer sighed impatiently. "You haven't read my report have you Ava. Oh you've read up about me no doubt, but if you'd read my report then you'd have known that I met the killers. One of them climbed naked into my bed. You'd have known that if you'd done what you said you'd done, now, how much do you know, how much have you read *really*?"

"Very little Terry I confess. I suppose if I'm honest, I spent too much time reading up about you. I wasn't sure if I wanted to work with you, I've heard so many things about you."

"Negative things, I take it?"

"Well yes, mostly negative, but, I decided to give it a try. If there is one thing I have learned in my career thus far, it is this, do not take anyone else's advice when it comes to assessing people.

Find out for yourself and make your own judgements.

"That's not a bad idea Ava, so what do you think of me so far?"

"Well, you've just bought me lunch, so that's a good start, you get a

plus for that Mister Mercer."
"Forgive me for asking Ava, but I must. Cruntze, is that German?"
"Got it in one Terry, my father, although I never got to know him, he took off on my third birthday."
"Bastard".
"How can I be a bastard Terry, I've just told you I have a father?"
"Mercer laughed. "Yeah, you'll do Ava."
"I'm so pleased to hear it Mister Mercer" said Ava, "Now, shall we attend to our business, now that we have established the fact that I am suitably qualified to be working with you?"

They entered the estate agents where, unlike Burlington and Hedgewood's they were greeted by a fresh-faced teenage girl at reception. The girl looked no more than eighteen and had obviously been trained in how to keep a cheerful smile on her face at all times. The fact that the girl wore a dental plate for straightening her teeth, gave the impression that the smile was false, and indeed wider than it actually was. There were small colourful jewels staggered around the dental brace which matched the small colourful stones that were visible throughout the massive thatch of the girl's thick ginger hair.
"Good afternoon sir good afternoon madam, how may I be of assistance to you today?"
Mercer could see by the smile on Ava's face that she'd picked up on the young lady's imperfections as well.
Mercer and Ava greeted the young lady politely, and then asked if they could speak to one of her superiors.
"Just one minute sir" replied the cheerful youth. "And may I ask what it's in connection with sir?"
Mercer produced his I.D.
"I see, I won't be a moment sir, would you like to take a seat until I find someone?"
The two detectives sat down on the extremely comfortable arm chairs. All around the office walls were portraits of male and female barristers, all business-like and wearing black robes, and which reminded Terry of his school days, or rather, of the days his father

had told him about when every teacher wore a black robe, and carried a leather belt, usually hidden from view just under the shoulder, producing it at lightning speed to thrash any unruly pupil into shape. Terry also remembered his father's rants as well.
*"Not like today boy. You don't know what punishment is, you fucking pansy bastards...fucking cry if the teacher looks at you the wrong way, you pink team fuck that you are! Policeman? You fucker...you'll never be a fucking policeman, you shit arsed pansy bastard that you are, get a grip you fucking clown!"*
The fact that Terry had only been fifteen years old when his father had said these things to him, and in that vicious hard-hitting soul-destroying way. But it only served to make him all the more determined to be successful in his ambitions. It was a pity the old bastard had passed away before Terry had the opportunity of ramming his words back down his throat and threatening him with a custodial sentence if he as much as once interrupted him in the middle of speaking with his mother, like he always used to do.
*"Never mind talking to your mother you gossip bastard, get out there and chop some logs for the fire you pansy pink team fuck...talking to fucking mummy, policeman? Dear Christ!"*
Terry rose up from his seat and walked over to one of the walls, staring in disbelief at the prices of some of these properties.
At least half a dozen of them would require that you won the lottery twice before you could even consider purchasing. He couldn't resist the opportunity of being witty in front of his new partner.
"Oh, here's one for you Ava, are you listening? This would do you. What do you think? A one-bedroom apartment with living quarters, a small modern kitchen and a petite bathroom, seven hundred and forty thousand pounds. How would that do Ava?
He put on his rendition of a spoiled teenage girl with filthy-rich parents. "Oh my, well that's me convinced then, I simply must have it. I'll talk to mummy and daddy and they'll sort out all the paper work for me. Rodney and I can use it for our nights out, or we could just use it as a store, because really, it wouldn't be much good for anything else now would it?"

Behind Terry Mercer's back an elderly gentleman had appeared at the desk with the young lady. He stood listening to Terry's rendition of a young lady, before clearing his throat when he thought that he'd gone far enough.
"May I help you?" said the smartly dressed gentleman. "I have been informed that you wish to speak to someone of authority. I am Reginald Saunderson, how may I be of assistance to you. I take it you won't be requiring your parents' signature to buy our Marble Arch apartment?"
The young receptionist's permanent smile momentarily widened. Mercer, now completely red faced, returned to reception.
"Mister Saunderson, we need to know if your office has had anything to do with an attempted sale of a certain Bridge Way Street apartment in the last few months, and if so, we would like to interview any members of your staff, who have had access to that apartment." Mercer glanced at the receptionist who was still smiling as broadly as ever. He surmised that he could tell this girl that he was going to pull her back by the hair on her head and force-feed her a whole breakfast bowl full of dog shit, and she would still be wearing her smile.
The old man looked at Mercer for a few moments, still not quite forgiving him for his joke.
"I can tell you here and now, that we have indeed attempted to sell that apartment, and on several occasions. We have decided to give up on it and have passed on the property to other agents. Would you like me to give you their names? The salesmen I mean."
"Yes please, and could you give me dates please of when they'll be available for interview, at the earliest opportunity of course."
"Certainly, take a seat please, I won't be a minute."
Mister Saunderson stopped in his tracks, "Or you could browse through our folders if you wish, see if any of our other properties tickles your fancy?"
"Oh dear, you've offended the old todger Terry haven't you, he's not very impressed with you is he?" said Ava grinning from ear to ear.
"Why didn't you tell me he was there?"

"What, and miss the opportunity of watching you shooting yourself in the foot? Load up the gun, and give your other foot a blast of buck-shot? No chance."

Ten minutes later Terry and Ava were making their way back to the car. Saunderson had shown them all the dates that his employees had attempted to sell the Bridge Way Street apartment. None of the dates had remotely coincided with any of the two murders. He had also given them a list of estate agents who were still attempting to sell the property.

"Well" said Ava, "It doesn't look like we're going to get any joy from Mister Saunderson and company does it. Where are we off to now?" Mercer lit up a cigarette. "We're off to the morgue Ava, they tell me they've fished out the body of one of those sickos, I'll believe it when I see him."

"This is one of the two people who abducted you I take it?"

"That's right Ava, although I would hardly describe them as people."

"I read what they done to you and inspector Neal...horrendous to say the least."

Terry looked into Ava's eyes as they walked.

"Yeah, to say the least."

"Do you think they belong in an asylum?"

"No, I think they belong in a grave, that's the only thing that could help those two, and that is why we're heading over to the morgue, I don't want to hear about the bastard being dead, I want to see him dead, and if she has killed him, then she's deprived me of my God given right to slash his fucking throat."

Ava shook her head disapproving of Mercer's profanations

"What? What are you shaking your head at?"

"Control Terry...self-control."

"Listen here, don't think-"

"Give me the car keys, I'll drive, you can smoke your cigarette as long as you open a window."

Terry looked intently at his new partner. "You've changed your tune, have you not?"

"You wanted me to cut you some slack, did you not? Don't mock it." He handed her the key. "I'm not...I'm very grateful, thank you."

They arrived at the morgue just in time to meet Polly Sheppard, who was exiting the building. She approached Terry and Ava.
"I know why you're here Terry, but I can save you the trouble, it's him alright. God knows what he's done, but whoever it was that wanted him dead were taking no chances. They've given him the full frontal lobotomy you were so keen to perform, then, after his death, they have proceeded to freeze his body and half him in two. Phillips says about three days ago, no more than four. Whoever it was, were not wanting to make any mess, hence, the freezing of the corpse."
"Whoever it was Polly? I can tell you here and now, that it was that sick fucking bitch."
Ava shook her head tutting.
Mercer ignored Ava's reaction to his swearing.
"Polly, I couldn't care if you told me the bastard was in a thousand pieces, I'm still going to take a look for myself."
Suddenly, it was as if Terry was not even there.
Polly addressed Ava.
"How are you getting on with Terry Ava? I know he can be a pain in the ass sometimes, but underneath that grumpy don't give a jot attitude he has, there is a decent man, hard to believe Ava sometimes, I know, but it's true."
"I know, you're right there Miss Sheppard, it is hard to believe."
Terry sighed.
"Do you mind? Can we go in and see the body now please? Once you've finished downgrading my personality."
"On you go Terry" said Ava. "I'll just wait here while you go and waste time in there. Our boss has just confirmed to us that the corpse in there is the man we've been looking for, so there is no need to go in. I don't think Miss Sheppard would lie to us, still, if it makes you feel any better, go and look at the dead man, parts one and two, and then we can continue to look for his accomplice, the female killer, who at this very moment could perhaps be in the process of killing again, on you go Terry." Polly and Ava stood smiling as Terry made his way up the steps of the morgue, clearly unimpressed with his partner's sarcasm, and shaking his head

muttering something about German arrogance.

### TEMPLE ROAD. LOCKSLEY ESTATE.

### EAST LONDON.

Sam Hargrieves sat outside of the flats in his brand new Volvo V 70. A car which Beth had insisted was far too young for someone of Sam's age, but Sam wanted it, and so, as usual, Sam got his way. He was here to see Mandy Smith, and as luck would have it, he could see her heading towards him now, laden with four polythene shopping bags. He had popped in for a chat with Tony Chrysler at Scotland Yard. Chrysler had asked him if he would deliver a document to the young lady. The document was confirmation for Mandy's insurance company, that her sister Jane, had indeed been murdered. There would be no further delays to Mandy being paid out. A payment that was long overdue.

Sam climbed out of the car laboriously, and smiling at the young lady. "Good afternoon Mandy" said Hargrieves, reaching out to relieve her of two of the bags.

"Is it?" said Mandy, "You could have fooled me."

"Oh dear, are you having a bad day?"

"A bad life would be more accurate. There is absolutely nothing in my life going right for me at the moment, and you detective Hargrieves are just about to make it worse, aren't you, cause I know that you haven't come all the way over here for tea and scones."

"Well yes I have Mandy, if you're inviting me for a cup of tea."

"Ah, so *now* I know why you're carrying my bags."

"I have been asked to deliver to you this document it's for your insurance company. Apparently you've been having a little trouble with them. They have been somewhat reluctant to pay you out, well, they'll pay you now Mandy."

"At last" Mandy sighed. "They want proof you see, in case I was lying to them. There were no such problems when I took out the

policy though, oh no, that took only about ten bloody minutes to do that, and that was six years ago. They didn't need any proof then of who I was, or who Jane was for that matter, bastards."
They reached the entrance of the flats.
"I wasn't joking detective Hargrieves, you're welcome to come up and have a cup of tea."
"Thank you Mandy, I will, I have half an hour to spare."
"To spare? So you're not married?"
Sam smiled at the young lady's humour. As they reached the floor level where Veronica's flat was, they stepped out onto the hallway. Sam had been educated in the art of pornographic graffiti all the way up in the elevator. Sexual insult and slander had been applied to every wall of the lift, including the ceiling. If it bothered Mandy, she didn't show any signs of disgust.
As they walked towards the flat, a young man came out from Veronica's apartment looking rather flushed.
"Fuck, you're dropping your standards Mandy are you not? Old fucking men now? Ah well, good business is where you find it, I was looking for you, but you were nowhere to be seen, so I had to do with Lizzy, still, she's not bad either, a fucking good blow job, I'll tell you that, hey mister, get Mandy here to give you one of her specials, you won't regret it, and it's worth the extra twenty, honestly."
"Simple Simon" said Mandy, "Allow me to introduce you to chief inspector Hargrieves, he is here investigating illegal prostitution."
The young man made off, and quickly broke into a sprint as he headed to the elevator. Sam only smiled as Mandy placed the key into the lock. "Poor bugger" said Mandy. "Lizzy and I are the only two working girls who'll go near him. He's nice though, in his own sweet fucked up way".
A description Sam had heard so many times when some people were referring to Terrance Mercer.
"I'm sure he is" said Sam, still smiling at Mandy's humour.
They stepped inside the apartment.
"I'll put the kettle on, Lizzy will be having a shower, we always do after we...well..."

"Quite" said Sam.  A few moments later Sam was sitting in the living room drinking a cup of tea with Mandy.

"Have you had any luck finding my sister's murderer then?"

"We haven't caught them yet, but we know who they are."

"They? There was more than one killer?"

"There was two of them Mandy, a man and a woman. The man was found dead just the other day, we have yet to apprehend the woman."

"Do you know what she looks like? Is she local? Would I know her?"

"Yes, well we have an artist's impression which seems to be quite accurate, as to you knowing her, I doubt it very much, and with regards to the artist's impression, well, she'll have changed her appearance quite dramatically by now I would imagine.

Officer Mercer, he em...he got quite a good look at her shall we say."

"I'm surprised he took the time to look at her face, the man is a colossal pervert, usually it's the legs tits and bums that get *his* undivided attention."

Sam, although smiling, shook his head. "Mandy, I have worked with that man for many years, and you'd be surprised as to what he's come through, and yet he still does his job with the utter devotion and dedication he always has.

His professionalism and his determination are second to none. He's not a bad friend for you to have around Mandy. He's out there doing his best to find your sister's killer, and that same killer brutally murdered his young partner. They have since proceeded in killing his lover and fellow officer inspector Sandra Neal. His life is in turmoil right now and whilst many other officers would take, medicinal leave, and they'd be entitled to, he keeps on going with that dogged determination that drives him and makes him one of the best detectives Scotland Yard has ever seen. I would go as far as saying he is probably the best they'll ever see. Before you point the finger at anyone Mandy, walk a mile in their shoes".

Mandy nodded her head. "I'm sorry Mister Hargrieves I have a bad habit of shouting my mouth off before I know the whole story. I've always been the same, but you see, in *this* game, you have to be

rock hard, and portray to people that you have no feelings, after all, most of them think that that's how we are anyway.
I didn't know about officer Mercer's situation. He puts on a good front, much the same as we do. It's a shame about officer ballet, oh, that's a little private joke between Officer Mercer and us girls."
"Oh yeah, officer ballet" said Lizzy, suddenly appearing fresh from her shower, and brushing her wet hair. "He was nice. I quite fancied a fu em...I wouldn't have minded going out with him."
"Yes, he was a nice kid" said Sam, rising to his feet, with a grunt, Mandy noticed.
"Is this your flat Lizzy?" the retired inspector said.
"No, it's Veronica's" said Mandy.
"Is she not here today?"
Mandy sighed wearily. "No, and she won't be here for much longer either."
"How come" enquired Sam, fastening up his coat buttons.
"Oh, because she's met this dolly-bird lady and she's asked Veronica to move in with her. Bloody money bags."
Suddenly Sam was very interested.
"She spent over ten grand on her the other day, huh, just like that, ten grand, stays in this fancy-assed house over in Knightsbridge, although, I can't blame Veronica for getting out of here, and being quite honest, the woman is rather beautiful."
"Really, said Sam, "Have you seen her?"
"Veronica has shown us a photograph of her, but I haven't met her in person."
"Would you recognise her if you saw her on the street Mandy?"
"Are you kidding? From one photograph"? You must be joking. Veronica says she changes her hair styles and colour just about every day of the week, you know, in those bloody cost-you-a-fortune hair salons, or boutiques, whatever you call them."
"So I take it your friend Veronica is in a bi-sexual relationship with this woman."
Sam sat down again.
"It's a long story Mister Hargrieves. It all started when this man picked up Ronnie for a bit of fun. He pays Ronnie over the top prices

for the pleasure of her company, and I'm talking way over the top, hundreds of pounds per night. Eventually he asks Veronica how she would feel if his girlfriend joined in with them. Well, if you know Veronica, then you'd know that she is up for anything, she'll give anything a try once. It looked like she was obsessed with this man. She stopped meeting with her own regular punters. She would sit around in here just waiting for her phone to ring. This new man in her life, had by now, stood her up a couple of times. Twice I think she got all dressed up to go and meet him with his girlfriend for three-way-sex. We could tell that he'd got to her, couldn't we Lizzy?"

"Yes, she would try and have a joke about it inspector, but we could see that she was completely hooked on him."

Mandy continued. "Yes, and then suddenly, this woman comes on to the scene, and Veronica's like, head over heels about *her*, she's infatuated with her, probably because she's spent thousands of pounds on her. Come to think of it, Ronnie doesn't even mention the guy now, it's all, her, and of course, now she's invited Veronica to move in with her."

"Is she going to?" said Sam, writing something down in a notebook.

"Yeah, she says she's going to give it a try, says she's got nothing to lose...and she's right."

Sam had sat listening intently as Mandy gave him all the details about Veronica and this new friend of hers. He stood up now producing the artist's impression of the female killer.

"Forget about the colour Mandy and even the hair style, but would you say that this sketch looks anything like the woman Veronica is meeting with?"

Without even looking at the sketch Mandy said, "You think that woman that Veronica is with is one of the killers, don't you Mister Hargrieves?"

"I can't say either way Mandy, it would depend on recognition, does that look like Veronica's friend?"

Mandy scrutinised the drawing and then handed it to Lizzy.

"I couldn't tell by that, I'm not going to say yes because that would be a lie. If I ever get the chance to meet her in person I could give

you a clearer description, a more accurate one, I'd be able to identify her then, and confirm."
"Hasn't she been in here with Veronica?"
"You must be joking" laughed Mandy, "she wouldn't lower herself coming in here goodness no. She pulls up down there in her fancy red Ferrari, and she whisks Veronica away to the west end, to the land of "I've-got-money.""
This time Sam couldn't help but burst into laughter at the young woman's light-hearted attitude to those people fortunate enough to have more than herself, and referring to the west end by the biblical quotation of "Milk and honey".
"Come and see this in here" said Lizzy.
"You watch at the window Mandy, in case she comes back, come and see this inspector."
"She won't be back for ages" said Mandy.
"Come and look at this Mister Hargrieves."
Mandy led Sam into Veronica's bedroom.
"She'll kill me for this if she finds out. She showed Sam all the top label dresses and tops.
The shoes, the boots the jeans and all the jewellery, the diamond-studied watches and bracelets, and necklaces.
"You see? Money is no object. Lizzy and I are dreading the day she moves out of here, but we know that day is coming.
We're bracing ourselves for it, but who can blame the girl.
Veronica is far too pretty to be living here. She deserves to be living in a better environment than this. It's not jealousy inspector, you understand, I think it's more a case of envy than anything else."
Sam had written down some of the names of labels of the clothing.
"Ok Mandy, I'll have to be off now, my half hour is almost up."
Mandy smiled.
"Your wife has you on a timer, does she?"
"So to speak Mandy, but, she has a point I'm supposed to be retired."
"Well don't knock it inspector, because I would love it for someone to care about where I was or what I was doing."
"I'm very lucky" Sam returned, "I know I am."

"Well you come back here any time you want, that is until Veronica gives this flat up to move in with money bags, hopefully by then, I'll be allowed to move back into my sister's flat.

Whatever, keep in touch though and let us know if you find anything out."

Sam boarded the elevator. He had gathered valuable information. Information he would pass on to Terry. All he had to do was put surveillance on to this street. It would only be a matter of time before they caught her, because he was almost a hundred per cent certain that the woman Veronica was seeing was the killer.

Sam stepped out of the elevator and strolled up to his car smiling broadly. He took out his mobile phone and pressed the digits for Mandy's phone.

"Hello Mandy, it's Sam again, could you please call me a taxi cab to come to your address, your neighbours have kindly relieved my car of all its' wheels, and? Yes, my stereo system as well, oh, and my engine, I could see why you would want to leave here ladies, I really can."

## FINLEY STREET.

## HOLBURN.

Terry Mercer was cooking himself a full English breakfast, consisting of grilled bacon rashers, fried eggs, sausages, French toast, grilled tomatoes and button mushrooms. He had grown tired of starting his days, anti-jentacular. Thanks mainly to Ava, he was beginning to dig himself out of the `hole` he'd dug himself into, and was now eating regularly and heartily.
He had never been one to worry about calories simply because he'd never had to. From a very early age his metabolism had seen to that. He'd spent almost every day of his young life, running around on his bike or playing football, and never staying still for long.
He'd spent many an afternoon running home from school from bullies as well, which had paid great dividends to him on sports days, allowing him to make fools of his opponents in the hundred metre races.
He sat down at his kitchen table to eat his breakfast, switching on the radio, and listening to two politicians verbally tearing lumps out of each other, each of them mocking the other's statements.
"You're not fooling anyone, you pair of dicks that you are", he ranted, turning the tuning to try and find some music.
He continued cursing the politicians. He had always been a soliloquist, blaming it on the fact that he'd spent too much time on his own and had no-one at hand to speak out to and hear his opinions. "We all know that it's just a fucking game you're all playing, because it's common knowledge to us all that you are in fact, pigs at the same trough, you're all rubbing shoulders and shaking hands and drinking with each other at the end of the day, and you're all treating your secretaries to nice bed and breakfasts in the top hotels at our expense, you forty-faced bastards that you are!"
The squabbling politicians had put him in a bad frame of mind, and not even Johnny Mathis's soothing voice singing When A Child Is

Born could bring him out of it. He tried the tuner again and settled for Abba's Fernando, only to find that after the song had finished, the D.J began talking to him in German.

"Fucking stupid thing!" was his reaction as he grudgingly switched off the radio.

He began to enjoy his food again as he thought about the information Sam had given him. Was it really going to be as easy as that? Put surveillance on Temple Road, and then just arrest her? Somehow, he just knew, it would not be as easy as that.

No-one as dangerous or as evil as *that* bitch would leave herself vulnerable like that especially following her recent endeavours. Maybe she *had* been pulling up outside the flats to pick up that Veronica girl, but there's no way she'd be making a habit of it, she just wasn't that stupid. As he finished his breakfast he thought it would be a good idea to go and visit Veronica's friends again. Hopefully she wouldn't be home, and he and Ava could explain to the girls just how dangerous this woman that their friend was seeing, really was. One thing was for sure. If this Veronica was as infatuated with the monster as Sam had suggested, then all he would have to do was put surveillance onto *her* then they would be guaranteed to find her. The only danger with that was, if the sick bitch found out that we were on to her, she wouldn't hesitate for one second in disposing of her. She must have fallen out with her sick lover, big time, and whatever they'd fallen out about, well, it would seem that it was unfixable. The damage whatever it was, was irreparable. She wouldn't think twice about killing a prostitute, and after all, she'd done it before. He lit up a cigarette and once more attempted to find some music on his radio. This time he was successful. He found one of those channels who played old and new hits. He finished his cigarette and then set about washing the dishes, listening to Annie Lenox singing Thorn In My Side. He was just drying the last of his plates when his mobile phone buzzed on his kitchen table. He picked up the phone and read the text message.

"*Mister Mercer, tut tut, shame on you, you didn't have much faith in Sandra, now did you? Did you really think that she would commit suicide, really? Shame on you, and all of your so called forensics, although, it has to be said, I am a bit of a clever girl, am I not? Bye for now. Xxxx.*

Mercer sat down at his table. He felt weak and broke out in a cold sweat, his stomach seriously threatening to reject the food he had just consumed. Suddenly he was taken over by a flood of emotion. Sandra hadn't been lying after all, she *had* been coping.

That fucking bitch had crept into her house again.

Pseudoautochiria.

Ava Cruntze stood at Terry's kitchen door, having got no answer after knocking several times on his front door.

"What the hell is it this time Terry" She said, as she observed him lighting up a cigarette with shaking hands, and then drawing hard on the cylinder of tobacco.

"Bad news never seems to leave you alone for very long, does it now. Tell me what's happened Terry, and then we'll both deal with it."

He showed her the text massage he'd received.

"Oh, she's a sick bitch indeed Terry. I can see now why you are so desperate to kill her."

Terry sat with his back hard against his chair, his head right back, staring up to the ceiling.

"Oh my God, forgive me Sandra forgive me for doubting you babes, I'm so sorry."

"She already has Terry" said Ava, putting on the kettle.

"I've got surveillance looking out for the sick bitch's Ferrari, and also looking out for the young lady called Veronica, although, she hasn't been seen for a couple of days. Her friends are expecting her back to pick up some of her clothes, but as yet, there's been no sign of her."

"No, and she won't show either. That sick bitch will have some kind of plan or scheme going on in her twisted fucking mind, and that poor girl will be clueless as to what's happening. I just hope we can manage to save her before it's too late. God knows what the evil bastard has lined up next. How the fuck did Andy Phillips and his men miss that though? They were adamant that Sandra had committed suicide. Normally, nothing gets by those guys, fuck he'll be gutted when I tell him."

"Not unless Terry, and I don't mean to downgrade Sandra in any way, but, maybe Sandra did commit suicide, and this em woman has read it in the papers. She calls you to claim that it was she who murdered her, trying to frighten you, or unnerve you further, and making out that she's superior to your forensic team, like, she could come and kill you if she so wished."

"But she could have Ava, that's just it, she could have, She was in here with that sick bastard of a lover, and I can't for the life of me figure out how they got in. They never even broke a pane of glass, there was no locks tampered with, nothing, and yet, she was lying next to me in my bed, with her accomplice pointing a fucking gun to my head. They could have killed me and I wouldn't have known a thing about it, fuck, unnerve me? Christ, she's done that alright. It's got to the stage Ava that I'm literally frightened to go to sleep. A couple of times now, I've got up, thinking she was in my house, and so convinced I was, that I got up and checked all over the place, I mean thoroughly Ava...oh she killed Sandra alright, make no mistake about that."

"Well, she's going to be in for the high jump soon Terry, she'll be spotted soon with that Veronica girl. You see, her mistake is, she thinks she's invincible, she thinks she's getting away with everything."

"Ava, she is, that's just it, and let's face it, if she hadn't told me she killed Sandra, then none of us would have been any the wiser, and that's the truth."

"Terry, listen to me. Very soon, surveillance will find out where she lives, that, I promise you, and then, her game will be over."

"Her game Ava? Fuck she's killing at will."

"I know Terry, I don't mean to make light of what she's been doing, but I'm afraid she is playing a game, and she seems to be playing it specifically with you."

"What do you mean?"

"Can't you see? She's playing psychological games with you. You've just said it Terry, you're frightened to go to sleep some nights, and you're right of course, she could have killed you, and she knows that'll be on your mind, so, to keep you in this game she plays, she kills the people who are closest to you.

First, she takes out inspector McDermot, she's obviously spotted you with him on numerous occasions and guessed that you were his supervisor. She would see that there was a bond building around you both. She eliminates him, just to start the ball rolling, to get you...unnerving you, then she notices how much time you're spending with inspector Neal. Victim number two.

All the time she knows you're thinking about the time in your house, when she could have killed you."

"Well, the sooner we hear from surveillance the better"

Terry sighed, finishing off yet another cigarette.

"No-one has heard from Veronica for a couple of days now. Her friends say that her phone has been switched off. As soon as Veronica *does* contact her friends, they are going to get in touch with us."

"How do you know all this Ava, have you been to the flat to speak with them?"

"No, your friend Sam told me. The girl called Mandy seems to confide in him, she's given him her word that as soon as Veronica appears, she'll contact us."

"I might have guessed they'd confide in that fucking old fossil. He always could get the females to talk to him, but me? I'm just a fucking pervert, that's what I get told from them."

"And aren't you? The girl told Sam that all you do is stare at their bums and legs...where there's smoke Terry." Ava smiled.

She handed Terry a cup of coffee.

"Listen, if they wear skirts as short as that, and I'm not joking, they were short, then how am I supposed not to look at them, Jesus, it's their trade. It's because I wasn't buying that's why, that's why they called me a pervert fuck. Huh, she's calling me that, and here I am trying to save her friend, and find her sister's killers."

"I know" said Ava, grinning.

Terry smiled devilishly at her. "You're as bad as they are Ava, do you know that?"

Ava's phone buzzed in her pocket. She took it out and looked at the message.

"Get your coat Terry. We're off to Temple Road, Veronica has just been spotted entering the flats. You see? I told you we would find her. We'll just ask Veronica the name and address of her lover, without alarming her of course, and then we'll set about levelling the scores between you and your sick friend, oh, and of course this will give you a perfect opportunity to have a good perve at the girls' legs and bums, you know, your hobby?"

"I'm glad she's turned up Ava, because that means that I don't have to drink this black piss you dare to call coffee, come on."

Ava's immediate task in hand was to keep Mister Terrance Mercer from cracking up completely. She already admired the man's strength in how he was handling everything, but everyone has a limit, even the strongest willed. This woman, whoever she was, seemed to have a personal hatred for him. Although Ava had her own ideas she would say nothing to Terry at this moment in time, but this woman was killing, not for the hell of it, nor was she just an opportunist, these killings were planned, and the victims were hand-picked, specifically to get to Terry Mercer, to unhinge him...but why?

TEMPLE ROAD.

LOCKSLEY ESTATE.

The Surveillance officers were parked about fifty metres down from the entrance of Veronica Wells' flat. Terry and Ava approached their vehicle and climbed in the back of the car.
"BMW boys? There's nothing like being conspicuous is there lads, just merge in with the locals huh?"
Ava spoke up for the two embarrassed officers.
"Never mind him lads, it's the wrong time of the month. This was all they could get Terry at short notice, and besides, Miss Wells has done nothing wrong, it's not as if we're staking out a bank robbery is it."
"How long has she been home?" Terry said to the two young officers.
"About three quarters of an hour now sir."
"How did she arrive?"
"Taxi sir."
"There was no-one else with her in the taxi?"
"No sir, just her, and the driver of course."
Mercer looked at the officer disdainfully. "Of course" he mocked.
"Ok let's go Ava, you guys stay here and let us know if anyone else pulls up outside of that block of flats, especially a red Ferrari."
"Ok sir, we will."
Terrance Mercer and Ava Cruntze made their way to the entrance. A gang of youths loitered around the double-doors.
"Hey!" One of the youths shouted to Ava, a scrawny looking young man who looked like he hadn't shaved for two days.
"Do you take it up the arse bitch, fuck bitch, do ya?"
Without flinching, she replied, "Occasionally, but I have to know the man really well, and he has to know how to do it properly, not like your mama takes it, although, having said that, it will be rather difficult to control an Irish Wolf Hound, at the best of times let alone when they are sexually aroused."

"Fuck off!!"

"Ooh, that's original isn't it. Now get out of my way, before I kick you in the testicles and make you cry in front of all your friends here, go and help your mama cope with the rampant canine."

"Fuck you, you scabby fucking whore!!"

"You will not." Said Ava smiling as she and Terry boarded the elevator.

"A little more caution Ava, they'll be carrying guns no doubt."

"I carry a gun as well Terry, and I'll bet you that I'm more efficient with mine than they are with theirs."

"You would use a gun on them Ava?"

Terry was attempting to test Ava's attitude towards juvenile offenders. He needn't have worried.

"They're just kids, teenagers."

"If they pull a gun on me Terry, then they die, or I do, it is as simple as that. I see a gun? Then I don't care what age the person is who's brandishing it. The gun doesn't care what age the person is who pulls the trigger, it'll still kill me."

Terry pressed the button on the panel and the elevator door closed. The youths began banging on it just before it ascended. Ava smiled as she read from the elevator wall, that *Melanie revels in spunk baths*, and that *Lizzie's fanny can take bull elephant cocks*.

"Lucky Lizzy" said Ava, as they disembarked.

"What?"

"Nothing"

They approached Veronica's door. Ava knocked loudly and heavy. They heard chains being rattled and bolts being slipped. Then a female voice shouted, "Who is it?"

Ava looked at Terry, and before he had a chance to reply, she shouted back, "It's officer natural beauty".

Terry stood shaking his head. The girls had obviously told Sam word for word, what had been said the last time Terry had interviewed them, and Sam had taken great pleasure no doubt passing on the information to Ava.

Mandy Smith opened the door.

"Is Veronica home?" said Terry, hardly able to stifle his smile.

"She won't be long she's getting ready to go out, is this your girlfriend?"
Before Ava had a chance to say anything, Terry replied, "Yes, yes she is Miss Smith, and she can vouch for me that I am not a pervert, can't you Ava, tell her, tell Miss Smith what I'm really like."
Ava only stood and smiled at Mandy, but said nothing.
Terry continued. "Is she going to be long, this is rather urgent you see."
"I'll go and get her" said Mandy, "take a seat in the living room."
"You're a fucking bitch Ava, do you know that?"
Ava only smiled back at Terry as they entered the living room.
Upon entering Ava heard Terry mumbling something like "oh shit." Much to Ava's amusement, Elizabeth Keaton sat in her underwear only, painting her toe nails. Terry cleared his throat.
It was supposed to inform the young lady that she had company and so she should cover herself up and put some clothes on, instead, she only looked up and said, "Hi."
"Hi." said Terry. Ava continued to smile.
The girl was pretty, she thought to herself, they all were, and it would be practically impossible for any red-bloodied man, not to take in an eyeful of the young woman in front of them, but she would tease Terry about this for days to come. To make matters worse for Terry, Mandy came into the living room and roared, "For fuck sakes Lizzy, put some fucking clothes on, you know what he's like, God almighty, he'll be coming in his pants before he even gets the chance to speak to Veronica. You know what he's like when he's confronted with natural beauty, and this is his girlfriend, how do you think *she* feels whilst you sit there flashing your fanny at him. Would you like some tea Mister Mercer, or are you quite happy to stand there with your tongue hanging out."
Ava burst into laughter. She couldn't help herself, although she did feel the embarrassment for the situation her colleague had been put in. It wouldn't matter what answer Terry gave, this feisty little vixen named Mandy, would have an answer for him.
Terry Mercer had met his match.
To cap it all, Veronica entered the living room, wearing the tightest

of dresses and one of the shortest any woman would dare to wear outdoors. Ava had to take over, because for the first time in Terry's entire career, he was speechless.

But, the light-heartedness was over. It was time for business.

She introduced herself to Veronica and explained to her, that they would require her assistance in clearing up a misunderstanding, and could she please escort them to her friend's house."

Veronica had then asked what the misunderstanding was, and so Ava had to tell her a story. "Someone is claiming that jewellery has been stolen from a store, and it was stolen by someone with you, or at least someone fitting your description...so, if you could take us to your friend's house."

Terry now stepped in. "Or, if you prefer Miss Wells, just give us the address, and that would save you any embarrassment."

Veronica looked at her brand new watch and said, "Well, she's supposed to be coming here for me in ten minutes, we're going to a show in the west end."

"A show?" said Ava, "What kind of show?"

"It's opera, I've never been to the opera, Victoria says that I'll know within the first ten minutes whether or not I'll fall in love with it."

"Victoria, is that your friend's name is it?"

"Yes."

"Don't you think you should be wearing an evening dress and not a mini dress, you know, to go to the opera." said Terry.

Mandy pounced.

"Hah, who are you trying to kid inspector Mercer, your eyes have never left her arse since she stepped into the room."

"That's what I thought Mister Mercer, but Victoria insisted that I wore this dress, she bought me it, and she bought the tickets to the opera, and so..."

"What do you want to do Miss Wells?" said Ava, ignoring Mandy's last sarcastic comment to Terry.

"I'll stay here if it's all the same. It'll be embarrassing enough for Victoria when she gets here."

"Does she come in here for you Veronica?"

"Does she fuck" said Mandy. "This place is not posh enough for her

expensive candy-ass, she'll pull up there and wait in her fancy car for our Veronica."
Veronica now spoke up for the first time in defence of her lover.
"If you think for one minute that Victoria has stolen jewellery, then I can tell you now, you are both seriously mistaken, what's she supposed to have stolen anyway?"
"We'll talk to her about that Miss Wells, now could you please write down her address just in case by some miracle, she doesn't turn up for your date."
"She'll turn up alright."
"I'm sure she will Miss Wells, may we sit and wait until she arrives?" said Ava.
Veronica responded, "Mandy, make the officers a cup of tea please." Mandy rose up from the sofa and made her way to the kitchen.
"I'll give her a hand" Ava said, rising and following Mandy.
As they entered the kitchen Mandy said "How am I doing?"
"You're doing just fine Mandy."
"Do you really think that this snobby bitch is my sister's killer? It'll break Veronica's heart if she is. My sister Jane and Veronica were the best of friends you see, God if Veronica finds out that it was her posh friend who killed my sister, well..."
"Listen Mandy, you mustn't say anything to anyone about this, nothing has been proved yet, ok? You're doing fine, just keep it up, we'll be in touch with you if it is her, but we have to catch her first."
"Well she'll be here in five minutes so she shouldn't be too hard to catch. And is that why you have two officers down the road a bit, are they waiting to catch this Vicky as well?"
Ava smiled, so much for surveillance.
"Sshh...yes."
They brought the cups of tea into the living room.
Mandy handed Veronica a mug. "Here you are babes."
"Thanks Mandy, do you know, inspector Mercer here has done nothing but look at the floor. I think he's frightened to look at me or Lizzy because of your comments about his perversity, and Lizzy refuses to put any clothes on until her nail polish is dry."

"Lizzies' a cock-teasing bitch Ronnie, just as you are, no wonder the perve can't look up from the floor."
"Are you alright Terry? Ava said. "And if you don't mind me saying Mandy, your friends are not giving him much option are they?"
The two officers waited for a half-hour.
"Well" said Terry, "It would seem that your friend is not going to show Veronica."
At that very moment Veronica's phone began playing a pop tune. She held it up and read the message.
Mandy and Lizzy could see by Veronica's face that it was bad news.
"That was Vicky. She's very sorry but she's had to cancel tonight's engagement, I hope you're all very fucking happy now!"
Veronica threw her phone down on to the sofa, almost hitting Terry Mercer, who had to duck.
"I'm going to get changed" she snapped, as she headed off to her bedroom.
"Right, well we'd better be off then" said Ava, "thanks for the tea ladies, and tell Veronica we are sorry about everything."
"Bye for now ladies" said Terry, as he and his partner left.

They drove into Millington Road in Knightsbridge.
Terry slowed right down so that Ava could read the numbers on the doors.
"There it is, got it Terry".
"I'll just turn the car round at the bottom of the road Ava."
Terry parked the car thirty metres from the house.
"I know she won't be there, but it's worth a try Ava, have you got your gun with you?"
"I'm not even going to answer that Terry. Give me some credit would you."
"I'm just saying Ava, because if by some miracle she is in here, well, she won't be intending to come with us, I can assure you of that."
"If she's in here Terry, then I'll eat my hat. Look, let's just see if she's here, and if not, we can put surveillance on to the street and they'll inform us if she returns. We'll go through the proper channels Terry, keep ourselves right. We'll come back with a

warrant and search the place thoroughly, the last thing we need, is to be face to face with one of her fancy-assed lawyers, and being torn apart in court with illegal entry, so, what do you say, do it my way?"
"Ok" said Terry, climbing out of the car. "Let's go and knock on the door, there's no law against that is there?"
Terry had intended to just bust their way into the house regardless. Five minutes later they were back in the car.
"Come on then Ava, let's go and put the wheels into motion for obtaining this search warrant, I'll phone Polly, and she'll see to it."."
Ava could see the disappointment in Terry's face.
"Look, we're not going to find anything in there Terry, nothing that would help us find her anyway. She could be anywhere, although now that she knows we're on to her, well that's the end of this pretentious life she leads. It's the end of her living here, and it's the end of her living with her husband, wherever the hell he is."
"We'll soon find out who he is Ava, and we'll find out who this bitch is. Obviously her real name is not Victoria, that's just been part of the game she's playing with Veronica."
Ava sighed, "Well, wherever she is Terry, her game is up now, she's on the run now, for however long it takes us to find her, and we will."
"This is the first time in my life Ava that I am actually looking forward to killing someone, that's how much she's got to me. Her death is my one and only goal in life."

As Terry drove through the north London traffic, he said,
"Do you think she's taken off now Ava?"
"I think she has Terry.
"What about Veronica?"
"She won't miss her, Veronica was just a pawn in Miss Psycho's little game, in fact, Veronica can count herself lucky that she escaped with her life. You say this woman is married Terry?"
"Well we don't know for sure yet, but Sam thinks he saw her at the theatre one evening. He said this woman was acting promiscuous towards him, right in front of the man Sam took to be her

husband."
Nothing more was said for a few moments, but then, "Anyway Terry, if this woman is as attractive as you say she is, then you'd better leave everything to me. You'll be unable to arrest her for staring at her figure, and God help us if she's wearing a short skirt, you really will have to stop this perversity Terry, it's going to lead you into deep water my friend, go and see a shrink or something, or take bromide with your tea, goodness me man."
Terry laughed and said, "So much for Ava Cruntze sticking up for me, and all that do-or-die-shit, huh? You encouraged those girls Ava, you enjoyed my embarrassment didn't you, in fact, you revelled in it, you're a sick bitch Ava, I hope you know that lady."
"It's not my fault Terry, no-one asked you to get an erection back there, and think yourself lucky I didn't point the fact out to the girls, then you *would* have been embarrassed mister."
Terry shook his head, smiling as he drove.

When they arrived back at Scotland Yard, they were greeted by Sam Hargrieves who was waiting for them in Terry's office.
"How are you coping" he said, smiling at Ava.
"Still managing to work with him Miss Cruntze, don't worry, he'll get to you soon enough, he'll have you depressed in no time."
Terry ignored the banter. "She's not there Sam, she's fucked off somewhere, she could even be out of the country. I can't check with the airports because I don't have a name."
"I have a name for you Terry" Sam said, who had filled the kettle before Terry's arrival.
"Haven't got time for coffee Sam, what's the name?"
Sam just continued to talk as though Terry hadn't said anything. He handed the detectives a cup of coffee each.
"Her husband is an instrument inspector on the rigs, and I mean all-over-the-world- on the rigs. He is some kind of engineer, a very highly paid one. His name is Charles Simpson. His wife's name is Rosalyn.
"You were right Terry" said Ava.
Sam continued. "He's a very clever man Terry, he was educated at

Eton. He also has degrees in English, history and mathematics, but he specialises in engineering."

"He's not that clever Sam, being married to that. Surely he can see that his wife is a raging nymphomaniac lunatic."

"He's away from home for long spells at a time. On average he's away from home about seven or eight months of the year."

Terry smiled. Sandra was right about that as well.

"So, her real name Sam, is Rosalyn Simpson, and where was *she* educated, dare I ask, Oxford?"

"Afraid not Terry, she just had an ordinary education at a comprehensive school, in Leicester."

Terry looked at Sam.

"You're joking Sam, tell me you're joking."

"No, why?"

"Because that's where I went to school, in Leicester. Which one did she go to, don't tell me Montgomery High."

"That's exactly where she went Terry, do you know her?"

Terry sat down with his coffee.

"Rosalyn, Rosalyn…Rosalyn Clark, that was a girl I went out with…we eh…"

Sam raised his eyebrows. "That's her Terry that was her maiden name, you went out with her?"

"It was a bit more than that Sam. We went out together for two years when we were at school." Terry pulled out a cigarette and lit it, closing his door. He sat back down.

"We were just kids Sam. We made a kind of secret pact. We swore we would never leave each other, that we would always love each other, hell, we wouldn't know the meaning of the word, but we bought each other a ring. We declared each other engaged, but we didn't tell our parents, Christ, we were only sixteen Sam, that can't be her, surely."

"Of course not" Said Ava, "hell Terry, there must have been a thousand Rosalyn Clarks went to Montgomery High in Leicester, of course it's her, remember the psychological games I told you she was playing with you, it's her alright, and what became of your engagement?"

"I started seeing other girls behind her back, and then I finished with her. I gave her my ring back."

"How did she react to the news?"

"She cried a bit, and then asked if we could get back together and that she'd forgive me, but I just wanted to move on, surely this isn't her doing all these killings?"

"Do you know any other Rosalyn Clarks who went to Montgomery High in Leicester Terry?" said Ava.

"Rejection Terry, some people just can't handle it, especially some people with mental health problems. This could manifest itself in the form of extreme jealousy. She's killed Sandra and Billy already, and she's tried to kill you."

"Tried Sam? She could have killed me in my bed."

"She wants you to suffer Terry, merely killing you outright would not satisfy her needs, and it seems to me that it *is* a need she has. I'm afraid you've hurt her more than you ever imagined, that's why she took you down the sewers. To drown is a horrible way to die, but to drown in sewage and sludge...she's a twisted cookie Terry boy."

"I thought you were supposed to be retired Sam, you've been more help to me in these last few weeks than you've ever been, what a bloody weight off my shoulders when you retired Christ, you've no idea."

Sam responded, knowing full well that Terry was well aware of the seriousness of the situation.

"Has he made a pass at you yet Miss Cruntze? He can't help himself you see. He sees a beautiful woman and he gets this crazy notion in his head, that somehow he has a chance of sleeping with them. He fancies himself as some kind of irresistible libertine. Please don't take offence Miss Cruntze if he attempts this with you, a short sharp blow to his testicles usually does the trick, however, he may have used hypnosis on previous victims, so, be aware of that. Also, lead him to believe that he is right sometimes, this will hold back his profanations, although to be fair to him, his brain does not contain enough logical information for him to be able to express himself properly...very limited vocabulary you see."

Ava smiled at the two men who she knew, thought the world of each other. She imagined the banter between them both when they'd worked together as a team. There would never have been a dull moment, and she also imagined the heated debates between them, both men being stubborn, and both men insisting they were right.

"She's running now Sam" said Ava, bringing the banter to a close. "But I don't think she's running scared. The fact that she's been forced to vacate her premises will be nothing more than a minor inconvenience. I believe she'll have other properties throughout the city, and whether she does or not, she has plenty of money. She just splashed out over ten thousand pounds on her plaything there like she'd just spent a tenner. The thing is, and this is what I'd be concerned about Terry, if I were you, she could be hell-bent on killing you. You said to me that killing her was your one and only goal in your life, well, what if *her* one and only goal is to kill you? She's already killed two people who were close to you."

Terry stubbed out his cigarette.

"Christ almighty, it was so many years ago, if that is her. Why would she spend her life plotting my downfall?" Terry tried to convince himself that she hadn't spent all this time doing just that.

"No, she's read about me and you Sam, some-time in the recent past, and it's sparked something off in her sick head, that's what's happened. Maybe we've prosecuted one of her lovers or something and it's tipped her scales, she hasn't been tracking me since high-school, no way."

Sam put down his empty mug. "Well Terry, I would proceed with extreme caution if I were you, and you too Ava, because if she's still trying to intimidate him she could quite easily attempt to take your life. She obviously took a note of your number Terry, the night she came to your place, is there anything else on your phone she might find useful?"

"I don't think so, I mean Ava's number is on there now, but I didn't know her then. Your number Sam, and your house number, but she hasn't contacted you about anything, has she?"

"No, but that doesn't mean that she hasn't taken them."

"I don't think that you come into the equation Sam." said Ava. "It's him she's after, the dirty two-timing pig that he is, I'm talking like *she* would refer to you Terry, you understand."
Sam looked at his ex-partner, smiling and shaking his head.
"Even at school Terry."
"I've already told him Sam." laughed Ava. "I've warned him that someday his perversity would land him in hot water, and lo and behold, that day has come, two-timing freak."
"You said deep Ava, you said I would land in deep water, and I already have, I've been there."
"Listen." said Sam, "just watch how you go kid, and you too Ava. If she has been watching you for a long time, then there's nothing to suggest that she's not now. Remember, if she can see you, then there's little chance of you seeing her, take care, I'll be in touch with you."

Terry and Ava made their way back over to Locksley.
"You don't seem to have much luck with the ladies Terry." Ava said, as they drove through the rush-hour traffic.
He didn't respond, he was in deep thought.
She tried again. "I said, you don't-"
"I heard you, there's just nothing to add to that, you're right, I don't have much luck with the ladies, there's nothing more to be said."
Ava could tell that he wasn't in a very talkative mood, and who could blame him. She decided to say nothing more until he spoke.
He was troubled, and it was no wonder. Had this Rosalyn woman set out to destroy his life? How long had she her sights on him? And could you *really* bear a grudge from as long ago as that?
As Terry had quite rightly explained, they were only sixteen, how on earth could she be possibly holding this against him.
Hell, millions of teenagers are pledging their allegiance to one another every single day of their lives, swearing their undying love to the boy or girl who they think will be their lifetime partner. It usually lasts a couple of months or so, and then the girl in question, suddenly becomes this uncontrollable nymphomaniac because she said hello to another boy in her class, or he becomes nothing but a

rotten no good two-timing fucking bastard because he's helped his friend's sister with her homework.
This was normality, it was part of growing up. We could all think of someone from our past who has done us wrong. It doesn't mean that we want to destroy their lives, or stalk them, or murder anyone who goes anywhere near them.
If that is what this Rosalyn woman was doing, then what a waste of a life. Why would you commit your whole life exacting revenge on someone for something they had done when they were so young, abnormalities in the mind? Over-reactions for the simplest of wrongdoings. Ava wrote something down on a small notebook she carried with her.
Terry looked at her, but still said nothing, only cursing when he had to manoeuvre around a careless driver. Fifteen minutes later, they pulled up outside of the Temple Road apartments. Not a single word had been spoken between the two detectives in that time. Even now, as they boarded the elevator, Ava wasn't quite sure why they were back here. For now, she would just go along with it. He obviously had a reason for returning. Perhaps Veronica could point them in the direction of the whereabouts of Rosalyn Simpson. One thing was for certain, when he did find her, she would die, the trouble was, she, it would seem, had similar plans for him, one of them would fall.

Mandy Smith answered the door. There was no verbal invitation to come in this time, Mandy simply walked away from the threshold back into the living room. Terry and Ava entered, closing the door behind them. They stepped into the living room.
The atmosphere was different now. It was sombre. Veronica sat on the sofa nursing a mug in her hands, the young lady called Lizzy smiled at the detectives.
"She knows." She said, nodding her head to Veronica.
"I'm sorry?" said Mercer.
"She knows...about the woman, she knows she killed Jane.
Your friend, Mister Hargrieves has been on the phone. He's told us everything she's done, he also told us what she's been doing to you,

and that she's sick in the head."

Terry cursed Sam inwardly. What the fuck was he doing telling them everything? And on the phone? Had he lost his fucking marbles or what?

That bitch could have a device on the telephone, a bugging device, the stupid man!

"Would you like some tea?" said Mandy.

"Em, yes please" replied Terry. Ava smiled and nodded.

Veronica looked to the two detectives.

"Jane was the best friend I ever had. She and I come through some things together. I was so pleased for her when she met Thomas, what a nice man he was, they made a lovely couple. Mandy was over the moon as well, because, for the first time in Jane's life, she had fallen in love. From the moment Thomas had moved in with her she began to wean herself off the heroin.

She didn't seek medical help, she done it her own way, and within two years or so, she was clean. We all respected Jane, respected and loved her. She gave up prostitution because she no longer had a habit to feed, she done it all herself without anyone's help."

Veronica looked right into the eyes of Terry Mercer and said, "Can you imagine how I feel right now? To think that I slept with the monster who killed my best friend? And not only that, but went shopping with her, laughing and joking, and cuddling, kissing this...this animal who took the life of the one and only person in my life who had shown me any affection. Can you imagine how I feel right now? I was going to walk out on these two as well, give the flat up, and just leave them behind to get on with it, and for what? Money? A better life? Huh, some friend I turned out to be?"

Veronica broke down and began to sob. She looked at Lizzy. "I'm so sorry girls, I really am, I don't deserve your friendship, I betrayed you."

Lizzy just continued rubbing her friend's shoulders, consoling her and then Terry Mercer done something that completely threw Ava and her opinion of him. It went against everything he'd ever been taught as a police officer. He got down on his knees on the floor in front of Veronica, took the cup from her hands, and then placed both of her hands in his. "Hey now" he said softly, "None of this is your fault Veronica. These girls don't hold anything against you. You weren't to know who that woman is, nobody can hold you to blame for any of this. This has nothing to do with any of you girls. You saw an opportunity to better yourself, who can blame you for that? These girls certainly don't, and I'm quite sure, if you ask them that if they were in the same situation that you were in, then they'd have done exactly the same, and just supposing this woman *had* been genuine, and you did move in with her, I just know that you would never have neglected your friendship with these two, hell, anyone can see that you all love each other, it stands out a mile, and I respect that, I respect you all, I really do. And as far as Jane's concerned, you hadn't even met that woman at the time Jane's life was taken, how on earth can you possibly be blaming yourself for anything Veronica. You are all very beautiful young women, and I can tell you here and now, that there'll be numerous offers given to you throughout the course of your lives. Some of those offers will be genuine, and some of them will be bull-shit, that's not anyone's fault, it's just life, and I'll bet you that you could all tell me stories of experiences you've all had in your short lives. I am not judgemental; I don't care what people do for a living. I don't care, and I don't know why you girls choose to do what you do, and I don't want to know, because it's none of my business. I know this much though, whenever I come to speak with you, I always leave here with a smile on my face, and I'll tell you something girls, there's not many people in my life right now, who can make me do that."

Lizzy gave Veronica a box of tissues. "He's right." She said. "He's right in everything he says."

Mandy came through with a tray of beverages and placed it upon the coffee table, and then, as Terry stood up, she wrapped her arms around his neck and cuddled him, just like she would have loved to cuddle her dad. Terry, who was quite taken aback, said;" What is this for?" Without releasing her grip, she said; "This is for all the nasty things I've said to you Mister Mercer, and for explaining something to my friend in a way that I could never express, please accept my apologies for my discourteous behaviour."

"Apology accepted, although there is no need for one."
They all sat drinking their tea, the sombre mood had been lifted. Veronica said, "She promised to take me to America. We were going to go shopping in California, she said we were going to Rodeo Drive, it's been my life-long dream." They all laughed as Ava said, "That's in Beverly Hills Terry in case you're wondering."
"Is it now, thank you for that Ava." A few minutes later they had finished their tea.
"If there's anything else you can think of Veronica, then please let us know, like if you suddenly remember something she said, or maybe somewhere she goes, people she meets, anything."
"I will." She replied. "Oh, what should I do with all these things she's bought me, it doesn't seem right to keep them you know, under the circumstances."
"Don't be silly." Said Ava, "They're yours, you keep them, get the use out of them, Terry here particularly likes to see you in that burgundy and gold dress, don't you sweetheart, that's his favourite, he's tried to get me to buy one just like it."
Yet again, Terry Mercer was smiling as he left this apartment, and yet again, Mandy threw her arms around him and cuddled him.
"Thank you once again Terry, I know you're a good man, really, considering."
"This time" Said Veronica, "you have got *us* smiling as you leave."
As the detectives entered the elevator, Terry caught Ava smiling at him, not to him.
"What gives?" he said.
"That was some speech Terrance Mercer, if you don't mind me saying. God at one point I had a lump in my throat. Now I know why you were so quiet on the way over here."
She kissed him on the cheek. "Full marks Terry, well done, I couldn't have said that any better myself."

# PARLOUR STREET.

## SOUTH KENSINGTON.

It was almost six-thirty in the evening, as Beth Hargrieves clambered out of the taxi laden with polythene shopping bags. The taxi driver made no attempt to leave his heated seat and offer her any assistance. She paid him the fare and gave him a generous tip for Christmas. The driver mumbled some kind of appreciation to her, and drove off.
It took Beth a couple of trips from the pavement to her front door to assemble all the shopping on her front step. Her house was in complete darkness. *"Sam must be down at Scotland yard"* she thought to herself, but then noticed that his new car, the one replaced to him by the insurance company, after his previous one had been taken apart in Locksley estate, was sitting in the drive. Having collected all her shopping from the step, the bags now were all assembled in her hallway. Sam had been complaining for some time now to her about the traffic in the city, and how it was so much easier just to take a cab and relax.
She had to constantly remind him that he was now retired, and there was no need for him to go there to Scotland Yard as often as he did. If she was honest though, he never refused her a trip anywhere, and besides, one couldn't spend all those years in the force and then just expect to shut off from it, after all, he'd been a detective for over thirty years or so, old habits and all that. She also knew that Sam was doing his best to assist Terry any way he could, obtaining little bits of information from people he knew, and passing it on to Terry. He was still looking out for Terry if truth be known, and she admired that, whether Terry Mercer would feel the same about Sam's assistance was another question. As she began to ferry the shopping bags into the kitchen she sniffed the air.
"Oh that's nice Sam, you've been polishing, good boy."
She smiled to herself as she loaded the fridge and the freezer, and her cupboards. Sam would scowl if the words hen-pecked were

ever mentioned to him, but in all honesty, he was, not in a soft way, but, well in a Sam Hargrieves kind of way which no-one would ever detect. She smelled the air again.
"What kind of polish is that? I don't recognise that fragrance."
She sniffed again.
"That is not polish, it's perfume, and it's absolutely beautiful. It's perfume, definitely, and whoever it is, it's lovely. I wonder if it's the nurse who comes to check up on him after his heart attack?"
She would have to remember to ask her the next time she was here what brand it was.
It was now time for a well-deserved coffee after her late afternoon exertions in the supermarkets, having negotiated shopping isles which were packed with distraught mothers and over-excited children trying their level best to test their resilience to the limits. Add to that, the countless charity workers rattling tins in your face every two strides you took, and looking upon you as if it were your duty to donate to their specific cause, even though they could see for themselves that the poor mothers were struggling desperately to control their offspring to the best of their abilities.
As she sipped her coffee, she decided that Sam was not hen-pecked after all, having explained to her long ago to not ever expect him to go food shopping. It was the one and only thing he refused to do, but, she smiled to herself, she was glad about that, acknowledging the fact, that if he did come shopping, their entire diet would consist of baked beans and pasta.
She finished unpacking, and opened the conservatory door. She smiled, she could see Sam's feet up on the old coffee table with his slippers on. The chair upon which he sat was at an acute angle, almost with his back to her. He had fallen asleep...again.
The perfume smell was in here as well, stronger.
Whoever had been here had not been away for long.
She decided to leave him until he woke up himself, or until she had his dinner ready.
*"He's hardly touched his coffee"* she said to herself. Since his heart attack he'd been having these afternoon naps which done him the power of good. She came back through to her kitchen and made

herself another cup as she set about peeling the potatoes.
This is what married life was supposed to feel like, having dinner together, talking to each other, and not having to worry about whether you were going to see your husband for bloody days at a time. *"Beth Hargrieves has had her share of that thank you very much"*.
Suddenly, she almost jumped out of her skin. Her front door had been closed with an almighty bang.
"Oh my God, what on earth?
I closed the door when I came in, I'm sure I did."
She headed down the hallway. "Hello?" She shouted. She opened her door and looked left and right down the street.
There was no-one walking close by, only traffic passing to and fro.
"Strange" she thought, as she stepped back into the house.
"Sam will be awake now for sure, and none too pleased in the manner in which he's been awoken."
And still, she could smell the perfume. She walked back through to the kitchen and then into the conservatory. Sam hadn't moved. She approached him. The light was dim in here.
"Sam? Sam, come on angel, it's time you were awake. Come on, I'm starting dinner, Sam!"
He didn't move. Beth turned and switched on the light. When she returned to Sam, she saw the reason he hadn't stirred.
Initially, she thought he'd had another heart attack, but upon closer inspection, she saw the small red and black hole, about half an inch in diameter in the centre of his brow. All of the back of Sam's chair was crimson, including the antimacassar. Beth took a sharp intake of breath and put her hand up to her mouth. She went back through to the kitchen, closing the conservatory door behind her. Tears streaming down her face, she continued peeling her potatoes. She peeled the whole five-pound bag, and then washed her hands and dried them. She then returned to the conservatory and pulled up a chair beside her husband's. She smiled at him.
"You promised me Sam, you bloody promised me angel, you said you'd always be here for me. Now what am I going to do? Oh my dear God Sam, I need you angel, Christ Sam, you know that, what

the hell am I to do with you. I've just sorted out all the shopping while you've been here sleeping. I'm making the dinner Sam, I took too long shopping I know, I couldn't help it angel those bloody queue's Sam, you can't bloody move because it's so close to Christmas. What Am I going to do without you Sam, I've waited for so long to spend time with you, and now look at you, it's too late angel, that's just it Sam, it's too late. I've got all the photographs from the Lake District."

Then, and only then, a full fifteen minutes after discovering her husband's body, Beth Hargrieves began to break her heart, clutching the right hand of the one and only man she had ever loved.

MILLINGTON ROAD.

KNIGHTSBRIDGE.

Charles Simpson had finally been located and had returned home at the request of Scotland Yard. He sat now on one of his Chesterfield sofas completely devastated, having just been informed of the horrendous crimes his wife had committed. At first, he'd shaken his head in total disbelief, informing detectives Mercer and Cruntze that there had obviously been some mistake, and that his wife was not capable of such atrocities, but after the evidence had been shown to him, he had to accept the fact, that it was all true. He rose from his seat and poured himself a large whiskey.
He took a large mouthful and then said as he turned to face the detectives. "I've known all along that she doesn't love me, I could even go as far as saying that she sometimes cringes when I touch her, but I love her, what can I say? Call me a fool, call me pathetic, but she is all that I live for. I am besotted with her, I can't help it. know that she only stays with me for the money, but it's a small price to pay to have such a beautiful woman in my life. I could buy the services of beautiful women, but it wouldn't be the same as having one at home, one you can call your wife.
I know all about the lovers she's had over the years, and there's been a few.
I made out to her that I knew nothing about them, but I knew everything, or at least I knew enough."
He took another sip of his whiskey, and then turned away from the detectives. "You'll never find her you know you've missed your chance."
"What do you mean!" barked Mercer. "Explain yourself you must know where she is."
"I'm afraid I don't inspector, but I do know this, all of her bank accounts have been emptied, and the house she owns in the Isle of Dogs has been sold. It's my bet she's been planning this for some time. In a nutshell detective Mercer, she's made sure that she is

financially secure. She's obviously planning in making a new start for herself...she's gone."

"You must have *some* idea of where she could be Mister Simpson" said Ava Cruntze.

" I only wish I did inspector. She could have gone anywhere. She may even be abroad for all we know, and heaven knows, she'll have enough money. Anyway, it looks like she's away for good this time."

"You're right about that Mister Simpson" said Mercer, "because even if we do catch her, she certainly won't be back here for a while, in fact I'd just get used to the idea of living without her if I were you."

Mercer's phone buzzed in his jacket pocket. He had a text message. The caller was anonymous.

"Oh it's a photo Ava, someone's sending me a photograph."

He pressed the reveal app on his screen. Ava watched his face change. Terry Mercer stood looking at his phone like he wasn't able to comprehend what it was he was looking at. He seemed to Ava, like he'd gone into shock. Ava stepped over to look at the screen. Terry moved so that she couldn't see it. He just stared at the screen in total disbelief. On the small four inch screen he held in his hand, Sam Hargrieves' face stared up at him with a single bullet wound in the centre of his brow.

"Terry? What is it?" said Ava, knowing that something was seriously wrong.

"What the hell is it Terry?"  Terry finally showed her the image.

"Oh my sweet Christ" said Ava, placing a hand up to her mouth. Then Ava's professionalism kicked in with precision timing.

"Terry, come on back to HQ with me just now, we can come back and interview Mister Simpson later, come on, let's go and see Polly."

Mercer switched off his phone and rose to his feet. He looked at the concerned old man and said, "I don't know what kind of a twisted relationship you have with that sick fucking mental whore, but I'm going to tell you something right now, this is your last chance to tell us where she is if you know, your very last chance, because if I find out any time in the future that you have played any

part in harbouring this fucking screw-ball, then I'll come back here, or I'll hunt you down to the four corners of the earth if needs be, and I will kill you, do you understand what I've just said to you?"
"Yes" replied a bemused Mister Simpson.
"Inspector Mercer, understand this, first of all I had no idea whatsoever that she'd been committing these crimes, I had no idea that she was, sorry is, mentally unstable, and now that I know how dangerous she really is, I give you my word as a gentleman, that if I should hear from her, I will call you immediately, you have my word on that. I take it by the reaction of your phone message that she's been back in touch with you."
Mercer stared at the man.
"Oh she's been in touch alright. The sick fuck has just killed a very dear friend of mine.
Mister Simpson, I'm going to be honest with you, I might as well. When I find that deranged fucking whore, I'm going to beat her until my fists hurt, and then I'm going to kick her until I can't stand, after that, if she recovers consciousness, I'm going to set her alight, that is an absolute promise, that's a solemn promise. I want to hear her scream and beg for mercy, so whatever you think of me, I really couldn't care less, but that, my friend, is what I'm going to do to her, and like I say, if I find out that you've played any part in hiding her, or covering up her crimes, then I'll do the very same to you. Now, don't you fucking dare take off anywhere, do you hear me, because if you do, I'll take that as a guilty plea, and I'll come and hunt you and kill you. Are we all clear on that? You just stay fucking put sunshine."
Ava looked at Mister Simpson with an ice-cold stare.
"For your own safety Mister Simpson, I would advise you to stay exactly where you are, and God help you if he finds out that you know something. If you have been protecting her in some way, and then he finds out, well then I seriously doubt that God *could* help you."

## PARLOUR STREET.

## SOUTH KENSINGTON.

Andy Phillips stood outside Sam Hargrieves' house on the top step, smoking a cigarette, something he hadn't done for nearly six years. This, apart from the day he'd lost his wife to cancer, was the worst day of his life. He had to come outside and leave his forensic team to perform all the necessary procedures.

He and Sam Hargrieves had been life-long friends, having begun their friendship at primary school. Both of them had been best man at each other's weddings. Sam and Beth were God-parents to Andy's two daughters. As far as he was concerned, Sam Hargrieves should never have been a target for that sick bitch to aim for, after all, the man was retired, but because of Terry Mercer's total incompetence, and lack of enthusiasm, the man lay dead, it was an absolute travesty. He was aware that although Sam was retired, he was picking up little snippets of information in an attempt to help Mercer, but Mercer had, in Phillips' eyes allowed himself to be continuously distracted, and hadn't followed up on crucial and important facts given to him. The result of all this negligence and negativity from Mercer lay in the house behind him with a single bullet wound in his brow. He shuffled on his feet agitated and frustrated at how sick our society had become.

He drew hard on his cigarette silently cursing this sick, greedy, contemptuous society that was now London. London today was not the famed national jewel of England that it once was. It was now a multi-national concoction of corrupted sludge that flowed through the veins of this once great capitol of the world. No-one today would as much as give you the time of day, and even if they would, more than fifty per cent of them couldn't greet you in coherent English. He stood thinking about his grandfather and how he had fought for his country, fought and gave his life like thousands of others, and for what?

As Phillips stamped out his cigarette, he sighed, as he pulled out his little pill box and took a hydroxychloroquine tablet, followed by a methotrexate, both tablets taken to ease the pain of his arthritis. He accepted the fact that he was xenophobic and would never deny the fact, he blamed it on the government and how they had planted into his brain and all the other kids of his age who would listen, that they should be proud of their country and to always be prepared to serve and assist in any way they could.

"Always be proud and patriotic."

He mumbled a soliloquy as he lit another cigarette, cursing this poisonous ungrateful, spoilt pretentious generation who had been left a free victorious proud country to build upon, but who had instead, grown to be a bunch of self-centred, caring-for no-one-but-themselves greedy bastards, who now had the audacity to blame everything that had gone wrong, on the youth of today. What the fuck had happened to the post war dream?

Every day he heard people referring to better times, when the people of London actually gave a damn about each other. Now, the majority of London's population kept themselves to themselves.

If anyone did hear about anything untoward going on, they kept it secret, and in most cases, they had to if they valued their lives.

This was a very different London as compared to what it used to be like in his younger days. Indeed, it was a different world than he used to know, and he had witnessed most of the changes personally, and the majority of these changes were not for the better.

London was now a city of greed and callousness, unmerciful. If you didn't have money, then London didn't want anything to do with you. Get out of the way. The sing-alongs he fondly remembered in some of his local pubs, were all just that, distant memories. There was not much hope of them ever returning either. Different culture, oh yes, very different. He'd lost count of how many headless bodies he and his team had come across in this city, or young overdosed men and women, the number of pensioners he'd came across, bound and gagged, beaten and raped, decapitated or burnt to death.

Newly-born babies, discarded like a bundle of rags, lying dead on waste ground, abandoned by girls who weren't probably at the age of consent yet...and now this, his one and only true friend in the city, his confidant, his mucker, his mate, lying dead within the city he'd spent most of his life defending. Phillips wiped a tear from his eye. He was on his own now, Sam was gone. His wife had been gone now for nearly five years. His two daughters were up and away now as well, married and both living abroad, one in Canada, the other in Australia, even they could not be further apart from each other.

In his fifty-eighth year Andy Phillips reasoned that he had served his purpose here on earth.  He and his wife had reproduced, and so they had done their bit to keep the world turning. He drew hard on his cigarette, wondering that, *if* or when his daughters decided to start a family, would he ever get to see his grandchildren. He sighed again as he exhaled smoke. The kids would grow up Canadian and Australian, they would learn nothing of this city.

His depressing thoughts were interrupted by one of his officers.

"Sir, there's someone would like a word with you."

"Who is it?"

"It's Miss Sheppard she's asking if she can have ten minutes with you."

"Miss Sheppard? When did she arrive? She didn't come past me."

"She's been here sir, since we first arrived."

Phillips had been on automatic pilot since he and his team had arrived here. It was like he was in some impenetrable bubble, completely isolated from the rest of the world. He could see out, but no-one could come in.

"Tell her I'll be there in a minute, have you men finished with Sam yet?"

"Just about sir" said the young nervous officer.

He was nervous, because he'd been warned by some of his colleagues to tread lightly in conversation with the head of forensics. Unpredictable, was the word they'd used.

"I'll tell her sir."

"Is he here?"

"Who sir?"

"Terrance fucking Mercer, that's who."
"No sir, not yet, I know he and Sam Hargrieves were very close sir."
Phillips looked at the young officer disdainfully.
"Do you now...is that what you know."
Phillips threw down the half-finished cigarette and stamped it on the ground.
"Back to reality" he mumbled to himself. Back to the business in hand, which is, to try and prove to the world that that sick psychopathic hedonistic venomous fucking whore had taken the life of his best friend.
*That bastard Mercer had even been in bed with her as well.* Maybe if he could have spent some time on the case instead of putting all his concentrations and efforts into trying to bed every female officer he was given to work with, Sam would still be alive. He very slowly made his way back into the house, his protective bubble completely burst now, and leaving him feeling extremely vulnerable.

Polly Sheppard stood in the living room holding in her hands a photograph of Sam and Beth's wedding day. A young handsome Andy Phillips smiled at her from the steps of ST Mary's.
"You wanted to see me" said the fifty-eight year old Andy Phillips as he approached her.
Polly smiled kindly at Andy as she replaced the photograph back onto the mantle shelf.
"Andy, I know how hard this is for you. I know that you and Sam have been friends for a long time. I also want you to know that-"
"How long do you want me to take off?"
"Andy I think-"
"How long? Just tell me, that's what you're about to say, isn't it?"
"Andy, give yourself a couple of weeks, at least, and then we-"
"You could give me a couple of months Polly, or a couple of years, if it's Sam you're talking about. I will never get over his death, especially when we all know that his death was down to someone else's incompetence, the same could be said for young Billy McDermot as well, and inspector Sandra Neal."

"Andy? You're not trying to tell me that you're blaming Terry for these deaths, are you?"

"Well, if the cap fits, wear it."

Polly looked at the senior forensic officer incredulously.

"Andy, I think you'd better take time off, I mean, really."

"Yeah, that'll solve everything won't it take time off and sit and brood about everything. You think that it was me and my men who were incompetent don't you, because we never doubted Sandra's suicide, well I'll tell you something for nothing, there wasn't anything to find. I don't know what that bitch wore on her hands and feet that day, but there was absolutely nothing we could trace. Of course, if Terry Mercer had been there, he would have found something I'll bet, because he's the best isn't he, he can do anything, he's the best, he would have found proof."

"Just hold it there Mister Phillips. I don't know where all this hatred towards Terry is coming from, and I don't particularly want to know, but you had better change your way of thinking. Don't you dare blame Terry for any of this, you haven't got the slightest idea of what that man has been through, you're so tunnel-vision in your hatred or jealousy towards him-"

"Jealousy? You must be-"

"Yes jealousy, and don't you dare interrupt me again whilst I am talking to you. Ever since I came here, I've heard nothing but negativity from you towards Terry."

" Pardon me" said Phillips. "You've just lost three very dear people, valuable people through total incompetence, and it's fair to say, that if a certain detective had been doing their job in a professional manner, then those three people would still be with us. Now that's not victimisation, that is fact Miss Sheppard, and fine well you know it."

"You just refuse to listen Andy, don't you, well I'll tell you what I'm going to do. I've changed my mind. Having had this conversation with you, I have decided that in fact you are well enough to carry on with your duties. I shall also make out a report of the same conversation, and I shall inform detective Mercer of your views and opinions on the present situation. Now I have no idea of just how

he'll be feeling at this moment in time-"
"Should that not be *who* he is feeling Miss Sheppard, I think that would be closer to the truth."
Polly Sheppard stared into the eyes of Andy Phillips.
"You can smart-mouth all you want Andy, but I think we both know that Terry Mercer would tear you from limb to limb, and as your superior, it is my duty to refrain my personnel from such behaviour, but in this case I'm going to turn a blind eye.
Now then, one final chance Andy, I am prepared to walk away from you now and not repeat one word of this conversation to anyone else, but if I hear you bad mouthing detective Mercer to any of my staff, I shall not hesitate for one second to inform Terry of your opinions, and then the two of you can sort it out in your own time. Now if that occasion should arise, then I can safely say, that you'll be off work for a lot longer than two weeks, I think we both know that, and oh, by the way, while we're on the subject of doing our jobs professionally, I think you should go through there and apologise to those men of yours for covering up for you. You see, I gave permission to two of your men to go back into Sandra Neal's house and do another sweep. They found three samples of Misses Rosalyn Simpson's DNA. I hardly think Mister Phillips that you're in any position to be accusing anyone of incompetence. Now on you go, back to your duties. See if you can find proof that she's been here as well. I am so sorry for your loss Andy, as I say, we'll all miss Sam, but don't you dare point the finger of blame at that poor bugger, who's shoes you could not fill. I'll expect your report from here on my desk first thing in the morning, and try not to miss any traces. Whatever you think of Terry Mercer Andy, remember this, right now, he's on your side. Whatever you do, for your own sake, do not lose his support."

SCOTLAND YARD.

BROADWAY VICTORIA.

Terry Mercer sat on a chair opposite Polly Sheppard. Ava Cruntze stood looking out of the window. Terry looked exhausted to Polly, as if he hadn't slept for a week. The man was stressed beyond belief.
"Why the hell is she doing this to me Polly? How could the actions of an immature school-boy, almost thirty years ago cause her to do these despicable acts? If she hates me that much, then why doesn't she just kill me and be done with it? Why does she have to be killing all these innocent people?"
Ava turned from the window to look at Polly, but said nothing, hoping that Polly agreed with her unspoken opinion...she did.
"If she killed you Terry, then you wouldn't be suffering any more, would you. It's like Ava said to you, it's all about torturing you. Like it or not Terry, this woman has been obsessed with you for most of her life, indeed I would go as far as to say consumed by you."
Terry sat shaking his head.
Ava spoke now as Terry cursed the fact that the one remaining cigarette left in his packet, was crushed and broken. Polly opened her desk drawer and produced a packet.
"You left these here a couple of weeks ago, I shouldn't encourage you."
As he lit a cigarette, Ava said to him; "Polly and I have come up with a plan Terry, of course, this plan will only work if she hasn't already taken off somewhere, if she's not left the country, and, if you are prepared to go along with it."
He sighed heavily. "Right now ladies, I would do anything to get my hands on that sick excuse for a woman, anything, what's your plan? Because I'm at a complete loss as to how I'm going to catch her...there's no-one left who is close to me, she's killed them all. In fact, I think she's going to come for me now, I honestly believe that, I think that's her next move."

Ava smiled at Terry, taking a seat beside him.
"She's too late Terry, you're already dead."
Terry had sat back in his seat with his head looking up to the ceiling. He snorted and said, "I fucking feel like it Ava, and that's the truth."
"Ok Terry" said Polly, leaning over the table, " here's the plan. Whenever they're planning Sam's funeral, then the following day, you are going to put a gun in your mouth, it's all been too much for you to bear. All the pressure from people like me, the loss of your partners, the press hounding you for explanations, and accusing you of not doing your job professionally, it all became too much for you, the photograph of Sam on your phone, everything, it all stretched you beyond your limits."
"She wouldn't buy that Polly, not after the way she disposed of Sandra, she'd see through it, thinking that we were trying to copy her trick, she wouldn't buy it."
"How do you know that unless we try Terry" said Ava, waving a magazine rapidly in the air, trying to keep Terry's cigarette smoke at bay.
"But just supposing for a minute Terry, she did buy it, after all, she's enjoying herself torturing you psychologically, and who knows, maybe that's how she's planning to kill you, like some kind of psychological strangulation, pushing you to the end of your tether until you can see no other way out."
"She's right" said Polly, and anyway, we have nothing to lose, it's worth a try."
"What if she's already left the country? It would all be for nothing, I take it you'd be having a funeral service for me, and everything."
"Of course, and if it turns out she's already left the country, well then that's our loss, but we'll never know unless we try. I think she's coming for you as well Terry, so what have we got to lose? Even if she has fled the country, which I doubt, we'll find her, eventually, but if she's still here, then I think that when she learns of your death, she'll just *have* to make an appearance, I think she'll have to watch them burying you."
"And supposing I go along with this, where will you bury me?"
Polly cleared her throat, unsure of how Terry would react to this

next suggestion. She glanced at Ava, for as much as to say, here goes. "Well, we thought, em...to make it look realistic, we thought we'd put you in with your mother, I know how sick that sounds, but it would be effective, it would look convincing."

"It would look like desecration Polly, that's what it would look like." Polly attempted to continue. "We wouldn't be disturbing your mother's coffin Terry, we would only be going down a couple of feet or so. No-one would be getting anywhere near the graveside, other than the selected people. We wouldn't disturb your mother's coffin Terry, I promise you."

"And where would I go? Where would I hide?"

"Well, there are two options. We could move you out of the city to somewhere in the country, although it would need to be somewhere really remote, or you could stay here, but of course, you wouldn't be able to leave the house."

"Which house? and for how long?"

"You could stay at Ava's apartment, or you could stay at my house, it's up to you. I know before you say, that we could put you in a hotel, but then you'd need a new identity, but even then, there'd be the risk of someone recognising you."

"I can't stay at your house Polly, because I'd end up beating that womanising fucking husband of yours up."

"He's not there Terry, I took your advice, we've separated, anyway, you've got a couple of days to think about it, but it seems to me that it's our best chance of flushing her out if she's still in the country."

"I'll think about it Polly, it's just the thought of it, you know disturbing my mother."

Ava tried to make light of the subject. "Well we could burn you Terry, we could take you to the crematorium if that's what you want sweetheart, we don't care, just as long as we get rid of you." She smiled, waiting for Terry's reaction. He didn't give one. He stubbed out his cigarette and rose to his feet.

"If I thought for one second that this would work, I wouldn't hesitate."

"That's just it Terry, we won't know until we try" said Polly.

"You said it yourself Terry, she's proving really difficult to capture, and I know what Sam would have said. Oh, I'm sorry Terry, I didn't mean that the way it came out, I'm sorry, I apologise."

Terry sighed, "It's alright Polly, don't worry about it." He turned and looked at his latest partner. "What do you think Ava? Do you think it'll work?"

"You know what I think Terry. This could be our only chance of bringing her out of hiding. At least, if we do this, we stand a fifty-fifty chance of getting our hands on her. Both Polly and I are certain that she would make an appearance either at the service, or even a day or two after the funeral, we're pretty certain that she'll visit your graveside at some point. What do you think Terry, do you want to give it a try?"

Terry nodded his head. "Ok, and like you say Polly, we've got nothing to lose. When I'm in hiding though Ava, who are you going to be working with, I don't want you wandering around out there on your own."

"That is so sweet Terry, thinking about my safety, and exposing your slight jealousy at the thought of someone else working with me."

Polly smiled at Ava.

"Don't be so fucking stupid woman, talking like that, I'm not jealous, what the fuck have I got to be jealous about? I couldn't care less who works with you, you stupid woman, for fuck sakes! I was merely concerned for my colleagues' safety that's all, and don't you be getting up on your fucking Krout high-horse lady."

"Of course you couldn't care less Terry" smiled Ava, "That's why you asked me."

## CHAPTER ELEVEN.

## PARLOUR STREET.

## SOUTH KENSINGTON.

Andy Phillips sat in the lounge with Beth Hargrieves drinking a cup of tea. Beth had asked Andy if he wished to take the head cord of Sam's casket at the funeral. He had thanked her and told her he'd be the proudest man in the country, performing such an honourable role. The two friends sat together now in silence. Only the sound of the grandfather clock ticking could be heard as they each sat with their thoughts. Eventually, Beth broke the silence.
"I thought that was it Andy when Sam retired, I thought that was the end of the danger."
"Beth."
"No, but you know what I mean Andy. All those years I've spent worrying at nights, hoping and praying to God, that he wouldn't catch a bullet, or be stabbed by some crazed villain's knife, years and years worrying myself sick looking at the clock at all hours of the night...him and Terry."
Andy blinked rapidly at the mention of Terry Mercer's name, as he sipped his tea.
"And then Sam made the decision and retired. The man was so selfless Andy, he retired for me, I know he did. He tried to make out that he'd grown tired of doing the job but I knew what he was doing. He even told me. He said that we were going to start living now. We were going to start going out again, meeting up with old friends. This...this was the last thing I expected."
Beth slipped the tea-cosy from the tea-pot and refilled their cups.
"It just shows you Andy, you just never know what's round the corner. This...woman, who you say has killed him, we met her, if it is

her. We met her at the theatre a few weeks ago. I knew Andy, when I walked in here, I subconsciously knew I'd smelled that perfume before. She must have worn it that night at the theatre. What I can't understand is, what the hell has Sam done to her for her to want to kill him? Why did she shoot him Andy?"

Phillips put down his cup and saucer.

"She done it Beth because she's a very sick woman, that's all, there's no other reason" he lied.

"Well Andy, I honestly don't know what I'm going to do now, really. We have no family, it has only ever been me and Sam, and now, I am going to be totally lost without him. We thought about adoption a few times over the years but never really done any serious research into it, I suppose, in hind-sight our hearts weren't really in it.

"She sighed. "Even when I was informed that I couldn't have children, he just accepted the situation. He would not have his dream, a baby girl, and that was that. He tried his best not to show his disappointment but I could see that he was cut to ribbons. He didn't make a fuss Andy, he just accepted the situation…that was the kind of man he was. We had your girls when they came along. I think that Sam and I poured all our parental love into them, they were our escape. You and Helen were always telling us off for spoiling them."

Andy Phillips had a lump in his throat. He was here to try and help Beth stay strong, but here he was, very close indeed to losing control of his own emotions as he remembered his little girls arriving back home, laden with presents and telling him tales of the wonderful times they'd had with aunty Beth and uncle Sam. Once again, all that could be heard was the sound of the grandfather clock. This time Andy broke the silence.

"Beth, I don't want you taking this the wrong way, but if you want, I could take some time off, you know, to spend with you, for comfort and support, you know, just like you and Sam done for me when I lost Helen."

Beth smiled. "You're so kind Andy you really are, but there is no need to worry, I'll be fine, besides, Terry already offered to do the same. That poor man Andy, sometimes I wonder where he gets the strength to carry on. This has devastated him. He was like the son we never had."

Phillips felt cut to the bone. Mercer had beaten him to it. Incompetent Mercer, womanising Mercer, the foul-mouthed hero. Everyone, but everyone had nothing but good things to say about him. The fact that Beth Hargrieves had just referred to him as the son she never had, hardened Andy's heart. Now, he couldn't care less how she felt. She had, albeit unintentionally, just insulted him more than she could ever know.

"I'll have to be getting back now Beth" he said, rising to his feet, "Thank you for the tea".

"You could stay a little longer Andy if you wish, and I really appreciate your visit, thank you ever so much."

He gave Beth a short hug and made his way to the door.

"No, I'll have to get back Beth, keep in touch with me, you know, about the funeral arrangements won't you?"

"Of course I will Andy, and if for some reason I don't get to phone you, I'll tell Terry to pass on the relevant information."

Andy Phillips felt sick to the stomach.

"Oh all right then, you just tell him everything Beth, and he'll pass it on to me."

"Are you alright Andy? You look a bit pale, you look drained."

"I'm ok, now remember, any time you need anything, then just call me, and I'll get here as quick as I can."

"Thank you Andy, you're a gem, you really are."

He made his way out, and couldn't wait to be back out onto the streets. Beth waved to him from her top step as he made his way into the night. He had tried his best not to show her how cut he was.

"Yes, you just tell that fucking prick everything Beth" he said to himself, "but little do you know, that if it wasn't for that fucking libertine womanising bastard, you'd still have your husband with you."

## WEST HILL CEMETARY.

## WINCHESTER.

There were more than two hundred people gathered together to hear Father Arthur Conroy's sermon and dedication to Sam Hargrieves. For once, in this wettest December since records began, the sun shone brightly upon the grieving congregation. More than fifty per cent of the people present were from the police force. Old acquaintances of Sam's were here as well as young recruits. The six poll bearers stepped forward as Father Conroy gave them the signal.
Terry Mercer stood at Sam's right shoulder holding the cord in his hands. At last, the signal was given to them to lower Sam's coffin. As they lowered the casket Terry was thinking about all his years in the C.I.D, working under the man he was now placing to rest.
Yes, they'd had their ups and downs, and many of them. Indeed, there had been many times when they'd held each other by the scruff of the neck, and on several occasions, they had actually exchanged blows. These disagreements were soon forgotten though. Neither man held grudges towards the other.
They had been a very successful team over the years, which had baffled their colleagues considerably.
Their personalities were like chalk and cheese. Whatever the chemistry had been, God alone knew...but it worked.
Now, it was over. All Sam would ever be now was a fond memory, but he would never forget him, he would not allow those memories to slip into oblivion. Terry watched tears flowing down the face of Andy Phillips. Sam had thought the world of this man, their friendship stretching way back to their childhoods.
Now Terry could hear Beth sobbing behind him.
Poor Beth, she had lost her soul mate, her husband, her lover, her confidante. Everything that she needed, Sam was.
Concentrating on Rosalyn Clark, or as she was known today, Rosalyn Simpson, helped keep Mercer's emotions in check.

The hatred he felt towards this woman was indescribable.
He had never felt anything like this throughout his whole career, but then, he'd never encountered a criminal as callous or ruthless as this. As he released the cord of Sam's coffin, he reminded himself of the fact that this was the third funeral he'd attended of dearly loved colleagues put into their early graves by this incontrollable evil psychotic time-bomb.
He would find out soon enough if she was obsessed with him or not. Tomorrow morning it would be in all the mainstream newspapers, that detective Terrance Mercer had taken his own life, having been under extreme pressure following the murders of three of his close colleagues. He would write a suicide note apologising to everyone concerned, having caused the families of these victims' extreme heartache and stress, and that the world would be a better place without him, particularly because the woman who had committed these murders, was the one and only girl in his life that he had truly loved, and still did love.
Separating from her so many years ago had been the biggest mistake he'd made in his life. If the suicide note was constructed well enough, then there'd be a fifty-fifty chance of this schizophrenic fuck head believing it, and just like Ava and Polly had said; "If she believes it, then she'll turn up at your grave, she'll have to. The odds of her resisting the temptation would be the same as a lame gazelle making it past a pride of starving lions".
Terry stepped back from the grave with the other poll bearers as Father Conroy spoke his last words of dedication to mister Sam Hargrieves, and then proceeded to commend Sam's soul to his God. Immediately after the service Terry wanted to go and comfort Beth but there were too many people around her.
Ava approached him, smiling gently and sympathetically, taking his right hand in both of hers, and squeezing gently.
"Are you alright Terry? I mean, I know you're not alright but-"
"I'm ok Ava, don't worry, and thank you for your concern."
He stopped and looked back to where he'd just laid his friend to rest. He stood and watched Andy Phillips who was standing at the graveside looking down at Sam's coffin.

Andy had no-one now, other than his work colleagues. Sam had been his last true friend. From where Ava and Terry stood, it looked like Andy's shoulders were shaking.

It was alright though, in here, in a cemetery, a man was allowed to cry. The world did not look upon it as a weakness, as it was when you stepped out of that gate. Out there, you were not permitted to show any signs of weakness, because if you did, you would suffer the consequences, one way or another.

"Come on" said Ava, "he'll be fine, he's just saying his last goodbye's to his buddy."

As they left the cemetery in Ava's car she said, "Your turn tomorrow Terry, sometime between now and tonight I'm going to come across your corpse."

"Is "everything in place Ava?"

"Yip, we're all ready to go."

Terry sighed, "I hope she buys it."

"So do I Terry. If she's in London, she'll buy it alright, in fact if she's anywhere in the country she'll buy it, and she'll be back in London before you can say, Terry Mercer is nothing but a two-timing bastard."

Mercer smiled, nodding his head at Ava's attempt to lighten his spirits.

## FINLAY STREET.

## HOLBURN.

Everything had been arranged and was running as planned. The forensic team had arrived, along with several police cars and an ambulance, just as they would have done if Terry Mercer *had* taken his own life. All newspaper editors had been interviewed by the Metropolitan Police Department, and all of them being forced to sign a government secrets act, which meant, that if any `false` information was leaked to the general public there would be serious consequences.

Terry Mercer stood in his bedroom changing into his forensic suit, complete with hood and face mask. He was to leave here as one of the forensic team, and just in case Miss sicko was watching from a distance, they'd placed a dummy in the body bag, forming a simulacrum, and was to be taken to the morgue, again, in case Rosalyn Simpson was watching.

Nothing was being left to chance. If Rosalyn Simpson *was* watching then everything would have to look convincing, which was why Ava Cruntze sat outside on the top step of Mercer's threshold, and looking like she was crying into her handkerchief.

If all went well Terry would be in Ava's apartment within the hour. Tony Chrysler, the chief of police had a meeting with the reverend John Muirfield at the church, where Terry's mother had been buried. It had taken Chrysler the best part of an hour to convince reverend Muirfield and three dignitaries from the Church of England to proceed with the fake funeral, but at last, they gave their permission. Much to their frustration, they too had to sign a secrets act, but in return for their kindness and cooperation, Chrysler had promised the church of St Michael a sizeable donation, which immediately seemed to take the sting out of their inconveniencies. All parties were happy and all shook hands with satisfied smiles. The dinner they were all about to share, in one of the city's highest class hotels was being paid for by the

Metropolitan Police Department, and no expense was spared from the five-star menu.
Chrysler smiled to himself as, for the first time, another fourteen dignitaries from the church of St Michael's had mysteriously appeared from nowhere as they all sat round the huge table.
"Yeah, praise the Lord and pass the spuds indeed." thought Chrysler.

By five o clock in the afternoon their plan had been executed. Terry Mercer sat now on the sofa in Ava Cruntze's apartment.
All they could do now, was wait. In the morning, the world would be informed on television and in national newspapers that detective Terrance Mercer had taken his own life. They would even publish his suicide note, word for word and hope that Rosalyn Simpson would respond. Ava was to go about her business as usual. They had even given her another partner to work with. All Terry had to do, was wait here in Ava's house, and "Keep away from the windows." It was all done. The trap was set. Ava sat with Terry in her living room.
"I don't think she'll buy it Ava. In my heart of hearts, I don't think she'll fall for it. Something tells me it'll all crash down."
"That's it Terry, you just look on the bright side, why don't you, always the pessimist aren't you, the glass is always half empty to you isn't it."
"Ava if you knew how my luck runs, then you wouldn't be so critical of me. Don't get me wrong, I hope with all my heart that she does fall for it, all we can do is wait. Wait and pray that she does, but all I'm saying is, she is not stupid, whatever else she is, she's not stupid, I'm beginning to think she's indomitable."

TEMPLE ROAD.

LOCKSLEY. 10am.

The three young women sat in total disbelief at what they had just read in their morning newspaper. All of them had eventually taken a shine to detective Mercer, particularly Mandy. None of them had ever had a kind word to say about any police officers, for obvious reasons, but since investigations had begun on the murder of Mandy's sister and her boyfriend, they had all taken to the officers who had promised them that they would find the culprits and bring them to justice.

Now, all three officers were dead. Although Mandy and Elizabeth had constantly reminded Veronica that she was guilty of nothing, she couldn't help thinking that she was at least partly to blame for all of this trouble, after all, she had slept with the monster. But, it was no surprise to her, or at least it shouldn't have been, that her plans had all collapsed around her, every other plan she had made in her life had ended this way. None of them had ended up as disastrous as this though.

Mandy had made coffee for the three of them.

"Do you think she'll stay in London Veronica" said Mandy, placing her friend's cup on the table.

"I haven't got a clue Mandy" she replied, picking up the newspaper and looking at the photograph of Terry Mercer. Veronica continued, "They're saying she's schizophrenic, she didn't seem mentally ill to me. I just find it hard to believe that she can kill as cruelly and callously as she does. If you could have seen her, and heard her talking, laughing and talking about every-day things just like we do, God she hid it well if she's schizophrenic."

"That's just it though Veronica" said Mandy, "A schizophrenic can and does have, well, two personalities, sometimes more. If you could have been a fly on the wall and watched her, twenty-four-seven, I'll bet you'd have seen the changes then but...whatever, she is one sick woman."

"I just don't understand it though" said Veronica "You've got all that money, a beautiful house, fancy cars, you don't have to work, you don't even have to worry about a bill, you can go anywhere in the world you want to go, why the hell would you jeopardise all that by killing people, I mean, ill or not, she's bound to realize that she'll be caught eventually, how many is that she's killed?"
"God knows Ronnie" said Mandy, "I'm just grateful you escaped with your life, because, as nice as she was to you, she'd have killed you at the drop of a hat."
Veronica sighed. "That poor detective, Mister Mercer, he obviously wasn't as strong as he made out to us."
"I think it was the murder of his friend Mister Hargrieves that tipped his scales, that and the murder of officer ballet" said Lizzy. "They've worked together for years Terry and Sam Hargrieves. He obviously blamed himself for Sam's murder. The poor man couldn't live with that, God, what a predicament to be in."
"*She's* killed Terry really." said Veronica. "It was *her* actions, *her* dirty deeds that made him feel that way."
"Well, just you remember what he said to you Ronnie, don't let his words go to waste, don't you be blaming yourself for anything that sick bitch has done." Mandy continued, "I wouldn't want to be in her shoes when they do catch her. Bad enough killing anyone, but to kill three officers and now, cause a forth to commit suicide, wow, to say she's in for the high jump would be the understatement of the year. God her poor husband as well, what the hell must he be thinking."
"Well" said Veronica, "What chance does she stand now? She'll be caught soon I would say, and then, that'll be the end of her life of luxury for sure. Her money will be of no use to her once they catch her."
"If they catch her." said Mandy.
Veronica nodded her head. "She told me once that she had friends in high places, very high places, she said I'd be surprised at who she knew."

## AVA CRUNTZE'S APARTMENT.

## 3 DAYS LATER.

Terry Mercer was beginning to feel claustrophobic. For someone who spent most of his time running around at high speed, and never in the same place for any length of time, this was proving harder than he had ever imagined. Up until this point, Ava and Polly's plan seemed to be failing miserably. Surveillance had reported nothing from the cemetery of St Michael's.
As far as he was concerned the whole thing had been a complete waste of time and money. He knew she would never fall for it, however Polly had persuaded him to stay put for another couple of days, just in case Rosalyn Simpson had been staying somewhere else on the island, outside of the city, which, if she had any sense, she would be.
"Give it time Terry" Polly had said to him. "If she's still in Britain, she'll arrive, she'll come to your grave you just have to be patient."
It was five o clock in the morning and Ava had not returned home. She explained to him that she wouldn't be home every night, and that she visited a friend from time to time, and sometimes stayed over. She had also given in to her dislike of smoking in her house, and had allowed Terry this one room where he would be permitted to smoke. The room he was in now. The room where he felt he was being strangled. This was the room where he was staying, sleeping, thinking, hoping, praying...suffocating...two more days. He made himself a cup of tea and lay down on his bed, looking, once again at the photograph of his wife and son, and yet again, he wondered why Carol had done that to him. Just up and away with his kid.  A man could take an enormous amount of physical pain he could harden himself to it. This kind of pain was different.  This kind of pain would slowly suffocate you, crush you like a constrictor, wrapping itself around you and slowly squeezing the life out of you with every breath you take, until, inevitably, your lungs would no longer contract, leaving you a lifeless form, and so easy to be

consumed.

How could she do that?

Not even as much as a single row, no heated discussion about a lover, nothing. Just happy and content, supposedly, one minute, and then gone the next, never to be seen again.

As he lay smoking and thinking on his bed, he heard the door down stairs.

"So, Ava has decided to come home."

When Ava had mentioned this friend of hers, he had not asked if they were male or female, it was none of his business.

"Whatever gender they were, they were very lucky".

The blonde jokes did not apply to Miss Ava Cruntze.

She was beautiful, but also rugged in her features, and ways, a well-trimmed body that had visited gymnasiums regularly, and yet this sweet femininity which was overpowering almost, making you feel grateful to even be in her company, and in some cases, as was the situation here, very grateful to be in her presence for long spells at a time, albeit on a working basis.

He listened now for the door to open. It didn't.

He heard the door, he knew he hadn't imagined it...or had he? Was this claustrophobic fifteen-by-ten room playing tricks on his ears now? He rose up from the bed and made his way to the hallway to investigate. He switched on the light and descended the stairs. Ava hadn't been at the door at all, but someone had.

A piece of folded paper lay on the floor directly underneath the letter box. He carefully and quietly approached the door, bending down to retrieve the piece of notepaper. Slowly, and somehow with an unexplained feeling of dread, he opened the note.

*Was that your attempt at being clever Terrance? Because if it was, you weren't very successful were you? It would take more than that to fool me, you should know that. Whoever heard of a coffin being lowered only two feet or so into the ground. If it hadn't been for that I may have been convinced, but there's no chance of that now, is there, you silly boy. That fiasco was nothing less than an insult to my intelligence.*

She had done it again. She'd outwitted them.
"Huh, she's obviously been in the vicinity watching. She's found herself a good vantage point and scrutinised the whole operation." What the hell were they going to do now, and more importantly, what was *she* going to do now.
"I fucking knew this wouldn't work" he said out loud as he made his way back to the room. He snatched up his mobile from the bedside cabinet. "Hello? Polly? Is that you?"
"What's wrong Terry?"
"Oh I'll tell you what's wrong Polly, I'll tell you like I've been trying to tell you all along, she knows, that's what's wrong. I fucking told you didn't I, She's not stupid."
"How do you know this, has she phoned you?"
"No, she hasn't fucking phoned me, she's dropped a note through the door, hand delivered if you please. I thought you told me you had a surveillance team watching Ava's house?"
"I have Terry, they should be there, haven't they been in touch with you? Surely they've seen someone at the house."
"Exactly, that's what I was thinking Polly, but obviously, they've fallen asleep, or they've fucked off home, anyway, it's all irrelevant now, the sick bitch knows what we were up to. I told you, didn't I? She was never going to fall for that. She's been watching from somewhere, because the bitch even knew that we only buried the casket a couple of feet into the ground. We had the immediate area covered. She must have a fucking good pair of binoculars that's all I can say. What I'm worried about now Polly, is what she's going to do next. She's not running scared, far from it, she's enjoying all this. She hasn't threatened any action on her note but I think she's going to do something nasty, we've offended her. We've offended her intelligence...fuck Polly...she's just toying with us. She's got us on strings here...oh my nasty bastard."
"Calm down Terry, I'm coming over, I'll be there in half an hour."

## TEMPLE ROAD. LOCKSLEY. 9 30am.

Veronica Wells had slept soundly for the first time in what seemed an age. She had sat up with her friends Mandy and Elizabeth, drinking until two o clock in the morning. This was the latest she had ever slept in. Normally she was up and about around six thirty, but aided by the amount of alcohol she'd consumed, she had slept coma-like until ten minutes ago.
Even now as she opened her curtains, she felt like she could go back to bed and sleep for another seven hours.
Dressed in her "Naughty-Pussy" dressing gown, she made her way through to the kitchen to put on the kettle, for her first of many cups of coffee she'd consume throughout the course of her day. She opened the kitchen curtains and then made her way to the living room to retrieve her cigarettes. As she made her way back to the kitchen she saw the scattering of letters lying in the hallway. "The postman's been early today" she said out loud, and then mumbled "huh, not that there'll be anything to get excited about." She brought the mail through to the kitchen and laid the envelopes on the table while she made her coffee.
Two minutes later, she sat at her table with her breakfast which consisted of, one strong cup of coffee, with two heaped teaspoons of sugar, a generous amount of full cream milk, and one king-sized middle-tar cigarette. Yet again most of the mail wasn't worth opening, and once again she cursed the TV Company for trying to entice her into adding additional channels to her existing contract. One of the letters was rather thick, like it was full of those good-for-nothing tokens offering you generous discounts on everything you see on their coupons, only when you attempt to purchase something at the discount price, you discover that it's only a fuck-you-up-the-arse deal that has expired the day before, or you need another ten tokens like these to be able to purchase at the sale prices.
She sighed as she opened the envelope, and was completely shocked at what she found inside.

Altogether, in one hundred pound notes, there was five thousand pounds.

There was also a passport complete with her photograph, and two first class flight tickets to the United States of America.

Together with these items, there was a letter.

Veronica drew hard on her cigarette. She was shaking.

Her emotions were in turmoil. She began to weep.

"You killed my friend you evil bitch" she whispered, remembering all the fun she'd had with this woman.

Still whispering, she said, "Why are you doing this to me?"

She attempted to extinguish the cigarette in the ash tray, but her hands were trembling so badly that she fumbled it onto the floor. She bent down to pick it up and struggled to get back to her feet. She sat back down on her chair. She looked at the folded letter and then began a personal psychological battle with her conscience. She was trying to decide whether or not to read the letter. She looked again at the tickets and the passport, and the money.

Suddenly Veronica had a flash-back to a certain evening when *she* had held her face in her hands, telling her that she was the most attractive woman she had ever met in her life, and kissing then her passionately.

Veronica shook herself out of her daydream.

"How can you be like this? You murdered my friend and her boyfriend, how can you be like this? Who the fuck are you? What the fuck are you?"

She picked up the hundred pound notes and spread them over her table, shaking her head. She found herself continuously whispering, "How can you be like this Vicky? How can you be kind like this, and then become this callous sick murdering bitch that I've read about in the papers. What the hell are you doing to me Vicky?"

Finally Veronica made the decision to read the letter, if for no other reason than curiosity, although, if she was honest with herself, it was for more than curiosity she was going to read it;

*Dear Veronica, I am deeply sorry for the way things turned out between us. You will by now have read all the terrible things I've* done in the newspapers, although they only tell half the story. If you have read recently about a CID officer committing suicide then you will also know that there was once a connection between him and I.

Let me start by saying that that was the last thing I wanted to happen. I did not want him to die. I loved that man like nothing I have ever loved before in my life. I had hopes of him and I getting back together. I hope you can believe this Veronica, because it's the truth.

Now, as far as we are concerned, I accept that there is little chance of you and I reuniting. If I am honest with you Veronica, you were only ever meant to be a play thing for me. I had initially intended to dispose of you after a while, but I grew so attached to you, and could never have hurt you in any way. Do you remember what we talked about? I hope you do, but just because I can't be with you, doesn't mean that you can't at least fulfil part of your dream, so please accept the gifts I have sent you. Take one of your friends with you, and even if you can't buy much, at least you'll be able to tell your friends that you were there in California, and that you shopped in Rodeo Drive in Beverly Hills.

Your passport is perfectly legitimate so don't worry, I told you I had friends in high places .Anyway, it is with regret that I must close now. We probably shan't ever meet again Veronica but I want to thank you for all the lovely times we had, I shall never forget them. I shall never forget you, how could I?

I understand that you had several meetings with detective Mercer and I know that you'll be feeling sorry for him and his colleagues, and rightly so. I knew him once Veronica and became besotted with him, and I am hurting beyond belief at his actions...I still love him, but now I will never find out if he and I could have started over again. I wish you well in everything you do Veronica. You will succeed, trust me. The secret of success my friend is, have no fear. Good luck and goodbye Veronica, from a very grateful lover and friend.  Ps. I always wanted to be called Vicky.

Take care and live your life well and think of the good times we spent together rather than the all those bad things you've read *about me. Best wishes, Rosalyn Simpson. Xxx*

Once again Veronica found herself in a state of quandary.
Plus, she had a problem. Should she tell her friends about this? Should she inform the police?
But, two tickets to America, and first class no less, a legitimate passport, and of course, five thousand pounds. She had never owned that amount of money in her entire life. She knew what her friends would say, and they'd be right, they would tell her to inform the police straight away. She made herself another cup of coffee and lit another cigarette, a two-course breakfast today.
Once again, she read the letter. The slight hang-over she was suffering was beginning to lift. It was amazing what two cups of coffee and a couple of cigarettes could do to bring you round, that, and a gift of five grand could change your physical condition for the better, in no time at all, certainly your train of thought. Whatever she decided to do, she was keeping the money that was not even up for debate. After reading the note for the third time she made her decision. She would inform the police and her friends, after all, if this so called Vicky hadn't taken a shine to her, she would be lying dead somewhere. Veronica placed the money and the tickets in her biscuit tin together with her passport. It wasn't important for the police or her friends to know about them, at least not at the moment, but she owed it to Terry Mercer to inform the police, the man had been doing his utmost to apprehend this dangerous woman and put a stop to her killing.
"What a shame for you Vicky that you have to live this Jekyll and Hyde type of existence, such a beautiful woman. Who would ever think for a second that you were capable of such atrocities.
I wonder what sparked that off. What kind of a childhood have you had? I guess we'll never know."

# SCOTLAND YARD.

## BROADWAY VICTORIA.

"I've got a good mind to suspend thee three of you for gross misconduct. I don't get it you're all staying in a good hotel and being paid a handsome salary. All you've been asked to do is keep an eye out on Ava Cruntzes' apartment, but it seems you're all incapable of even that, have you got anything to say for yourselves?"
Polly Sheppard stared at the guilty parties standing before her. One of the three officers cleared his throat and mustered up the courage to ask the question.
"May we ask mam what has happened?"
In total frustration Polly removed her reading glasses and gently threw them onto the table.
"Yes you may. Because you have not applied yourself to the task, the very simple task, that you are being paid to do, a certain Misses Rosalyn Simpson was able to walk up to Ava Cruntzes' house and post a note through the letter-box for Terry Mercer to read.
The frightening thing is, just suppose she'd had a key, or some means of entry, she'd have been in there, and you lot, thanks to your complete unprofessionalism, would have known nothing about it, and Terry Mercer would be dead. You have all been informed how dangerous this woman is and how important it is for us to stop her. Are you aware of how many police officers she's killed? As well as civilians? And you three let her march up there unchallenged with the same freedom as post-man Pat, get out of here the three of you, get out of my sight. Go and report to your superiors, maybe they can find something useful for you to do, because you're certainly not capable of surveillance. Maybe you could go to the shop for them or something, make them coffee, I don't know, just fuck off out of my presence, and you'd all better keep out of my way if you see me coming, otherwise you might not even have a job, now disappear!"

The profanation that Polly had just used was the first in her entire career as a police officer.

The three shamed, and somewhat confused officers left her office, each of them swearing to the other that no-one, other than authorised personnel had entered Ava's apartment from their vantage point.

Polly hated being like this. Cold and sarcastic, heavy handed, but she had to be, the officers had let her and themselves down.

She felt frustrated. She was certain the plan would have worked. Obviously it hadn't, and now Terry would be more frustrated than she was. Was this woman really that clever? "No she's not" she exclaimed out loud as she picked up her car keys from her desk. "It's us, we're so stupid, that's what it is." She knew she should have lowered the coffin deeper. The bitch had obviously been watching and witnessed the whole procedure. It should have worked. We should have had her, and if not for three dummies lying reading or watching TV, we would have.

Polly was bracing herself for Terry Mercer. She was just going over there to face his anger. He was right, she was too clever for them, and now she would have to face his red-hot anger. He despised this aberration and had made his views clear to herself and Ava. He had been hidden away from society for this half-hearted, weak, unconvincing plan.

She was just about to leave her office when her telephone rang. She snapped it up in complete frustration. "Hello, who is this?" she said, almost spitting the words out. Her frustrations grew almost into rage.

"It's sergeant Davis mam, I was just wondering if you knew where Ava Cruntze is?"

Polly gritted her teeth and fought back the flood of anger washing through her. She took a deep breath. "No I don't know where she is, but may I ask you a question? Why are you calling me about such a trivial matter, don't you have her mobile number?"

"No I don't mam, it's just that we've had a certain Miss Veronica Wells on the phone asking for her. She's asking for Ava because Misses Rosalyn Simpson has been in touch with her.

Veronica seems to think that the matter is urgent."
Polly almost threw the phone down as she made her way out of the office and began the journey to Locksley estate.

Twenty minutes later Polly Sheppard sat on a sofa listening intently to the details of the letter sent to Veronica.
"Read that bit again Veronica, I just want to make sure I'm hearing this correctly."
Veronica read out the section Polly was referring to. "*I am hurting beyond belief at his actions, I still love him but now I will never find out if he and I could have started over again.*"
Polly said nothing to Veronica to let her think any differently to what happened to Terry but in her head she was saying to herself, "So she does think he's dead."
If this was true, and it did seem to be genuine, then this changed everything, and they now had an even bigger problem than they'd thought, because this meant that someone else had written the note to Terry, and whoever wrote it, knew about the plan. It had to be one of their own. There was little chance of it being one of the newspapers, considering what was at stake, someone obviously with a grudge on Terry Mercer.
It didn't take much working out.
Polly left Veronica's flat and made her way down to her car. On her arrival she'd been approached by two young men who had offered to look after her vehicle for the princely sum of twenty pounds each. She was informed that if she declined their offer, then they couldn't guarantee what condition her vehicle would be in upon her return. She had paid the young men their asking price having remembered what had happened to Sam's car. Sure enough, when she returned her car was in one piece.
Once seated in the car, she took out her mobile and called Terry. His phone rang constantly for almost a full minute.
Finally, a bad-tempered rough-voiced Terry Mercer croaked, "What!! Who the fuck is this?"
"It's me Terry, it's Polly, don't you leave that house Terry whatever you do, I'm on my way over."

"Leave the fucking house Polly? Have you lost your mind?"
"Terry I can't explain on the phone, I'll tell you when I get there, just don't leave that house please."
"Well you'd better bring me some cigarettes on your way over because I've ran out."
"Ok I will, see you soon, everything is still on Terry."
"What the fuck is that supposed to mean?"
"Terry I am your chief inspector, language please."
"I know who you are, what the fuck is that supposed to mean?"

Half an hour later Polly sat in Ava Cruntze's house with Terry Mercer. Ava had not yet returned home.
"What the hell is going on Polly, you sounded frantic on the phone."
"I honestly don't know Terry what's going on, but I can tell you this, that note that you received was not written by Rosalyn Simpson, I know that much."
"What?"
"Someone else wrote that Terry, your friend Veronica has received a genuine letter of apology from the monster, and I assure you it is genuine. On that letter she expresses her disappointment of the news of your death. She goes on to say that she had hopes of her and you reuniting, something like that, but it is genuine Terry...she thinks you're dead."
Terry tore the cellophane from the packet of cigarettes Polly had purchased for him. "If that is true Polly, then who wrote the note, and why? You know it's someone in the force don't you."
"Yes I know Terry, and I'll get to the bottom of it, the most important thing is, she thinks you're dead. Our plan may yet work."
"Where the fuck is she"?
"Was there a post-mark on the letter?"
"No, it was just a hand-written note."
The stupid whore, what the fuck is she doing?"
"Keeping out of the way that's what she's doing. Now then, she's informed Veronica that they shan't ever meet again which gives me the impression that she intends to fly off somewhere, and soon. I will inform all airports of her name should she be stupid enough to

book a flight in her own name. But she may not, she may feel safer staying wherever the hell it is she's staying. If she feels safe where she is, she might just stay put.

Terry was enjoying his cigarette when Ava's front door opened. They heard her fumbling in her hallway and then she shouted, "Terry, are you up yet? I've bought some morning rolls do you want a bacon roll for breakfast?"

Ava entered the living room. "Oh my God, you've got the house stinking with those bloody cigarettes, Miss Sheppard, you shouldn't be letting him smoke in here, hell Terry I gave you a place to smoke, come on, stump it out, play the game Terry, that smell is disgusting."

"I've just made a pot of tea Ava, would you like me to pour you a cup, you must be exhausted after your all-night excursions. Here have a seat Ava while I get you your tea."

"Nice try Terry, now come on, cigarette out...now."

Polly smiled at Ava as Ava winked back. She hadn't expected Terry to pay a blind bit of notice to her request, but was pleasantly surprised when Terry rose up from his seat and extinguished his cigarette

Ava made bacon rolls for the three of them, and as they all sat around her kitchen table Polly explained to her everything about the note and how it had been someone else who had written it, someone in the force to be precise. After they had eaten Polly said to Ava, "I want you to stay here with him Ava, and make sure that he does not leave here under any circumstances whatsoever."

"I'm sitting right here Polly, and I know I have to stay here, but I won't be staying here for too much longer I can tell you that for nothing, I'm about climbing the walls here."

"I know Terry" said Polly, "but the thing is, she's convinced that you're dead, we're half way there, she'll come, sooner or later Terry, she'll come. In the letter she expressed her love for you."

"Fucking sick bitch, love, fuck."

"Terry, we are all well aware that the woman is sick, but she doesn't know that, and she gave the impression that she had some kind of plan in her head for you and her to get back together. Now if she feels that kind of love for you, then we can be assured that she'll visit your graveside. She'll feel drawn to pay her respects to you, you mark my words Terry she said she loved you like she's never loved anyone or anything in her life before."

Terry rose to his feet shaking his head and smiling sarcastically at the thought of this monster speaking of undying love and sentiment after the gruesome murders she'd committed.

"Where are you going?" said Ava, smiling at Polly. He replied sarcastically, "I'm going to my room to smoke a cigarette, any objections Ava?"

"Yes I have, there's a heap of dishes here to wash, and I don't have a dish-washer, so it would be the decent thing to do, for me cooking your breakfast, for you to wash them, don't you think?"

"I'd love to oblige Ava, but you see Polly has given orders that I am to steer clear of the windows, remember?"

Ava smiled. "I'll close the blinds, you're doing them mister."

Polly put on her coat. "Well, I'll leave you two to battle it out for domestic supremacy I have to be going, thanks for breakfast Ava. I'll stay in touch, and I'll let you know if I hear anything new."

She looked at Terry. "I've put a new team on Terry, so don't worry, no-one will be posting any more notes through Ava's door. There is also a surveillance team over at St Michael's cemetery. We'll be informed immediately if she appears there."

As Polly reached the door she said, "I know how frustrating this must be for you Terry, but believe me this is the best chance we have of capturing her. If, for some reason she fails to appear at the cemetery, then I honestly believe we'll have lost her forever, she'll be off somewhere...but she will appear, I just know it."

"Is that a statement Polly, or a prayer?"

"A bit of both Terry, I'll be in touch soon. I have to go and sort something out first."

Mercer looked at his superior. "Don't be too hard on him Polly, he's just lost his best friend."

Polly smiled. "I won't Terry, but this bitch is proving hard enough to apprehend without Mister Phillips throwing spanners into the works all over the place. I'm going to give him something to think about, his actions could have destroyed our plans completely...stupid bugger."

"Polly, he's vulnerable, don't go too far, he's just like me now, me and Phillips have finally got something in common, neither of us have anyone to care for us."

"Listen to this pathetic specimen Polly" said Ava, "nice try again Terry, now start taking these plates over to the sink!"

## HENSLEWOOD ROAD. BURLINGTON.

## LONDON.

Polly Sheppard opened the gate at the side of Andy Phillips's garage, having got no reply after ringing his door-bell three times. His garden was very well kept, even for this time of year. Everything looked like it had been carefully planned out, and although she was no horticulturist she could tell that there would be a blaze of colour come the spring.
She heard the sound of an electric tool being used somewhere at the back of the house, like a sander or a grinder of some description.
As she approached Andy's rather over-sized workshop the volume increased. The workshop door was open. She looked inside to find Andy clad in a bottle-green boiler-suit complete with mouth mask and protective goggles. He was sanding down a coffee table which looked to her to have been skilfully crafted. He was obviously a very keen DIY enthusiast. Polly stood at the door waiting for Andy to switch off the sander. When he finally did, she cleared her throat and was about to say, someone is a very clever boy, but she only got the first two words out.
Andy dropped the sander with fright.
"Jesus fucking Christ what!!"
"Sorry did I startle you Andy?"
"Fucking hell Polly, what the fuck? Christ Jesus I nearly had a heart attack. What the hell's wrong, I put my sheet in, they know I'm taking a couple of weeks off, Christ almighty!"
"We need to have a little chat Andy, can we go inside I'm getting rather cold standing here."
"Yeah no problem, I'll make us a cup of tea, hell Polly you shouldn't creep up on people like that." He took off his goggles and mouth mask.
"I didn't creep up Andy, I've been standing here for about five minutes now, it's not nice Andy is it? When people just appear

suddenly and unexpectedly remember when I was in my car and you thumped the window like Thor."

"That was completely unintentional Polly, I didn't mean to startle you."

"I didn't mean to startle *you* Andy."

"Come on, come in."

Polly followed Andy Phillips through his conservatory which had an abundance of beautiful potted plants, all neatly perched on well-crafted miniature tables. If he had made these, then he was more than just an ordinary enthusiast. He seemed to be a very skilled man, unlike the man she had just broken up with, he couldn't even change a light bulb, or rewire a plug.

He was however exceptionally good at removing the undergarments of desired women, he had a masters' degree in that department. "Good luck to him, he is no longer my concern."

A couple of minutes later Polly and Andy Phillips sat at his kitchen table each with a cup of tea. Polly was thinking to herself that he was calm and collected considering what he'd just done to Terry Mercer, and his fellow colleagues.

"Would you like a biscuit Polly" he said, opening a tartan cookie jar.

"I never eat the bloody things, it's a habit of mine, Helen used to like them. I just find myself buying them when I shop. I don't know why I buy them, it's not as if she's coming back."

Polly detected a break in his voice towards the end of his sentence.

"How long has it been Andy?"

He took a sip from his mug. "Coming up for six years, they say that time is a great healer Polly, well not for me, it feels more like six weeks. The pain won't go away, Christ I keep her slippers at her side of the bed, still have her dressing gown hanging in the wardrobe, bloody bath-salts and everything."

"It must be very difficult for you Andy, with your girls living abroad."

"The girls Polly, yeah, I never hardly hear from them. Oh I phone them or talk to them through the internet, but if I don't contact them first, well I eh, I don't think they'd bother, of course they've got their own lives to lead, I can't expect them to put me at the top of their to do lists. It's just me Polly, I miss Helen so much. Is there

such a thing as loving somebody too much Polly?"
"I don't know, but if there is, don't beat yourself up about it.
I think Andy, if it had been the other way around and you had gone first, she would be feeling the very same as you feel now, you obviously loved each other very much."
Andy sighed, nodding his head. She spotted a tear in his eye.
She decided to give him some time to compose himself.
"Andy, may I use your bathroom please?"
Andy bounced up from his chair as if he'd suddenly been jolted with an electric shock.
"Of course Polly, let me show you where it is.
Even in the bathroom Andy had kept some of Helen's things.
Skin cream, talcum powder the body sprays, all kinds of beauty products, ornaments and trinkets, things that women buy to put that finishing touch to a room, that special skill, that only women could apply. She had read somewhere that men who had lost their wives would use things like perfume sprays, deodorants, things like that. They would spray the perfumes around the house. It was like they were still there. It helped them, it calmed them, reassured them. She wondered if that was what Andy was doing, like he didn't want Helen's memories to fade, as if he feared that one morning he would awaken and not think about her. He would feel that he had betrayed her, hence the slippers and the dressing gown. Did Andy have other issues though? Why would he do that to Terry? He must have known what Terry had been through, Sam would have surely discussed it with him, but, whatever his issues, and no matter how sorry she felt for him, she was here on official business, and the subject would have to be dealt with. When she returned to the kitchen, Andy was standing in his conservatory with his back to her.
"Do you see this Polly?" he said, pointing to something outside in his garden. Polly stepped into the conservatory and joined him.
"That rose over there, the one in the middle. That was the first thing we bought for the garden when we first purchased this house, Helen chose it. That was twenty-two years ago Polly, and it produced the most beautiful red roses you'll ever see.
Every year, without fail for seventeen years."

He sighed and looked at Polly. "I am going to tell you something that I haven't told anyone, apart from Sam, probably because they'd all think I was making it up."

He took another sip from his best-husband-in-the-world mug, and then, holding the mug in both of his hands he nodded with his head referring to the rose. "Helen was buried on the twenty-ninth of July Polly. I went out there on the morning of her funeral. All of those rose bushes out there were in full bloom, they were beautiful, especially our rose, with its' lovely deep red blossoms. Two days later, our rose began to deteriorate. I couldn't understand it, greenfly hadn't got it, slugs, nothing. The other roses beside it were fine, they continued to flourish." He finished off what was left in his mug, and then said, "She hasn't bloomed since, five years Polly, and not a single flower. The plant isn't dead, there is nothing scientifically wrong with her, it's just, when it gets near the time for blooming, she just seems to shut down, her leaves are perfectly healthy, the buds are there, but then nothing. All the other roses around it all come to life in their own spectacular way. Strange don't you think Polly?" He smiled and looked at her again.

" Sam told me once, that it was Helen, and she was letting me know, that she refused to let it bloom again until she could see that I was happy. Once I get myself out of the doldrums and start to live again, then she'll let it bloom...the silly bugger. Anyway, I'm glad you're here because it gives me the chance to apologise for my behaviour, I've been-"

"Andy, I need to talk to you-"

"Please Polly, let me finish, and I apologise for interrupting you. It's just that I've been doing a lot of soul-searching lately, and I've been looking at my behaviour, particularly my attitude at work. I've been short tempered with my men, snapping and biting at them like a bloody puff-adder. Terry Mercer as well, I've been really unfair to him. Hell I go on about how much I miss Helen, but Helen's gone, she's dead. Sam told me how Carol had left Terry, and took his bloody lad away from him as well. I don't know what that pain must feel like, to wake up in the mornings, knowing that somewhere out there in the world , the woman you love still exists, only she's lying in another man's arms, laughing and talking about every-day things, planning out their lives, as if Terry Mercer had never even existed...and his boy? He must wonder how his kid is doing, I think Sam said the boy would be ten or eleven now. I moan about my daughters not contacting me enough, but they have jobs and they have husbands, and most of all Polly, they have happiness and contentment. They are living out their lives with the people they love, poor Terry, doesn't even know where his wife and son are. According to Sam, she hasn't even filed for divorce. Is she happy? Is his boy happy? Is he doing well at school? Does his mother treat him appropriately? Does the lad now have a strict step-father? All these things that I took for granted Polly. I saw my daughters grow up right in front of me. I was there when they performed in their first nativity play at school, I saw them growing from children into adolescence, and then into young women. That poor bugger is missing out on all that. I'm going to make amends with him Polly, I feel so sorry for him. You know all that cursing and swearing he does? Well that's just a front. He refuses to let the world see how he's hurting, he puts on this hard-as-nails act, but believe me Polly, that boy is hurting bad. This crazy bitch who is murdering his partners isn't helping his cause. Off the record Polly, keep an eye out for him, he may look like he's coping, a man can only take so much, just keep an eye out for him."

Polly wasn't one hundred percent certain that what Andy was saying was genuine. She decided to tackle the matter in hand with a cold-as-ice attitude and with a sledgehammer approach.

She would watch for a reaction in his face, and so, with both hands firmly on the heavy hammer, she said," Andy, why did you send that note to Terry, making out that it was from Rosalyn Simpson?"

He looked at her with a puzzled expression.

"A note?"

"Yes Andy, a note, you put a note through Ava Cruntze's letter-box didn't you. You were trying to torture Terry further weren't you, telling him how stupid he was, only burying the coffin a couple of feet into the ground, and how hopelessly incompetent he was, or words to that effect."

Phillips stared into her eyes. "Is that why you're here Polly? Someone has sent Terry a note, and you automatically think it's me who's sent it?" Once again he sighed, this time with exasperation.
" You fucking bitch. I've just opened my heart out to you Polly, about things that are really dear to me and things that are tearing me apart inside. I have been a criminal forensic officer for over twenty years and have seen sights that you would not be able to gaze upon without turning out your stomach. I have been professional and have done my job to the best of my abilities, and have applied myself into that job one hundred per-cent, but if you think that I would lower myself to do something like that, that I would even consider doing something like that, to a fellow officer, then obviously your opinion of me as a human being...well, I'm actually stuck for words. Even when I misunderstood Terry Mercer, and yes, hated him, I would never dream of lowering myself to that level. You obviously think differently. You are not welcome here anymore, don't ever come back here, just fuck off, go away and die somewhere you fucking bitch, thinking I would do that."
"Andy, I had to ask you, I have to find out, I didn't-"
"Just fuck off Polly would you, I don't want to talk to you anymore. Get me sacked, I don't care, I couldn't give a fuck about you or the fucking job. You give the best years of your life to the force, and then, one day, your chief inspector accuses you of something so despicable, it beggars belief. Just fuck off and don't ever come back here. How the fuck could you, of all people think for one second that I would do something like that, just fuck off!!"
Andy Phillips walked out of his conservatory, throwing the mug that Helen had bought him onto the paved area, and making it smash into a thousand pieces. He made his way over to the rose he'd told her about. Either he was a better actor than Lawrence Olivier or this man was completely innocent.
As Polly reached the gate, she heard the sander being started up again. As she climbed back into her car, she said,
"I'm so sorry Andy, I will make this up to you."
As she started the car she thought to herself, If Sam had meant what he'd said to Andy about the flowers, then, because of what

she had just said to him, there wouldn't be much chance of Helen's rose coming into bloom this year either.

## BETHWELL STREET.

## AVA CRUNTZE'S APARTMENT.

Terry sat in his room smoking a cigarette and studying the notes that he and Sandra Neal had put together. "Poor bugger, she'd been telling the truth all along." He cursed himself for his initial reaction at the news of her `suicide`.
Without giving the matter any thought he'd gone in to one of his tempers and called the woman everything, accusing her of cowardice and taking the easy way out. In hind-sight, when he thought about it, he'd reacted like that because of fear and frustration. It was about *him*. It was because she'd left him on his own again. He'd been very selfish, condemning his actions as immature to say the least. Sandra had been right concerning everything she'd said about the killer, the money, the life-style, everything."
He found himself wandering back in time to when he was a teenager in Montgomery High in Leicester. What the hell had he done to deserve this? Surely he wasn't the first kid to go out with other girls behind his girlfriend's back. Why had it made such an impact on her so early in her adult life? It was like Sam said though, she wasn't just an ordinary sixteen-year-old school girl, and whether or not it had been detected at that point of her life, she quite obviously had some serious mental health problems.
He hadn't noticed any deficiencies. There didn't seem to be any abnormalities in her behavioural patterns when things had been alright between them, although there had been one or two mood swings, sudden mood swings, but he'd put that down to her menstrual-cycle. A smile formed on his face as he read one of Sandra's foot-notes. : *Must remember to rub Terry up about Kathlene Oconnor's infatuation with him. That wee Irish girlie would bed him in a minute "Over my dead body".*
The smile disappeared from his face. Terry suddenly felt alone again. Sandra's last words on her foot-notes, albeit in jest, Over my

dead body. He lay down on the single bed.
Billy, Sandra, and now Sam, when would this crazy woman stop? Would she stop now that she thought he was dead?
Only time would give him the answers to these questions.
He needed to get out. He needed fresh air. He would ask Polly if she would get him some kind of disguise, but he had to get out of here, even if it was just for a couple of hours.
He lay back looking up at the ceiling.
God knows where that sick woman was now. She's probably just travelled there only to post her letter and throw the police a red herring. At this point of time he couldn't care if she was next door, he needed to get out of here it was as simple as that.
He heard Ava entering the house. When he got down stairs she was standing in the kitchen, shaking water from her coat and cursing the weather. He made her a cup of tea and both of them sat down at the kitchen table.
"Why are you not out working Ava?"
"I have to stay here with you remember? I think Polly was spooked after the letter and everything, she went to town with that surveillance team I can tell you that."
Terry scowled, "It's that stupid bugger Andy Phillips, huh, the man just does not like me Ava, although I've done nothing to him."
"Are you sure? Maybe you've bedded one of his girlfriends in the past or maybe even his wife before he met her."
Terry frowned at her.
"I'm only saying Terry that's all, you know what you're like." Mercer got up from his chair and put his empty mug into the basin.
"Fuck you Ava."
As he was leaving the kitchen she said, "Perhaps you will Terry, but not just now, the time isn't right yet. Perhaps once we have this monster out of the way we can review the situation."
Mercer stopped in his tracks, hardly able to contain his temper.
"What the fuck are you saying Ava, don't you think I have enough shit to deal with?"
"I didn't think I was shit Terry."
"You know what I mean. I know what I'm like you say? Yes I do Ava,

I do know what I'm like, but you don't. You're like so many others over there in Scotland Yard, you think you know me, but you haven't got a clue, and what was all that shit about our relationship only ever being a working one? Now you're telling me to give it time, and maybe I'll be able to bed you. Is that what you think I'm about?
Is that what you think, that I spend all of my time trying to bed women? I'll tell you what takes up most of my thoughts. I spend most of my time wondering how my little boy is doing, and how his mother took him away from me with no clue as to why.
 Most couples when they break up come to some kind of arrangement for access to the children, but oh no, not for me, not for Terry fucking Mercer. He kisses his boy goodnight one evening, and without any warning whatsoever, he never sees him again. That's the kind of things I think about Ava, that's what I'm like, and I still fucking love her, can you believe that? After all she's done to me, I still love her. If she walked in that door right now, I wouldn't even ask her where or why, because I just can't stop loving her, there, there's the truth. You want to know what I'm like, well I've just told you about everything I have ever cared for in the world. Sandra Neal was the first woman in five years that I had been out with, five years. I kept thinking that Carol would come back. Five years, and yet all you lot refer to me as a womaniser, well, thanks for all of your moral support, you bunch of hypocrites."
He left the kitchen and headed to his bedroom. Ava sat at her table feeling lower than she had ever felt in her entire life…almost.
"Terry I didn't mean anything-"
"Fuck you Ava. It's nice to know you have the backing from your friends and colleagues. Gives you a sense of pride in the job you do."

## SCOTLAND YARD.

## BROADWAY VICTORIA.

Polly Sheppard had summoned every officer working on the Rosalyn Simpson case into one of the conference rooms, and anyone who'd had anything to do with the fake burial of Terry Mercer, including Andy Phillips. In total there were twenty-four officers in the room when Polly and Tony Chrysler the chief of police entered.
Polly removed her jacket and laid it upon the table in front of her. She stared around the table at each individual, as if she was seeking out the guilty party before she had even began to speak.
Eventually, she sat down beside Chrysler who was busy studying a file in front of him. There was silence in the room as the twenty-four officers around the table sat waiting to hear what this meeting was about. The vast majority of them had no idea.
She cleared her throat.
"One of you, at least one, have just about come to the end of your career. One of you is a traitor and a disgrace to the force and everything that Scotland Yard stands for. I know first-hand about all the corruption that goes on within your little groups.
I have witnessed money changing hands in order for a blind eye to be turned. I've seen large quantities of confiscated drugs being sold off to the very people we are supposed to be eliminating.
I said nothing, not because I didn't want to, but because I knew if I did, I would be out on my arse within a month of my report. Corruption, the place is rife with it. Well, now that I am chief inspector, I no longer have to keep my mouth shut. I call the shots now. I suppose that a few of you voted for me to replace Sam Hargrieves because you thought that I'd be easy-going and that I'd continue to turn a blind eye on everything that goes on out there. I'm afraid you're all in for a shock. The corruption stops, as from here and now. That means that any confiscated drugs that are bound for the incinerator will go exactly there. There will be no more selling them off to your buyers at cut-down prices. If it is no

longer required for legal purposes, then it gets incinerated, all of it. Furthermore, I do not want to hear any tales of officers bribing prostitutes for their services in order to keep them out of the courts. It all stops today, and it stops for good. I'll ignore everything that has happened prior to today, accepting the fact that some of you were in a similar position to mine and had no option but to keep quiet."

She sighed heavily as she continued staring around the table.

"One of you however, has already stepped way too far over the line. There will be no reprieve for you, whoever you are. There will be no escape. You have let your fellow officers down and you have let yourself down, because, very shortly you'll be...out on your arse. As detectives our lives are in danger from time to time depending upon what we're investigating. Some of our ghost workers have to live among this scum in order to win their trust.

They have to become just like them. Their lives are at risk practically every day of the week. Some of them have no contact with their families for months on end. Perhaps one of you in here will be skilled enough one day to become a ghost. First of all though, you have to prove yourself. You have to prove you are worthy and devoted and dedicated to your work."

Again Polly looked around the table, careful not to stare at any one person for too long. "One of you in here today is dedicated to bringing Terry Mercer down. Only the guilty party or parties will know what I'm talking about, and only the guilty party will know why they are doing it. However, I will give them one chance to walk away from their job with some dignity. If you post me an e-mail or send me a note telling me your name and rank, and the reason you have done this, then I will not hold back on any references for any future employment, in fact I will enhance your chances. If you don't, then when we find you, expect to be dealt with harshly, and I mean harshly. This is your last chance of leaving here with any dignity. Have the guts to be decent just for once in your life. Believe me, it would be the best thing you could do for yourself, otherwise I will make your life a living hell, you are all dismissed."

Gradually the officers made their way out of the conference hall.

"Do you think they'll own up Polly?" said Chrysler rising to his feet.
"No chance Tony but at least they'll know we're on to them and that we know it wasn't Rosalyn Simpson who sent the letter."
"Why the hell would they do it Polly in the first place?"
"God knows, jealousy perhaps, or some grudge, who knows."
Polly spotted Andy Phillips making his way out of the hall.
"Andy? Could I have a word with you please?"
Tony Chrysler who was placing a document into his briefcase looked up suddenly as Andy Phillips replied,
"You can go and fuck yourself, that's what you can do, go and lie in your piss."
"Phillips!!" roared Chrysler, "get your arse up here now!"
"Oh you've got me quivering in my boots Tony boy, send me my termination form in the post, see if I care, I've had enough of the fucking lot of you, you bunch of fucking clowns that you are, and don't bother coming to my house Polly either, I may not be responsible for my actions, I might take my sander across your arse."
Before Chrysler had a chance to say anything else, Polly told him that it was alright and that she would deal with it.
"I know what this is all about Tony, leave him, I'll deal with him."
Chrysler's face was burning with rage. "Well you make sure that you do Polly, because I've had it up to the back teeth of my staff talking to their superiors in this manner, bloody Terry Mercer and now this? Talking to us like we were bloody dogs, I've had enough Polly."
"It's alright Tony, he'll apologise eventually."
"Eventually? Polly, he should be made to apologise right now."
"Tony, the man is at the point of a nervous breakdown, I'll have to deal with him with kid gloves, he's on the verge Tony, Christ he's just lost his best friend in the world...the man is down."
Chrysler closed his briefcase and began to walk out of the room.
"I mean it Polly, even if he apologises I want him punished for his outburst. Hell, we're all vexed at what's happened to our officers, that's no excuse for him to speak to his superiors in such a way, you make sure you punish him Polly, or I will."
Chrysler left the room. Polly stood looking at the door, thinking,

"Andy is already being punished beyond belief Tony, if only you could see. Terry Mercer and Andy Phillips are not so far apart. One of them has lost their wife for good, and the other has lost his wife for no good reason."

## CHAPTER TWELVE.

## SOUTHPORT.

## SEAFRONT HOTEL.

It had taken Rosalyn Simpson a couple of days to get down here from Glasgow, choosing to use public transport instead of driving. It was much safer for her, and allowed her to change routes in an instant. She had gone all the way over to Dundee to post Veronica's letter, and upon her return to Glasgow she'd booked into a different hotel. She was going over Terry Mercer's suicide note in her head. The emotional confession he'd made, admitting that she had been the best thing in his life, and how he had still loved her. She stood at her hotel bedroom window now, looking down onto the shore. She imagined deck chairs and towels strewn across the beach in the summer months, people swimming, children building sand-castles, eating iced lollies and playing beach-ball games.
It would be a very busy little town in the summer time.
Today though, five days before Christmas, the beach was deserted, save for a couple who were out walking their Golden Labrador. She smiled to herself as the wind blew off the man's hat, and the dog taking off with it in its' mouth, thinking it's master was playing a game. She came away from the window and took a seat on one of the three chairs in her bedroom. The hotel wasn't the classiest by any stretch of the imagination, but it was clean and it was adequate. It served her immediate purpose. Her mobile phone buzzed on the double bed. She picked it up to read the message that had been sent to her. It was from her `source` in Scotland Yard. She'd been expecting a message, but certainly not the one she was about to receive. The last couple of days had been spent thinking about herself and Terry Mercer, and of all the things they could have achieved together, if only he'd made good to his promise to love her only for the rest of his life.
She'd spent the best part of the last couple of days feeling

melancholy and brooding at *her* loss, smoking a cigarette at her bedroom window, which she had opened, and enjoying the cup of tea she had made herself. Her expression changed completely as she read the message.

"*I expect to be rewarded handsomely for the following information, are you ready? Terry Mercer is not dead. It was all a hoax to fool you. Send my payment to the usual bank account. Oh, and by the way, in case you think that you no longer need to pay me, I happen to know that you're staying in the Seafront hotel in Southport. I'll be keeping an eye on you, and as long as you keep my payments coming, I shall keep you informed as to what they are up to. As it stands now, they're expecting you to visit the cemetery to pay your last respects to Terrance Mercer esquire. It's up to you how you respond to this information, bye for now.*

Filled with rage, she picked up the newspaper which contained Mercer's `suicide` note. A wry smile formed on her face.

"You really think you're a smart boy don't you mister. When are you going to learn? Well, I'll have to hurt you some more then, won't I, one way or another, you're coming back to me Terry Mercer, but first you must learn a lesson. I'll just keep taking people away from you, until you are truly on your own, then you'll learn the errors of your ways."

She took out the ring that Terry had bought for her all those years ago, and studied it. She remembered the day he'd placed it on her finger, and kissed her passionately in her bedroom. Although she was frustrated at the thought of being outwitted by him, she couldn't help but feel at least slightly exhilarated at the thought of him still being alive, because this meant that her dreams were as well. "You swear an oath of love to Rosalyn mister, then you keep it." She had another problem now. Her source had someone watching her. They were collaborating with someone else.

How else would they know she was here. She was being tailed, and the fact that she was being tailed meant that they could more or less call the tune. In effect, what she'd been doing to Terry Mercer all these years was now being done to her.

Somehow she would have to gain the confidence of this person and arrange a meeting...in person. Harder than it sounded because whoever this was that was giving her the information were putting themselves at great risk, not only from their job but indeed their lives. Scotland Yard had ways and means of disposing of unwanted trash that much she knew.

She sat back down on her bed and contemplated her informant. Already she knew their personality. A back-stabber, an instigator, a turn-coat, selfish, greedy, but full of self-confidence, at least outwardly phlegmatic, but with an eye as keen as a Tercel to spot an opportunity. She had to ask herself some questions as well. Why was this individual so keen to give her the required information about one of their fellow colleagues?

Had Terry Mercer done something against them? Was it merely jealousy that drove them to try and aid his downfall? Or was it just simply that they spotted an opportunity to enhance their bank account with super-speed. And was their intention to lead her along until they felt they'd taken enough of her money and, then set a trap in which they would become something of a hero in the force, after all, they had her where they wanted her. They knew where she was. Her plans involving Mercer would have to be put on hold for the time being, there were more important issues to be dealt with. If she couldn't arrange a meeting with this person then she was the one being played along, not Terry Mercer. Was there more than one tail involved? Was she being followed around the clock? If she was, then they'd have known that she'd been in Glasgow, and Dundee, and anywhere else she'd laid her head. Someone was playing games with *her*, and now it was an absolute necessity to find out who they were. They had started this little charade by contacting her with juicy snippets of facts about Mercer, and she had unwittingly climbed right into the spider's web of deceit.

" Well then, I'll just have to offer the spider something irresistible to entice them down into their own parlour."

BETHWELL STREET.

AVA CRUNTZE'S APARTMENT.

Ava tapped lightly on Terry's bedroom door. Like so many others she'd been wrong about him, and in so many different ways.
"Terry? May I come in? I wish to apologise to you for my stupidity."
"It's your house, although I won't be staying in it after tonight."
"Terry, I'm deeply sorry." Ava opened the door and stepped into the room. He was sitting looking at the photograph of himself and Carol and his son Daniel. Ava pulled a seat up beside his and placed one hand on his shoulder, half expecting him to throw it off.
He didn't.
"I haven't known you for that long Terry, but already I have misjudged you. I am sorry for that, and from what I can gather, I am not the first in the department to do that. I knew you were hiding something painful, and you are good at convincing people that nothing gets to you. I could see from the beginning that you were anything but gregarious, and I know that if you were permitted to, you would work on your own. You hide your pain well Terry, and now that I know just what that pain is, then I sympathise with you, I think I told you that once before, but I had no idea that it was ripping you apart the way it is. Now I fully understand your outward audaciousness, in fact, you use it like a self-protective weapon, and I now understand why you do. No-one else in the world is going to hurt you the way Carol has. Just for a few days though, Sandra Neal did, until the truth came out about how she died. No wonder you're hurting the way you are, you're getting absolutely no reprieves whatsoever. Everywhere you turn there are people criticising you, or condemning you, and like I just done there, judging you. It will never happen again Terry, I give you my word, whether or not you wish to work with me in the future or not. I will never do that again to you, or anyone else for that matter."
Terry placed the photograph back on to the bedside table.
"I shouldn't let it get to me Ava, but it does. Maybe if I didn't have a

son I would feel different, I don't know, but I still feel like I love her the same as the day we got married, that's why it hurts so much, and I am not convinced that she didn't love me when she left, but therein lies my stupidity...she did leave me, so she couldn't possibly love me could she."

"Maybe she did still love you Terry, but maybe she fell in love with someone else who she loved more, it's possible."

"Who knows Ava, she's gone and she's been gone for some time now, so I should just move on. Even if she sent me a letter telling me not to worry about Daniel, and that he's doing fine without me, even that would help me...but nothing, absolutely nothing...it's fucking torture Ava."

Ava rose to her feet smiling softly at Terry.

"It's a cruel world Mister Mercer, a very cruel world. I have something that I lock away as well. My mother left my father because of all the beatings she received. No-one could blame her for that, but at least she could have taken me with her, but she didn't, and I would never forgive her for that. I was fourteen years old Terry. My father treated me like shit. I was his slave and the target for all of his frustrations and anger.

I was a slut like my mother, and a tramp, a whore and a painted wretch. I had to hide the bruises before I could go to school some days. And then came the day, at the grand old age of fourteen years and thirty-one days, I lost my virginity. My drunken father Terry, not even a step-father, my father, my blood-father and two of his drunken associates took my virginity away from me.

The ordeal lasted more than four hours. It haunts me to this day. I knew someone who could get me across to Britain. I heard that my mother was over here, she had a sister in London. I came over here and stayed with my aunt Agnes until I could find her. I needn't have bothered. My mother made it clear to my aunt that she didn't want anything to do with me and that I would have to learn to stand on my own two feet...and so I did Terry.

Yes, it's a cruel world.

Now I am going down stairs to make a pot of tea. I'll be honoured if you will join me Mister Mercer, so that we may sit together reminiscing this and that, what do you say you nasty scoundrel." Terry Mercer and Ava Cruntze stood in a locked embrace for more than two minutes, not kissing or whispering sweet-nothings to each other, but just holding on and crying their eyes out, as if their very lives depended upon it, and in many ways, it did.

## SCOTLAND YARD.

## BROADWAY VICTORIA.

Officer John Smedley had many duties to perform around the various offices in the department where he worked, including delivering coffees and other assorted beverages to the staff on request, and taking messages for otherwise busy colleagues. Today however, John Smedley was about to discover something, albeit serendipitously that could enhance his career and gain him respect from his colleagues. The forensic officer to which he was now delivering the bottle of orange-juice to, had momentarily abandoned their desk and left their computer on.

Smedley was a devoted officer and had never been tempted to read anyone's private mail, not only for fear of facing the consequences, but also for honour and self-esteem. However, the flashing word URGENT on the officer's screen convinced him to press the reveal button.

The e mail read; *I now know who you are, and as you can see, I also have your e mail address. If you know what's good for you, you will call off your tails immediately. You will also meet me tonight in The Pilgrims Rest at 9.30. If you fail to appear, then I guarantee you that your career will be well and truly over by this time tomorrow. I have paid you a handsome amount for the information you gave me concerning Mister Terrance Mercer, and I will continue to pay you, if you comply with my instructions. You have made a huge mistake my friend in trying to bribe me and frighten me. However, I am prepared to let sleeping dogs lie if you do as I ask. Also, if you are stupid enough to bring anyone else with you tonight, even if you think they are out of sight,(I'll have people watching) then the deal will be off, and you will be exposed, and your friends will be executed. Please note that this is not an idle threat. I am deadly serious, see you at 9.30.*

Smedley quickly flicked the screen to where it had been and left the desk. He was shaking from head to toe. This was big. This was

serious, it was huge. Some of the officers in the department began shouting out to him, demanding their beverages and telling him to `get his finger out` and wake up.
He finished delivering the drinks and then made his way to the latrines.
He had to calm himself down. He splashed his face with cold water several times and dried it with paper towels.
"Jesus Christ" he now knew who the snitch was. This officer was the traitor. He had worked under them for short spells.
They were regarded with the highest of respect, and here he was, with the information that would bring their career to a shocking end. He had no idea where Polly Sheppard was but was informed that she'd be away for at least three days.
This couldn't wait for three days. The trouble was, there was no-one in here that he could trust, not with this, and what did the e mail say? Call off your tails? So, there was more than one traitor involved. There was only two people who he could really trust and they were Terry Mercer and Ava Cruntze, and he knew there was little chance of any of them making an appearance in here in the near future. Somehow, he would have to get the information to them.
He couldn't phone Ava's house because all the lines were bugged. He couldn't trust surveillance to get the message to them, for obvious reasons. What the hell could he do? He would have to think about this at home. He was due to be going off duty at three o clock this afternoon. He would have a few hours to come up with some kind of plan. Still reeling from the revelation of who the guilty party was, he stared into the bathroom mirror at his reflection. His face was almost crimson. He almost jumped out of his skin as two detectives came bursting into the toilet, almost knocking the door off its' hinges. He had seen them around the offices but had no idea of their names. One of them, a tall man who reminded him of the character Basil Fawlty shouted out loud to him.
"What the fuck's wrong with you smiggy, you've not been wanking off in here have you? You look flushed bum-boy, you haven't got one of your fellow cadet's in one of those cubicles have you?

You want to suck cock boy, then you do it in your own time, you're looking flushed as fuck, you've been up to something phlegm-wad, come on, spit it out, the sperm I mean."

Smedley responded in his usual humble manner by smiling and taking the insult on the cheek. He was used to the verbal onslaught directed to him throughout the course of his working day, and had grown innocuous to the insults.

The other detective, who was about five ten in height and who was built quite solidly with shaven head and a day old growth around his chin, looked a bit like Phil Collins the rock singer.

His cream suit had seen better days and hadn't seen a drycleaners for some time. He turned to look at Smedley as he urinated.

"You keep your eyes off my John Thomas Smiggy do you hear me? I've heard all about you toilet-boys. You'll be offering me aftershave and shoe-shine you cunt that you are. Get yourself away to fuck out of here, you're making me nervous lady boy. There's plenty of nice ladies out there in the offices around you, so get out there and try and lay one of them instead of sniffing me and Joe's cocks in here like the fucking male whore that you are. Huh, detective? You couldn't detect a fucking wet day, go on, get to fuck out of here, can't piss now 'cause you've got me guarding my arse with my back to you. You're flushed about something...you're a wanking bastard, now get to fuck!"

John Smedley stepped back in to his work place. The officer whom he discovered was the snitch had returned to their desk. He began to make his way to the other side of the offices when the two detectives returned from the bathroom, and much to his dread, one of them, the one who looked like `Phil Collins` began to shout out to everyone; "Hey everybody, we just caught Smiggy in there pulling one off for Polly. He's got a photograph of Polly Sheppard and he goes in there to bang one off the wrist, look how flushed he is. He's Polly's frock-boy and dogs-body and he's infatuated with her. He can only go so long before he has to go in there and relieve himself, look at him, he's Polly's little ass-wipe so he is. You'll go blind boy, you will, you'll have to find yourself a proper girlfriend kiddo instead of making love to girls in magazines and photographs. Can none of you ladies here help him out for goodness sakes, the poor boy can't get any work done for thinking about Polly Sheppard. He's been in there sniffing a pair of Polly's knickers, and where he's got them is anyone's guess, and stroking off, me and Joe had to make him clean the floor up, bloody jizz everywhere, look at him, it's no good feeling embarrassed boy, if you've got a sexual hang-up about Polly, you'll just have to see her and explain to her that you're infatuated...maybe she'll help you out there.

Now, go and get me and Joe a coffee and don't take all day about it, and no stopping off in any of the other bathrooms on your way there, come on move, two coffees, today."

John Smedley made his way red-faced and embarrassed as usual to one of the canteens to get the detectives their coffees.

He would take all the flack dished out to him just now, it was part and parcel of the job, but some day, one day he'd have his revenge on them, and not just verbally. His karate lessons were coming on fine and he'd reached his black-belt status. He was going further than that though. He was taking advanced lessons now and was aiming for his fifth Dan. As it was he was almost certain that he could have taken the two officers who had just ribbed him, without losing breath. He could have embarrassed them, but then that would be the end of his career. No, there was plenty of time to put them right, and when he did, he would make sure there was no-one else in the vicinity. Meanwhile he had a lot of thinking to do.

The first thing he had to find out, was where this Pilgrims Rest was. If he couldn't get word to Ava or Terry, he would have no alternative but to go there himself and watch from a safe distance. The threat on the e mail about having them `watched` would mean that he'd have to be extremely careful. He'd have to wear some kind of disguise, and it would have to be very convincing, or he and the snitch would be lying dead in some ditch by the morning...or standing up at the bottom of the Thames wearing concrete shoes.

## BETHWELL STREET.

## AVA CRUNTZE'S APARTMENT.

Polly Sheppard had made a brief appearance at Ava's apartment and had praised her and Terry for their patience, particularly Terry, because she understood how difficult this was for him to be stuck indoors. Of all the detectives operating from Scotland Yard, Terry was probably the most active. Under normal circumstances he was a very hard man to find. What he was doing here was completely against his nature. She also assured him that it wouldn't be for much longer. They were expecting Rosalyn Simpson to pay a visit to the cemetery any day now.
The temptation would be too great for her not to at least observe his resting place, after all, she had spent so much of her time disrupting his life any way she could. For him to end his life this way would affect her, or at least her plans, quite drastically.
Her game was over.
She could do no more to hurt him. If she hadn't exacted enough revenge up until this point, then it was too late. Whatever way she looked upon it, Terry had inadvertently put a stop to her tortuous inflictions.
Polly left the apartment having informed her favourite detectives that she would be away for a couple of days, giving them a phone number where they could get in touch if there were any new developments. She also instructed Ava to work from HQ and observe any odd behaviour within the staff, particularly surveillance and forensics as she felt sure that the traitor worked for one or the other. Either way, Ava was to work from the inside. She couldn't afford to take any more chances with officers' lives and with Ava being the last one to work with Terry, there may be some kind of vindictive killing on Simpson's mind. She would have to take out her frustrations on someone. It wasn't going to be Ava Cruntze.
"I'm so sick of this Ava, I am. I've had it up to the back teeth, she's not going to show, I'm sure of it. I don't care what Polly is saying,

the woman is too intelligent to be pulled in with a stunt like this. She's spent years scrutinising my career and watching every move I make, she'll know that this is a trick."

Ava Cruntze and Terry Mercer sat in his room.

Polly's car would hardly be at the corner.

"Terry, you saw the letter she sent to that Victoria girl, she believes you're dead alright. I know you've got every reason to be pessimistic, but that's because we've never been this close to catching her before. Up until recently, it's been her calling the shots and causing the trauma, but now she's done.

Even if for some reason she doesn't attempt to visit your grave, her actions are now limited, she'll have to proceed with extreme caution. Apart from trying to destroy Terry Mercer's life, she has killed numerous police officers as well as three citizens, and that's only the ones we know about, God knows what else she's been up to on her travels. You mark my words Terry, her days are numbered."

"Two more days Ava, and then I'm out of here, whatever the situation, she can transfer me to another department somewhere else in the country, I just have to get out of here, never felt so bloody useless in all my life, sitting here smoking and drinking tea and coffee all day, my blood pressure must be hitting the roof."

"And what would I do then Terry, if you leave here to work somewhere else? I can't have that, and besides, Polly would never permit it, you're too valuable Mister Mercer."

"Ava, it's not just this sick bitch who's gunning for me remember, one of my own colleagues has it in for me as well, bad enough a bloody maniac chasing my arse, but I've got one of our own trying their best to fuck me up as well, at least one, there could be more."

"Terry, I promised you something at the beginning of our working relationship. I said I would protect you with my very life.

Nothing has changed there my friend. I will Terry, I will find out who it is who is collaborating with her and they will pay for their actions, trust me. Why do you think Polly wants me in there?

She knows I'll find them. In the meantime, let's just see what happens with the sicko, let's see if she visits the cemetery, because

I can tell you here and now, that if she does, and we catch her, I'll have the name or names of her accomplices faster than any woman can say Terry Mercer is a two-timing Casanova bastard."

He couldn't help but burst out laughing at Ava's comment. He sat shaking his head, smiling. "You're so fucking sweet Ava."

# CHAPTER THIRTEEN.

# SCOTLAND YARD.

# BROADWAY VICTORIA.

It was 2.40 pm and officer John Smedley was closing his locker in the changing rooms wondering how on earth he was going to manage to disguise himself convincingly enough to be able to observe proceedings in `The Pilgrims Rest`.
He'd discovered that the pub in question was in the district of Westminster. Ideally he would have liked to at least have scrutinised the place and find out what kind of clientele frequented the bar, at least then, he would have some kind of idea of what code of attire to wear. He had looked on the internet at the references but he knew that some places were not quite up to the standard of ratings that the internet had given them. This particular pub had a three star rating. A three star rating in Westminster meant that there was no way he could disguise himself as a junky or a down-and-out.
He would not even be permitted entry. Just at the point where he was beginning to panic, and as he was leaving the changing rooms, he witnessed a minor miracle. Ava Cruntze came walking down the corridor towards him. His troubles were over.
Now he could disclose his information in total confidence and privacy. There had been three different officers in the changing rooms and so he kept looking back to see if they were coming out behind him. As Ava approached him she could see that the young man in front of her was flustered about something. Again Smedley looked behind him and whispered to Ava, "Could I have a word with you in private please Miss Cruntze please." He kept looking behind him nervously at the changing room doors.
"Yes you may" she replied, "as long as it's about something important I am rather busy at the moment."
"Oh it is Miss, is there somewhere we can go where we won't be

disturbed." Again he looked at the doors of the changing rooms.
"Come with me" said Ava, wondering what on earth the young officer could possibly want a meeting with her for.
She about turned and began walking in the direction she'd came.
"Do you have some information for me Mister Smedley, I mean worth-while information."
"Yes Miss, I do. I have found something out which has totally shocked me. I knew you were with Mister Mercer in your apartment and there is no-one in here that I can trust, and when I inform you of what I know, you'll see what I mean, I am so glad you came in Miss Cruntze because I was at my wits end as to what to do."
Ava looked at the young man with curiosity as they made their way down the corridor. "This had better not be about someone stealing cakes out of the canteen Smedley, because you know if it is, I will kick you hard in the testicles, your eyes will water, I guarantee it."
"No Miss Cruntze it's not. This is crucial information, and I came across it quite accidently."
Smedley looked at his watch. "I'm afraid I'm not giving you much time to act on this information. I was about to proceed with a plan on my own and I wasn't even certain on how I was going to execute the plan if truth be known, I'm so glad you've arrived you've no idea."
Ava smiled at Smedley's choice of words particularly at the reference of her having `no idea`.
She stopped and knocked on a door before entering.
"Come in here Smedley, and get off your chest this bit of information you think is crucial, let's hear it."
She closed the door behind them.
"Take a seat Smedley, you have my undivided attention, and there's not many people who get that I can tell you, so, come on, spit it out, and I warn you here and now, it had better be important."
Fifteen minutes later officer John Smedley had unloaded all of the burdens that had been placed upon his shoulders.
"You've done well officer Smedley, very well indeed and I will personally see to it that you will be rewarded for your work."

She explained to him how important it was for him to carry on around the place like nothing had changed.

"Act normal" she had told him. "Don't do anything out of character...just be yourself, I will deal with everything from here on in, do you understand that Smedley?"

He said he did.

"If anyone asks you what you were talking to me about, tell them to mind their own business and refer them to me."

## THE PILGRIMS REST.

## WESTMINSTER. 10:15pm.

Ava Cruntze sat in her BMW parked about thirty-five metres down from the public house. The fact that Rosalyn Simpson would undoubtedly be armed meant that her colleagues within the pub would have to proceed with extreme caution.
Cruntze had selected a team from another area so that there would be little chance of any of the targets recognising anyone.
Three of that team were now in the pub enjoying a glass of beer and sitting only two tables away from their targets, laughing raucously at their pre-whispered joke.
The purpose of the raucous laughter was to annoy Misses Simpson into making some kind of comment to them, and therefore begin a conversation with them. Their plan worked.
"Do you mind? We're trying to have a private conversation here" said Simpson with venom.
One of the officers replied, smiling, "I am so sorry, we didn't mean to offend, it's just that we haven't seen each other in such a long time and I'm afraid we got carried away with our stories, sorry if we offended you, we apologise."
Simpson sighed. "It's alright, forget it."
She turned back round to face her companion at the table who sat smiling nervously and looking embarrassed.
"Excuse me" persisted the officer, "Allow me to buy you a drink for causing this distraction, it's the least I can do."
"Look" said Simpson, clearly tired of the situation. "We don't want any drinks thank you. Your apology has been accepted now please, just leave it at that will you? There's no need for any drinks. Now, do you mind if we continue with our private conversation?"
Once again she turned back round to face her companion.
The second officer now stepped into action. He had arisen from his chair and approached Simpson's table.
"Allow me to introduce myself, I am Andrew"-

"Look, I really couldn't care less who you are, or any of your childish colleagues for that matter, just leave this table immediately or I'll be forced to call on security, now please, go and sit down and at least try to behave like normal human beings...go and enjoy your reunion with your friends and leave us be, is that too much to ask, I mean I only asked you to keep your volume down."
"It's Ben's fault miss, he can't hold his drink you see, and as soon as he's confronted with beautiful women like yourself and your friend here, well, he can't help himself he really can't, let me get you a drink, it's-"
"I've had enough" said Simpson rising to her feet.
"I'm going outside for a cigarette" she said to her friend. She looked at the three men. "But before I do, I am going to make a formal complaint to the Landlord about these bafoons. I'll be back in five minutes."
She looked once more to the three gentlemen all standing now by her table.
"If you are not away from this table by the time I get back, then I assure you, you will regret ever being born, that's a promise."
The first officer then persisted. "Look, I know we've all got started on the wrong foot here, but honestly, we're nice guys, there's no need for all this hostility."
Rosalyn Simpson completely ignored the comment made to her by the third officer, and made her way out towards the back of the pub to have her very much needed cigarette.
There was a small cabin-like structure provided by the proprietor specifically for the smokers. Although open-ended it contained tables and chairs as well as ash trays and beer mats. One could have been easily mistaken that she had been transported back in time to a more civilised time in Britain, when people were allowed to make decisions for themselves and were able to choose whether or not they would like to smoke or not in a public house.
The smoking ban was supposed to cut down the number of people who had been contaminated by passive smokers and that it would cut down drastically, the number of cancer sufferers.
The fact remained though, that although cancer survival rates had

gone up, the actual number of people contracting the dreaded disease, had actually gone up.

"More bull-shit from the government then" she thought to herself. And that was another thing, cigarettes as far as she could remember, never used to stink the way they did today.

They were putting something in the tobacco these days that was making a cigarette stink to the high heavens. As she inhaled her cigarette she could feel her nerves being soothed and her temper calming down.

It didn't matter where you went these days, there would always be some idiot doing their utmost to spoil your evening. She wasn't going to be here for much longer anyway. She would tell her informant the situation and threaten her once again with her job if she as much as breathes another bad word in her direction.

She had already informed her of how lucky she was that she wasn't lying very still in some dark alley-way like a sewer rat.

What she needed now from her informant was the location of where Mister Terrence Mercer was residing. Once she had obtained that information there would be no need for any more correspondence. Rosalyn Simpson sipped her drink and smoked the rest of her cigarette completely unaware that as she did, her informant was being led outside to the waiting police van at the front of the pub by the annoying gentlemen who had so rudely interrupted their conversation. Simpson had half expected Kathlene Oconnor to follow her outside even though she didn't smoke.

"No doubt the bimbo bitch was being entertained by the baboons within, and probably accepting copious amounts of alcohol from the over-dressed clowns masquerading as men."

She stumped out her cigarette and drained her glass of the remaining vodka and coke and then made her way back in to the pub. Two of the men were still seated where they had been, but the other was gone, and so was Kathlene Oconnor.

Thinking perhaps that Oconnor had gone to the ladies room, Simpson made her way to the bar to order more drinks for herself and her `friend`. The young gentleman who was serving her informed her that her companion had to leave in a hurry and that

she would be in touch with her soon.
"Did she say where she was going? Did she leave any address?"
The smartly dressed young man only smiled and said "I'm afraid she didn't Miss, sorry."
Simpson sighed heavily. "Forget the drinks" she said dryly, and turned to leave the premises.
She had only taken a few steps outside of the pub when Ava Cruntze's arm grabbed her from behind, along with the annoying gentleman from the pub.
"Taxi for Simpson" Said Ava, as she clipped on the handcuffs around Rosalyn Simpson's wrists and relieved her of her handbag.
"At last, we meet, Miss Simpson, I've waited for so long for this privilege you've no idea honey. This has made my day, honestly. We've got your friend in another taxi and she's on her way to Scotland Yard even as we speak. I hope you enjoyed that drink in there Rosalyn, because it'll be your last for a very long time I can tell you that babes. Your game is up. Terry will be so pleased about this, he tells me he can hardly wait to have a conversation with you, you know, to catch up on everything that's been going on in your lives, he'll be so excited when I phone him now and tell him that we have you here, in the flesh."
Simpson said nothing. She only looked disdainfully at the officer who had annoyed her in the pub. An unmarked police van appeared from nowhere and pulled up directly in front of them.
"Come on then Rosalyn, time to book in to your new address honey. It won't be five-star accommodation I'm sure, but it will be your home for a very very long time…you'll soon settle in."
Still Simpson did not respond to the detective's sarcasm, but only turned to give her a wry smile as she was escorted into the vehicle. The cold look gave Ava Cruntze a strange kind of tingle down her spine, momentarily knocking all sense of humour from her.
It was a strange kind of look thought Ava to herself as she made her way back to her car. One that said, "Ok, I know you've caught me, but the game is far from over".
Ava tried to put all negative thoughts away from her mind. They'd caught her hadn't they? What possible damage could she

cause now?

All the way back to H.Q. Ava drove directly behind the police van. That last look Simpson had given her, the steel in her eyes.

Then, Ava came to her senses. "No no Miss sicko, you're caught baby, you can't do anything else now, and I'll make sure of that." Fifteen minutes later, and half way through her journey, Ava began to think again about that disdainful look, and the smile. For no apparent reason, she began to fear for Terrence Mercer.

## BETHWELL STREET.

## AVA CRUNTZE'S APARTMENT.

Terry Mercer was loading the last of his luggage into his car and ready to make his way back to HQ. Ava had informed him of the situation regarding Rosalyn Simpson. At last, they had apprehended her, although it had to be said, it had nothing at all to do with the plan they had devised.

Officer John Smedley had been in the right place at the right time and had discovered the e mail that had led to Simpson's arrest.

Ava had also informed him who the informant was, and that really rocked him. Of all the people he had suspected in his mind, Kathlene Oconnor would have been the last one he'd suspect, but then, wasn't that always the way? It's always the last one you'd think it was.

This would be an interesting interview he would have with her. Oconnor was second in command in the field of forensics, next to Phillips. Why on earth would she get involved with a sick-minded woman like Simpson, and for what reasons?

He began to think to himself of anything specific he'd done or said against her. Maybe the way he addressed her had displeased her. He remembered Sandra joking with him and informing him that *"wee Irish lassie would sleep with you in a minute mister Mercer."* Whatever her reasons, he would soon find out. Rosalyn Simpson as well, this was going to be weird to say the least. The last time he'd had any kind of conversation with her, other than the time she'd slipped into his bed beside him was back when they were sixteen years of age. How the hell could she hold a grudge for as long as she obviously had, and not just a grudge, a compulsion, a driving force of evil, an obsession to inflict as much heartache and misery as she could into his life, and boy, had she done that. Killing Sandra Neal, Billy McDermot, Sam Hargrieves and God knew how many others. She'd had the chance to kill him when she and her accomplice had broken into his house, and although she'd left them in the sewers,

she had given him a chance of survival.
When she had lay beside him naked in his bed, he knew she was getting some kind of buzz out of the situation. Infatuation, Ava had suggested, possessed even. No matter now, there would be no place for sentiment. She would be sent down for the rest of her life and that would be the end of it, and deservedly so.
She was a monster, a ruthless monster who had numerous psychological problems and some might say, unfixable problems. It would be best for all mankind if she was just locked away in some institution for the criminally insane. The young sweet Rosalyn Clark he'd once known had disappeared from the face of the earth and would never again be seen. The trouble was, Misses Simpson would argue that it was because of Terrance Mercer's insatiable appetite for the female flesh that had encouraged her to depart from this world.

## SCOTLAND YARD.

## BROADWAY VICTORIA.

Tony Chrysler sat in one of the interview rooms with Polly Sheppard and Ava Cruntze awaiting the arrival of Terry Mercer so that they could proceed with the first of the interviews. Chrysler ran his fingers through his pure grey hair and breathed a long sigh of relief. "Thank Christ we've got her ladies, I was beginning to think we'd never be successful. Still can't believe Kathlene Oconnor would do something like this, collaborating with this bloody mental woman, what the hell was she thinking, she had her whole career in front of her, stupid girl."
Ava looked at her watch and not for the first time in the last fifteen minutes.
"What's wrong Ava?" said Polly Sheppard. "You look flustered, agitated."
"I just want Terry to be here, I'm concerned about him."
"Concerned?" said Chrysler, rising to his feet and proceeding to pour himself a cup of coffee. "What are you concerned about Ava, we've got her here, and she sure as hell is not going anywhere. Terry is safe from her now, and his colleagues I might add Ava, you've got nothing to be concerned about. Our troubles, as far as Misses Rosalyn Simpson is concerned, are over."
Ava glanced at her boss, and nodded politely, as if accepting everything he'd said as truth, when all the time she felt very uncertain about the whole situation.
What was more frustrating to her was the fact that Tony Chrysler should have been correct in everything he'd said. They *did* have her here, and she wasn't going anywhere, but still this feeling of uncertainty consumed her. She felt uneasy, almost nervous. Perhaps she would feel better when Terry got here.
"Come on, get a cup of coffee Ava." said Chrysler, "you've done amazing work as usual in apprehending this monster, well done girl, you've excelled yourself again, hasn't she Polly?"

Polly smiled at Ava as she answered Chrysler.
"She always does."
The office door opened and Terry Mercer stepped into the room and immediately made his way over to the coffee machine.
"Good news Terry at last huh? said Chrysler, "we've got her, and her accomplice, Miss Kathlene Oconnor, can you believe it? Who would have thought that Terry?"
Terry didn't answer his boss at first.
He looked at Ava and Polly and shook his head in disbelief.
"She's one of the best forensic officers we have, next to Phillips, she *is* the best." He sipped his coffee. "I don't get it, I mean, was she in with Simpson from the start? And if she was, then she is just as much responsible for the deaths of all these people, her own colleagues included."
Chrysler sat back down on his chair. "Well, we're about to find out Terry. Which one do you want to interview first, I'm leaving it up to you. It's been you and Ava who have dealt with this, and by the way, we appreciate you going into hiding the way you did, you handled it well Terry, and-"
"No I didn't handle it well sir, and I'll tell you something right now, I will never do it again, I was just about going up the wall, and to cap it all, it wasn't even that half-assed plan which led to her arrest, Christ it was a rooky who led us to Simpson, or we'd never have found her. It's young Smedley you should be praising, not us."
"Well, be that as it may Terry, the main thing is, she's here and she's killing no-one else, her game is over."
Ava excused herself to go and have a cigarette before the interviews began. Terry Mercer picked up his cup of coffee and proceeded to follow her. They both descended the elevator to the ground floor and exited the building at the rear. Mercer had lit his cigarette before they were outside.
"What do you think Ava?" he said as they reached the designated smoking area.
"About what Terry?"
"About Kathlene Oconnor, Christ, I can't believe it, she's so nice, what a bloody shock, and why? Why would she get involved with a

woman like that? Do you think she was blackmailed ?"
"All will be revealed Terry. We'll find out everything in due course no doubt, but as far as being shocked with her is concerned, well I'm afraid there's nothing much would shock me now, with anybody. Unless Kathlene's family have been threatened or held to ransom, then she has no excuse for her actions and will face the full penalties of the law. She'll go down Terry, and not for a short spell I might add. This woman could have been conspiring to kill you Terry, however nice she's been or, seemed to be.
You have to forget about sentiment here. For all we know, she could have been the reason that Sam and Billy were killed, or your friend Sandra. She would know where they all were and at what times, making it easy for Misses Simpson and her sick colleague to dispose of them. In a nut-shell Terry, she's every bit responsible for these people's murders, you said so yourself. She's dangerous Terry, to everyone around her, especially colleagues."
Mercer inhaled his cigarette deeply as he leaned against the wall, with one of his legs tucked up against it supporting him.
To any onlooker he would look more like a drug dealer than a detective, standing there with his faded jeans and black tee-shirt complete with his hair slightly jelled and waved back over his brow. On closer inspection she noticed that he hadn't shaved today either, or yesterday.
"Terry, I think we should postpone these interviews until tomorrow morning, you look like you could do with a good sleep. It would benefit us all I think."
Terry nodded in agreement.
"Don't think I could trust myself Ava in my present state of mind, I'd end up beating the shit out of Simpson. We'll start the interviews first thing in the morning, and it will be first thing, I don't want the bitch getting a lie-in, her fucking fancy days are over, mental bastard."
"You were doing so well Terry, you've been here for more than fifteen minutes and you haven't uttered a single swear word, but as soon as you even think about Rosalyn Simpson, then off you go with your uncontrollable profanations."

"I know Ava" he sighed. "I'm sorry, and you're right, I do need a good night's sleep."

Ava looked at her colleague, and smiled. "You've been through a lot Terry, but this particular hardship will soon be over for you. Do you want to speak with Kathlene Oconnor or Simpson, before you go home? You could pour on the discomfort to Simpson now and inform her of what belies her fate. Torture *her* like she's tortured you, and God knows, no-one could blame you. She took Sam away from you and your new recruit Billy, as well as Sandra Neal. Polly told me how much you thought of her, and of course, I didn't exactly help matters there by storming in with my sledge-hammer sarcasm did I?"

"You weren't to know Ava Christ. No, I don't want to speak with them yet, I'll leave it until the morning, I'm heading off home now, and I mean home, my home, bloody sick to death of hiding from the daylight."

"Well Terry, as far as my half-assed plan was concerned, Simpson bought it actually. She genuinely believed you were dead. It would be your little Miss Kathlene who would no doubt inform her of the truth, so, less of the half-assed if you don't mind."

Mercer held up his hands in a gesture of apology.

"I'm sorry Ava, I am. I know your plan worked, and no matter how frustrating it was for me, I wouldn't have agreed to it if I didn't think it would work...and it did. Anyway, I'm off Ava, we have a busy day in front of us tomorrow."

The following sentence surprised Terry more than a little.

Ava finished off the last of her cigarette and then said, "I'm going for a couple of drinks Terry before I go home, would you care to join me"?

"That'd be nice Ava, thank you, I think I will. I will only have a couple though, because I couldn't possibly keep up with hardened drinkers like you, I'm just not used to it, I could end up blabbering about all kinds of things if I have more than a couple."

"Blabbering about what precisely?"

"Oh, just things, stupid things."

Ava pushed the boat out.

"Feelings Terry, is that what you mean? Specifically about how you feel about me, dare I ask?"

"Come on Ava," said Terry Mercer smiling at her. "Let's go and have a couple of night-caps, my little German friend, "Ich bin thirsty sweetheart."

Ava smiled back at him. "So am I Terry."

## SCOTLAND YARD.

## BROADWAY VICTORIA. 7am.

Terry Mercer had been in his office for almost an hour, as Ava Cruntze arrived. As she approached him he seemed transfixed, almost hypnotised by the two weapons placed on his desk. Without looking up he said to her,
"Look at this Ava, fucking bitch, A Glock G-19 semi-automatic, and this bastard here, a forty-four Magnum Colt Anaconda with six inch barrel. Jesus Christ Ava, she wasn't intending to take any prisoners was she. Hell if she hits you with this", he picked up the Magnum, "bloody thing is going to half you in two, the Yankees call it The Cannon, and no wonder."
Ava sat down opposite her colleague, and took the Magnum from him. She shook her head as she studied the weapon.
Terry continued.
"That's what she had in her hand bag, Christ, it makes you wonder what she'll have at home, probably a couple of cruise missiles in the garage, a couple of anti-tank rocket launchers, fuck it wouldn't surprise me Ava...sick bitch."
"We've got her husband here Terry, would you like to interview him, poor bugger didn't know a thing about all these killings, he's in shock Terry. He's kept her like a whore knowing she was seeing other men, but he didn't for one minute suspect anything like this was happening. He's breaking his heart down there in one of the interview rooms."
"Yeah I was a bit too harsh on him I think Ava, but under the circumstances...we didn't know what the hell was going on, I'll go and talk to him shortly."
Ava placed the giant pistol back onto the desk.
"We've got two different psychiatrists coming in today to interview her. If they pronounce her sane she'll spend the rest of her life in jail. If they judge her to be insane, she'll spend all of her life in an institute, a high security institute, either way, she's finished with

society, or rather, society's finished with her. She's had her chips as they say Terry."

"I don't know what the hell to think concerning her Ava, I really don't."

"Chrysler's suggested that I do the interviews with both of them, you know, Simpson and Kathlene Oconnor, would you have any objections about that Terry?"

"If I'm honest Ava, you'd be doing me a favour, because I wouldn't even know where to start with either of them, especially Kathlene, I'm absolutely gutted about her, what a waste of a good forensic officer, not to mention her career."

"Well Terry, it was her decision, it's her look-out, she'll have to face the consequences of her actions. She more than anyone knows that there is no room for sentiment, she shouldn't be looking for leniency Terry, and don't you go feeling sorry for her either, you could have easily been killed because of her, she deserves everything that's coming to her."

Mercer had wandered over to his coffee machine and was proceeding to pour himself another cup when there was a slight tap on his door. A secretary poked her head through briefly and introduced a Mister Henry Rogerson, one of the two psychiatrists who would be interviewing Rosalyn Simpson. A tall gentleman about the age of sixty entered the room carrying a black leather valise. He had very thin grey hair which he'd swept over his entire head giving the impression, or at least trying to give the impression that he was still able to grow a full head of hair. Unbeknown to Mister Rogerson, his attempts were completely unsuccessful. Mercer smiled at the gentleman politely. He could have been looking at Jack Charlton, one of Mercer's father's heroes from the football world, such was the resemblance.

"Good morning sir" said Mercer, "would you like a coffee before you begin your interview."

"Thank you that would be lovely" replied Rogerson relieving himself of the burden of the valise and unfastening the buttons of his long raincoat. "I take it you are detective Terrance Mercer."

"Indeed I am sir" replied Mercer, "and this here is Miss Ava Cruntze detective Ava Cruntze, herself and I have been working together on this eh...case, the em Rosalyn Simpson case."

"Yes, quite a character by all accounts Mister Mercer she's been leading you all quite a merry dance has she not."

Was that sarcasm from the shrink? Mercer thought to himself.

"Not any fucking more she won't Mister Rogerson, no matter what your verdict of her mental health is, she's for the high jump now, she won't be leading anyone else a merry fucking dance, that's for sure."

To save any further embarrassment Ava suggested to Terry that he might go and find Tony Chrysler to come to his office and meet Mister Rogerson before he begins his interview. As she was saying this Rogerson was bent over extracting a document from his case, his bald head shining beneath the strands of thin white hair, his head almost crimson in the heat of the room.

Even though Terry knew exactly why Ava had suggested he should find Chrysler, he still couldn't keep himself from his next comment, which was, "I hope you're a good shrink Mister Rogerson for your own sake, because if you're not, she'll lead *you* a merry fucking dance I can tell you that, she'll do your fucking head in, I kid you not...I'll go and find Chrysler Ava."

## 11:50am.

By 11.30am both of the psychiatrists had completed their interviews with Rosalyn Simpson. The second psychiatrist was a woman of about forty years of age. She had been far more courteous to Mercer and had praised him and Ava for the way they had handled the case. She had also expressed her condolences for the loss of all the officer's lives that had been taken throughout the course of their inquiries. The two psychiatrists had left individually having both informed Tony Chrysler that they would be in touch in due course regarding their interviews with Simpson.

Terry Mercer sat now beside Ava Cruntze in one of the conference rooms. Tony Chrysler had called a meeting with all officers who had had anything at all to do with the Simpson case. The press had been hounding certain members of staff for information regarding the names of the guilty parties. They had been informed that two women were being held in custody and that as soon as the appropriate interviews had been completed, they would be informed of the verdict concerning the two suspects, but, at this moment in time, they were only that, suspects.

There was a total of twenty-seven people gathered around the table as Chrysler swore them all to secrecy and that punishment would be administered if anyone here let out any information regarding their prisoners. Everyone around the table knew for certain that Rosalyn Simpson was as guilty as could be and that the interviews were in fact, nothing more than a formality. The only question now was where she would serve her sentence. Depending entirely what the psychiatrists had thought of her mental welfare would determine where that would be. In short, asylum or prison, as far as Terry Mercer was concerned, it was as simple as that.

All they had to do now, was wait for their reports, or rather their decisions on whether Simpson was sane, or insane. He knew what he thought it should be.

2:30pm.

Misses Rosalyn Simpson had been officially charged with murder on numerous counts and had acknowledged the charges. Ava had dismissed the witnesses necessary to observe the charges administered. Now, it was just Rosalyn Simpson and herself.
"Would you like another coffee Misses Simpson, before we continue our interview?"
Simpson, dressed now in denim jeans and tee-shirt, her long auburn hair tied back and with all jewellery and make-up removed replied,
"I would love another coffee, but, I'm afraid as far as any interview is concerned between yourself and me, well it's not going to happen. I have said from the minute you brought me in here that I will only talk with Terrance Mercer, and he alone. I am well aware of the charges pressed against me, so there is nothing more that you need to inform me of. So, any further interviews you wish to have with me will only be taking place between Mister Mercer and myself, unless of course he suffers from a serious bout of gutlessness."
Ava smiled at the prisoner who seemed, even at this point, to be calling the shots.
"I'll inform him of your decision, but I warn you now, don't hold your breath, he doesn't think very highly of you at this particular moment in time as you can understand, you know, with your sick murderous ways, killing innocent boys and various other members of staff you have disposed of, he's just glad we've got you in here. I think he said that he hoped that you rot in jail, and that you contract some long-suffering illness that would bring you lots and lots of pain, it was something like that he said, I can't quite remember word for word, but it was something along those lines, and I must admit Misses Simpson, having seen the photographs of that poor McDermot lad and the mess you left in Locksley estate, well, I tend to agree with him."
Rosalyn Simpson smiled sarcastically at Ava.
"Yes, quite, you'd agree with Terry Mercer if he told you that Hitler was a sweetheart, wouldn't you Ava. It's ironic wouldn't you say?

Here's me making jokes about Hitler, and you being German and all, it wasn't very tasteful of me was it, but I suppose you'll be used to all the Krout jokes by now I dare say. I wonder what your mother saw in you that made her take off like that and leave you so vulnerable. Most of the women I have come in contact with absolutely adored their little girls, but not your mummy Ava, huh? She just took off and left you, such a bloody shame don't you think? Has she ever been in touch with you? Has she ever attempted to find you and see what became of the little vulnerable girl, so hurtful Ava, isn't it, rejection I mean, it's a crying bloody shame if you ask me, of course, on top of all that, your own mother then adds to your misery by practically abandoning you, now that couldn't have been much fun for you, goodness me, total rejection from both parents, that would knock the stuffing out of anyone, but never mind, all's well that ends well, you've got your family here in the Metropolitan Police department haven't you, this is all the family you need. Come to think of it, it's the only semblance of a family you actually have. Perhaps Terry and you can make a fresh start together, you can console each other on winter nights and trade stories and opinions of how your parents rejected you, and why his lovely wife Carol took off and left him, hell she even took their son away with her did she not? You'll make an ideal couple don't you think? You've got enough heartaches there to keep you warm and grateful to have each other, because it would seem that no-one else wants you, so sad."

Ava could feel the fire burning in her belly. An almost uncontrollable urge to beat the living daylights out of this excuse for a human being surged through her body. It took all of her might to fight off the urge to hurt this woman seated in front of her.
She sat staring at the wretch. Simpson's words had cut her to the bone, and how on earth did she know about all of that childhood stuff. As far as she was concerned, the only person who knew about that was Terrance Mercer. The nasty bitch even knew about Terry's wife leaving him, and taking his son with her. Just who the hell *was* this woman? How did she know all this information? After a few uncomfortable moments, Ava rose to her feet.

"Still full of yourself Rosalyn, aren't you. Even in the circumstances you're in, you still have this, I'm better than you complex don't you, you still think you're the bee's knees, well I think the ladies in the prison you'll be going to will soon sort out all that nonsense for you. They'll bring you back down to earth with a bump.
You're nothing more than a whore, taking that poor man's money from him administering favours to him no doubt in between your murdering innocent people, you sick bitch that you are, I hope Terry comes in here and kicks the shit out of you, scrubber, I've a good mind to do it myself here and now you nasty cow."
Ava pushed her chair back under the desk and informed the monster that she would pass on the information to Mister Mercer.
"We're searching your house right now Misses Simpson to see what else you have hidden away. We'll find all your weapons and your kinky underwear, all your love letters, everything, our officers are looking forward to having a good search around your house, or should I say, Mister Charles Simpson's house. He's in one of the interview rooms just now having a laugh at your predicament. Do you want to know what he said about you? He said he was getting a divorce from you anyway and that you made it so much easier than it would have been. He knew all along that you are a whore who bends and manipulates people to your own advantage.
He and Terry were laughing their heads off when Terry informed him that you'd be out of his life forever, he's so happy.
I'll just go and tell him everything you said. You'll have to excuse him Rosalyn if he keeps bursting out into laughter, it was something your em...husband told him, regarding plastic surgery, oh, and while we're on *that* subject, whoever the surgeon was...well, he's not the best in his profession is he deary. It's a pity you're stuck in here, you could have sued the bastard, see you soon Rosalyn, and oh, by the way, Hitler was not German Misses Simpson, he was Austrian, so, no offence taken."
Ava had done well to control her temper, but she was still sickened at the thought of that monster knowing all those details about her childhood. Perhaps this bitch had more than Kathlene Oconnor helping her out by giving her information, but even if she did, no-

one else knew about her relationship with her mother, and how that relationship had ended. Only Terry Mercer knew about that, and he had only been informed of that recently, Simpson had spoken to her as though she'd known about it for quite some time.

When Ava arrived back at Terry Mercer's office, he and Tony Chrysler were discussing the case. Ava informed Terry of Simpson's insistence that he, and he alone, would be the only one she would conduct any interview with.
Chrysler rose to his feet.
"Don't worry about it, Ava, we don't need any confession. I have already informed the forensic team to gather up all their evidence ready for a court case. Her D.N.A has condemned her anyway, we've already got all the evidence we need, don't worry about it, either of you."
Again, Ava smiled to her boss as if accepting the facts as they were, and that Simpson's DNA had indeed condemned her.
So why this uneasiness, this doubt, apprehension almost.
It was as though, even under the present circumstances, even with the inevitable outcome of her court case, she still had something up her sleeve. One thing that really got to Ava was the fact that Simpson knew so much about her.
Where on earth did she get that kind of information? There was no-one inside Scotland Yard who knew anything of her past, but Christ, this woman even knew about her childhood, and how the relationship with her mother had ended.
When she moved to London, where she stayed, who she stayed with, when she was finally accepted into the CID, and now, here in Scotland Yard.
How long had she been scrutinising *her*?
Worse still, if she wasn't important to her, then what the hell did she know about Terry? She had obviously been watching him when this Carol had left him. She would see that he was devastated. That would turn her on. She would also see that after some time he'd begun the relationship with Sandra Neal.
That certainly wouldn't turn her on. But it was this frame of mind

she was in that bothered Ava. She sat silently reading in her cell any time anyone had attempted to speak to her.

Her laid back attitude, complete calmness, her languid demeanour certainly got to Ava. Here was a woman knowing full well, that before very long, one way or another, she was going to spend the rest of her life behind bars, and it didn't seem to bother her one bit. It was almost as if she were executing some kind of preconceived plan, and that, in fact, it was she who was in control.

There was certainly good reason for Ava being in a state of quandary. Whatever the hell had happened to Rosalyn Simpson, it certainly wasn't Terry dumping her that had caused it, although perhaps that had sparked off this tunnel-vision hatred she had towards him, and not just him, anyone at all who remotely annoyed her would or could be subjected to her wrath.

As well as this, we have her promiscuousness, and an abnormally high sexual drive, certainly for a woman of her age, her depravity perhaps another symptom of her broken brain.

Maybe the psychiatrists could enlighten her more on that subject, but the fact remained, anyone who stood in her way was in danger. Her confidence and audaciousness surprised Ava.

Simpson, for years had been living a celebrities' life-style, her fancy cars and restaurants, her shows, her top-of-the-range hotels.

They were all going out the window, and here she was, apparently unconcerned about it. Obviously, something had gone wrong with Miss Simpson, and at an early age, and it most certainly had gone undetected.

Perhaps it had even been something teratogenic, something malfunctioning in the brain which had worsened as she grew older. Whatever it was, it was plain for anyone to see that the woman was in fact knitting with one needle. As Ava rose to her feet and began to make her way down to the car park she wondered if Terry, just for the hell of it, would be prepared to have an interview with her. Perhaps, if she was permitted to sit in at the interview she just might be able to find out from the way she spoke, just what it was she was about to bestow onto Terry. Something was coming his way that would not be very pleasant. One final infliction of pain delivered to Terry, before she would become completely powerless...but what?

## 48 HOURS LATER.

Ava and Terry had spent the last couple of days going through Rosalyn Simpson's belongings. Simpson's husband had left them the keys to the house and had gone to stay with friends down in Kent. Together, Ava and Terry had scrutinised letters received by Simpson over the years, documents from various banks, statements of accounts, withdrawals and deposits etc.
Terry had scrutinised her computer to try and find out who her friends were, but there was nothing to be found, nothing of any great interest. She wasn't on face-book or any of the other chat sites.
Ava discovered that she possessed an enormous collection of pornography. After checking some of the discs at random she was surprised to say the least, that it was all heterosexual. There was no child pornography or dominatrix as Ava had expected, in fact, apart from the size of her collection, she would seem to be a normal human being. There were no films of torture or brutality, again as Ava had expected. Judging by the way this woman had executed people, inflicting as much torture and excruciating pain to the victims, she was certain there would be visual diaries either of her acts, or films from around the globe where torture had been administered, a kind of adrenalin booster for her, but nothing.
There was no kinky attire in her bedroom either, only the usual stockings and see-through underwear. Every garment of clothing she possessed though was of the highest quality.
There were no common clothes department-tags in Rosalyn Simpson's collection thank you very much.
So apart from that, nothing out of the ordinary.
The only other weapon they discovered was another Glock pistol, which had been strategically placed under the driving seat of her Ferrari.
Again, Ava and Terry had expected to find an absolute arsenal in her garage.

As far as they knew Simpson hadn't filmed any of her escapades or sexual depravities. To all and sundry, you would think that this was just another average woman, apart from her bank accounts.

There were the usual photographs framed, and hanging around the walls of the living room of Simpson and her husband taken on various vacations around the world.

One of the photographs showed her standing looking over the Grand Canyon.

Another showed her standing with her arm around her husband dressed in skiing attire, red faced and laughing at whoever had taken the photograph in Aspen. Yet another photograph boasted her standing directly in front of the Sphinx. The woman had been well travelled. She had used her skills of deception to achieve many things in her life.

Exotic holidays were the norm for her, and judging by her bank accounts, she certainly wasn't suffering from plutophobia.

Tony Chrysler entered the room.

"Oh you're back you two. Did you get any joy in her house, did you find anything else to add to her collection of horrors."

"Nothing at all sir." replied Ava. "It's a good job we have this damning evidence on her, or else we'd be struggling, she seems clean as a whistle."

Chrysler took a seat opposite his favourite detectives.

"I've just received the results from the psychiatrists, and they are both overwhelmingly in agreement that our Misses Simpson is indeed completely off her rocker, but having said that, the psychiatrists both used PolyGram tests on her and guess what, she beat them both, can you believe it?

Mister Rogerson says she suffers from a condition known as Hyperthymesia"

"What the hell is that when it's at home." exclaimed Mercer.

Chrysler smiled, as if he'd been expecting Terry to come out with some kind of profanation with reference to the afore-mentioned illness.

"Hyperthymesia is a rare condition Terry that gives a person an abnormally good memory. So, all those years ago when you broke up with her would quite easily seem like yesterday to our Misses Simpson, hence the hatred and grudge towards you, and of course, that being the case, her pain of your departure would never leave her."

Ava put in, with a smile, "You'll always be nothing but a cheating bastard Terry, a two-timing cheating bastard, in *her* eyes, you understand."

Chrysler smiled at Mercer as he rose from his seat to the coffee machine. "That's right Ava" said Mercer, dryly, better not ever date me, you know what to expect if you do…just ask Rosalyn, or my wife Carol, or Sandra Neal."

Ava nodded, smiling back at Mercer.

"Yeah, I'm sorry, I asked for that Terry."

## 24 HOURS LATER.

The trial of Misses Rosalyn Simpson had been set for ten days from now. Normal procedure would have been to place Simpson into a high-security prison until the time of her court case, but because of crimes committed and the fact that two different psychiatrists had pronounced her insane, Terry Mercer, Ava Cruntze, and Tony Chrysler were all in favour of keeping her where she was in one of the holding cells right here in Scotland Yard. They had no intentions of letting her out of their sight. Most of the high security prisons had an immaculate record of security, but still they all decided unanimously, that nothing would be left to chance with Rosalyn Simpson.

Because of her acharnement, nothing would ever be left to chance with her, especially when she was admitted into a mental-health establishment, and all said and done, that's where she would end up. There would be no prison sentence for Misses Simpson, just a luxurious laid back mental health establishment for her.

If she behaved, she'd be treated practically like royalty.

Mercer sat now at his desk looking to Ava to be in a state of quandary. In front of Terry, placed neatly on his desk were the photographs of Billy McDermot, Sam Hargrieves, Sandra Neal, Jane Smith and Thomas Felton. These were just some of Simpson's victims. His best friend for more than fourteen years, Sam Hargrieves, looked up from the photograph, smiling directly at Terry. Sandra Neal as well, the first woman he had had any connection with since his wife Carol had left him. He and Sandra were making progress, until Simpson had decided that enough was enough, and had then killed her. Pseudoautochiria, a very sinister and cruel act by Simpson, which had for a while convinced him that Sandra had taken her own life. He still felt the shame of doubting her. If truth be known, he was finding it increasingly difficult to trust anyone these days, because as soon as he did, it somehow back-fired on him, one way or the other. Kathlene Oconnor as well, who he would soon interview had sold him down the river to that monster, and not just him. Sam's details she'd probably passed on to Simpson as well, and Sandra's no doubt. Ava had offered to interview her but Terry now had a change of heart. He felt strong enough now to face the truth and ask Kathlene face to face why she had betrayed her colleagues, and more importantly, threw a very promising career down the drain.

The girl seemed so sincere, both as an agent and a colleague, no wonder the news had hit him for six. He still found it hard to believe, which was why he'd decided to interview her.

He was curious to say the least, because whatever else Kathlene was, she was not stupid.

He continued to scrutinise the photographs.

Ava approached him and placed an arm around his shoulder.

"I know Terry, I know. I can't for one minute try and understand how you feel, but she can't do it to you any more honey, she can't get to you anymore."

"Look at this Ava, she can't get to me any more you say? Look at her victims here, young Billy, bloody Sam, poor Sam, and poor Beth, I haven't even been round to see her since the funeral, and Sandra, God almighty Ava, are they trying to tell me that because I broke up with her all those years ago, it's sparked off this bloody murderous frenzy, Christ nobody can get that hurt surely to goodness."

"It's got nothing to do with the break-up Terry, both of the psychiatrists are in agreement that she's insane, and by the looks of things, she's been insane for some bloody time it would seem.

She may be using that as an excuse but it's more than lame. She's just a very sick woman Terry, and you just happen to have been unlucky enough to have come into contact with her at some point of your life."

"No no Ava, she's been targeting me for years, you said it yourself, she's all but been consumed with the idea of getting even with me, killing Sam and young Billy, Sandra, I mean what the hell have *they* done to her to deserve that? They didn't even know her. Christ she even sliced up that cunt-pig of a lover of hers when she grew tired of him, and threw him in the fucking Thames."

Judging by the increase of his profanations, Ava could tell he was well on the way to getting himself into a state about the bitch again, so she calmly put it to him that Kathlene had been asking to speak with him. She had only asked for ten minutes, just enough time to explain to him what exactly had happened, and why she had done the things she had.

Terry Mercer sighed, regaining his composure, and looked at Ava. He sat back in his chair staring at the photographs of his deceased friends. After a few moments, he stood up, nodding his head.

"Yes Ava, I think I will speak to her, I think she owes us an apology."

"She just wants to speak with you, alone Terry, she was practically begging for the opportunity."

"Well, I'll give her the opportunity Ava, huh, this'll be interesting to say the least. How can she possibly justify her actions, but, we'll see, we'll see what she has to say for herself, because after her court case, we won't be seeing her for quite some time I would imagine."

Terry made his way down to the holding cell where they were keeping Kathlene Oconnor.

The cell consisted of one single bed, a small table, one chair. The small toilet was semi-concealed behind a wooden partition which allowed the prisoner some privacy. One or two cheap prints of various types of flowers hung on the walls around the cell. The floor was carpeted. All said and done, it wasn't a prison cell. It wasn't meant to be.

Terry closed the door behind him and walked over to the table where Kathlene Oconnor sat, tapping her fingers on the table nervously, her knees bouncing up and down as though keeping the beat to a song. Kathlene's blond hair was tied back and kept in place by two multi- coloured butterfly clips, her face looking as though she'd been crying.

"Hello Kathlene" said Mercer, "Ava tells me you wish to have a conversation with me, but I can't for the life of me think of anything that we could possibly discuss, apart from maybe how you've managed to throw your life down the drain but, I'm here, and I must say I'm curious as to where our conversation will take us."

Kathlene looked up briefly and smiled gently at Terry before putting her head down again, and staring at the table.

"I'll just go and get another chair, won't be long Kathlene."
Kathlene Oconnor wore a white blouse with blue denim jeans. Someone had provided her with slipper-like footwear.
She looked to Terry like a scorned school-girl awaiting the dreaded headmasters return.
As Mercer re-entered the holding room, he was surprised to find that Kathlene had made two cups of coffee. One of the cups already sat opposite where Kathlene would sit.
She knew exactly how Mercer liked his coffee having made him many a cup over the years. She came and sat down at the small table and placed her beverage on top of a newspaper.
"I haven't got a lot of time Kathlene, so, whatever it is you want to say to me, go ahead, I'm a very busy man, as you know, and very lucky to be alive young lady, as you also know, so, let's hear it, what do you want to tell me, and thanks for the coffee."
"May I show you something please Mister Mercer" she said, her voice sounding like it was close to breaking.
"By all means Kathlene."
She bent down and opened the small hand bag she'd been permitted to have in here with her, and produced a photograph. She placed the seven-by-four photograph on the table, slowly turning it around for Mercer to see.
Mercer sipped his coffee as he glanced at it, and then back at Kathlene Oconnor.
"This is my young sister Mister Mercer, and these are her two children, Debbie and the girls are all I have in the world. Her husband-to-be took off and left her when he fell in love with a colleague he worked with. He left her with nothing, no forwarding address, nothing. She's received no child support from him or anything. I've been living with her, or rather, she's been living with me for the past four years, they em...they depend on me."
Mercer was unmoved.
"Yeah, I know how she feels Kathlene, I depended on you too, as did all your colleagues. I'm afraid if this is an attempt at the sympathy vote young lady, it's far too late. You knew what you were doing Kathlene. How much did she pay you for the

information required, not that I'm in the slightest bit interested you understand, it was really a rhetorical question."
Oconnor looked at him straight in the eye.
"I know that, and I'm not looking for sympathy. I asked to speak with you for the simple reason that I needed to explain to you, why I done what I did. When I got home from work one night, about six months ago, I found Debbie sitting crying her eyes out and cuddling her little girls on the sofa. Clutching them like her life depended upon it, and it did. Rosalyn Simpson had paid her a visit and had threatened to kill her children if I didn't respond to her requests, which were, names and addresses of certain people within the force. Sam Hargrieves' address was top of the list, followed by Sandra Neal's address and William McDermott's.
She left the list with Debbie and promised her faithfully that she would kill me and her children if I did not comply."
Mercer raised his hands to stop her.
"Don't you dare, don't you fucking dare go down that road with me lady, you know full well the procedure in a case like that, you'd have got protection from the force and fine well you know it, don't you go down that blackmail road, and that you had no choice. I lost my best friend through your disloyalty you fucking little bitch, not to mention a young lad and another colleague, fuck sakes Kathlene, you used to share the canteen with Sandra, you used to laugh and joke with her all the fucking time, how can you sit there and blame some-one else for your treachery. You regret it all now that you've been caught, but how long would you have gone on with the deceit? When would you have stopped?" Kathlene Oconnor looked at Terry Mercer with red eyes.
"I would have stopped when Rosalyn Simpson told me that she wouldn't kill my nieces and me, that's when I would have stopped. As I say, Debbie and those girls are all I have in the world, and I would do anything to protect them, and I know about all the procedures, but you more than anyone knows about Rosalyn Simpson's ways and what she is capable of doing.
If I didn't help her out with those addresses, then those little girls would have died without a shadow of a doubt, and you know it.

On top of that, I didn't know she was going to kill these people when I gave her the addresses...I had no choice Terry, I really didn't, I was stuck between a rock and a hard place."
"You still should have come to us Kathlene we deal with blackmail all the time you know that. And if you *had* come to us, chances are, we probably could have reeled her in before she was able to do any more damage, but, you said nothing, you just proceeded to sell your colleagues down the river.
Your actions killed them Kathlene.
Your aberration from loyalty to your colleagues sealed their fate Kathlene."
Oconnor said nothing. She only looked into Terry's face and held his stare. She'd just been shattered by his cutting words moments before and was more than aware of the consequences of her actions. Still looking into his face, she said," You know her Terry, and if I had come to you for help she'd have found out, and she would have undoubtedly murdered those little girls before killing me.
I have had to sift through the remains of what she's left behind at murder scenes. Myself and Andy Phillips and his team have had to plough through flesh and bone, brain tissue and matter. We've pulled bullets out of eye sockets we've examined the remains of kidneys which have been cooked in ovens. The sperm in young Billy McDermott's throat was put there by Rosalyn Simpson, it had been in her mouth first though, her saliva was present in the sperm.
She is capable of any number of hideous crimes.
Murder means nothing to her. She has no thoughts of consideration towards other people or their feelings or predicaments, or their fears, in fact fear is what turns her on.
She likes to know that people are frightened of her. Her beauty is her mask, she could-"
"Hey! You don't have to convince me of what she's capable of, I was her fucking target remember, most of the people she murdered was to get to me. You tell your tales to the judge lady, but do not look to me for sympathy because you'll wait a long time.
You got close to me Kathlene, or at least you tried to.

Hell you flirted with me in front of Sandra, and you did it to gain my confidence that's why, so as you could go back and help that sick bitch with her sick games. You were her accomplice madam, and don't you forget that, fuck you and your sympathy vote, you devious little bitch that you are. How dare you sit here and cry to me for assistance, you effectively killed off three of your colleagues, and I'm not listening to any more of your shit, she's going down, and you are going down with her, you fucking little snake in the grass."

Mercer stood up and placed his chair neatly under the table.
"You asked for ten minutes, and I've given you them, good luck in court Kathlene, and I hope they throw away the key, so that you can sit and reflect on all the dirty deeds you've done against the very people who helped you with your career. You were a very good forensic officer Kathlene, and you had a long way to go. They were set to promote you to head of forensics, did you know that? They were going to have you replace Andy Phillips when he retires next year. That would have been you at the top of the tree in your career Kathlene, you were set to have it all girly, but, because of the treacherous little fucking rat that you are, you'll rot in jail now for the rest of your life."

Mercer turned to exit the room.
As he reached the door Kathlene Oconnor quietly spoke half a dozen words to him that made his spine tingle and the hairs on the back of his neck stand on end.
With one hand on the door handle he heard her say, "She's not finished with you yet."
Mercer had stood rooted to the spot while Kathlene Oconnor had spoken the words. Trying his best to sound unmoved, he said, still with his back to her, "We'll see about that Kathlene", as he exited the room.

Half an hour later, Terry Mercer and Ava Cruntze sat in the canteen discussing his interview with Kathlene Oconnor.
"What the fuck is she going to do Ava? What has she planned out? Whatever she has premeditated, God knows, but it's not going to

be pleasant that's for"-

"Terry, calm yourself down, she's in here, she's under lock and key, and she's going nowhere."

Mercer completely ignored the smoking rule, again, and proceeded to light up a cigarette, his fingers fumbling with the lighter as he did so. Ava sat smiling at Mercer as he inhaled the smoke deeply.

It was a smile of sympathy, because in her heart of hearts, she knew that somehow Terry's troubles were not over. She had racked her brains trying to think of what the monster might have lined up for him. Perhaps she had another accomplice in here. Right back from the moment Ava had spoken to Simpson on the night she'd arrested her, she'd had this feeling of uneasiness. The woman was full of self-belief. She was so self-assured, as if her being arrested made no difference whatsoever to what she'd planned for him.

Ava looked at Terry, as he smoked nervously and stared out at the laden skies looming over London. It was as if she wasn't even in the room. He'd gone in to a trance-like state of meditation.

Mercer was comparing the heavy skies with his own life.

There was no sign of a break in the grey gloom overhead, and there was no sign of the relentless torture that this evil mental bitch was continuously inflicting upon him, coming to an end.

After a few minutes he pulled himself out of the doldrums he'd gotten himself into, and spoke to the windows rather as look to Ava.

"I'm going to put an end to this Ava. I've changed my mind, I am going to interview her. You're right Ava, she's in here and she `aint going anywhere. She's not going to intimidate me anymore, the mental fuck that she is. I'll find out what the fuck she has planned out for me, if anything, it could just be a bluff. I'm going to do it Ava, I'm the one who's in charge in here, not that wretched witch. I'll force the answer out of her, one way or another, I'll find out what she's done, or going to have done to me."

As Terry was going on about how he would extract the answers from Rosalyn Simpson, Ava was trying to sort something out in her own head. Rosalyn Simpson and Kathlene Oconnor had both been arrested on the same evening, only minutes apart.

From the moment of their arrest, neither of the two women had been permitted any time together, so, since they'd been brought in here they had not had the opportunity to utter as much as a single word to each other. That being the case, then how did Kathlene Oconnor know with any certainty, that Rosalyn Simpson wasn't finished with Terry? There had obviously been something said in previous conversations between the two for her to know that. More to the point, she may even know what exactly was coming Terry's way. Ava excused herself from the room as she headed down to Oconnor's holding cell. Surely with a little bit of `friendly persuasion` she could find out from Kathlene Oconnor what exactly was going to happen to Terry. It obviously concerned something she'd done in the past, something that she could use against him if the worse should happen, and now, of course, the worst *had* happened. Whatever it was it undoubtedly involved other people. Who would stoop so low as to help her?
Kathlene Oconnor for one, so if *she* was capable of such treachery, then anyone in here could be suspect, anyone at all.
When Ava entered the holding cell, Kathlene was sitting up on top of the single bed reading a novel. Ava studied the girl's face as she approached her. Kathlene had lost her aplomb. Her eyes were tear-stained and heavy. She would be regretting the fact that she'd allowed Simpson to inculcate her into her ways.
Ava had sat in discussion with Kathlene Oconnor for over forty minutes. Oconnor, if she was telling the truth, knew nothing as to what Simpson had lined up for Terry. Ava even tried to bribe Oconnor with leniency and have whatever sentenced imposed upon her, cut dramatically. Still Oconnor insisted that she knew nothing, other than the fact that Simpson had told her that she was far from finished with Mister Mercer, and that even if she were arrested, it wouldn't make a blind bit of difference to the heartache he would suffer. "In a nut-shell" said Oconnor, "she is one hundred per-cent dedicated to destroying his life, destroying him."

Tony Chrysler entered Mercer's office. Mercer had been staring out of his window watching the city traffic ebbing and flowing

continuously for almost an hour, his mind totally focussed upon what he would say to Rosalyn Simpson, and how he might extract the information from her.
"There's been a meeting Terry, and there won't be any trial for Simpson. We cannot try an insane individual in the courts, and I should have known that."
"What does that mean Tony?"
"It means Terry that they're coming for her the day after tomorrow and they're taking her up to Birmingham to a high security mental institute. Apparently this place is brand new.
All of the country's worst offenders are going to be kept here. I'm told the place is gigantic. All the extremely violent criminals are going there, and once they're in, then there's no way they're coming back out. If you're admitted, then you're admitted for life, there's no parole in there Terry, and from what I've been told, it would take an expert cagopholist just to get into the reception lobby, your troubles are over Terry.
Don't worry about interviewing her either, she'll only put doubts into your mind, and God knows she's done enough of that in the past few months, she's caused us all nothing but bloody misery, but, Mister Terrence Mercer, as from forty-eight hours' time, she'll be out of our lives forever, we'll never set eyes on her again."
Throughout the time Chrysler had been speaking to him, Mercer hadn't taken his eyes off the traffic on the streets below, his mind taking in all the information from his boss. Finally he turned to look at Chrysler.
"She's saying that it doesn't matter, the fact that she's locked up. Whatever she's got planned will still go ahead, and she's-"
"Terry, she's bluffing. What can she do? Her perspicaciousness is nothing more than a front. She's not intelligent Terry, she's, she's...to put it in your words Terry, she's fucking off her rocker, we have nothing further to fear from our deranged little friend, she's gone Terry, in every sense of the word, in two days' time, she becomes history, she's gone forever, and on top of that, it hasn't cost the tax payer a penny for expensive bloody court cases. She'll be taken from here to her new home, and then we can wash our

hands with the whole thing, she will no longer be our responsibility. And it can't come a minute too soon Terry, we've all had it to the back teeth with her."

Terry opened the window slightly and proceeded to light up a cigarette. Once more, looking down at the traffic, he said to his boss, "What do they call this place they're taking her to, does it have a name?"

Chrysler sighed as he pulled a sheet of paper out from his inside jacket pocket and studied it.

"Pleasant Meadows Terry, that's what they're calling it Pleasant Meadows, that's a nice name isn't it? This place where the inmates have committed some of the most violent crimes in British history, violent sexual cannibalistic murderers, and they name it Pleasant Meadows."

Mercer snorted laughter through exhaled cigarette smoke. He nodded his head at Chrysler in agreement.

"Yeah, they've given that a lot of thought Tony haven't they...Pleasant fucking Meadows...very fitting wouldn't you say."

"It doesn't matter to us Terry what the hell they're calling it, our little Felidae will be going there forever...forever Terry."

Terry stubbed out his cigarette and squashed it inside a paper towel. He closed the window and put the finished cigarette in the bin.

"I thought they might have taken her to Broadmoor, that's the highest security prison in the country isn't it? It's full of her kind in there."

"Not any more Terry, this new place is supposed to be the highest quality mental health institution in the country. Apparently it cost more than seventy million to build."

"Jesus Lord all that money to build a place for insane people, who would kill their keepers in an instant if they turned their backs on them."

"I know Terry, but the law insists that we put them somewhere."

"I know where I'd fucking put them Tony, a little slit across the trachea would do the job nicely, and then we could put them in a nice high security coffin, and then bury the bastards, that's what I'd

do...wouldn't cost seventy million pounds either, twisted fucks."
"Terry, please, stay in control man, like I say, she'll soon be history, out of your life forever, stop your swearing man."

BETHWELL STREET. SOUTH LONDON.

AVA CRUNTZE'S APPARTMENT.

Ava had taken a day off for two reasons. One, she would catch up with some house work which was long overdue, and two, she was to meet up with Terry at mid-day for a bar lunch.
Tomorrow, they would drive behind the armoured car that would take Misses Rosalyn Simpson to her new permanent address which was Pleasant Meadows, on the outskirts of Birmingham.
They were to supervise her admission and whilst there, interview the head of the establishment and explain to them, "as if anyone could ever be in doubt", just how dangerous this woman was, and to make it painfully clear to them, that under no circumstances whatsoever was she to be left unattended, unless she was in a secured room. Ava smiled to herself as she went over Chrysler's words in her head. The people in question would undoubtedly take offence at such remarks, making them feel incompetent or worse, inadequate, but, they had to be informed, Chrysler had insisted.
Ava knew that Tony Chrysler had given Terry this job to put his mind at rest, and to actually witness first hand Simpson's admission, so that he saw for himself rather than be told that she was completely out of society, and more importantly, out of his life forever.
It wouldn't matter one jot to Terrence Mercer, her actions would forever remain ineffaceable to him, that was just something he'd have to learn to live with, though she had to admit to herself that

would be easier said than done.

Ava spent all morning cleaning her house and rearranging furniture to suit her fancy. She also took down the curtains in the spare room where Terry had spent those agonising days awaiting Simpson to fall into the trap. Although she had taken the curtains down and washed them three times in an attempt to remove the stench of the cigarette smoke, she decided that they would be thrown out. The same fate befell the bedding and the antimacassars around the chairs in the room.

She couldn't help herself, she just despised anything to do with cigarettes and the smell they left. It was probably the fact that her *mother* had smoked so heavily, and so did most of the men she brought home, and there were many.

As Ava showered, she shuddered involuntarily as she remembered listening to her mother's groans and moans as she screwed through the nights. Oh God and the money too, sometimes lying on the kitchen table, right beside her packed lunch, which she had made herself because her mother was far too busy giving her friends extra blow jobs, just to secure future transactions.

She turned on the radio in an attempt to rid her mind of the disgusting actions of the woman she had once referred to as her mother. There would be a rare moment from time to time when Ava would give her mother a couple of seconds, wondering what had become of her, or even if she was still alive. She would never make any attempt to find her though, there were too many bitter memories for her to have any emotional connections now, and anyway, too much time had gone by for any real chance of reconciliation.

At 12.00 pm, Ava and Terry rendezvoused as planned for lunch. It didn't take Terry long to bring her out of the mild depression she'd got herself into, with his usual profanations and his sledge-hammer wit concerning Chinese restaurants.

He wasn't a fan of Cantonese food that was for sure.

He never failed to amuse her, or surprise her either, using words in between his blasphemous outrages that quite literally left her gobsmacked. All said and done, Terry Mercer was an educated man. Today's surprise came about when she had suggested going for Italian food.

"Not today Ava, today I think we'll just head to off to my favourite cafe, I'm feeling ichthyophagous."

Ava burst out laughing thinking he'd just made the word up, but later found out when she got home that the joke was on her. After consulting her dictionary, she discovered the word. Ichthyophagous simply meant, fish-eating.

After their meal, they spent half an hour or so discussing the events of the next day, and how they'd planned to go for drinks to celebrate the removal from society of that wretched woman. Terry then again surprised Ava by informing her of where he'd spent his morning.

"The mind boggles" she jokingly mocked. "Have you been licking Polly's ass again Terry to gain her affections, you're really quite transparent you know. We all knew you'd be back in her office now that she's back from vacation, we were all quite surprised that you didn't go with her actually."

The smile faded from Ava's face as Terry said, "I went to see Deborah Oconnor today, I had to Ava, she-"

"Terry? What did I tell you, you can't have any sentiment, her sister nearly killed you. She gave information which endangered your life and took the lives of three of your colleagues might I add. Don't let them play on your soft side, she's going down Terry, and I for one will be making sure that she does, so I hope you haven't put any hope into this sister of hers, because it's not going to happen, fuck her and her sob stories, and you get a fucking grip. You were the same with the whores, they had you round their little fingers." Did he detect a little jealousy there?

He had never heard Ava quite so outspoken, or so determined.

"Ava, calm yourself" he said quietly. "I had to go and see for myself if Kathlene had been telling the truth. I've known that girl for quite some time, she is an excellent forensic officer and her work is flawless, she has through her professionalism helped solve a number of cases. I know what she done was wrong, and I know

there are rules that she should have followed concerning blackmail, and ordinarily I would have agreed that she'd breached those rules, but not where Rosalyn Simpson is concerned.
She gave the bitch the information to save herself and the lives of her sister's children, and having visited her sister, I can confirm that she was indeed telling the truth. Hell Ava, think about it. She loves her career, she lives for the job." Terry sighed, thinking that his words would go in one of Ava's ears and out of the other.
The two detectives sat in silence for almost a full minute, just scrutinising each other's faces.
Eventually Ava nodded her head and smiled at him.
"Ok Terry, ok, maybe I'm being a bit ruthless, but it's just that I can't for the life of me understand how one of our own could put so many people's lives at risk, and, albeit inadvertently, cause the deaths of three very highly respected detectives. Even if she were reinstated Terry, she wouldn't be working here in the yard. I have to tell you that more than a few in here have rejected her to a state of non-existence. What she done Terry, was unforgiveable, certainly in most people's opinion. Whether or not she was being blackmailed is by the by as far as they are concerned, and I understand perfectly their venomous attitude towards her. She would have a life of hell in here I don't need to tell you."
"She won't be working in here Ava, I'll see to that. I will also see to it that every person present at the meeting will be informed of just what an impossible position the poor girl was put into, bearing in mind that when that ruthless maniac promises to kill someone she keeps her promise. It wouldn't have mattered to Simpson if Kathlene had given her the information or not, she would still have found out what she needed to know. Look what she found out about you Ava, and I sure as hell didn't tell her anything. She got to you Ava, and she got to me, and every single person whoever comes into contact with her. She's not finished with me? Huh, she's in jail, she's going to be put into a mental institute for the rest of her life, and still she's saying, she's not finished with me?
I'll be doing my utmost to make sure that Kathlene gets reinstated, bloody girl knows she's done wrong but do you know what Ava?

She managed to save the lives of her sister's children, and truth be known, if it was my son's life at stake, I would have done the very same, without a moment's hesitation."
" Alright Terry" Ava gave in, smiling. "I'll put in a letter supporting yours...but she won't be in here Terry, and she'll have to face the disciplinary hearing, it won't be easy for her, and if they allow her to continue, she'll be on probation for quite some time. It'll take some time before they can bring themselves to trust her, she's shot herself in both feet Terry...I know you like her."
"What the hell is that supposed to mean, you know I like her. Yes I like her, but not in the way that you are insinuating."
Mercer rose from his chair and headed over to the counter to pay for their meal. They walked the short distance to the car park without saying a word to each other. As they drove through the city back to Ava's apartment, Terry Mercer once again said something to her that completely took her by surprise, and made her flush.
"When all this is over I'd like to take you with me on a holiday, would you be up for that? I'm asking you as a friend you know, I'm not trying anything stupid here I mean, I'm not compulsive if that's what you think. Would you be up for that Ava, the holiday I mean? Would you come with me?"
Still flushing, and now blushing, Ava replied, "I'd love to go on holiday with you Mister Terrence Mercer, it would be an honour."
"Ok, that's' that settled then, I'll look forward to it. Is there anywhere in particular you'd like to go, I mean, you can choose, it doesn't have to be me who decides."
"I trust your judgement Terry, surprise me."
Moments later, he was back to his blasphemous ways cursing bad drivers along the city streets.
"And by the way Ava, the whores as you call them did not have me round their little fingers, and they're not whores either, I've told you before they are working girls, and a bloody fine job they do too...sisters of mercy, that's what they are, don't you forget that...just because I like them...fucking wrapped round their fingers...Christ Ava."
Ava Cruntze just smiled as they drove through the city, Terry

Mercer was a very unique man indeed, and if truth be known, she was beginning to fall in love with him...more than a little.

# PLEASANT MEADOWS PSYCHIATRIC CLINIC.

## STOURBRIDGE. BIRMINGHAM.

The day had finally arrived. Terry and Ava had followed the armoured car all the way up from London and were now entering the grounds of the psychiatric hospital where Rosalyn Simpson would spend the rest of her life.
Very little had been said between the two detectives as they followed close behind the truck.
Off and on they spoke about things in general, about crime and punishment, and how the crimes committed these days seemed to be more and more brutal and callous.
People in general, were less forgiving than they used to be.
There seemed to be no boundaries in the crimes committed today. The woman in the armoured car in front of them had extracted the kidneys from a victim and then proceeded to cook them.
She had strung a young helpless woman up onto a wall, by means of the use of a nail gun, and then slit the young girl's wrists, making love with her perverted accomplice in the spill of the girl's life-blood. She had cut the young detective Billy McDermot practically into pieces. She had pierced the knife into him more than a hundred times, and then had proceeded to deposit sperm from her mouth into the dead detective's mouth.
Misses Simpson had then murdered her accomplice for no apparent reason and then sliced his body into pieces, dumping the bundles into the Thames. She had left Terry and Sandra Neal for dead in the depths of a sewer, and then murdered Sandra by means of Pseudoautochiria. Then to cap it all, she'd killed the best friend Terry Mercer had ever had in his life. She shot Sam Hargrieves in the head. Cold and callous were not the words to describe a person like this, and Pleasant Meadows was not a title she'd have given to a place where the inmates were as dangerous as the plague.
There was a silence between Terry and Ava as they climbed out of the B.M.W. They both watched in silent fascination as the monster

was escorted out of the armoured car and up the long strip of concrete steps that led to her new home. With her hands cuffed behind her back and an armed guard on each of her arms, she actually looked quite vulnerable, helpless, and if not for her violent history almost...innocent.

A team of nurses and doctors and psychiatrists awaited their new guest, at the top of the steps, standing outside two huge oak doors that must have been four metres high. The building was massive and looked to Terry like an ordinary hospital, rather than a home especially built for the criminally insane.

The place looked...normal, but then, so did its' guests.

They looked like normal people, until whatever triggered off their demonic behaviour kicked in, and then...look out world, but all said and done, if the people in here done their jobs, and he'd been assured that they would, then they could do no further damage to society. Society would be safe, from the lunatics that were in here at least, the trouble was, there were thousands more like those in here, who had still not been detected, or apprehended and so the hideous crimes would continue to be committed, and innocent people would continue to be slaughtered violently...for no reason other than being in the wrong place at the wrong time.

Ava looked at Terry just as Simpson was being led into the building.

"You fucking evil bitch fuck," Mercer whispered as Simpson finally was led in through the huge doors.

"What the fuck happened to you Rosalyn."

"Come on Terry, let's go inside and have a coffee with the doctors, I'm sure we'll feel a lot better once we've had a conversation with them, and once we've seen the inside of this place, it certainly looks secure enough doesn't it."

Terry didn't answer his colleague, but began to walk slowly towards the steps almost reluctantly, as if he was dreading even entering the building...and perhaps he was.

As they climbed the steps Kathlene Oconnor's words kept ringing in his ears. *"She's not finished with you yet."*

"What's wrong Terry, come on, it's over, she's doing nothing more, she's here. We leave here Terry today, and we leave her and her hideous crimes here with her. It was horrible I know, but her goose is cooked, she's home, and she's here forever."

Ava and Terry spent the next fifty minutes in an office having a conversation with the two psychiatrists who were in charge of all proceedings within the premises. Once again they emphasised to the two detectives that she'd be well looked after, and by well, they meant that there was no chance whatsoever of any of the inmates ever escaping from here.
"None whatsoever." said Mercer, rising to his feet.
"Absolutely no chance whatsoever Mister Mercer, I can assure you." The very tall Doctor Andrew Mullard replied.
"You can leave here with the sure knowledge of knowing that Rosalyn Simpson will never again show her face in public, to all intents and purposes Mister Mercer, she is, obsolete."
The two detectives shook hands with the two psychiatrists and excused themselves from the room. It took them the best part of ten minutes to even find the lobby and the front exit.
They had been led through a labyrinth of corridors before they'd entered Doctor Mullard's office, and it had been he who had done all the talking. The other psychiatrist who's name Terry had already forgotten had sat and said practically nothing throughout the meeting. A woman in her early thirties, very slim with pale skin and raven hair, held up with colourful clips. If no-one had told him, he would have surmised that the woman was a librarian or a manageress in one of the more expensive hotels.
She had sat stern-faced and only cracking a smile occasionally when her colleague had said something that *he* thought was humorous.
At one point, Terry got the feeling that she was assessing *him*.
She had glanced, or rather, stared into his eyes from time to time, over her large red glasses, making him feel quite ill-at-ease.
As they descended the concrete steps Terry let out a massive sigh of relief.
"I'm glad that's over Ava, I can tell you that, Christ I'm more than ready for a cigarette, they go fucking on and on about the same old fucking shit, do they not?"

"Circumlocutory it's called Terry, very annoying."
"Circum what?"
"Circumlocutory, it just means that they use a whole lot of words describing or explaining something, when a few words would do. They stretch it out Terry to look or sound impressive, I'm afraid it doesn't work with me, to me they're just long-winded, quite tiresome actually."
"You can say that again. Let's get to fuck away from here Ava, I could use a drink, how about you?"
"Sure, we can go when we get back home, do you want me to drive?"
"Yes please Ava, I think I'll smoke about thirty fags before we get back...I'll open the window of course."
"Yes you will Terry" replied Ava grinning at him "You're right there."
Ava pulled up the B.M.W. to a halt at the perimeter gates, where they were greeted by two armed officers. One of the guards stood about six foot six at least Terry thought. A huge man and built in Terry's words, like a brick shit-house. The other guy was no midget either, he would be at least six two, and again, heavily built.
"Look Ava" said Terry, "they've hired two night-club bouncers for security."
"Stop laughing Terry, they're looking at us."
The tallest guard approached the car and bent down as Ava opened the window.
"Can I see your pass please Miss?"
Ava smiled at the guard and politely produced her I.D. wallet, showing her C.I.D. status.
"That's not it Miss, I'm afraid I can't let you leave until I see your pass, you have to have a pass you see."
"We're detectives man, for God's sake, we're C.I.D. Christ, let us out of here we're having a bad enough day."
"No way I'm opening these gates until I see a pass, didn't anyone issue you with a pass in there?"
"No they didn't" Terry snarled.
"Well then, you'll have to go back and get one and it had better be signed by one of the doctors or you're not going anywhere, no

matter how bad your day has been. I have list of strict rules that must be withheld and I'm afraid your status means nothing to me. And rule number one is, that all visitors, or staff for that matter must produce their identity pass on entering and leaving these premises, so I would suggest that you go back in there and have one of the staff print you out a pass, and once you obtain it please keep it with you for any future visits, I know it's an inconvenience to you, but as you can understand, we have to be exceptionally careful regarding who comes in and out of here...sorry."

Terry was about to go into one of his blasphemous rages when Ava, immediately spotted the danger and said, "Terry, you wait here and I'll go and see to the passes. Enjoy your cigarette.

Go and wait in the guard's little cubical, I'll only be ten minutes or so."

Mercer was undoubtedly relieved at Ava's suggestion and kissed her on the cheek. "Thanks bud" he said, climbing out of the car. I need some fresh air Ava."

As Terry was walking around the car Ava summoned him with a movement of her head. He bent down to hear what she wanted to tell him.

"I'll be as quick as I can Terry, but I don't know how long that will be, in the meantime, don't start anything with these two here to land us in any trouble, do not start any swearing or cursing especially at them. You want out of here, then you'll have to behave and be patient, ok?"

"What are you doing?" said the tallest guard to Mercer,

" You can't come in here, you'll have to go back up there with your partner, you'll have to have your photograph taken for your pass, you can't stay here, away you go and get sorted out, you're not coming in here, and there's no smoking anyway, you're not even meant to be smoking on these premises, you'd better put that out or you'll be reported."

Words could not possibly describe the temper that was rising inside Terry Mercer. He knew he had to keep his mouth shut no matter what, but the thought of re-entering the hospital made his skin crawl. He reluctantly climbed back into the car beside Ava who was praying that Terry could control his temper. If he couldn't there would be repercussions which they could both well do without. Terry waved his hand at Ava as though he were a Lord ushering his chauffeur to move onward. He flicked the unfinished cigarette in the direction of the tall guard and stared at him intently as he pressed the button to close the window.

"See you soon" the guard shouted, smiling at the two detectives. One hour and twenty-five minutes later Terry Mercer and Ava Cruntze finally left the grounds of Pleasant Meadows. Ava drove all the way back to London and hardly a single word was spoken between the two, not because of any fall-out between themselves, but rather that they had both come to the end of their tether with the staff and the premises at Pleasant Meadows. A place where neither of them had any intentions of ever returning to, other than perhaps coming to confirm the death of a certain Misses Rosalyn Simpson.

## CHAPTER FOURTEEN.

## SCOTLAND YARD.

## BROADWAY VICTORIA.

The day had come for Kathlene Oconnor to learn what exactly her fate would be regarding her punishment, and indeed, her career. Polly Sheppard had come to see her and had informed her that she would do whatever she could to help her case and to point out to the board, exactly what her circumstances were when she had given Simpson the information. Polly had also explained that Terry Mercer had been to visit her sister and had changed his opinion completely. He and Ava Cruntze would also be putting forward positive references regarding her work and her loyalty towards her colleagues. Andy Phillips had also put forward to the board a list of crimes that had been committed, and if not for Miss Oconnor's professionalism, would never have been brought to a close.
"Try not to worry too much Kathlene, and if the worst comes to the worst, we'll appeal against any negative decision, and I'm quite sure we would be successful...they'll be lenient I'm sure. I'll come and see you after the trial...don't worry."
Polly left the holding cell and returned to her office.
One hour and twenty minutes later, Kathlene Oconnor walked out of the conference-room, practically a free woman.
She had sat listening to the charges pressed against her, and was acquiescent to whatever would come her way, after all, she had disclosed information that was highly secret and so was at least aware of the seriousness of the situation. If it didn't go her way, she'd just have to do the time and move on with a different career when she'd completed the sentence.
However, the board had taken in all the information given to them, the plusses and the negatives. Finally they came to the decision that Oconnor would be given a three year suspended sentence, and that she would be permitted to continue in her field on probationary

grounds, which meant that, at least for a while, she would not be permitted to work on her own. Jubilation was not the word to describe how Kathlene Oconnor felt at this moment in time.
Thanks to Polly Sheppard, Terry Mercer, Ava Cruntze and Andy Phillips, she would be able to go home to her sister and the kids, and her life would now go back to normal. She had learned crucial lessons throughout this experience, and would never again allow herself to be put into a situation like this.
She had been very lucky, and was now indebted to those people who had helped her escape the severe sentences that would have been given to her if not for their kind character-reference compliments.
Kathlene Oconnor headed straight down to Polly Sheppard's office where she was permitted entry. Polly embraced her as the young forensic genius broke down and sobbed bitterly on her superior's shoulders, trying her best to express her gratitude. Just as Polly had the girl almost back in control, Terry Mercer and Ava Cruntze entered the room, and so it was a further ten minutes before Kathlene could speak coherently. The fear of what could have been, the vituperation thrown to her by colleagues who'd had a less compassionate opinion upon her crimes. Their criticisms had been excoriating and so, even with the support of Polly Sheppard, she'd half expected to be dealt with quite severely. Once again Kathlene Oconnor thanked everyone in the room before departing to the lobby where her sister awaited her arrival, along with her two children. One thing was for sure, if for some reason she ever had to give up this career, she'd have a bloody good chance of making it as an actor.
Polly gave the girl a final hug and said, "On you go now Kathlene, use these two weeks to get all that negative stuff out of your head. I shall e mail you when we require you back, now don't worry about anything else just now, you just go home and enjoy your sister's company, and remember Kathlene, no matter how hopeless the situation seems, you come to us and you tell us everything, ok?"
Kathlene Oconnor nodded briskly, tears beginning to flow again.
"I will." She managed before leaving the room. "Thank you all so

much" she said as she closed the door behind her.

"What changed your mind Terry?" said Polly Sheppard, as she poured her two detectives a cup of coffee each.
"The last time I spoke to you, you were all for hanging her, and you as well Ava, your opinion wasn't much different from his."
Terry sat down in front of Polly accepting the beverage gratefully.
"I went to visit Kathlene's sister, that's what done it. I hadn't realized just how much the young girl depended on her. At first I thought it was just another sob story about circumstances and predicaments, but it soon became clear just what a nasty situation Kathlene had been put into. That bitch, she knew, would have killed those children, and if she'd came to us she was almost certain that the witch would have found out, and so there-for putting the children first, she decided not to inform us about her situation. On top of that Polly, she is a bloody good forensic officer. Phillips has gone to pieces since Sam has left us and I happen to think that he'll retire very soon, I mean even before next year, and so, as far as I'm aware, there is no-one else with the skills or dedication to their work on our books, certainly not in this department to take over from him. She's perfect. I know Polly that that decision will be made by the board, and so I'm asking you not to be dissuaded from what the truth of the matter is, and that is, that Kathlene Oconnor should be made head of forensics. They'll be lining up outside of your door to be considered for the post Polly, all these sycophantic bastards, "Oh yes Miss Sheppard, Oh I couldn't agree more Miss Shepard, anything you say Miss Shepard grovelling nauseating twats, they're all fucking sycophants, the whole lot of them, criticizing the poor girl with their fucking excoriating remarks and accusations..."
"Terry I get your point, please, no more swearing. I know about everything, just calm yourself down, I'll deal with everything. You just get away for a few days somewhere, enjoy your time off as well. Why don't you and Ava go away somewhere together, that's if Ava can stand your continuous profanations."
Polly looked at Ava smiling. "If you can keep him calm Ava, then there's worse people to spend time with you know."

Although Polly had been joking with the two, it came as no surprise to her when Terry informed her that that was exactly what they were going to do.

"I'm glad" said Polly. "The two of you need to get away and get that monster out of your heads. My God, she has done some damage to us all has she not, psychologically I mean, as well as her murderous escapades. Get yourselves away from work, because God knows, when you come back, there'll probably be another Rosalyn Simpson to take care of, although I find it hard to believe that there's anyone out there who could inflict as much horror into society as she, the abysm from whence she came, is where nightmares crawl."

Two days later, Terry and Ava boarded the euro-train and took a trip under the English Chanel heading for Paris, where they would spend the next eight days, building their relationship to a point where they had both accepted, that they would indeed be quite lost without the other. Apart from Sandra Neal, Ava was only the second woman in his life since Carol had decided to depart from his life. Sometimes, while Ava slept, he would go through the course of events regarding his marriage, and try and work out where he had gone wrong. Without being chauvinist, he'd failed to see where he had derailed the train. Carol had seemed happy, apart from the length of time he would spend at work, although she had accepted that, or so she said. Obviously, there had been something wrong with their relationship, or she wouldn't have just up and left, but no matter how he scrutinised the situation, he couldn't for the life of him, find the reason. Sam had told him not to knock himself out about it and not to let it rankle him, and that, sometimes women or men for that matter would or could just suddenly fall in love with someone else and find themselves besotted by that person, to a point where they felt that they just couldn't live without them. Carol had taken off in that manner because she wouldn't be able to find the words to explain just how she felt about this other man, or woman.

"You'll just have to accept it Terry, she's fallen in love with a guy, and that's it. There's no excuse I know about your wee boy, I know that, but, she's away Terry, and that's the end of it, you know she'll look after the kid, so, just live your life now kid, you've done nothing wrong."

He rose up out of bed as stealthily as he could so as not to awaken Ava, and made his way through to the kitchen in the small apartment he'd rented. Smoking was forbidden in here, but he opened the window and stood drinking his tea enjoying his forbidden cigarette whilst listening to the Parisians going about their nightly routines. It was just the same as London.

Different languages being spoken, but it was just the same.

The police sirens, the distant screams, the laughter, the car horns, the hustlers, the whores, the pimps, the pushers, the murderers, the victims, the Rosalyn Simpsons, yeah, the screw-balls, who had long since rusted their hinges. The lunatics, they would all be here in Paris, just as they would in London, or Reo, or anywhere else in the world for that matter. And you'll never know who they are. You go for a pint in your local. Same faces as there has always been, you even know them by name...but you don't them.

There they stand with their vacant expressions, leaning against the bar, where the speechless unite. The depressed the gamblers, the lonely, the lost. All standing there staring into their beer silently contemplating their lives. There in their harmonious silence.

It could be them. They could be keeping someone prisoner in their basement for all you know.

How do you spot a psychopath? Answer? You don't, you can't, unless you actually catch them in the act.

He sighed as he observed the activities below him. Two young men were in dispute about something. He could not make out obviously what was being said, but eventually, the two young gentlemen made up and shook hands and walked away, with the young lady in the middle of them, holding both of their hands on the narrow street. Terry closed the window and returned to bed where he found Ava in the very same position she was in when he left the room. He smiled as he carefully climbed back into bed with her. Two more days here in Paris, and then it would be back to the grind-stone. At least young Kathlene would be there, he'd helped to save her job...and then her voice in his head, *"She's not finished with you yet."*

## SCOTLAND YARD.

## BROADWAY VICTORIA.

Terry and Ava had been summoned to Polly's office as soon as they arrived back from holiday, summoned being the correct word judging by the urgency in the officer's voice who had informed them. As they entered the office, Polly was busy scrutinising the screen on her computer studying the information Kathlene Oconnor had given her.  She, and of all people, the young promoted Smedley, who had disclosed her activities with Rosalyn Simpson, had been sent down to a village called Kilndown in Kent to investigate a certain gentleman's activities.

The gentleman in question was a surgeon, an ex- surgeon to be precise. He had been struck off the list because of numerous fatalities which had taken place in one of the hospitals where he had worked.

There had been seven deaths involving people who had been admitted for routine operations. Their deaths had all occurred within three months. Although there was insufficient evidence of any wrong-doing on the surgeon's part it had been decided by the chief of staff and his administrator to let him go, on the grounds of negligence. This way, they would apologise profusely and compensate the families of the deceased financially, but that would be the end of the matter, and there would be no more coincidental misfortunes with surgeon Alexander Stineman. Mister Stineman was no ordinary surgeon. He specialised in brain surgery.

What had saved him from any further investigations was the fact that he had performed some major operations throughout his time and had saved numerous lives applying his inimitable skills, bringing people out of comas and achieving wondrous results with patients who had suffered strokes, helping to give them back speech and use of their hands. The man had been looked upon by the people he worked with as some kind of modern-day medical messiah, such was his credibility. His record and his professionalism were exempt.

A man in his late sixties, he was due to retire in a couple of years and that being the case, as far as the board of inquiry were concerned was the reason Mister Stineman had not appealed against the decision. As far as the public were concerned, that is exactly what had happened, the man had simply retired.
The letter that the board of inquiry had sent him was very different to that which was written in the newspapers. But, there was no appeal, no complaints about loss of pensions, nothing.
It was as though he had been acquiescent to the matter. Mister Stineman however had recently disappeared and hadn't been spotted for at least three weeks. Nothing unusual there one would have thought, except that a number of people from around this area in Kent had mysteriously disappeared along with him, or at least at the same time. Ten people in all had been reported missing, most of them young teenagers but also a couple of elderly people as well. Where, Alexander Stineman lived, just a mile or so east of the village Kilndown was where Kathlene Oconnor and John Smedley were now.
After Kathlene had reported that Mister Stineman was nowhere to be seen, she was instructed by Polly Sheppard to search the premises. It was while she was doing just that, that Oconnor was shocked beyond belief. Because what she discovered rekindled all kinds of fear into her. Throughout the search, she found women and gentlemen's clothing. The women's clothing looked to belong to young girls rather than older women. She also discovered wallets and purses, all of which contained money and bank cards. Mobile phones were discovered but had been destroyed and sim-cards removed. It was when Kathlene began her forensic work that she was shocked beyond all belief. But there was no mistake, the proof was here and she had kept records of all investigations and samples taken from suspects up in London concerning Simpson.
But here it was...how on earth was she going to inform Polly Sheppard of this? How the hell could this be, but all over the house, including the bedroom, especially the master bedroom was the D.N.A. of a certain Misses Rosalyn Simpson.
She knew that Simpson was locked away safely up in Pleasant

Meadows in Birmingham, but she also knew that there would be some kind of sinister connection between that evil bitch and this missing surgeon. It had obviously been quite some time since she'd been here, but the fact that she had only frightened Kathlene even more. What the hell was going on here, and how long had they known each other. Worse still, *how* had they got to know each other? Under what circumstances had they met? This was going to be serious Kathlene knew. She kept thinking about the woman who had quite calmly informed her that she would kill her sister's children if she did not comply to her requests. There would be a team sent down here just shortly, Polly would see to that.
The fact that Rosalyn Simpson's D.N.A. was all over the place simply meant that there would not be a stone left unturned down here until they got to the bottom of it. If this surgeon was a friend of Simpson's then it didn't bear thinking about what they might find down here. Was this going to be what the bitch meant when she said that she wasn't finished with Terry yet? Was this the reason for her smug-faced confidence? Something pre-arranged was going to happen to Terry. Simpson couldn't do anything, that was for sure, but someone else could, and Terry would undoubtedly be sent here, of that there was no doubt whatsoever. The question was, where the hell was this Mister Stineman? It was of the utmost importance to find out where he was, and to get him to explain who these clothes belonged to and all the other possessions he happened to have in his house, and ,of course, how on earth did he know Rosalyn Simpson?

Polly Sheppard looked up from the screen at Terry and Ava. "You're not going to believe this you two. I have some news that could be very disturbing to us all, and it concerns Misses Rosalyn Simpson. We sent young Kathlene down to Kent to investigate a certain gentleman's activities. Kathlene landed down there accompanied by young Smedley, only to discover that the gentleman in question it would seem, has absconded."
Terry shifted uneasily on his seat, muttering something incoherent. "She found traces of Simpson's D.N.A in several parts of the house.

This gentleman by the way, is a surgeon.
For want of the use of better words, he's been forced to retire, apparently there wasn't enough evidence for him to be convicted in a court of law. Several people have lost their lives undergoing routine surgery. Needless to say, all the operations were performed by this man. He specialises in brain surgery and has done sterling work throughout his career, and was, until recently, a very respected man indeed, which is why, I'm guessing, that no further inquiries were made after his mishaps."
Terry and Ava sat listening intently to every single word their superior was telling them. Mercer knew instinctively what was coming next. It was inevitable. He braced himself for Polly's next sentence.
"I'm afraid Terry, you and Ava will have to go back to Pleasant Meadows and interview this Simpson. See if you can find out anything else about this surgeon, or where he might be found. I know this is not ideal Terry, and if push comes to shove, I can send some-one else up there with Ava if you feel that you're not up to the task, and God knows, we would all understand if you weren't. We have to find out what the connection between the two is. She might be able to tell you where he is. There has not been a trace of any of the people who have been reported missing, not a thing. Kathlene informs me, and this is what's worrying me, that she's found clothing belonging to teenagers, female teenagers. She's informed Mister Phillips of her discoveries and the clothes are on their way to the labs. We will then find out if the clothes belong to any of the missing people...and God help us if they do."
"I knew it, I just fucking knew it...that bitch has something to do with this surgeon fucker, and it's my guess that she's got something to do with these people disappearing, the fucking termagant that she is."
Polly Sheppard burst into laughter, she couldn't help herself. She and Ava had been glancing at Terry as the information had been given to them. The outburst of profanations from Mercer had been long overdue. Ava placed a hand upon his shoulder.
"Calm down Terry, you don't have to go back up there, I'll take

someone else with me, but it has to be done."
She smiled at Polly as though Mercer wasn't even in the room. "It's not just the bitch that's bothering him." She whispered, "it's the bloody security men on the gate, they and Terry both started off on the wrong foot shall we say."
"I'm sitting right here Ava, what the fuck am I, a mirage? Of course I'm going with you…wouldn't miss it for the world."

## KILNDOWN VILLAGE.

## KENT.

Kathlene Oconnor and John Smedley had completed their search of the house. She had sent for extra help and so now there were no fewer than six forensic officers in the premises. They had done everything that they could do and now it was up to the detectives to find out where this missing surgeon was, and of course, the people belonging to the clothes they'd found. It would only take a couple of hours for the lab technicians to determine if the clothes belonged to any of the missing people.
Oconnor waited until the other four officers had departed before locking up and heading over to the car, where Smedley waited patiently.
"I'm sorry about everything Miss Oconnor" he said, as she climbed into the vehicle.
"Sorry about what exactly John? You were doing your job, that's all. I made the mistake of trying to deal with it myself without informing my colleagues. I've been lucky John, they understood my predicament, they were lenient. I shan't ever make that mistake again. So, there's nothing for you to apologise for, and I hope you'd do the same again if it were to reoccur, anyway" she smiled, "you got a bloody good promotion out of it all did you not?"
"Yes Miss, but I still feel a bit like...like I've let you down, it was never my intention to cause you harm or get you into trouble, I hope you know that."
"Come on Mister Smedley, back to London my friend, let's go and make Terry Mercer's day, he's gonna` love us for this, rekindling his affectionate affair with Misses Simpson, can't wait to find out what he'll get us for Christmas.

As Smedley drove back up to London Kathlene kept searching her mind trying to remember if Simpson had ever mentioned anything about this surgeon. As far as she could recall, she'd never mentioned him, but still the reference to not being finished with Terry kept jabbing her. She was locked up in that mental institution but still spoke with the arrogance of being a free woman...as if she were still in control of proceedings. The frightening thing was, that if this surgeon and she were working together, or had something premeditated, then as long as he was at liberty...she *was*.

Kathlene also surmised that it would be a good idea not to inform her colleagues that Misses Simpson had delivered a hand-written note for her to read, prior to her arrest.

## PLEASANT MEADOWS.

## BIRMINGHAM.

"Here we go" muttered Terry as he and Ava approached the main gates of the highest security mental institution in Britain.
"Look at them, chomping at the bit, hoping we've forgotten our fucking passes so as they can fuck us off again, well they're shitten` on today...it'll break their poor hearts...bloody passes indeed."
"Terry, don't start, don't be riling them up, it took us long enough to get out of here the last time. Now, Polly has already informed them of our arrival and why we're here, so there shouldn't be any problems. When we're in here Terry don't make contact with her eyes, look at her neck or something when you're asking her any questions. If you look her in the eyes she'll mess with your head, anyway, I'll be asking her most of the questions, and so just to remind you, losing your temper with her won't get us anywhere...so, we play it cool ok?"
"Yeah, I know Ava, I won't lose my temper. There's more chance of me losing my temper with these twats, look at them."
The tall guard who had rebuked Terry on their previous visit approached the vehicle.
"Good morning to you both, do you have your clearance passes with you?"
"Right here bud." replied Terrence Mercer, smiling broadly at the giant officer, and producing his card pass, almost sticking it in the officer's face.
"She's got hers as well, would you like to see it?"
"Of course I'd like to see it, what kind of stupid question is that?"
Ava produced her pass and smiled at the guard who's face did not alter from the deadly seriousness etched upon it.
"Will we need to produce these cards again when we leave" said Terry, knowing full well he would annoy the officer, who just exhaled impatiently through his nose and nodded.
"Ok then, let's go Ava, we don't want to be holding the gentleman

up from his duties, goodness knows how many more visitors could be coming here today, he'll have lots of cards to check, we'll see you soon bud, take it easy."

"Terry, don't please, said Ava as they drove up the long drive. Please don't annoy them anymore. This is going to be unpleasant enough talking to this sick bitch in here without making things any more difficult for ourselves, so please Terry, no more sarcasm…to anyone, ok?"

They entered the building having been greeted by Mister Thomas Graham, the head psychiatrist who gave them a short lecture on the terms and conditions of their interview with Misses Simpson. As well as having to follow a strict code of conduct, there would also be a member of staff present throughout the duration of the interview, and anything they asked Misses Simpson, would, of course be recorded. Terry found it extremely difficult to stop himself from speaking out in protest but then thought that perhaps it would be best for everyone concerned that there was a third party present at the interview.

Thomas Graham was a man in his late sixties immaculately dressed in a navy-blue suit and white shirt. The silver tie he wore matched his thick well-kept hair. Perhaps because of his line of work, he wore a permanent sympathetic smile which never at any point disappeared from his face, giving the impression that he felt sorry for everyone he spoke to, or that he had just listened to your heart-rending story and was undoubtedly giving you his support.

He uncrossed his legs placing both of his hands on his knees and rose to his feet, straightening his trousers as he did.

"So, are we all clear on that?"

"Yes, thank you Mister Graham, and thank you for allowing us to speak with her, we appreciate it very mush indeed." said Ava, as she rose from her chair. The psychiatrist once more shook hands with the two detectives and then proceeded to lead them down one of the building's many corridors to a room where he introduced them to the member of staff who would take them to see Rosalyn Simpson. Mister Graham looked at his colleague, a young man about the age of thirty, and said to him, "I'll leave them in your very capable hands Mister Foster, any problems, just give me a buzz, good day officers." And with that, he left the room and disappeared down another corridor. Finally, having been in the building for more than twenty-five minutes, they were led into an interview room where Rosalyn Simpson sat at a table in the centre of the room accompanied by two gentlemen both of whom were almost as tall as the gateman, standing either side of her. To Terry's astonishment, Simpson had been permitted to apply make-up and must have also been permitted to send for some of her clothes. She sat in the centre of the long table wearing a beautiful crimson blouse, her hair set up in what Terry would describe as a pony-tail, held up with two silver butterfly clips, her makeup immaculate. If they hadn't discovered overwhelming forensic proof of this woman's crimes, then it would be difficult indeed to imagine the person in front of them having any kind of involvement in criminal activities. As much as Terry hated to admit it, the woman looked extremely attractive, her curvaceousness obvious to anyone, including, of course, herself. The crimson blouse was worn to accentuate her hair. Even in here, she couldn't resist to flirt herself ostentatiously, "*Whatever good it would do her in here*" thought Terry. As the two detectives sat down opposite Simpson, she smiled, looking down at the floor momentarily and then attempted to look into Terry's eyes.

He looked away.

The two tall gentlemen stood back and informed John Foster, the man in charge of all internal security that they would be in the adjoining room if there were any problems. Mister Foster assured them that there wouldn't be and that the interview would last no more than fifteen minutes, the last piece of information was for Ava and Terry's benefit only.

The two giant men left the room, closing the door behind them. Now there was silence, as Mister Foster retrieved a chair for himself and sat it down just a few yards from the detectives.

He then pressed a button on a small recording device he'd placed earlier on the table. "Ok?" he said to the detectives.

Terry and Ava nodded their heads.
"Ok then, you have fifteen minutes, just ignore me sitting over here I won't interfere with any of your questions, unless I think there's something been said that I'm not happy with."
Simpson smiled continuously into Terry's face as she sat with her cup of tea, the cup raised to her mouth and held in both hands.
Ava began the conversation. "Well now Rosalyn, it would seem that you finally got your wish, an interview with Terry at last, although not quite under the terms that you proposed, how are you keeping dear?"
Terry cringed at Ava's words. Wasn't she the one telling him to be cautious regarding what he said to her, and yet, here she was being openly sarcastic.
If Ava's words had got to Simpson she did not let it show.
She continued to smile into Terry's face and completely ignored Ava. "It's been a long time Terry, has it not? I mean apart from the time I was naked in your bed, and I must admit, I enjoyed your attentions whist you dreamily thought that I was your lover Sandra...you have very skilful hands I must admit, you certainly know how to arouse a woman."
Terry looked over at Mister Foster expecting him to intervene in some way, but was astounded to find that he had no intentions of stepping in at this moment in time.
Instead, Ava stepped in again.
"Of course Rosalyn, the man was semi-conscious and so could be forgiven for his actions, you on the other hand suffer from some form of encephalopathy which the doctors here will eventually get to the bottom of, anyway, we won't keep you for long, just a simple couple of uncomplicated questions, and then we'll be out of your way forever. Do you know anything about a certain gentleman who goes by the name of Alexander Stineman?"
The smile momentarily left Simpson's face.
She took a sip from her cup and then smiled again as she continued looking into Terry's face.
"Oh my goodness Terry, you're getting *so* close to finding out the truth about everything, really warm."

She placed her cup down gently upon the table, and then rubbed her hands together vigorously, as though she were cold.
"Not long now Terry, before the final infliction, your final lesson in how not to mess with people's feelings and disappoint them bitterly, completely spoiling their lives, nay, ruining their lives."
She took another sip from her tea-cup.
"To answer your question Miss Cruntze, it is still Miss isn't it? Hard to find a good man after you're thirty-five dear, never mind, you can always try and find someone who has fallen off the bandwagon perhaps, anyway, Mister Alexander Stineman, yes I know him well. We can all be bought for a price Terry, wouldn't you say? It certainly was the case with your Miss Oconnor wasn't it. She sold you all down the river. Oh I know you have had the decency to reinstate her, after all her sob stories. All is forgiven Terry huh? After her lachrymose performance, I bet she had you all in tears."
Ava continued. "How long have you known this man?"
Still looking into Terry's face, she replied, "Long enough deary, long enough for him to do what I wanted done. It was quite a long process as well, and none too cheap I hasten to add, but, as I'm sure you'll agree someday, a very thorough performance, and one that will knock all the stuffing right out of you Mister Mercer, and cancel out Miss Cruntze, any chance you may think you have of living a life with him."
"Do you happen to know where we can find this Mister Stineman, he doesn't seem to be at home, and hasn't been for quite some time. Does he own any other properties in Britain that you know of?"
Still she smiled in Terry's face.
"That would be telling now wouldn't it Miss Cruntze. Let me ask you a question Terry, how is Beth Hargrieves doing, is she keeping well? I don't suppose you know seeing that you haven't been round to see her since your best friend lost his life, don't worry, he felt nothing, I done it really quickly...he certainly didn't deserve to suffer, God rest his soul."
Terry couldn't contain himself any longer.
"You sick fucking bastard, if you've had anything done to Beth I'll kill

you with my own two hands, you sick pathetic bastard that you are. Look at you, fucking mutton dressed as lamb, you scabby whore, you're nothing but a sick fucking whore, you nymphomaniac bastard, I would fucking fry you in a minute if I had my way, you deserve to burn you nasty cow, and you forgot to mention that you'd blackmailed that poor girl into giving you the information, you were going to kill her sister's kids, because that's the only way you can get attention isn't it, by inflicting misery into people's lives, well, you can't inflict any more misery now, you're here for the rest of your scabby life you fucking rat that you are, I hope you rot in Hell you fucking witch, blaming a teenage relationship for all of your sick deeds...mental bitch!!"

John Foster rose to his feet at this point. Before he got a chance to say anything, Mercer roared at him.

"Don't worry I'm leaving, I've heard and seen enough.

Is that supposed to be helping her? Letting her wear makeup you fucking idiots, how is that going to help her realize she's in cuckoo land? You should fucking hang her by the neck and be done with it, or use her for medical experiments instead of rats, come on Ava, let's get out of here, fuck, she's not the only one who needs help around here. I was informed that your methods were unorthodox, but Jesus Christ, letting them dress up and wear makeup like they were going out? I would question your psychiatrists methods if I were you buddy. If that bitch there has done anything to my friend Misses Hargrieves, I'll come back here with a gun and I'll blow her fucking head off, and just see what happens if you try and stop me. You can't help her in here, she's beyond any help, and she'll get out of here if you turn your backs for just one second, I'm warning you, and God help you if that should ever happen, I won't be responsible for my actions if she gets out of here, she's playing you for fuck sakes, gaining your confidence, Jesus, letting her wear makeup and shit, and letting her dress up. You just turn your backs and she'll carve you up like prime beef." He turned to look at Simpson, Won't you, you sick fuck, you know all about cutting people up into pieces, taking out their kidneys and everything you disgusting wretch that you are."

Simpson drained the remainder of her teacup, licking her lips and smiling at Terry Mercer.

"Mister Foster" she said, "You must forgive Mister Mercer here for his blasphemous outburst, he doesn't take very kindly to defeat you see, he's so used to getting his own way, but you mark my words Mister Foster, the next time I see Terrence here there won't be a trace of this arrogance, or self-assurance I can tell you that, he'll be a very different man, and in fact, I would go as far as to say, he may not have enough spiritual strength to continue in this line of work, but we'll see, he's certainly handled everything I've threw at him thus far, though I doubt if he'll get through this last little change in his life which I have arranged."

She looked at Terry menacingly now. "I doubt it very much indeed."

## PARLOUR STREET.

## SOUTH KENSINGTON.

Beth Hargrieves had come to a decision about her future, and where she would spend that future. She and Sam had no family and so as far as she was concerned, there was nothing left for her here in London. The house in which she lived was far too big for a single person, especially an ageing single person, not that she thought of herself as old…but. Certainly she had plenty of friends here, she and Sam had accumulated quite a number of acquaintances over the years, and all of them very nice people. But the climate here in Britain, and especially London did not help her asthmatic condition, and so she'd decided along with a close friend of hers, to buy a house in southern Portugal and emigrate there.

The house they were buying was easily as big as the one in which she lived now, and there was more than enough room for she and her friend to live in separate apartments if needs be, allowing each other the breathing space they would need from time to time, and still have their feeling of independence.

She and Sam had discussed on many occasions what she must do if anything should happen to him. He had insisted that she moved on with her life and live it to the full, and not to brood and continuously reflect on the past and become a recluse.

Nothing had ever been mentioned about emigration but Beth assumed that "living life to the full" meant anything her heart desired, and she certainly desired living in a better climate than this.

Her friend was a gentleman Sam knew well, who had lost his wife through a car accident three years prior to Sam's death. John Pearce was one of the nicest men she had ever met. She and Sam had John round for dinner on quite a few occasions. It was Sam's way of trying to keep John active and involved with people. John was fifty-four years of age, his wife Elizabeth, tragically, was only forty-seven years old when she died. Her death had devastated the man beyond belief. One or two of his other friends had invited him round to their homes for dinners and card nights. John was a lover of bridge, and many other card games.

She and John had begun going out for drinks soon after Sam's death. She felt comfortable in his company.

There would not be a man walking on God's good earth who could replace Sam Hargrieves, but this was not about replacing anyone, this was about moving on with her life, just as she and Sam had discussed, and so she certainly wasn't going to feel guilty about moving away with a man who had been a friend of her husband's. They had discussed over drinks one night the prospect of emigrating and the benefits to their health living in a friendlier environment, friendlier meaning air-quality, John was also asthmatic.

Within two or three weeks, they had both decided on Portugal. She and John had visited the country on holidays with their loved ones, and coincidently had both visited a little village on the south coast called Cascais. They had both enjoyed their visits there, Beth for the lovely white-sand beaches and John, because there happened to be a casino in the nearby village of Estoril, not that he was an avid gambler, but like lots of people, he enjoyed a little flutter on the roulette wheels, and of course the black-jack tables. The climate was perfect for them both and so they agreed that it would seem appropriate for them to start a new life together away from the places they'd spent their married lives. No doubt there would be some who would deprecate their decision, but that was never going to matter to either of them, simply because they wouldn't be around to hear their disapproving remarks.

Because Beth had no family, there would be no-one except friends to leave her estate to in her will. She was financially sound for the rest of her life, Sam being well-insured as well as the two of them having quite a handsome nest-egg set aside. She had also cashed in Sam's shares, of which there were many, not that Sam knew anything at all about trade markets, but Sam being Sam, knew people who did, and so throughout the years having been well-advised, he had invested heavily into certain businesses.

Her solicitor had summoned her to his office recently having been instructed by her to withdraw the shares.

Beth was quite pleasantly shocked, when she was informed by Mister McGregor, one of Sam's golfing enthusiast friends, that the total amount due to her was one point three million pounds.

Sam had invested into some of these shares more than twenty years earlier, and in recent years the stock prices had soared through the roof accumulating a nice sum of money, and in all honesty, money she felt she didn't really need, and so, for this reason, she had come to another decision.

She wouldn't sell her house here in Kensington she would give it to someone as a gift. Sam Hargrieves was one of the most genuine men she had ever met in her entire life, and she felt honoured indeed to have been lucky enough to share all these years with him. His judgement on people's character was second to none.

He would share stories with her of people who had impressed him, of people he admired, and sometimes those people were criminals, but there was one particular time he informed her of three young women living in Locksley Estate. He explained to her what it was they done for a living, and how one of the girls' sisters was a victim of Rosalyn Simpson's wrath, of course, he didn't know at the time her name was Rosalyn Simpson.

The girl and her boyfriend had both been brutally murdered.

He'd got to know them throughout his investigations and had become quite friendly with them to the extent of sharing jokes and having cups of tea together. Sam also told her of the unity between the friends, the camaraderie between them.

"These girls are so close Beth" he'd said. "They would do anything for each other without question." Having spent quite some time in their company, he'd been gifted an insight into just exactly what it was like to be a working girl. His opinion on prostitution had changed completely when he'd heard their stories and the reasons why they done it, although he never disclosed those facts to her.

He would laugh out loud sometimes whilst they watched T.V. remembering something one or the other of them had said, particularly when they informed him that they'd christened officer

McDermot officer ballet.

Beth knew he had a soft spot for the girls and a fondness for them that most other wives would not even begin to understand, or even attempt to understand, so for that reason and that reason alone, she would gift the house in which she presently lived, to the girls who had warmed her husband's heart. What they done with the house would be their business and their business alone, but she was giving them the deeds for the property assuring herself that Sam would be proud indeed of her actions. She could always tell when Sam was secretly rooting for someone, and she certainly knew he was rooting for them. She would give them a break in their lives. Beth smiled to herself at the thought of the girls moving into Kensington if they decided to continue in their present line of work, that would certainly give the neighbours something to talk about, but again, it wouldn't matter one jot to her, she wouldn't be here..."and good luck to them," she said to herself, as she boarded the taxi to take her to Locksley Estate.

KILNDOWN VILLAGE.

KENT.

Forensic officer Kathlene Oconnor and detective John Smedley had returned to Alexander Stineman's property.
They had been instructed to do so by H.Q. following a telephone call by someone who claimed they used to work with the surgeon. She claimed she was a nurse working with his team for almost two years. The call couldn't be traced, but Scotland Yard's Chief of Police, had decided to investigate further on the "nurses" advice. Her exact words being, "He's a lunatic, a brutal lunatic, he should be found and executed for the things he's done, the Nazis have nothing on this bastard, get him."
Smedley had been chomping at the bit to be assigned to his first case, but the investigation of Alexander Stineman was not going to be that case. Mercer and Cruntze would be appearing sometime today and from then he was to return to HQ for instructions. Perhaps they felt that this case was going to be too big for him to handle.
As he and Kathlene Oconnor climbed out of their car, the van containing two carpenters pulled up behind them. They were here to lift up flooring so as thorough investigations could be made, forensic investigations from below the ground floor level.
The woman on the phone, claiming to be a nurse had informed Scotland Yard that doctor Stineman had a basement and it was in this basement that he would perform his illegal operations.
As it turned out, the carpenters were not needed. Under one of the Persian rugs at the far end of the luxurious living room, there was a hatch-door. Kathlene Oconnor instructed the workmen to stay put and not to come down into this basement unless she required their assistance. She would come back outside to their van if that should turn out to be the case.
The reason the carpenters were here at all was the fact that, up until now, doctor Stineman had done nothing wrong whatsoever,

and so the tradesmen were here to remove floor-boards or wood panels carefully so as not to cause any damage. The fact was, they had no proof thus far of him having any connection at all regarding the missing people. The only thing perhaps mildly pointing to some kind of guilt, was the fact that the man had just mysteriously disappeared from the face of the earth, but that fact was about to change.
Smedley lifted up the hatch door and peered down into the darkness. "I'll go and get my torch" he grunted to Kathlene as he awkwardly clambered to his feet.
"Hang on, what are these", He said as he approached a panel of switches on the living room wall. He flicked on all four of the switches and suddenly blazing light shone up from the basement below them into the crepuscular room.
There was a small stair-case leading down to the basement floor. Oconnor headed down first having put on the usual polythene gloves. Half way down the carpeted steps she stopped in her tracks. Apart from the steps, everywhere down here was tiled, floor and walls, just white tiles. In front of her and along the long wall were four operating tables exactly like the ones you'd see in any hospital. In between these tables were computers, their screens displaying electrical animated images of the human brain.
On two of the operating tables there were blood stains.
"John" she shouted up to Smedley, "call for the team, tell them I need the full forensic team here as soon as possible, and just stay up there just now, stay there until the team get here, hand me down the shoe covers please. She placed the polythene covers over her feet and began to slowly walk over to the tables. In between the tables there were trays of instruments and appliances of which she had no idea whatsoever of their identity. She recognised several surgical instruments, but there were instruments here that *only* brain surgeons would know about. Beside one of the operating tables there was an appliance that at first hand looked just like an ordinary fridge, but upon closer inspection she could see that the good doctor had been busying himself with cryosurgery.
Oconnor wondered if the D.N.A samples from these tables would

match those of the missing people from around here. If they did, and she had a gut-feeling that they would, then they were going to be in for one hell of a roller-coaster ride with this one, either that, or a laborious peregrination.

## CHAPTER FIFTEEN.

## M1. Near London.

Both Terry Mercer and Ava Cruntze had been bitterly disappointed with themselves. They should have known better than to get caught up with Simpsons antics.
They'd come away from Pleasant Meadows with only the one fact, and that was that Simpson admitted knowing the doctor, although the D.N.A samples had undoubtedly proved that fact anyway, so in effect, they'd come away with nothing.
"What do you think she meant Ava, when she said she'd paid money for him to do something for her, something that she had said was well worth it in the end, or whatever the fuck she said, she's done my head in."
"God knows Terry, it could be one of her many mind games. She doesn't seem to be suffering does she, and I must admit, I agree with you Terry on their methods, letting her wear makeup and nice clothes, hell when we walked in it looked as though she was sitting there waiting for the waiter to bring her her starter course."
"Well, hopefully Ava, this time we can say that we don't have to go back there, I mean there's no bloody point anyway, is there? All she does is rile us up with her subtle deprecations and her vituperative attacks. Anyway, I'll just refuse to go if they send us again Ava, this time I mean it, I'm not going back there, unless she's died, and God speed." As Terry drove on they both became silent, each of them contemplating what Simpson had been saying to them. It was very easy to pretend to your partner that something or someone hadn't got to you, but if truth be known, Ava was, if anything, even more concerned for Terry than she had been before regarding Simpson's threats. She doubted that he would have enough spiritual strength to even continue in his present line of work? As far as she could tell, the only two people left in Terry's life now that would get to him, would be either Beth Hargrieves, or, dare she say it, herself, but by

the way Simpson was talking, whatever the deed had been, it had already been done, and done being the key word, not planned, but already completed. The damage, whatever it was, was done. On top of that, she had boasted that it had cost her a princely sum of money. *"But it was well worth it."* She glanced at Terry's face as he drove. Worry was etched now into his facial features, they were part of his identity, the lines were here to stay, and most of them scribed there by a psychopathic lunatic who was stopping at nothing to destroy his life. From this day hence though, Beth Hargrieves would be put under observation. Ava would explain to Polly just what Simpson had said and so would understand the necessity of her being put under surveillance. Beth of course would not be informed, it would only make her feel uneasy and perhaps afraid to go outdoors at all, and that was the last thing they wanted. Terry would visit her soon anyway.

LOCKSLEY ESTATE.

EAST LONDON.

Veronica Wells' apartment.

Veronica would never have known the woman standing in front of her if she hadn't been to Sam Hargrieves' funeral.
She remembered well the emotional wreck sobbing bitterly as the minister had performed the sermon. Veronica watched that day in fascination at the woman's despair, a genuine loss of love.
She wondered what it would be like to be *that* close to someone, and how it must feel to lose them. She could only imagine that it would be like losing a part of yourself, it would undoubtedly leave a massive void. She remembered as well the affection Sam had of his wife, jokingly informing Mandy that she was the boss in their relationship, but it was clear that he gave his wife his love uxoriously, of that there was no doubt.
"Hello I'm Beth Hargrieves, I believe my husband came to see you on several occasions regarding those horrible murders".
Veronica at first was unsure of what to do, whether to invite her in or to query why she was here, but she found herself saying, "Yes, we eh...we had a few conversations regarding the crimes, em Mandy's sister was one of the victims, he was very sympathetic and helpful to us all, we were all fond of him you know, and Mister Mercer, would you like to come in Misses Hargrieves, I'm afraid we weren't expecting any guests and so the girls are sitting in there in their underwear, I'll chase them to their rooms to get dressed, come in, please."
Beth Hargrieves stepped inside the flat not really knowing what to expect, judging by the graffiti she'd just read on the walls of the elevator but had braced herself for at least, `rough and ready`.
To her genuine surprise, the place was immaculate.
She could tell that the furniture was second-hand, and that some of the pieces didn't match, but everything they owned was clean and

extremely tidy. Veronica introduced Beth to her two friends, and with a wave of her right hand, gave the signal to the two of them to go and clothe themselves. Mandy had been sitting in bra and pants painting her toe-nails, Elizabeth her fingernails, also in her underwear. The two young ladies greeted the woman and then left to see to their attire.

"I'll put the kettle on for a cuppa" said Veronica as she made her way into the kitchen. Ten minutes later Mandy and Elizabeth had reappeared fully clothed, complete with their fluffy bunny slippers. Beth sat smiling at the girls, remembering what Sam had told her about them, and he'd been one hundred percent correct in his character-assessment. She wondered when their sense of humour would make an appearance, Sam had told her about the young lady named Mandy. She didn't have long to wait.

Mandy spoke now as she sat there on the sofa looking like she was fifteen, knees together and head slightly bowed, as if she were an awkward adolescent.

"I'm afraid we're not used to nice people coming to visit us, that's why Lizzy and I were dressed the way we were, usually the people who come here are here to make business transactions with us, regarding certain favours concerning the female anatomy, you must have read the graffiti on the elevator walls, that might give you an insight as to what we do for a living, but believe me, there's no-one in here capable of taking an elephant's —"

"Mandy! I'm quite sure Misses Hargrieves is aware of what we do, and I'm equally sure she's not here to discuss our customer's preferences, for goodness sakes girl, I'm so sorry Misses Hargrieves, our Mandy has to be kept right from time to time, she forgets the meaning of good manners, and indeed how to apply them."

Beth only smiled and said there was no need whatsoever to change the way they portray themselves on her part., and that she was here to give them a gift. Forty minutes and two cups of tea later, she explained to them just exactly what that gift was.

It was a gift that could potentially change their lives for the better. "I have been fortunate enough to be left quite comfortably off for the rest of my days ladies, and I know how hard it has been for you three. I also know the reasons why each and every one of you do what you do...Sam and I were very close you know. He admired you more than you'll ever know and I was flattered when you all made the journey over to his funeral, it was very much appreciated, and I felt honoured indeed that Sam had touched you deep enough for you to attend, especially when most people there were from the police-force, you know, in your line of work there isn't much chance of you all becoming friends any time soon."

Veronica and Mandy looked at each other and then to Lizzy, wondering what on earth Misses Hargrieves was going to come out with next.

"So, I have decided to do something to improve your lives. As I have already said, I am fortunate indeed to be in this position, although I could hardly say that my wealth is incomputable." There was a short silence until Beth said, "I have decided to emigrate I'm going to live in Portugal, where the weather is kinder to my asthma. I am emigrating with a gentleman friend of mine and we are to live together for the rest of our days...hopefully, so, I won't be needing that big house in Kensington, and so, as a gesture of good will and a testament to the friendship you all shared with my husband, I'm giving you the house to do with as you see fit. You can all discuss it among yourselves what you want to do with it, but it's yours, all three of you. As far as market price is concerned, that's if you wish to sell it, I think as it stands now, it would go for around two maybe two point five million pounds, that's not including furniture and fittings of course, which I will also be leaving. Of course, you're all welcome to live in it or rent it out, you can discuss that with a solicitor about rates of renting and the likes, but, at the end of the day, it's all yours to do with as you wish, and personally speaking? I couldn't think of three nicer young ladies to give it to.

So, you all have a think about what you want to do with it. Here are the deeds of the property ladies, oh, and I've paid the rates for a few months to give you some time. The rates are quite expensive I must warn you, but I'm sure you three girls would handle that, after all, you'll be paying quite a bit for renting here are you not? Anyway, I need you three to sign these just as soon as you can."

She produced a small bundle of documents. "I presume you'll allow me to live there until January until John and I finally leave the country?"

In all of their wildest dreams, none of the three women sitting in front of Beth Hargrieves could have even began to dream something like this. Mandy had arisen from the sofa to go and make cups of coffee. Standing in the kitchen, as she waited for the kettle to boil, she recalled one particular day when Sam had come to visit her, and how she had been having a bad day.

She remembered how he'd taken the shopping bags from her to relieve her of some of the burden, and how he'd hinted that a cup of tea would suffice for payment. She also remembered how he'd smiled at the young boy who had just had sex with Lizzy when she informed him of inspector Hargrieves' identity, and how he'd ran off. How he had defended Terry Mercer when he'd seemed to come over harsh and masculine. And now, right here in this room, his widow had bestowed upon them, or was just about to, unless she suddenly woke up, a gift so unbelievable it beggared belief, and all because of the friendship they had built up together with Sam Hargrieves. All three girls had prayed for a break in their lives, something that could get them out of here, and away from this degrading occupation, and none of them with any qualifications whatsoever between them…and here it was. Sam Hargrieves' fascination with them, and his widow's generosity had disposed of any necessity of qualifications…they were going to get their break. The gesture, if anything had made Sam's death even more tragic, if that was possible. As the kettle boiled, Mandy burst into tears. All the harsh things her parents had said to her, the name-calling, the rejection, the blasphemous inflictions which had cut into her soul, the reasons for getting into prostitution in the first place, the loss of her sister and future brother-in-law, Terry Mercer taking Veronica by the hand and down on his knees , saying openly that he respected us all, the christening of officer McDermott into officer ballet, everything. Her head was whirling. Veronica came through to the kitchen. Seeing her emotional friend she approached Mandy and placed an arm around her shoulder, giving her a cuddle.

"What about this Mandy huh? Who could have guessed *this* would happen to us, Sam must have thought a lot more of us than we realized babes. Listen, we are to get ourselves ready and then Misses Hargrieves is ordering a taxi to take us over to Kensington to see the house, God Mandy, it's a five bedroomed house, it must be massive." With tears still streaming down Mandy's face, she nodded her head vigorously, smiling. The two friends embraced tightly. "I know Mandy, I know darling, but all the bad stuff could be behind us now, the three of us are going to be alright."

# SCOTLAND YARD.

## BROADWAY VICTORIA.

Polly Sheppard had sent Terry and Ava down to Kilndown village to assist with the forensic officers that Kathlene Oconnor had left there. Kathlene sat now in front of Polly with detective John Smedley. Polly had a worried look on her face, and for very good reasons.

Extensive investigations had been carried out throughout the country led by forensic expert Andy Phillips. He had visited several mental health institutes across England having been instructed to do so. He and his team were to take D.N.A samples from various patients in these premises who had no identification, and worse still, had no knowledge of who they were.

This phantom caller to Scotland Yard was assuring them that there were several victims who had been afflicted by Doctor Alexander Stineman's handiwork within these premises, particularly around Wolverhampton and Coventry.

The only high security mental health hospitals in these areas were Smithfield near Kenilworth which was close to Coventry, and Karringdale, near Perton, which was close to Wolverhampton. Phillips was informed by the chief surgeon in Smithfield, that they had four patients in their care who had severe brain damage.

One of the four was completely immobile and had to be fed by staff. The other three could move slowly, their sloth-like movements due to muscular disabilities, although they were able to feed themselves, but had no idea whatsoever of who they were or where they had come from. One of them, a woman in her late thirties or early forties, no-one was quite sure, was found sitting on a pavement on the outskirts of Coventry in the early hours of the morning, three weeks ago to this day. She was capable of speech to a point. Her words were jumbled and slurred. At first the doctors here thought that it was a case of autohypnosis, but after x-rays, it was discovered that the woman had been victim to brain surgery.

He used the word victim because of the damage inflicted upon her cerebellum, the part of the brain which coordinates and regulates muscular activity. It was undoubtedly malicious, deliberate.

Phillips had asked if it would be possible to see the woman, and was granted ten minutes, but no more than that, as she tended to get nervous and restless when being asked questions continuously, and by different people.

Doctor Muller, was very helpful indeed and had assisted Phillips in every way he could, within the rules of course.

"Does she have a name, I mean does she know her name?" said Phillips as they entered the lounge.

"I'm afraid not, although she sometimes mumbles the words Cal and Dal, especially Dal, she seems to say that regularly, and then sometimes cries, so there is still some normal activity in her brain, but there has been extensive damage done."

"Irreversible damage doctor Muller?" said Phillips, already knowing the answer to his question.

" I'm not a hundred percent certain Mister Phillips, but it would certainly seem that way, considering the damage that has been done to her cerebrum as well as damage to her temporal lobes. If we could just discover her identity then perhaps we could then find out who her enemies were, or who it was who performed the operation to put her into this state…a crying shame."

Phillips entered the lounge with the doctor, and observed the woman in question. She sat on the easy-chair staring out of the window, looking at birds feeding off tit-bits thrown out to them by the kitchen staff, or at least, she was looking out in that direction, whether or not it was the birds that had caught her attention would be hard to define. Dressed in a sky-blue track-suit and slippers to match, the woman looked pitiful, as she stared outside not even acknowledging the fact that the doctor was here, for the simple reason that she didn't even know who he was, even though the man spent half an hour with her each day.

"There's someone here to see you Cal, that's what we call her mister Phillips. He's come to ask you some questions, would that be alright?" The woman turned to look at the doctor, but gave no facial or verbal reaction."

As she turned, Phillips felt a twang of recognition, as if he knew the woman. Had he met her before somewhere? For a brief moment, just a fraction of a second, he thought she recognised *him* as well, but then, the bland expressionless face again.

Why had he felt like that? *Had* he met her before somewhere? And if so where? Perhaps it was he who was suffering from prosopagnosia. He informed Doctor Muller that he wouldn't be questioning her today having seen her present condition.

"It would just be a waste of time Doctor Muller, I hadn't realized how bad her condition is.

I'll take D.N.A samples from her, and then we'll take it from there, and you say there has been deliberate damage done? Someone has actually purposefully caused her this brain damage?"

"Undoubtedly Mister Phillips, the operation, or operations were performed by a skilled surgeon, judging by the scars on her cranial cap. There are three scars on her skull. When we x-rayed the brain, we discovered that the cerebellum had been pierced in several places, hence the slow movement."

Phillips decided to have lunch here in the hospital having been invited by Doctor Muller. The two men sat discussing the condition of the brain-damaged patients and how anyone could bring themselves to inflict such atrocities to a fellow human being, but during the course of Andy Phillips' career, he'd seen enough to convince himself never to trust anyone outside of his family and friends. Nothing but nothing would shock him now.

Fifteen minutes after he'd finished his lunch Andy Phillips thanked Doctor Muller for his assistance and cooperation. Muller reminded him of a young Paul Simon, both in looks and stature, although it would be hard to imagine Paul Simon having a strong German accent and a pencil-thin moustache.

"And here's to you Fraulein Robinson".

"If there is anything else Mister Phillips that we can help you with, please don't hesitate to call me or any of my staff, although I get the feeling you'll have to return here at some point, whether or not you find out the identity of these poor souls."

"Probably Doctor Muller, but I'll let you know, I'll keep in touch with you...and if I do find out who they are, you will of course be the first to know, though I must admit, it's a difficult task indeed, but, you never know, their D.N.A could perhaps give us some valuable information."

As the two men were passing the lounge where the mystery woman was, a nurse came running out of the door.

"Doctor Muller, she's having one of her turns again."

Phillips turned and looked into the lounge as the doctor entered. "Come on now Cal, calm down calm down, everything's going to be alright. The woman sat, almost screaming at the top of her voice, shaking almost convulsively with her right pointing finger jabbing her chest. She was repeatedly shouting Cal, Cal, Cal, I Cal, I Cal."

As Phillips left the institute, he felt heavy with grief and sympathy for these poor people who, to all intents and purposes had lived a perfectly normal life, until recently.

The task for him and his team now, was to find out if a certain Doctor Alexander Stineman was responsible for the damaging surgery. At this moment in time, Phillips was thinking that his task was a Sisyphean one. Just when he thought his day could not get any worse, his mobile phone buzzed in his pocket. It was one of his team, Trevor Giles, whom Andy had sent to Perton near Wolverhampton along with two other forensic assistants.

Next to Kathlene Oconnor, Trevor was undoubtedly one of the best there was in his team, so when Trevor had said to him on the phone, *"You need to come and see this."* Then he knew that something deeply distressing had been discovered. He shuddered to think what that might be.

"Does it concern patients with brain damage Trevor?" he said sighing, and climbing laboriously into his vehicle.

"I'm afraid so Andy, and it's bad, I mean it's really bad, you have to see this. We've identified three of the patients here as those of the missing people at Kilndown and the surrounding area, it's definitely Mister Alexander who's been at work here.

Their D.N.A matches the samples we took from the operating tables in his basement."

Andy sat nodding his head at the steering wheel of his car. He had been almost certain that this would be the case, and now, his dreaded assumptions had been confirmed.
"Right Trevor, I'll be with you shortly, see you soon bud, you'd better inform Polly."
"I will Andy, but there's something else.
We identified two teenagers who were reported missing, two young girls, but there's a boy here, I would say around the age of twelve or thirteen, something like that. Well, his D.N.A doesn't match up with anything that we've got, and he's been affected the worst, I mean our good Doctor has gone to town on this wee fella, poor bugger, what a bloody mess Andy, wait until you see the state of this poor boy."

Polly Sheppard sat with Kathlene Oconnor and John Smedley.
"Our, what should I call her? Informant, has been on the phone again Kathlene, and according to her, Mister Alexander has been spotted in the Dagenham area. I want you two to go over there and check out the area. She said he's been residing in a hotel there somewhere although she couldn't give us a specific name. If he has then he will undoubtedly be using a different name, so you may have to go on visual descriptions if you're showing photographs to hotel staff. Just hang around there in that area for a few days, I'll tell you if I need you to go somewhere different, or if I get any other information concerning him."
As the two detectives made their way to the door Polly said to them, "Listen, this is not a punishment you two, I'm not sending you over there just to get you away from the forensic teams Kathlene, and you John, I can't fault your work, so please, don't you two leave here thinking that you're not needed or appreciated, because believe me, you are. I will need your skills Kathlene before long, but we need to find this man, and so, everything our informant is advising us of, we're checking it out, after all, everything she's told us has been true, thus far, so, please go over to Dagenham and see if you can spot this man, and by the way Kathlene, off the record girl, there is no way you're on probation,

ok? As far as I'm concerned, that unfortunate incident did not even happen.
How's your sister and the kids coping, I'll bet they're happy bunnies now."
Kathlene smiled at her boss, "You have no idea mam, and thank you, thank you for understanding my predicament, I will never make that mistake again."
Smedley and Oconnor would hardly have been out of the building when Polly's phone rang on her desk. It was Andy Phillips. He had been to Smithfield and then had proceeded to visit Karringdale near Perton and had made gruesome discoveries.
He wouldn't tell her on the telephone what he'd discovered but it was of the utmost importance that she got up there as soon as possible.
It was those last few words that Phillips had spoken which had really frightened Polly, and she didn't scare easily.
"What the hell has he discovered up there" she thought to herself, as she collected her car keys from the desk and slipped on her jacket.

## PARLOUR STREET.

## South KENSINGTON.

Forty-two year old Inspector David Sewell sat in his Ford GT about thirty-five metres from Beth Hargrieves' house.
He had been watching her movements closely now for three weeks as Terry Mercer had instructed him, but as far as he could tell, there was no-one watching her or following her.
No-one suspicious hanging around her house, not even any visits from would-be salesmen or bogus gardeners or landscapers, nothing.
She usually returned home at around six pm in the evening with a gentleman friend who spent the night with her most of the time. On the occasions that he didn't spend the night, he was usually away by about ten-thirty. Having made inquiries Sewell had discovered that this gentleman was the person Beth was going to emigrate with to Portugal, John Pearce, a widower for three years, and with no criminal record whatsoever.
He watched now with a wry smile on his face as Beth Hargrieves climbed out of the taxi with three young ladies.
By the way the young ladies were dressed he figured that it wouldn't take a Philadelphia lawyer to work out what they done for a living. *"But why the fuck would Misses Hargrieves be inviting them into her home?"* It was none of his business at the end of the day, and as long as they weren't posing a threat to Beth's well-being he wouldn't be looking into the matter any further, although he had to admit, the situation was rather a comical one. Here they were in Kensington in a well-respected area where money spoke in volumes. Goodness knows what the total value of these houses would be in this street alone, if they were all put on the market at the same time.
The first thing one of the girls done as soon as she was out of the cab, was to light up a cigarette and make a half-hearted attempt at pulling her ridiculously short skirt down. David Sewell smiled to

himself with more than mild curiosity at the sight before him.
The girls stood pointing at Beth Hargrieves' house, laughing and shaking their heads, before finally cuddling Beth and hugging her. He sat shaking his head and smiling as he watched the four women enter the house. Were these girls going to be buying Beth's house? Business must be bloody good girls, if you can afford that beauty, *"Christ they must be working around the clock."*
He would inform Terry of all events and await further instructions, but as far as he was concerned Beth Hargrieves' life did not seem to be in any danger. Sewell also knew how much Terry thought of Misses Hargrieves and knew instinctively that he'd be instructed to continue observing her movements, at least for the time being. To see this type of women in this particular area humoured him immensely, and right on que, as he drove out, one of the girls scratched her behind as she entered the house. His smile suddenly burst into uncontrolled laughter.

## MILLINGTON HOTEL.

## SOLFORD. MANCHESTER.

Alexander Stineman had changed his appearance completely. He'd had his head shaved and removed his moustache as well as replacing his spectacles with contact lenses. News of the CID's discoveries down in Kilndown had been broadcasted on all major TV channels. No matter how dramatically he'd changed his appearance he knew now that his time was nearly up.
There would be no leniency for him regarding his experimental brain surgery.
At one time in his career he'd been awarded with honours and titles and commended for his brilliant work, but something had happened to him that he could not explain, even to himself. He'd developed this greed, an urgency to expand further in his field, to be the best, to be the pioneer of all brain surgery.
Before he knew what had happened to him, he'd become this manic obsessed with surgery, eager to explore the realms of surgery never before attempted by anyone who had preceded him. He would go down in history.
At first he had paid `scoundrels` to obtain experimental patients for him, pulling down-and-outs from society, nobodies, from the darker regions of the cities, no-one would miss them, in fact he thought that he was doing society a favour by disposing of them, disposing, if the surgery went wrong, which from time to time, it inevitably did. He hadn't actually counted the people he'd `used` but guessed that it must be well over fifty. He'd been performing operations for his own experiments long before he was dismissed from the board of health, and that had hurt him, because even now if he succeeded in what he was doing there would be no-one prepared to listen to him.
Anyway, it was all too late now. It was over, there was nowhere left to hide. It was only a matter of time.
From his room in the hotel, he phoned his brother and informed

him that there were important documents in the safe at his house in Kilndown that he must read, as he was going to be away for quite some time.

He then proceeded to send a number of text messages to certain people he knew thanking them for their friendship throughout the course of his life, Rosalyn Simpson being one of them, although a wry smile etched on his face as he sent *her* message.

That done he poured his fifth glass of gin and tonic and checked that his Glock pistol was fully loaded.

Stineman felt no remorse for anything he'd done, and why should he, there had never before in history been any progress made in the medical world without sacrifice.

His only regret was that he hadn't managed to achieve what he'd set out to do in his field of surgery.

He smacked his lips having consumed the last glass of gin he would ever drink, and then made his way to the bedroom window.

Sliding the window open, he casually stepped out onto the sill, one hundred and seventy two feet from the ground.

Below him he could hear the buzz of the city traffic and hoped above all, that there would be no innocent passers-by who would suffer a premature end on account of the weight of his body slamming into them. He put one foot out into the fresh air, and then placed the gun inside his mouth, closing his lips around the barrel, he uttered the words, "You tried Alex, you definitely tried, no-one can hold that against you."

For one fraction of a second Alexander Stineman felt a stabbing pain in the top of his head but then felt nothing at all as his limp body fell at a ferocious speed down onto one of the taxi-cabs outside of the hotel.

Miraculously, for Sandra Knox, a twenty-six year old taxi driver, mother nature had decided that she would have to go to relieve her bladder and so was not in the car as Alexander Stineman's body completely wrecked the year-old vehicle, spraying several shop windows with his blood in the process and causing several passers-by to scream out with fright and shock, and for one old lady to faint.

## PERTON.

## KARRINGDALE MENTAL HEALTH INSTITUTE.

## WOLVERHAMPTON.

As Polly Sheppard pulled into the almost deserted car park of Karringdale institute she spotted Andy Phillips standing alone in the distance. He looked like a really old man from where she was.
He stood hunched over, with his long winter coat which was as grey as the sky above him. His complexion was pale and faded, like the skin of a dying man.
As she climbed out of her vehicle and approached him.
She observed the colour of his hands, almost bright purple. Acrocyanosis, a condition Andy had suffered from for quite some time now, caused by poor blood circulation.
Polly had known Andy for some years now, and had nothing but respect for him. He was one of the old school, and his work sometimes unorthodox to say the least. He'd investigated many crime scenes impromptu and had pulled off some remarkable results. His career had spanned well over thirty years as a forensic officer, and the last ten of those as chief forensic officer.
As Polly approached he placed his hands into his coat pockets and stared down at something on the ground. She instinctively knew something bad was coming. Andy had put on this stance ever since she'd known him. It was going to be difficult for him to talk about it, whatever it was, so that meant it was personal to him, or to someone in the force, someone in the team.
She wasn't wrong.
"What the hell is it Andy? What's happened? What have you discovered?"
The chill wind seemed to be adding years on to Andy by the minute. His face looked more weathered now than it had ever done.
Tears were in his eyes from the chilly breeze biting into his face, making him look more upset than he actually was, although that would be difficult to do. Polly wondered if the tears were emotional or due to the weather. At this point it was hard to tell.

With the wind on their backs, Andy Phillips led the way into Karringdale mental health institute.
Polly broke the silence.
"There's someone in here we know Andy, is that it?
Have you identified somebody we know Andy, don't keep me in suspense."
At first Andy did not answer her question, but eventually, he half spoke half whispered, "I've had enough sweetheart, this time I've really had enough. I'm not doing this anymore Polly, this is…oh Christ this is beyond belief Polly."
"But you're still not telling me Andy what the hell it is, are you."
"You'll see soon enough. It's not just what's in here Polly, it's what's over at Smithfield, the connection, it was…devastating, and it will be devastating for someone we know…I've really had enough Polly, this world stinks to the high heavens, it's rotten to the core. Society has gone to the dogs Polly, we have no-one we can trust now, politicians, priests, ministers, doctors, police officers, and now, fucking surgeons, brain surgeons, corruption Polly, from the top to the bottom, and if not corruption, then undetected bloody maniacs roaming around slicing people to pieces, fucking cooking their body parts Jesus Polly, we can't trust anyone, and if they're not doing that, they're interfering with little bloody kids, the whole world has fucked up Polly, and as far as this country is concerned, well we now lead the way in all of these fields. We've got British citizens doing deals with Eastern Europeans in connection with human trafficking, Christ Polly, there's more than a thousand people each year going missing from Britain, and twenty-eight percent of them are never heard of again, they're kidnapping young British girls and selling them like cattle to these vermin, and not thinking twice about it. Poor Sam Hargrieves as well Polly, shot in the fucking head in his own home, in his own home Polly."
Andy's voice broke off as they continued to walk towards the building.
"I know Andy, I know, it was a tragedy to say the least."
She could see that her colleague was all but ready to burst into tears. She could also see that this time, he actually meant it, he

would retire, and who could blame him, hell, thirty odd years of experiencing the sickening aftermaths of inhumane actions. Horrendous inflictions onto fellow human-beings, and he and his team having to sift through the gunge and blood and broken bones, and decapitated heads and legs and arms, and yes, it is bound to have an effect on your opinion of `human-beings`.
She found herself linking arms with Phillips as they walked the last few yards up to the steps of the building, and Andy did not even question why she suddenly had done this.
It was a silent recognition. She felt sympathy for him, and he felt her sympathy, and was grateful for her affection.
As they climbed the steps Andy said, "We'll have to see a Mister Morgan, Doctor Alistair Morgan, he is the head psychiatrist in here. He tries to work with the patients and improve their mental well-being. He'll take us to...em...he'll show you."
Andy trailed off.
Polly squeezed his hand. It was this unspeakable discovery again. Just when Polly had begun thinking about what this could be, he said to her, right out of the blue, "Where's Terry just now Polly?"
For some unknown reason, she felt a stab of fear, shock. She tried to remain calm and not show him that she was in fact, frightened beyond belief on Terry's behalf.
"He's em...he's down in Kilndown with Ava, why, what has this got to do with Terry?"
As they reached the front doors of the hospital Andy turned and looked at Polly.
"Plenty."
Fifteen minutes later, Polly Sheppard was sitting in one of the waiting rooms of the hospital breaking her heart and sobbing bitterly. It was Andy's turn to console *her*.
Doctor Morgan had shown them into a room where they met a young boy, or at least the remnants of a young boy.
His brain damage was severe to say the least.
He sat rocking his head back and forwards like an old woman on a rocking- chair, his arms folded looking like he was fastened into a straight-jacket. He made noises from his mouth, more like

animalistic noises than human ones.

The boy was not even capable of uttering one coherent word. Neither was he capable of showing any emotion whatsoever, happiness or sadness. He was just here, here in a world that he could not comprehend. He was fed by staff, spoon fed, and from time to time, he could not even chew. The staff had to move his mouth until something triggered in his brain to remind him how to eat. Doctor Morgan had painstakingly explained to Polly, and again to Andy Phillips just what had happened to the lad, and how the malicious damage had been inflicted. The boy was also blind in his right eye due to the damage inflicted upon his occipital lobe.

There was damage to the boy's right and left hemispheres of the brain, the lateralization. There was also damage to the part of the brain called the Broca, the region of the brain which contains neurons, and which is involved with speech function. Lastly, he explained how there had been massive damage inflicted upon the cerebellum and the cerebrum. As sorry as Polly felt for the young boy, she failed to see how this would affect Andy the way it had. She made the mistake of asking him just that. It was the look on Andy's face when he asked her again where Terry was.

Suddenly, she realized who she had been looking at in the ward. No wonder Andy kept asking where he was.

The young boy was Daniel Mercer. Andy spoke now very softly as he explained the completion of his gruesome discovery.

"The boy's mother is in Smithfield in Kenilworth."

The woman Andy had seen there was Carol Mercer.

"Cal`...I Cal...I Cal."

Polly had quickly excused herself from the doctor's presence and made her way to the waiting room where she sat now.

The monster had paid this madman surgeon to do this to these poor people.

Carol hadn't left Terry at all.

No wonder no-one could find her, she'd been held captive by the lunatic, probably in his basement. No wonder Terry felt hard and turned to stone, but in his mind, the most tortuous thing that would eat away at him, was the fact that the action had been so out of character for Carol...it just wasn't her way of working, of doing things.

She would have undoubtedly come clean if she had met someone else and wanted to make a fresh start, and she would have made arrangements for Terry to see his son regularly. All these years he'd been tortured. The evil bitch had even seen to it that Carol's clothes and Daniels had been removed from the house, as well as the bank account being emptied.

No wonder Andy was cut to pieces.

Yes, he and Terry had had their falling outs from time to time, but at the end of the day, they were colleagues, and that part of their relationship had never once been an issue between them.

She could now fully understand why Andy was now retiring as well. Maybe she would too. In all of her years in the police force Polly had never felt anything like this. This was worse than a bereavement, far worse. When someone dies, a healing process kicks in, sometimes it takes weeks, sometimes years, and sometimes the person left behind never heals at all, but at least the pain recedes enough for them to continue with their own lives, but this, this situation here that poor Terry Mercer had been left in was beyond healing.

She remembered how he'd cursed Sandra Neal when he thought she'd committed suicide and deserted him, and then how hurt he was when he found out the truth. Now, after all these years of cursing Carol for taking off with their kid and leaving him with nothing, he would find out, yet again, that he'd been wrong, and when he discovered their conditions, God knows how he would react.

Doctor Morgan entered the waiting room carrying three cups of tea. He handed one to Andy and Polly, and then sat down with a heavy sigh on the chair opposite the chief inspector.

Morgan, a man in his early forties, with a full head of black jelled hair opened the buttons of his tunic.

"I understand from what Mister Phillips has told me that you are very close to this Terrence Mercer, the husband and father of these two very unfortunate individuals. I'm afraid the damage inflicted on this young man is irreversible. If I request a surgeon to attempt to repair the damage, he could quite easily worsen the boy's condition, although..."

Morgan had no need to finish his sentence, Polly knew what he meant. The best paediatric surgeons in the country could do nothing for this poor boy, and from what Andy had told her about Carol Mercer, her condition wasn't much better.

Doctor Muller had informed Andy that Misses Mercer suffered from a condition called Agrammatism, among numerous other things, meaning that she would attempt to form sentences, but unable to form the correct inflectional structure, as a result of her brain damage, sometimes occurring to patients who'd been involved in car accidents or had received sudden massive blows to the head. Some days she could actually pronounce a few words in the correct order, the next, she was as bad as ever, hardly able to function at all. Whatever Doctor Stineman had done, or what he'd attempted to do, he had undoubtedly messed up big time, leaving the woman in a semi-vegetated state. The damage to her son Daniel was even worse than that, the poor boy only able to make noises with his mouth.

He had no control whatsoever over his bladder or his bowels and had to be hand fed by the staff here, and it was this that was tearing Polly to pieces knowing how much Terry loved his little boy. It would have been hard enough for him to see his son again after more than five years even under normal circumstances, but what he was going to see in here...

"When are you planning to inform inspector Mercer of your discovery Mister Phillips." said Morgan as he placed his cup upon the coffee table. Neither Phillips or Polly Sheppard made any attempt at a reply, they just both sat in silence shaking their heads at the thought of the task in hand, and both knowing that when Mercer was informed, that it could quite possibly finish the man. Ironically, her eyes were focussed on a poster on the wall containing a photograph of a young couple running along the sand with their little boy and girl, mother and father pulling on the strings of a kite, and informing whoever would look upon it the value of a close family.

All said and done, it would have been easier if they'd discovered mother and son dead, because that would be the end of the matter, but now? Now Terry Mercer would make the hardest decision he would ever have to make in his life, for him to come in here and witness first-hand the result of Alexander Stineman's handy-work. How could he compare the photograph of the bright-eyed little boy he carried around with him in his wallet, to this bloated puffed-face human-being having to be fed and changed like a baby every few hours, and completely unable to communicate in any form, and then to discover, that the damage has been done deliberately, that someone paid someone else to do this to his son…and his wife.

Polly sipped from her teacup.

"We'll tell him when we get back to HQ."

Her mobile phone buzzed in her coat pocket.

"Excuse me" she said as she rose to her feet and walked over to the far end of the waiting room.

Of all the discoveries Andy Phillips had made throughout his career, these were the worst by far. Everybody had felt sorry for Terry Mercer when they'd heard of what had happened between him and his wife, and although Terry would never gain any points for uxoriousness no-one could have foreseen anything like this coming though. Sam Hargrieves had even paid a PI to investigate further, and to try and locate Carol and Daniel.

Andy watched Polly intently as she spoke softly on her mobile. Was it Terry on the phone to her now? And if it was, it would be hard for her not to burst into tears with what she had to tell him.

As it turned out, it was the C.I.D in Manchester.

They were informing her that Doctor Alistair Stineman had taken his own life by jumping off the ledge of the hotel where he'd been staying. Polly had returned to her seat and told Andy about Stineman. There was no jubilation like there should have been, simply because his suicide had only made matters worse for them. For a kick off Terry had been denied the opportunity of killing the bastard his own way, and secondly, it would now take an eternity to find out just how many people had fallen victim to the deranged surgeon, some of them would never be discovered she feared.

As Andy Phillips had rightly pointed out to Polly Sheppard, we were now living in a world of corruption and dishonesty, and the Metropolitan Police Department were no exception.
Someone had passed on information to Terry Mercer and Ava Cruntze that there was something that would be of great interest to them both at Smithfield Mental Health Institution in Kenilworth, and that it would be very beneficial to them to take a trip over there. Having no idea whatsoever what their informant was going on about, but curious none the less to find out, Terry and Ava had made their way there and were now at the gates of the premises awaiting permission from Doctor Muller to be able to gain entry.
Polly Sheppard at this point in time was back at HQ in London and frantically trying to get Terry on his phone. The last three attempts had her talking to his answer machine. Of all the bad habits Terry Mercer had, driving whilst talking on his phone was not one of them. He wouldn't even install a hands-free system, claiming that that too could distract a driver. After six attempts, she was finally successful. "Hello? Terry? Where are you?"
"I'm at Smithfield Mental Health Institute, apparently there is something of great interest for me and Ava to see here."
"Who told you that Terry?"
"They wouldn't say, but it was one of our own, I don't think they were bullshitting us."
"Terry? Don't you go in there, do you hear me, don't you go in, put Ava on the phone please, I want to speak with her."
"Ava's talking to one of the security people here at the gates Polly, we're waiting for a Doctor Muller to give us the go-ahead.
Look we'll only be here for an hour or so, probably not even that long, then we'll head back to London, I'll let you know how we get on."
"Terry? I'm forbidding you to go in there, do you hear me, don't you dare enter those premises without me there, I'm warning you."
"Keep your knickers on Polly, we're here now, it won't take us long, like I say, we'll let you know if we find out anything beneficial, oh I

heard about our good friend Doctor Stineman, good news huh Polly? I'll talk to you soon, bye for now."

"Terry, I'm warning you, don't-."

Mercer's phone went dead. The only other thing Polly could do now was to contact Doctor Muller, and inform him not to let Mercer or Cruntze see any of his patients but all she had was the number for the hospital itself, which put her on to reception, where she was informed by the secretary that Doctor Muller was a very busy man and that if she wished to have a conversation with him she would have to go through the correct channels.

Not even when Polly explained to the girl who she was and that it was of the utmost importance that she speak to him did it make any difference to the young lady's attitude. "I'm afraid I can't help you there Miss Sheppard, I cannot leave my post here and anyway, I doubt very much if the Doctor could take time to come and talk on the phone to someone he doesn't even know, like I say, you'll-."

Polly switched off her phone, exasperated. It was useless.

Without Muller's personal number there would be no chance of contacting him, and therefor Terry would enter Smithfield with Ava totally oblivious to what lay in wait for him, and Doctor Muller would be completely unaware of what he was about to do to the man.

Phillips entered the office.

"Oh Andy, do you happen to have Doctor Muller's mobile phone number."

"Yes, I have it here Polly."

Forty-five seconds later Polly was listening to the ring-tone of Muller's phone. "Come on come on Doctor, please pick up, come on, please."

Doctor Muller's phone played out his wife's favourite song in the drawer of his desk where he kept it whilst he was doing his rounds with the patients. Doctor Muller himself was presently welcoming detectives Terrence Mercer and Ava Cruntze having cleared them with security. Terry, in all of his years in the force had faced many obstacles and had overcome them, sometimes with the help of others, and sometimes steadfastly through his own metal, but what

was about to happen to him here would to say the least, test his very own sanity. The first thing Terry Mercer noticed was the look of sympathy on the doctor's face. His solemn expression, hardly able to look him in the face, and choosing instead to look more towards Ava, and then, the sledgehammer blow that whacked Mercer so hard, it took but all of the air right out of his lungs.
"May I say Mister Mercer how much I admire your bravery in coming here, I know how difficult this situation must be for you, especially as how you thought that your wife had left you, Mister Phillips explained everything to me when he discovered that Cal was your wife, a complete tragedy Mister Mercer."
Mercer looked confusingly at his colleague.
"What the hell's he going on about Ava?"
"Would you like to see her now Mister Mercer although I'm sure that Mister Phillips will have told you about her appearance, and of course, her condition."
"What on earth are you going on about man? We're here to investigate-"
Muller looked at Mercer, realizing now, that the detective had not been notified of Phillip's discovery and wondered now which path to take. Did he tell him now or wait until he'd spoken to one of his superiors.
"Mister Mercer, your colleague Mister Andrew Phillips was here, and took samples of D.N.A from the patients, our unidentified patients. He then got back in touch with me to inform me that a certain female patient we have turns out to be your missing wife, surely he's been in touch, I mean I told him to inform you immediately, hasn't he been in touch with you?"
"My missing wife?
Are you telling me that my wife is in here? Is that what you're telling me?"
"I'm afraid so." said Muller, too late now to wait for Mercer's superiors to inform him.
"She was brought in here quite some time ago, I think they found her sitting on the pavement on the outskirts of Coventry.
Mister Mercer, she has severe brain damage."

Mercer stood completely benumbed, staring at the doctor unable to completely comprehend what he'd just been told.

"I'm so sorry Mister Mercer, I understood you'd been informed, I thought that that was why you were here, both of you."

"My wife's here? My wife Carol is here, that's what you said didn't you? You said that my wife is in here, and she was sitting on the pavement at Coventry, wasn't that what you said, you said Carol was here, she's in here. Isn't that right Ava, didn't he say that, my wife."

Ava Cruntze was shaking, almost as much as Terry Mercer was. Doctor Muller attempted to at least bring some sanity back into the room.

"Mister Mercer, I think we should all have a cup of tea and a little chat before we continue any further with this most unfortunate situation, I can only-"

"My wife's here? Christ Ava, she was sitting on the bloody pavement in Coventry...Christ, and is my son here as well doctor, what bloody pavement was *he* sitting on, was he beside her? Was *he* with her in Coventry, and she's got brain damage did you say doctor, my wife's here and she's got brain damage."

"Please inspector Cruntze, get in touch with your superiors, and get them here as quickly as you can, this man is in trouble here, he's struggling, please inspector, as quick as you can."

Unbeknown either to Ava Cruntze or Terry Mercer, Doctor Muller had pressed an emergency button underneath his desk. Any minute now, the door would burst open and at least two security guards would enter and hold down detective Terrence Mercer long enough for the anaesthetist Doctor Morgan to administer a sedative which would render him quite helpless long enough for the Metropolitan Police department to explain to him why this man had been sent here and why he was not previously informed of his colleague's discoveries.

Forty minutes later Ava Cruntze sat outside on one of the benches in the garden, reeling from the shock of what had just happened. Poor Terry was now lying semi-conscious in one of Doctor Morgan's recovery rooms. Polly Sheppard was on her way up here along with Andy Phillips and Tony Chrysler. The shit was going to hit the fan this time. Someone was going to pay for this.

Muller had explained to her what Mister Phillips had discovered, and how he had informed Mister Phillips that the damage done to Misses Mercer had undoubtedly been malicious. As he explained all these things to her, she remembered what Rosalyn Simpson had said when they'd visited her at Pleasant Meadows.

*"He may not have enough spiritual strength to continue in this line of work by the time I'm finished with him, in fact I doubt it very much."*

So this was what she meant. This is what she'd had done to Terry's wife. The woman hadn't left him at all, and what about his son? What had she had inflicted upon him? Had the woman's evil no end? Was there no limits to her deeds? This evil termagant was slowly tearing Terry Mercer's life to pieces, and stripping away the man's will to live. Ava found herself lighting up a cigarette and inhaling deeply, having taken Terry's jacket from him once he'd fallen asleep. "Get ready to be dumped again Ava" she said to herself.

"Just when I think I've hit the jackpot."

She only hoped with all of her heart, that she meant enough to him for her to be able to at least try and assist him through this nightmare, a nightmare that would undoubtedly get worse before it got better...and what *had* she done to Terry's boy, she wondered.

SMITHFIELD MENTAL HEALTH INSTITUTION.

KENILWORTH. COVENTRY. (Two hours later.)

Polly Sheppard sat at the huge table in the conference room beside Tony Chrysler. Opposite them were Doctor Muller, Terry Mercer Ava Cruntze and Andy Phillips. All of them sat stone-faced as Polly attempted to apologise to Terry for the course of events that had just taken place. She explained that this was why she'd insisted that he and Ava were not to enter the premises until she arrived, that she might have the opportunity to explain to him about Andy's discoveries.
By now, Terry had been informed of the condition of his wife and son, and how they had been operated upon by the lunatic surgeon Stineman, and of course, the real reason Carol had deserted him. Everything had been set up to make it look like she'd taken off when in fact, they'd been kidnapped and held prisoner by Stineman after he'd received payment from Rosalyn Simpson and instructed by her to perform this surgery that would render them completely incapable of natural function. Muller had gone through Polly Sheppard and Tony Chrysler like a hurricane accusing them both of incompetence and neglect, and lack of consideration towards a fellow officer of the law.
Polly had apologised to Muller unreservedly and swore that this would never happen again and that it was merely a lack of opportunity that had caused this unfortunate event, stating that she had tried on several occasions to contact Mercer but had not been successful.
As the reasons and excuses were given to Doctor Muller Terry Mercer suddenly broke in with the words,
"I want to see her."
There was silence for a few moments as those around the table ingested what he'd just said. Then Tony Chrysler said, "Do you think that's a good idea Terry, considering what Doctor Muller has just told you? Do you think that's wise Terry? Maybe you should give it a

few days to come to terms with the situation, prepare yourself properly for em, for the shock you will undoubtedly receive, I mean you know she's not how you remember her Terry, she's been-"
He's right Terry." Put in Polly Sheppard, "we can come back here soon and you can see her then, but for now I would recommend that you give yourself time to-"
"I want to see her now. I don't care what condition she's in, she's my wife and I want to see her, and none of you are going to deny me that privilege…none of you. You can all sit there and advise me what you think is best for me and give me all the reasons why I shouldn't go and see her, but I have waited for over five years to see her, and I'm going to, whether you think it's the right thing to do or not, and I shall not be leaving here until I *have* seen her, are we all clear on that?"
Again there was an awkward silence as all those around the table sat with heads bowed, not in shame, but in complete sympathy for Terrence Mercer and the thought of the task in hand which they all knew would devastate him.
Finally, Doctor Muller sighed and said, "If you're sure Mister Mercer, I'll take you to her now, but I must warn you, she is not a pretty sight."
Mercer rose to his feet and pushed his chair under the table. "Ready when you are Doctor."
Ava was unsure of what to do. She so wanted to be a comfort but was frightened of rejection if she offered to accompany him, however she managed to pluck up the courage to ask.
"Terry? She said softly, "Would you like me to come with you for em…for-"
"Thank you Ava that would be lovely, I think I'll need you with me."
Ava almost let out a sob of relief at the compliment Terry had just given her. She approached him and squeezed his hand gently as Doctor Muller led them out of the room to visit the woman that Terry Mercer had built the best part of his life around.
The woman he had cursed for over five years.
The woman who had given birth to his dream-son, the woman who had, through no fault of her own ripped away a huge chunk of his

very soul.

Ava walked side by side with Terry as Doctor Muller led them down a long corridor which seemed to Ava to be endless, probably because what lay at the end of it could change the man she loved forever, and possibly even end the relationship she presently had with him. She loved Terry, there was no doubt in her mind about that. The question was, did Terry love her, and if he did, how much did he love her, because in just a few seconds the two of them would be face to face with the woman who had the divine right to his heart. How could she cope if Terry decided to call it a day with her and spend time with his *real* love, his true love.

All the doubts Ava had in her mind about their relationship, all the fears of losing Terry, everything, were all put to the test when Doctor Muller led them into a room.

There, sitting at a small table was a bloated puffed-faced woman with lank brown hair, wearing a dark blue cardigan opened up revealing a cream vest which had soup stains all down the front. When Terry set eyes upon her he let go of Ava's hand and let out a pitiful exclamation. He stifled a sob and turned his head away momentarily, trying his best to contain his emotions, because Carol Mercer did not have the slightest trace of recognition as she looked up at the ceiling. Even Ava put a hand up to her mouth in total shock. She hadn't really known what to expect, but this, this was worse than she could ever have imagined. Terry looked at the doctor, waiting for him to start some kind of conversation regarding her condition, but he said nothing. He only stood, solemn-faced as he let the reality of the situation sink in to Terry Mercer.

The doctor then proceeded to bring a chair for Terry and sat the chair opposite Carol Mercer.

Terry nervously accepted the seat offered to him and sat down. Three feet across the table, sat the love of his life.

Had the doctor not informed him of who the woman was, he would never in a thousand years have guessed that this was his beloved wife. Her face bloated, her eyes bloodshot.

She sat there looking vacantly into his face now.

There was no recognition whatsoever, not a flicker.

He instinctively reached across the table with his two hands.
Carol did not move.
Doctor Morgan came round behind her and gently placed Carol's hands in front of Terrys'.
Terry picked up her hands in his and squeezed gently, rubbing the back of her hands with his thumbs, something he used to do with her when she ever felt stressed, or needed assurance.
Looking now into Terry's eyes, she shouted, "I Cal…I Cal."
Ava had to leave the room.
She closed the door behind her and sat on her hunkers in the corridor breaking her heart.
Doctor Morgan spoke softly to Terry.
"She has no concept of who she is, where she is, or even why she is here. She doesn't know you Mister Mercer. Her brain damage is so severe it-"
"I can see that for myself man, Christ let me have five minutes with her before you go into all the bloody medical details would you? I can see how she is, God this is my wife, this is the mother of my son, and she does know who she is, she's trying to tell you that her name is Carol. Cal, that's what she's attempting to tell you, can't you see that, Christ *you're* the psychiatrist, can't you see that. I Cal, that's what she's saying."
Carol Mercer pulled her hands away from Terry's having heard his voice being raised.
"I Cal…I Cal…"
"Carol? Can you hear me? It's me babes, it's Terry, it's Tel, can you see me?" By `see` Terry meant recognise. "Can you see me Carol? Christ what have they done to you baby?" He picked up her hands again and looked longingly at his wife, and then whispered again, this time in her face, "It's me baby, it's Terry, don't you recognise me? It's me Carol, please baby, you know who I am don't you, I'm the silly bugger from the registry office, come on babes, just say something to me…I'm Terry."
There was no response. No response whatsoever. Carol was neither looking at Terry or Doctor Morgan but just staring again up at the ceiling.

"I Cal…I Cal." She kept shouting, staring up at the phosphorescent strip-light. Terry stood up and turned to the doctor.
"She knows me she does, I can see it in her eyes, she definitively knows me, there is recognition there doctor, I can see it in her eyes, Christ that's my wife doctor, and here was me thinking she'd up and left me, that's Carol, that's my Carol doctor, hell, she recognises me alright, there's no doubt in my mind."
Mercer's voice broke off as he clenched his fists and began beating them into the wall. "It's my wife doctor, that's my Carol alright and she knows me, it's my wife, Christ Carol I'm so so sorry my baby." He fell finally to his knees as his mind gave in to the facts.
Before he broke down completely, he managed one final thump into the wall with his right fist before crumpling down, begging his wife to recognise him and to forgive him for doubting her.
Doctor Muller pressed a button on the wall and three seconds later, a male nurse came into the room and escorted Carol Mercer away as she continuously shouted the only two words she was able to form, "I Cal."
Another male nurse entered the room and looked at Doctor Muller who nodded his head. The tall young nurse moved over to Terry, lifting him up from under his oxters and raised him to his feet.
"Come on sir, let's go and have a nice cup of coffee shall we?
I know I know" he kept saying sympathetically as he led Terry out of the room. "Let's go and get a coffee bud."

Everyone in the waiting room could see that Ava Cruntze had been crying. She entered the room without knocking and sat herself down on the chair where she'd sat before.
Both Tony Chrysler and Polly Sheppard spoke in unison.
"How is he Ava?"
Ava stood up again and retrieved Terry's cigarettes from her handbag, moving over to the window. She opened it and lit up a cigarette. No-one in the room protested.
"I couldn't stay in the room long enough to find out how he's doing, the sight of that poor woman broke my heart, I had to leave him in there. Doctor Muller informs me that he's been taken down to the

canteen for coffee, other than that, I have no idea how he's coping, and I was supposed to be his support."
They could all see that the sight of Carol Mercer had undoubtedly affected her. She was quiet in a way that Polly had never seen her before. She looked almost sinister as she smoked, staring out of the window. It was as though she was contemplating some kind of plan in her mind, and as Polly continued observing her she had a good idea what that plan might entail. She would have to make a point of never sending Ava back up to Pleasant Meadows, ever.
Doctor Muller entered the room once more and sat himself down on his seat. He let out a long exasperated sigh as he did so.
"How is he doctor?" said Polly Sheppard.
"He's doing fine Miss Sheppard, considering what he's just witnessed. He's down at the canteen standing at the back door smoking his cigarette." As he had said the word cigarette, he looked over briefly to Ava, but said nothing more.
"What's he going to do now?" Polly said, "Will he be able to see his son? He does know that his son is here now as well doesn't he?" Muller nodded.
"Yes, he knows, and as soon as he's had his coffee he's intending to go and see him. I must admit, he recovered well from the shock, quickly, he recovered quickly. He kind of lost it there but he regained composure soon enough. He is a very strong man indeed, however, when he sees his son and the condition he is in, well, let's just say he's going to need every bit of that strength to see him through it. Doctor Muller had kindly travelled up from Smithfield with the boy and one or two of his staff, when you are all ready we shall go and see him and the boy. I must say Miss Sheppard, what this Mister Terrance Mercer is experiencing today I would not wish upon my worst enemy if I had one, I can tell you that. This is one day he will never forget for the rest of his life, in fact I would go as far as to say that it may be in his best interest to seek psychological help, I think he'll need some kind of counselling, you might want to point him in that direction when all this is over, although I use the word over metaphorically, this I'm afraid will never be over for him."

Again, Ava was warmed by the next words to be spoken which were said by Polly Sheppard.
"He has Ava, she'll help him, he's in love with Ava."
Ava looked over to Polly, smiling.
"He does Ava, he loves you to bits, he told me, in fact I think his exact words were, that that German bint is all that's holding me together, f knows what I'll effing do if she f's off Polly."
As they began to leave the room, even Doctor Morgan had a smile on his face.

Doctor Alistair Morgan led them all down a now familiar corridor to the room where Terry had been introduced to his wife. Having seated them all, he excused himself whilst he left the room to find Doctor Muller. Morgan sat now in the adjoining room to where the Scotland Yard staff sat patiently awaiting further instructions.
Morgan had also sent for Terry Mercer. As Mercer was brought into the room Doctor Muller introduced Morgan to him and explained to him that this was the man who'd been looking after his son Daniel since his admittance into Karringdale.
Terry had a multitude of questions to ask both doctors.
He began by asking Muller *who* had brought his son in to the hospital.
"Your son was found sitting outside a baker's shop in Wolverhampton Mister Mercer. The CCTV only showed a car pulling up, a B.M.W. and someone wearing a hooded jacket climbed out of the passenger seat and opened the back door, pulling out your son, and sitting him down on the pavement outside of the shop.
The person quickly climbed back into the car, and they drove off. Whoever it was would probably know about the cameras because the car had no number-plate whatsoever, that's it, that's all we've got. The B.M.W. was black. That's it, nothing else, it was three o clock in the morning, the boy had just sat there for three and a half hours until someone came to open the shop.
Your son has been with us now for a few months Mister Mercer, I have looked after him as best as I could. Has Doctor Muller explained to you just how bad the lad's condition is?"

"Yes."
"Well, having now seen your wife's condition, all I can say is, your son is maybe five times worse than her...I'm sorry.
We've had the best psychopharmalogicalists in the country looking at your son. We have tried giving him psychotomimetic drugs to see if they could enhance activity in his brain, we've had the best paediatric surgeons in the country trying their best to improve the lads' condition, and having taken numerous x-rays, but I'm afraid the damage is far too severe. The surgery performed on him is, I'm afraid irreversible. I'm only telling you these facts Terry, to prepare you as best I can for the shock of what you are about to see."
Mercer stood looking at Doctor Muller slowly nodding his head, and taking in this gruesome information. Muller continued to break his heart further.
"Your son is incapable of speech. He is no longer in control of his bladder or bowels. He has to be spoon-fed. He also suffers from an illness Agranulocytosis, which is a deficiency of granulocytes in the blood, in other words Mister Mercer his vulnerability to infections is high. He has practically no immune system.
There has been surgery performed on his Broca, that's the region of the brain which deals with speech. He has had massive holes pierced into his cerebellum. All four lobes of his cerebrum have been subject to massive damage as well. At some point in the near future we'll have to discuss the boys' future and what you think is best for him." Muller took a long breath. "I'm so sorry Mister Mercer that I have to explain to you these facts. I have been informed of your unfortunate circumstances. This, my friend will be the hardest thing you will ever do, that's if you still wish to see the boy having been informed fully of his condition...I'm so sorry Mister Mercer, I really am."

Forty minutes later Terry Mercer sat outside on one of the many benches situated around the grounds of the hospital trying to come to terms with what he had just seen. He looked at the bright-faced laughing little boy smiling up at him from the photograph in his hands. The photograph he'd carried around with him for all these

years which was the only thing sometimes that could help him continue, to keep fighting, keep hoping, and that perhaps one day they could once more be reunited as father and son and perhaps build up again that special bond that fathers and sons have.
But now it had all been finalized, brought to an ungodly end, by a deranged surgeon who didn't even know the lad, but had left him in an all but cabbage-state, not even worthy of calling an existence. The boy's mother too, the love of his life, who had done nothing wrong whatsoever, but was reduced to a state of vegetation.
There was no other description for their conditions.
He lit up a cigarette as he stared around the hospital gardens listening to the crows squawking as they prepared for the oncoming evening, settling themselves down for the night, together, in two's, the way nature intended it to be.
The sight of Daniel had shaken him badly.
The doctors could explain to him all day until they were blue in the face about all of that medical stuff, but when you have that dreaded fear of what you think the person may look like, and then discover that they are ten times worse than that, there are no words to be said. There are no words to describe how you feel, there is no description for that...other than complete devastation.
A depressing grey mist hung over the carpark as he smoked his cigarette, a colourless landscape all around him.
It matched perfectly his life, certainly since Carol and his son disappeared, and now they were back, at least in body form, but the child and the woman he had just seen were nothing like the two people who had exited his life. He recalled the young lad sitting there rocking two and fro muttering incoherently.
He stood up from the bench as if he'd suddenly remembered he should be somewhere else, and then sat back down, a reaction from the devastating image he'd just encountered. Just as he was about to break down again, Ava Cruntze appeared like a welcoming angel through the gloomy mist and drizzle, bearing a soft smile, not of sympathy but of admiration. He was ready to crack, and it would be alright to do so in front of Ava, because she understood what he was feeling, how he was feeling. The smile remained upon Ava's

face as she stood directly in front of him. He was just about to give in to his emotions and `cry upon her shoulder` when Ava took her hand and smacked him hard on his face, and then repeated the action.

"Listen to me , I need your full attention. I'm here with you Terry Mercer, whatever you decide, or whatever the world decides to throw in your face in the future, I am here with you until you tell me to leave. Whatever you decide to do, I will stand by your decisions and I will never, repeat never leave your side. If there is one person in the world you can depend on, then that person is me, even if you decide that we should part company as a couple I'll still be here for you, although it will never stop me loving you, that much is now out of my hands. So, do you want to go inside where we can get a coffee and a comfortable chair to sit on, or do you want to sit out here getting soaking to the skin in this bloody drizzle, and by the way, you'll need to get some cigarettes soon, there's only four left in your packet, I've smoked them all, it's with all your bloody cursing and swearing and fucking about, your bad habits have finally worn off on me, are you coming?"

Terry squeezed her hand gently and escorted Ava back to the hospital. As they walked he said, "I've got cigarettes here", producing a packet from his jacket pocket.

Ava smiled at him, now linking his arm and nestling into his shoulder.

"You're a lot tougher than even I thought you were Mister Mercer, I have to admit. Polly told me about how you referred to me as a German bint, and how your world would fall apart without me, was she telling me the truth Terry?"

"Ava, Ava, I have never in my life depended upon anyone for anything, I can tell you that for nothing, and I'm proud of the fact." As they reached the door where Terry held it open for her, he said, softly, "That was of course, before I met you Ava."

"So, did she tell the truth?"

Perhaps she was pushing him too far and coming over rather selfish in her wishful thinking, her hoping, for she knew at this stage that in fact, she needed *him*.

A slight pause, and then he said, "Polly doesn't tell lies Ava, hell even you know that".

## CHAPTER SIXTEEN.

## PARLOUR STREET.

## SOUTH KENSINGTON.

All the documents had been signed, all the paperwork regarding the ownership of the house had all been completed, and everything was in place for Beth Hargrieves and John Pearce to begin their new lives in Portugal. John Pearce, who now sat beside Beth in the lounge had been so impressed with Beth's kindness towards the girls that he had decided to `chip in` to help give them a start in their new home. He had once been the proud owner of a small accountancy business and had accumulated his fortune over thirty years of hard work.
Having been told everything by Beth about how Sam had taken to the girls and how they had brightened up his darkest days in the midst of very depressing investigations, he decided to gift the girls a further sixty thousand pounds.
Beth had placed the cheque into the girls' bank account, the joint-account she had opened for them when she had placed the money in advance to help them with their rates. Veronica, Mandy and Elizabeth sat opposite the couple who had in so many ways, changed their lives for the better. All Beth asked for in return was that they made sure that Sam's gravestone was cleaned and kept tidy, that was it, that was the only condition. The taxi was coming for Beth and John in about twenty minutes' time to take them to the airport. John Pearce smiled at the girls yet again, as they thanked him and Beth for this opportunity in their lives, to be able

to make something of themselves, an opportunity they could never dream they'd be given.
Mister Pearce arose from the chair upon where he'd sat and asked if any of the girls had a driving license.
Only Veronica had a license.
"Well. I'm quite sure girls if you ask Veronica nicely, that she'll take you wherever you wish to go, you see Beth already informed me about this, and so I have taken the liberty of changing the ownership papers of the Mercedes outside into her name."
He handed Veronica the keys for the six-month old automobile.
"It's all yours sweetheart, make sure you take care of your friends as I'm sure you all will take care of each other. I have only known you for a few weeks but it has been a privilege and an honour to meet you all, I wish you all the very best of luck for the future and that you have nothing but good luck throughout the course of your lives." Beth admired all the girls equally, but she had a particular soft-spot for Mandy. This was the one Sam had said had an amazing sense of humour even through all adversity.
The loss of her sister had shaken her badly, but still she remained strong for her friends. Mandy had told Beth how her parents had been towards her and how she was classed as scum to them and had been disowned. Beth had told her that as long as they all remained friends and looked out for each other, that they could all be each-others' parents and guardians. "Send her a picture of your new house Mandy and invite them for tea, that'll annoy them." Mandy was tough though, Beth knew, and she knew that you'd have to be tough in that profession and that being thin-skinned would get you nowhere, whether or not they planned to continue in that line of work would be entirely up to them, she kind of half-hoped that they would. Behind all of their false made-up faces and short skirts and fast-talking, there was three rather special ladies that the world would never have recognised. She could plainly see how Sam had taken a shine to them and had no regrets whatsoever about leaving them the house, in fact, it pleased her enormously to think that they could live here and in comfort, away from those terrible flats. Perhaps now the world would see the girls in a

different light, they'd certainly get noticed that was for sure. This had been her and Sam's home now for quite some years and so she felt happy in the fact that she'd gifted these girls a place where they could live quite comfortably. Something neither of them had ever had in their lives before, luxury.

## PLEASANT MEADOWS.

## BIRMINGHAM.

Against Polly Sheppard's advice Terry Mercer had arrived at the institute to have a final meeting with Misses Rosalyn Simpson. His visit was for no other reason than to show her that he and Ava Cruntze were deeply in love and that they planned to live together for the rest of their lives, and that her dastardly deeds had failed miserably to destroy his life, and to point out, once again that *she* would be spending the rest of her life, here with the rest of the fruitcakes, where she belonged, and that every day he would think about her and her miserable existence here in the funny farm. Mercer pulled up at the gates with his ID pass ready for inspection in his hand.
Steven Smith, the very tall guard who had given Terry so much grief in the past, had read in the papers all about his ordeal and what had been done to his wife and son, and now had a very different approach to the Scotland Yard detective.
"Good morning sir, on your own today sir?"
"Yeah, just a short visit today, my last visit in fact, so you won't have me here annoying you any more, disrupting your procedures."
"I must apologise Mister Mercer, I had no idea of what you were going through sir, I thought you were just being purposefully arrogant."
"Well, we're all aright now then, your apology is accepted."

Smith handed the card back to Mercer.
"You have yourself a good day now sir."
"Oh I will officer, you have a good day yourself."
"Thank you sir I will."

Mercer was greeted once more by Doctor Andrew Mullard, the man who had informed him that there was no chance whatsoever of any of the `inmates` in here escaping, and that anyone who'd been admitted here would never be leaving. As he walked with Mercer down the corridor he spoke business-like again and with his authoritative tone he said, "Now listen Mister Mercer, we do not want a repeat of what happened here on your last visit.
Your seniors have moved mountains on your behalf to allow you this visit, so I hope you will conduct your behaviour accordingly. I know what this woman has done to you, or rather has done to your family, but please, no more magniloquence, and anyway there shall be two security nurses present in the room with you and Misses Simpson, and they will not tolerate any continuous profanations, so, are we all clear on that? I can't for the life of me understand Mister Mercer why you would even wish to see this woman again, but, you will have your fifteen minutes as we arranged."
Mercer thanked the psychiatrist again as they reached the door.
"Now remember Mister Mercer, stay in control ok?"
Once again Mercer entered the room.
This time there was no-one seated at the table in the centre.
One chair had been placed either side of the table.
Mercer sat himself down where he had sat the last time he was here. He had Ava with him then. This time he had chosen to face the monster alone.
The walls of the room were immaculately painted in magnolia bearing pictures and photographs of peaceful landscapes and ancient clippers tackling rough seas, a bit like the minds of some of the people who were in here he surmised, then suddenly a flash-back in his mind, "*I Cal...I Cal.*"
He composed himself, and braced for the challenge ahead of him

which was, to stay cool in front of the monster and prove to her that she did not defeat him. The door at the far end of the room opened and a male nurse stepped in, followed by Rosalyn Simpson and then the second male nurse. What the hell was going on in here he thought to himself. They had allowed her to dress once more as though she were going to a function.

She approached the table dressed in black skin-tight trousers with a royal blue silk blouse, opened up to mid-way down her chest, exposing a deep plunge-line which was far too provocative for his liking.

Once again she had been allowed to apply make-up and had done that to her usual immaculate standards. Her hair had been cut short now and even that looked like she'd had it done by some fancy hairdresser from one of London's highest fashion salons.

Simpson sat herself down on the chair opposite Mercer.

"Nice of you to come and see me Terry, and on your own as well, you're getting brave in your old age are you not?

Haven't you got your German sperm-bank with you for encouragement, or should I say, assistance?"

"I don't need anyone's assistance Rosalyn to face you my sick friend. I have only come here to show you or to prove to you that you did not win. You have failed to destroy my life, and in fact have only succeeded in destroying your own."

Simpson smiled across the table and reached out with her hands in the same way he had done with his wife Carol.

Mercer pulled his hands away from hers shaking his head in disbelief that, even having done what she'd had done to his wife and family, thinking that he would even consider such an act.

"You really are a fruitcake aren't you, you don't seem to realize just how sick in the fucking head you really are, the only place my hands would be making contact with you, would be round your scrawny little neck, you evil bastard that you are."

"Mister Mercer." shouted one of the security nurses, "I must warn you sir to please refrain from that kind of language. Doctor Mullard has warned you of what will happen if you continue."

Mercer raised his hand as an act of apology. He thought he would change the subject with Simpson. "You know that we've seized all your assets Misses Simpson, and that we will be using them as reperation, that is, payments to the families of your victims.
The money will be spread out evenly, of course we've had your husband's permission to do this, or should I say cooperation, we were going to do it with or without his permission.
So, that'll be the end of your flamboyance and your pretentious living, believing yourself to be someone of importance or influence, it's all gone now, little Miss nothing."
"Have you paid Carol a visit lately Terrance, doesn't she look wonderful, and your lovely son, Alexander sent me photographs of them both when he had finished their surgery...I hardly recognised them, did you?
Mum mum mum mum mum mum mum Terry huh?
What age is your son now, can you remember?
Such a shame they don't even know that they're born, such a tragic course of events, but you must admit Terry, I am very clever, I mean I had you convinced that Carol had actually left you didn't I?"
It took Terrance Mercer all of his will power not to blast his fist straight into Simpson's face, but remarkably he kept control of himself.
"I Cal, I Cal I Cal".
Instead he hit her with the irrefutable truth, which was; "This is it for you Rosalyn, this is where the bus stops. You're home sick lady, and you are home for good, all tucked up nice and safe where you can't do anything to anyone, you can't inflict your repulsive acts upon innocent human beings, how on earth did you manage to eat someone's kidneys you sick fuck that you are, and there certainly won't be any chance of you escaping from here, you won't be able to pay anyone to help you now, because you now have nothing.
There'll be no chance of the guards entering your room, or should I say cell, to find a simulacrum formed on your bed and to find you gone, oh no madam, this is it, and when I stop coming here then you'll have no-one. Your ex-husband wants nothing to do with you and everyone else you've ever had contact with, all of them, out of

your life. It's just you now Rosalyn, just poor sick Rosalyn Clark who the world will forget ever existed.
You paid that madman to get to me by destroying my wife and family, you shot my colleagues and tortured them, you committed pseudoautochiria on Sandra Neal, and God knows who else, you even murdered your accomplice when he overstepped your rules, yeah, you're in the right place bitch and no mistake."
He leaned over the table and smiled at the woman who had destroyed everything he'd ever lived for and said to her; "You didn't win Missy, you tried your level-best to destroy me, but guess what bitch, I am stronger than you, I have a stronger will than you, and I can start again, I will start again, me and Ava, but you, you have nothing Rosalyn, absolutely nothing.
Everywhere you go in here you'll have guards escorting you around, they'll be like your stinking rotten shadows, me and Ava, we'll be doing just fine while you rot away in here like the fucking sewer rat that you are."
Simpson said nothing at first, but then informed him that they only made it look like they'd eaten their victim's kidneys.
Then she continued to smile in his face, turned to one of the male nurses and asked if she may have a cup of tea.
"I wouldn't bother if I were you Rosalyn, I won't be here for much longer, as I say, I just came to let you know that *you* are the loser in all of this, just to rub it in about me and beautiful Ava who I enjoy making love with immensely, I mean she's a real woman as opposed to the evil sick-minded bitch in front of me."
Still smiling she said; "And no wonder you enjoy, my goodness me she's had plenty of practice from what I can gather from Scotland Yard but I would recommend that you stay a little while longer Terry, it's in your best interest, honestly, I have some very worthwhile information for you, and as you say, this will be your last visit, so, will you join me for this final beverage? Please?"
"Come on then, five minutes more but I can't for the life of me, imagine what this information could possibly be that will interest me so much."
Five minutes later Rosalyn Simpson and Terry Mercer sat across the

table from one another with their tea. Simpson spoke now, still smiling at Mercer. "You remember I told you once Terry that we humans can all be bought for a price."

"Humans, fuck, what would you know about humans, you're a fucking felidae, and it's not just me either is it, it's all men, tell me, at what point in your life did you discover that you were misandry? Did you have to work at it?"

 She ignored his remarks and continued.

"As I was saying Mister Mercer, we can all be bought for a price, oh and by the way with reference to your earlier statement about me having nothing? They can only confiscate assets that are in my name Terry. I have lots of bank-accounts all over the world, all in different names, lots of money Terry, lots and lots, and you'd be surprised who has access to some of those accounts. How much money would it take Terry for someone to kill someone else? One million? Two? maybe three million?

Think what you could do with three million pounds Terry, you could have a wonderful life with three million pounds don't you think?"

"I'm not listening to anymore of your pointless fucking banter, I have a life to live and enjoy, you just enjoy your stay here Rosalyn, and I promise you I'll think about you when I'm sunning my arse out on the Caribbean, me and Ava."

He rose up from the table and nodded to the two male nurses.

"That's me finished lads, me and Rosalyn have had our last little chat and very nice it was, simply because I won't have to look at her cheap tarted-up face again, you know, her mutton-dressed-as-lamb face, full of acne punctured holes. Now you keep her nice and secure boys, do you hear me? You fucking follow her even to the toilet, and keep all sharp harmful objects away from her, we don't want her dying before her time."

He had reached the door by now and had one hand on the handle.

"That's a good word Terry" she said, still with the arrogant smile on her face. "Time, we take that word for granted don't you think? Carol thought she had all the time in the world, now, she doesn't even have a thought, isn't that sad Terry, and your little boy, well, he's not so little now, he's more like a great big-headed bloated

baboon isn't he, still, he's your son and I shouldn't mock should I, mum mum mum mum mum mum, such a shame, Doctor Stineman was so meticulous with those scalpels of his wasn't he, although by the look of your wife and son, I think rather that he used a blunt butter knife instead of his medical instruments."
Mercer shook his head disdainfully.
"You are one sad fucking excuse for a human being are you not? Goodbye forever you little sewer rat, and when you die, I hope you burn in Hell, you nasty sick fuck that you are."
He opened the door, and was half way through when she said, quite calmly and reassuringly, I'll see you soon Terry."
"That's what you fucking think bitch."
"That's what I know Terry, three million pounds is a lot of money." She looked at the giant clock on the wall. "I'm not finished with you just yet I'm afraid, we'll see each other pretty soon Mister Mercer, meanwhile you go and enjoy your time with Ava, where is she today Terry, do you know?"
Mercer slammed the door and headed back to Doctor Andrew Mullards' office where he signed himself out, thanking the doctor for his time and for allowing him this final interview with Simpson. As he drove down towards the security gates he began to go over in his head some of the things the monster had said to him, and how she had emphasised the word time. Time. Three million pounds. *"We can all be bought for a price." "Where is Ava today, do you know?"* She had that I-know-something-that-you-don't-know look upon her face. *"I'm not finished with you just yet I'm afraid."*
Five minutes later, he found himself speeding back towards London, as though he were running against the clock, like there was no time to spare, but why? Why was he speeding? He reduced his speed and pulled off the motorway to a layby.
The first thing he would do was text Ava, better still he'd call her. He pressed the call button on his phone. "Hello? Ava? Are you alright? Where are you?"
"Wow, slow down Terry, where's the fire, what's wrong?"
"Nothing, nothing's wrong, where are you?"
"I'm in the Millington hotel in Salford why? I've been sent here with

Smedley and Kathlene Oconnor. Is there something wrong Terry?"
"No, nothing, I'm eh, I'm just heading back to London now."
"How did your meeting go with Miss fucked-up, you didn't let her get to you again did you?"
"No, not this time Ava, but do you know something?
She said she wasn't finished with me just yet can you believe it?"
"It's just to scare you Terry, she knows she won't be seeing you ever again. It's just her way of trying to frighten you one last time."
"Yeah I know that Ava, Christ, it was just the way she sits there so matter-of-fact, you know, like she does, as if...as if..."
"Terry? Don't. Don't let her get to you, it's her last chance to hurt you and it's gone, and she's gone, and after Kathlene and John and I are finished here then you and I are taking some leave and we're going on a proper holiday this time, for three weeks, I've already organised it, and we're going all-inclusive Mister Mercer, and I've paid for first class tickets. This is where we begin our new lives Terry, she can say she's not finished with you all she wants, but we are undoubtedly finished with her, and if you as much as mention her name to me again I will kick you so hard in the balls, you'll be speaking the rest of your life in C-sharp, got it?"
"Yeah I've got it Ava, you're right it was her last opportunity to get to me, I told her as much, anyway I'll be back in London shortly I'll see you when you get back to HQ."
"Ok, we're nearly done here Terry, just going over the final details of how the nasty Doctor Stineman decided to end the world's misery, see you soon babes."
Terry smiled to himself as he put the phone back into his pocket. Carol was the only woman in his life to call him that.
He looked at his unshaven face in his rear-view mirror and laughed out loud. "Babes indeed, Christ Ava."

## M1.

### Forty-five minutes later.

Terry drove back towards London feeling a new lease of life, or at least, a fresh outlook. He and Ava were set to start afresh.
They had both contemplated leaving the force and trying something else, something away from this profession that constantly put their lives in danger. They were perusing very dangerous people who would kill you at the drop of a hat. You enter worlds that the average man on the street has no idea even exists.
Drugs and sexual crimes run by invisible `syndicates' of whom you have no idea whatsoever where to begin to search. They lie hidden in the cities, an underground population who Joe Blogs, if he's lucky, never even encounters in his or her life-time, but they're there, almost omnipresent. You could be rubbing shoulders with one of them as you stand in your local enjoying a beer. The lovely quiet man next door to you, who never bothers a soul, could be one of them. He even offers to cut their lawn for them if they're at work. The young fresh-faced girl in the baker shop who always smiles and wishes everyone who enters the shop, a good day. That was the problem, you can never tell, hence whenever you are investigating a crime you have to look upon all witnesses as guilty, until such time as you can eliminate them from your enquiries. It's not nice for the innocent parties, but that was just how it was. Although Ava and he had discussed leaving the force he struggled to see himself in any other line of work. This was his life, grimy and unclean as it was sometimes, it was all he knew, and for all of these years, it was all he wanted to know. He had learned his trade well from Sam Hargrieves and had been to Hell and back with him in their pursuit of the invisible criminals.
They always appeared though, some time, and when they did, he and Sam were waiting. He began to reflect on how Sam and him used to fall out from time to time, and sometimes rather heated discussions took place, so much so that the staff in the canteen they happened to be in would quickly make themselves scarce. Terry found himself singing along to the song that he loved best in the

world from the CD he'd inserted, and how very fitting it was in reference to Sam Hargrieves as David Gilmour chanted angelically the words that Roger Waters had written for Pink Floyd,
*"How I wish, how I wish you were here, we're just two lost souls swimming in a fish-bowl, year after year, running over the same old ground, but have we found, the same old fears, wish you were here."*
Terry wiped a tear from his eye, smiling to himself at the fond memory of his best friend. Before he knew it tears were flooding down his face as once more, the remains of that beautiful human being he married came to him in a flash.
*"I Cal...I Cal...I Cal."*
Nothing in the world could have devastated him so badly as what had happened to his wife and son...but it had happened, and he knew that somehow he just had to go on, it's what Carol would have wanted him to do, he knew that, just the same as he would have wanted it for her if the circumstances had been the other way round. They had discussed it many times. But it was very difficult indeed to move on when the person you truly loved and cherished was still present in the world, albeit in physical form only. He wiped his eyes and took control once more of his emotions.
"Have to move on, I have to."
His phone rang again in his pocket, another petty hate of his, people expecting him to answer them when they knew fine well he was driving. He looked at the phone. It was Polly Sheppard.
"What the fuck is it Polly, I'm driving."
"Terry? Where are you?"
"I'm on the M1 and heading back, what's wrong?"
"Pull into the next available service station and tell me where it is, stay there until I arrive, are you clear on that?"
"What the fuck is wrong Polly, you sound flustered, calm yourself down, I'll be-"
"Just fucking do it Terry, and do as you're told this time, do you hear me, now pull into the next service station and then tell me where it is, and wait there, do I make myself clear?
"Yes Polly, fuck sakes woman calm down Christ I'll do it I'll do it ok,

keep your hair on. What the hell is-"
His phone went dead. His heart pounded like a bass drum.
It is one of the worst feelings in the world to be frightened and you don't know what you're frightened for...but he was, he was very frightened indeed. Once again, Simpson's words rattled his brain like a jack-hammer; *"We can all be bought for a price Terry. Three million pounds is a lot of money. Where is Ava today Terry, do you know? Oh I will see you again Terry."*
He pulled in to the Northampton Roadchef service station and parked the car and then phoned Polly on his mobile phone, informing her of his whereabouts.
He tried again to find out why she had spoken to him with such urgency but was only informed to stay where he was until her arrival, and that she'd be there very soon. Yet again in the middle of him asking what all the fuss was about, Polly had hung up on her phone, making him all the more anxious. Now he knew something was wrong, and by the way Polly was talking it was nothing trivial. He found the number for Ava and pressed the call button. There was no answer. He waited a few minutes and then tried again, still no reply. "She must be driving" he thought to himself. He tapped the steering-wheel frustratingly as he waited another five minutes, then he sent Ava a text message asking her to call him as soon as possible, and did she know what the hell was bothering Polly Sheppard. He left his car to get refreshments from one of the diners and returned to his vehicle, checking his phone yet again.
Nothing.
Finally, he decided to call Andy Phillips to see if he knew what the hell was going on. Andy answered straight away. "Andy, it's Mercer here, what the hell is happening down there bud, I've had Polly on the phone telling me to stay put here until she gets here, I'm in Northampton service station. I've to wait here until she arrives, what the hell is happening Andy?"
Terry could hear nothing. "Hello, Andy?" Finally Andy spoke.
"I can't tell you Terry, I'm under strict orders not to tell you, Polly will tell you when she gets there, Christ Terry son...I...I...honestly, I can't tell you anything, Tony Chrysler is coming to see you with her,

just stay where you are son."
"Andy? I'm asking you as a friend, please tell me what's happened."
The signal was dead.
A surge of temper from Mercer attracted attention to a passing couple with their two children as they saw him first punch his steering-wheel repeatedly and then exit the car and begin to kick the back bumper ferociously, cursing and swearing as he did so. The couple instinctively protected their children from the madman and hurried past as quickly as they could, as one of their two little girls burst into tears. Mercer was completely oblivious to their presence at that point and burned out his temper with his fists pounding on the back of his car. Finally he regained control of himself and shouted after the family that he was very sorry.
They continued walking a brisk pace until they reached their vehicle. Only the husband looked at Terry as they all climbed into the car and drove away. Terry Mercer felt ashamed of himself having frightened them so badly. Inevitably he lit up a cigarette and leaned his back against the back of his car. He tried Ava's phone again, still no answer. He opened the can of fruit-juice he'd purchased and sipped from the tin. What the hell was going on? Why was Ava not responding to his calls? Had *she* been informed to tell him nothing as well? Maybe that was why she wasn't answering her phone.
It would be easier for her if she didn't speak at all to him until Polly had seen him, knowing that she'd probably give in and tell him, whatever the hell it was he was not supposed to hear.
He stood sighing impatiently as he awaited Polly's arrival.
He was sick of this. Every time he opened his mouth these days his comments seemed to be vituperative or vociferous, clamorous and accusing. He seemed to be snapping at everyone.
He knew what had made him this way as well, beginning with the disappearance of his wife Carol. Even then, he had automatically assumed that she'd taken off with another man. Christ what kind of man had he become? He was supposed to be a pursuer of the truth, of justice and honesty, but he'd turned into this bloody madman with uncontrollable temper fits frightening people half to death.

All the time it had been that sick woman Rosalyn Clark or whatever she called herself. She had made him this way. As he smoked his cigarette he looked around the car park only to discover that some other people had witnessed his tantrum, and probably frightened to leave their vehicle to go to the diners.
A police car pulled up not far from where he stood.
"Oh for crying out loud" he mumbled to himself. "Jesus Lord, have mercy." Just as the two police officers approached him Chrysler's Mercedes pulled up along-side the patrol car. Polly said something to the two officers who'd been heading towards him. They about-turned and headed back to their vehicle and drove away.
Polly Sheppard and Tony Chrysler approached him.
"Well? What's going on Polly, what the hell is this urgency all about, no-one will talk to me, no-one answers my calls, not even Ava, what the hell is happening?"
He could see in Polly's face misery and pain, it was etched there. Chrysler too now stood with his head bowed, as if ashamed, his grey hair now looking positively white. Chrysler looked down at his shoes with his hands in his pockets unwilling or unable to inform him of what was wrong, because he knew, something was.
"We got it wrong Terry." said Polly, leaning on Mercer's car.
"We got it horribly wrong I'm afraid. Kathlene...eh...oh fuck we got it so wrong Terry...there's been, em...at first we thought there'd been an accident but it turns out, oh Christ Terry-"
"What? What the fuck is it Polly spit it out, just fucking tell me would you?"
Polly looked into Terry's face. There seemed to be an eternal silence before she finally managed; "Ava's dead Terry, she's been...and John, young John Smedley he eh...he's dead as well...John was...oh God Terry, Kathlene Oconnor killed them both...she's em...she's missing."
Mercer was down on his hunkers, his head between his knees, his arms rested on his thighs, hands together. He looked up at Polly and smiled, nodding his head. Chrysler came round and joined him in a similar position.
"I'm so sorry Tel, really I am, we all are. We've got teams searching

all around Manchester and the surrounding areas, she can't have got far, it's only been an hour ago...not much more. We can try-"
"What happened Polly" interrupted Mercer. "I was just speaking with her half an hour ago what happened?"
Polly sighed, bracing herself having to give out these details.
"She em...Ava, she was pushed from the balcony from where Alexander Stineman had jumped.
Whether Smedley had walked into the room and discovered what was happening or whether he was just...but she shot *him*. Ava it seems was pushed though...she died instantly...and so did an eighteen month old little boy...Christ with his mum at the shops, the girl was injured but her baby died at the scene.
We can't find Oconnor...I'm so sorry Terry."
She leaned down and cuddled her favourite detective.
She cuddled him like his life depended on it, rubbing his hands with hers and nestling her head on his shoulders.
"We got it so wrong Terry. We should never have given in to her sycophantic pleading. She fooled us Terry, she fooled us all.
She's still been under the influence of that evil woman."
"No...no way Polly, not just her, there has to be someone else, there has to be. She's away in that loony fucking bin so there has to be someone else, Oconnor couldn't do this by herself."
"There is someone else Terry, you're right, and we think we know who it is."
"Who?"
"Simpsons' husband Charles. We made some enquiries and discovered that he has emptied some bank accounts, taking out huge amounts of money."
Mercer looked at Polly.
"How huge? Like three million pounds huge?"
"How did you know Terry?"
Mercer placed another cigarette into his mouth.
"Because the bastard told me Polly, that's what she was telling me. We can all be bought for a price she kept saying."
Polly nodded her head.
"Worse still Terry, that sister of Oconnors' well, it turns out it's not

her sister at all, she's disappeared as well, no doubt been paid by Oconnor to play the act."

Again she exhaled exasperatingly. "She's done us good Terry, we're searching frantically believe me, but if this has been pre-planned, and I think it has, then our chances of finding her, to say the least, are slim."

Before Terry Mercer could say any more Polly told him that she was driving him back down to London, which was why she'd came here with Tony Chrysler.

If Terry had been devastated before he was now positively defeated, he was down and Chrysler doubted that even Mercer as strong-willed as he was could possibly rise from these ashes.

He hadn't even protested when Polly had said she was driving them back to HQ. Chrysler observed the broken man as he rose to his feet shaking his head despairingly. He would no doubt blame himself for this most unfortunate outcome, but Oconnor had fooled them all, hook line and sinker. Mercer paced around the car slowly with his hands in his pockets looking at the ground as if he were reliving everything that Oconnor had told him. God alone would only know what he was thinking. Here was a man who had lost everything in his life, and every time it looked even remotely like he was picking himself up, the world would throw something else upon his shoulders. He and Mercer had had their differences over the years just the same as Terry and Sam had, but he could never fault the man's dedication to his work. He continued observing Terry Mercer as he finally rested his backside on the back of his car, oblivious to the rain which had begun to fall, adding more misery, if that was at all possible to this very bleak day indeed. He stood now with his arms folded looking down to the ground. Would this be it for Terry? Would this be the end of his career? Only time would tell. He would do his utmost to help him through this, but then there is only a certain amount of pain that a human being can endure, and perhaps the events of the past few months had finally taken their toll on him. Ava and he had made plans for their future but the deranged woman in Pleasant Meadows had had other ideas about that, and had finally pulled the keystone of his life that would be his foundation to happiness away from under his feet. Everything had tumbled down, yet again around him. He watched as Mercer lit up another cigarette. This time, there was nothing anyone could do to help him. There would be no words of encouragement from colleagues that could help to pull him from this. Ava meant the world to him, simply because Ava was all there was in the world for him, she was his future, but now, he didn't have one. He didn't have anything, not even the job, because, in the end it was doing the job that had destroyed his life, that and a teenage crush all those years ago in Leicester at Montgomery High with a girl who looked no different to that of any other teenage girl, but who would go on to slowly dissect anything in his life that would make him happy and who would think nothing of disposing of innocent people in her path, just to torment him hellishly.

Whatever it was that drove Rosalyn Clark to do the things she done to this poor man, God alone knew. Whether it was just pure evil or psychological deficiencies or just plain revenge, she had surely succeeded in her plans. Apart from being locked up for the rest of her life she had succeeded in destroying his. Terry Mercer was beaten. He was a broken man.

Charles Simpson was a very influential man. He knew many people in high places, he also knew people who could knock up a false passport in no time whatsoever which is what he'd had done for Kathlene Oconnor who sat next to him now on the jumbo 747 on their way to Marrakesh.

In less than four hours Oconnor would begin her new life in Morocco with her grand total of just under three and a half million pounds which had been paid to her by Charles Simpson and his `ex wife`.

Oconnor was crying as she sat at the window seat of the plane in first-class. Guilt had overcome her, albeit briefly, about what she had just done to the people who had given her the opportunity to forge a career in forensics.

That part of her life was now over though, and no matter how she felt, it was too late to turn back. She had just relived those horrible moments in Manchester, just over two hours ago. First as she approached Ava from behind and pushed her over the balcony to her death, and then having to shoot John Smedley in the head as he had entered the room just as she had committed the sickening crime. Her plane was just taking off when the police had arrived at the airport. Everything had been timed to perfection.

Charles Simpson was waiting for her at the airport as she disembarked the taxi-cab she'd hired to take her there.

Even after Charles Simpson had been informed of his wife's despicable acts, he'd stayed loyal to her, and had executed every plan that Rosalyn had written out for him in the letter she'd left him in their safe. He did not question why she wanted to inflict this much pain on any man or why he was to pay so much money to a certain young lady named Kathlene Oconnor simply because he loved his `wife` far too much. Whatever this man had done to her in the past he had no idea but he thought that it must have been something horrendous indeed for her to do these things, even going as far as purchasing a house for Oconnor in Morocco. He knew he would never see her again and that she'd be kept in that mental institute for the rest of her days and so in an act of sentiment he'd proceeded with her wishes. She'd explained to him that there was a reliable source in Scotland Yard that would give all the necessary details to her and that she'd pass on the information to Oconnor...and now the job was done, complete. Oconnor had kept her side of the bargain and everyone was happy. Charles Simpson knew he could never go back to Britain which was why he'd chosen a country where extradition was not an option for the raging-mad British detectives who'd be hounding himself and Oconnor with ruthless revenge in mind. He was used to travelling the world and so that part of his new life-style wouldn't bother him one bit. His only regret was that he would not retire down in Buckinghamshire with his horticultural favourite past-time, but, he'd done this one last thing for Rosalyn, after all, she was his wife, albeit in the broadest possible sense of the word. The stewardess interrupted his thoughts as she cheerfully brought refreshments to the passengers all happy and light-hearted to be heading off on their holidays.

Kathlene Oconnor had ordered a tonic-water and sat sipping from the glass as she contemplated her life here on in. Having a new ID and passport was all very well, and even a place to call her own, but she also knew that Scotland Yard would never rest.

They had people who were referred to as ghosts.

These were people who worked for MI5 but were nowhere to be found on their books. These people would live among drug dealers, even participating with the merchandise and befriending the most dangerous of them.

They would live in the world of human trafficking sharing information about the sales of innocent girls. In other words, they literally put their lives at stake with each and every passing day, their goal, to bring down the highest of the high in all of these horrendous crimes. They would come looking for her, and she knew it. How long it would take them to find her was anybody's guess, but they would come. It would all depend on how good her false name would stand her in stead. That was another thing, she'd have to get used to her new name, because for all intents and purposes, Kathlene Oconnor no longer existed, at least the Kathlene Oconnor who had worked in Scotland Yard in the field of forensic science. That Kathlene Oconnor could never forgive herself for what she had done to the people who had done so much for her. The rest of *her* life would be spent looking over her shoulder. No good, this maudlin now. Now and for the price of three million pounds, she would have to live like a fugitive, and for what, money? But the temptation had been too much. She wouldn't be the first, and she most definitely wouldn't be the last. For some unknown reason, she'd succumbed to Rosalyn Simpson's offer. Everything she'd ever learned in the world of forensics had all now just been a complete waste of time. She wondered how Terry Mercer would be feeling, having lost yet another love in his life. The last straw, his only hope for a meaningful future, and she'd taken it away from him...now he had nothing...Rosalyn Clark had achieved her goal.

## CHAPTER SEVENTEEN.

## FINLAY STREET. HOLBURN.

## LONDON. ( SIX MONTHS LATER.)

Terry was still on compassionate leave. There was no time limit put on to the amount of leave he required. It had taken him these last six months to even venture out into the city again.
He had been benumbed by the murder of Ava. She had been his only hope for some kind of purposeful future. He had no-one left now that he could call a `friend`, Beth was off to live in Portugal, Sam was dead, Sandra and Ava also dead. He had absolutely no-one, or so he thought.
He received a visit from three rather charming young ladies who now resided in Parlour Street Kensington thanks to the kindness of a certain lady named Beth Hargrieves. Through their cheerfulness and determination they had succeeded in getting him round to their house for dinner and drinks. It didn't take that long for them to work their magic on him and having him feeling that he was the luckiest guy in London.
He remembered on one occasion he'd burst into laughter as Mandy had said; "This opportunity has made us change our ways Terry, I can tell you that."
What had made him laugh so much was the way Veronica had responded by putting in; "No Mandy, it hasn't deary, it has made us change our prices sweetheart it's made us change our prices, not our ways'. We have a higher class of clientele Terry, no more of those poor penniless lost souls, no sir, not around Kensington. Lizzy was quite unsettled at first when we moved there, slightly

neophobic in fact, but then we're all a bit like that are we not Terry, when it comes to change, but after one or two clients offering her substantial amounts of money for her services she soon lost all apprehensions about the move, and Mandy, well, she was the first of us to realize just how much money could be made here, and so after some quick mathematics we all decided not to give up what we done or rather what we do for a living. We have the opportunity to make ten times at least the amount of money we used to make over at Locksley, so...why look a gift horse in the mouth Terry, that's what *we* decided."

It was the girls' attitude to life that so enthralled him. For whatever reasons they had decided to take up prostitution God alone knew, but he'd never really looked upon them as 'working girls'. He saw them more of just friendly, sometimes sarcastic friends who could share any topic of conversation with him and quite surprisingly, intellectual conversations. They too had had their tragedies as well, beginning with the murder of Mandy's sister Jane, and in all honesty, it was those horrendous circumstances which had sparked off the friendship he now had with them, and it was a friendship that they had no intentions whatsoever of relinquishing, even trying their level-best to get him to go to America with them. They had given him two weeks to think about it and had given him their solemn promise that he would have the holiday of a lifetime with them. Whether or not he would go with them, he had learned from their attitude. There was something to be said for the friendship they had forged between themselves. They were more like sisters than friends, really close sisters, like the closeness one assumed that girls like the Bronte sisters had, sharing all their experiences of life with each other, all their ideas, although the subject matter of those ideas would be very much different to that of what the Bronte's would have discussed. All said and done though, it was through these pretty young ladies' encouragement and enthusiasm that kept him determined enough to continue working in the force. Whatever could life throw at him now? What more could be bestowed upon him? He had lost everything he'd ever loved or lived for.

Now, he had to live for himself. He would have to find the inner strength to continue doing the job, for he knew only too well, that somewhere out there, there could quite easily be another Rosalyn Clark, or a Doctor Stineman, ripping people's lives apart and destroying hopes and dreams, or just another manic mad-man injecting Ketamine or Atropine into some poor unsuspecting victim's lunch.

He needed the job, and the job needed him because they had become one and the same. He sat now at his window alone in his house, the house that still haunted him of that cheerful girl he'd married and who had given him the son he so longed for.

That real-life princess that he used to cuddle up to after a long frustrating day, the house where he remembered that little boy giggling with his mum after playing pranks on him, mixing HP sauce in his custard, just to make the kid laugh, placing basins of water just inside doorways throughout the house, so that he would step `unwittingly` into them...just to make his kid laugh.

He would visit that princess as often as he could, or as often as his soul could cope with. His son as well, how strange to visit him and see him in the condition he was in, a far cry from the little boy he could still hear laughing hysterically as his father's feet got wet, or the face he'd pull from eating the `custard`, a far cry indeed. But it was for these tortuous reasons that he felt he must carry on, and hopefully prevent anyone else going through what he had just gone through, and indeed was going through.

If there had been any consolation for Terry Mercer, it would be the death of Rosalyn Clark. It had turned out that the good Doctor Stineman had in fact trusted no-one, no-one at all, including Rosalyn. He had poisoned her with a deadly substance called Dimethyl Mercury, a lethal poison which takes weeks, if not months to kill. By the time symptoms show, it is far too late for treatment. He wondered what her final thoughts would have been as the end of her life approached. She would feel defeated surely at the thought of Stineman getting the better of her. Did she feel as though she'd accomplished something by ruining his wife and son's lives, completely destroying them, and leaving them both in a state of vegetation? Ironically, the man she'd hired to do the damage had ended up poisoning her with that lethal substance.

Doses as little as 0.1ml had proven fatal and he would know this, that it would take a while for death to triumph, but he knew that it inevitably would. This woman who had inflicted so much misery and pain to so many others had been disposed of by a man who had been even more deranged than herself. He thought now of the young fresh-faced teenage girl he'd secretly got engaged to all those years ago. What the hell had happened to her? What made her turn out like that? She had in fact succeeded in ruining his life and utterly destroying all his self-belief. She had almost succeeded in killing him, in so many ways, but now she was dead and he had to move on. Now, right here and now, he had two decisions to make. One, does he go to America with the girls, and two, when does he return to work? He sipped his tea and stubbed out his cigarette in the familiar overflowing ashtray, and then, in his usual blasphemous manner he proclaimed out loud as he came to his decision, "Fuck it, I've got nothing to lose." And this time he was right. "I'll call Veronica and ask if they'll come over and help me pack...Viva Las Vegas ladies. C'est la vie."

# THE END.

Printed in Great Britain
by Amazon